FAE'RYNN

Sundered Moon

Mechanized Hearts Book One

First published by Fae'rynn Books 2024

Copyright © 2024 by Fae'rynn

All rights reserved. No part of this publication may be reproduced, stored or transmitted in any form or by any means, electronic, mechanical, photocopying, recording, scanning, or otherwise without written permission from the publisher. It is illegal to copy this book, post it to a website, or distribute it by any other means without permission.

This novel is entirely a work of fiction. The names, characters and incidents portrayed in it are the work of the author's imagination. Any resemblance to actual persons, living or dead, events or localities is entirely coincidental.

First edition

Cover art by Benjanun Sriduangkaew

This book was professionally typeset on Reedsy.
Find out more at reedsy.com

Contents

Acknowledgement	iv
Prologue	1
Gilded Cage	33
Secrets in the Garden	53
Phantom vs Bansidhe	73
Forged Bonds	89
Dancing Wolf	100
Mothers in Law	113
Battle Stations	130
Futch for Breakfast	142
Cradle of Humanity	159
Lesbians on a Train	175
Ordinary Day	188
Battle of the S-Tiers	206
Slip Space	225
Promises	240
Epilogue	255
Coming Soon	266
About the Author	269

Acknowledgement

Benjanun, without you, this book would simply not exist. I would not have the community that I do now, either. Your unwavering support and encouragement made all the difference.

Talia, your hardass ways and brilliance taught me so much that made it into this book. You are an inspiration.

Vyria, thank you for sitting with me in the late hours of the evening. I wrote so much while listening to you rant about Honkai.

Emily, you were always there to listen to me vent or bounce ideas off of when I needed someone to talk to. You downplay how you are a great friend, so let it be immortalized that this is not true!

Writing is a lonely endeavor, but you all made it fun.

My love to all of you, my dearest friends.

Prologue

"X10Z-Witchblade, Maeve Mirren, launching." I feel the clamps of the launch sling attach to my mech's feet. The force pushes me back into my seat as I am hurtled into the blackness of space. I move my hands along the sticks and press my feet on pedals that control the chrome frame. Plasma ignites from my back engines, propelling me forward. I take a moment to admire the stars, simply enjoying the small pinpricks of light against the inky black quilt of the universe.

The frame is an extension of myself; metal is now my skin, its sensors and optics work alongside my own senses to paint an even broader scope of reality. The Witchblade is me. I am the Witchblade. Yet, I am still aware of my own soft flesh. We are the same. We are separate. It's a surreal experience that is maddening if I think about it too much. I turn my head, the others of my squad are flying behind me.

There are five of us. Zeke, a young kid who's fresh out of training; he was just assigned to this squad. Alex, the best sniper I've ever worked with, can nail the joints on an enemy mech at 1500k and make it look easy. Morrigan, an absolute wild pilot who is more like a blender in a fight. Jax, a hardass brother-in-arms; good to have in a brawl. Then there is little old me, their commander. Our target is the supermassive structure a thousand kilometers ahead of us.

The Slip Gate.

"Post up here, Alex," I say into the comms. "You and the Artemis can watch our ass."

"Roger," comes her reply. "Maybe something exciting will happen today."

I roll my eyes. "Don't hope for that."

"How else am I supposed to keep my skills sharp?" she asks. "Come on, Commander, I can hope for a small pirate crew, right? I won't kill anyone, promise!"

"Alexandria!"

"Ma'am." Her voice is sulky, but I can hear that she's speaking through a smile.

The rest of us go forward towards the gate, leaving the brown and green Artemis behind. She takes position behind a small asteroid, ready to snipe any enemies that might come out of the gate.

Morrigan takes the front position with her two massive glaives on her back. Her frame, the Scarlet Queen, is a rich, dark red with gold trim along the joints. It's more svelte than most frames and incredibly agile.

Zeke is piloting the Phalanx, a bright gold frame with black trim. He takes his position on Morrigan's flank.

I stay in the middle of the pack. My frame is the most well rounded of the bunch because I can integrate directly into the Witchblade's systems. She's equipped with a single massive beam sword on my back, an anti-material rifle and twelve swarm-bits I control with my mind to slice my enemies apart.

Jax, piloting the Balor, a green bodied frame with white and orange trim, takes his position at my back. Balor is what I can only describe as living artillery, wielding a massive beam-cannon that capital ships would envy. We're a good team with over a hundred successful sorties, apart from Zeke, and I trust these people with my life. Most sorties end with no combat and today is not likely to be an exception. Still, I always make sure we are prepared and in proper formation.

It's always when you're relaxed and comfortable that disaster strikes.

As we approach the gate, it bursts violently into life. The engine at the center whirs rapidly, golden light pours out of the structure. A hole opens in the very fabric of space. The light that emanates from it is so intense and blinding that it's impossible to make anything out within the tunnel. A moment later, a small fleet of ships pop into existence and the hole seals itself shut. The horizon goes dark again, save for the stars.

"Commander Mirren to Osiris Fleet, welcome to Central Space. We'll be your escorts today," I say, a smile on my face. It's always a good day when people leave the war-torn territories controlled by the corporations of the Milky Way.

"This is Admiral Winters," came the reply. "Confirmed, Commander. Just lead the way."

"Are there any aboard that require medical aid? I know a journey through the gate can be harsh on the body," I ask.

The comm crackles to life. "No injuries or problems have been reported, Commander. We are hale and whole."

"Wonderful." I turn my back towards the fleet, signaling my comrades to follow me, guiding the fleet towards Charon Station. It's usually a quiet job, making sure refugees got into Central Space safely. I enjoy it—the lack of death, the promise of helping others find a new life.

An alert flashes across my screen.

"Not a quiet day after all," I mutter into the comms. I watch as the gate once again bursts into life and another three ships appear. I recognize the insignia painted on the side of the ships, a skull with twin serpents coiled around it. The Toxic Knights, a group of pirates that operate just outside of Central. Rumor is one of the corpo states finance them—the Fomorian Armory. "We got incoming."

"I see 'em," Alex responds.

Several more flashes appear on the screen as mechs sortie out from the ships' launch slings.

"This is Commander Mirren of Central's Fifth defense fleet," I say into the comms on all channels. "You have entered Central Space with what appears to be aggressive intent. Surrender and no harm will come to you."

No response.

The pirate ships' guns take aim at the refugee fleet, opening fire on them. Jax, quick as ever to jump to the defense of others, deploys a massive shield generator that blocks the ships' energy cannons. Alex is likewise quick to respond, sniping one from behind cover, the head of the mech exploding in a bright flash.

"Damnit. Alright, take them out, but do your best not to kill anyone," I say. "We capture them and their ships."

"I know the drill," Alex replies, taking down another mech with a well-aimed shot.

The fight isn't a particularly long or difficult one. Scarlet Queen makes quick work of anything that gets within range of her glaives. Artemis picks off several mechs one by one, a single shot for each mech. Jax looks out for Zeke, who is the only one to have a bit of trouble—expected, considering this is his first proper battle.

I ram an enemy mech so hard that the pirate mech stops functioning briefly. The swarm-bits surround and dismember them, leaving the cockpit well intact. Jax blasts off towards the ships, booster fire leaving a trail of light behind him. He unleashes his cannon on them, practically evaporating the engines while leaving the main body of the ships intact.

I'll never understand why people attack us here or what they hoped to gain by doing this. Surely, they knew they were following a refugee flotilla into Central. Perhaps they didn't and just assumed they were chasing cargo frigates? Whatever. The fight is over almost as soon as it begins; the others come along to take the pirates into custody.

"T-thank you," the Admiral says into comms. "We didn't realize we were being followed. Apologies for the fuss."

I chuckle. "Not at all. I'm just glad we minimized loss of life."

"What will you do with them?" he asks.

"They get sublimated back into society," I tell him. "We'll even relocate families if needed. We aren't interested in punishment for the sake of it."

"That's remarkably charitable," the admiral replies. "Is Central really all they say it is?"

I take a moment to reply. "We aren't perfect, but we do our best, Admiral. Your people are in excellent hands."

I think back to the motive for this attack, and I wonder if maybe that was the reason: did they know we'd take them alive and give them a new life? But then why attack at all and put people at risk? It doesn't make much sense to me. Then again, a lot of things make very little sense, like why the corpo states still work against us when all Central wants is to make life good for humanity. It's been three hundred years since the Secession War. One would think they'd get over their grudges.

It takes an hour to lead the fleet to Charon Station, a massive facility attached to a small rocky moon named Cerberus. The planet Cerberus orbits is your standard fare nameless gas giant. Nothing special about it except that it's a rather beautiful azure. It reminds me of Neptune, several hundred light years away.

As usual, this goes without incident, though I linger for a few moments just to make sure. Occasionally a corpo agent will slip onto a refugee ship and cause problems, though those incidents are exceedingly rare. Still, the pirate fleet from earlier has me slightly on edge. I get all clear from Charon and turn my mech back towards the Danu, the capital class ship I launched from.

Another good day.

My chrome feet stomp along the interior hull of the ship as I enter the hangar. The others follow behind me as I walk the mech back into my normal place among the hundreds of others. Clamps attach themselves to the frame, and I feel myself being pulled back into place and locked in. I end the link between me and the Witchblade, feeling a rush as my consciousness realigns with my body.

I take a moment to breathe, my brain connecting to the cybernetic lungs and heart in my chest. For a moment, time slows as my mind and body adjust. I open the cockpit and get out. I cast a glance back at her, just standing there looking so pretty.

The Witchblade is mostly black with white trim along the arms and legs. She's humanoid with a sharp face and defined indigo eyes that emanate light when she's active. The panels on her chest, arms and thighs are powered down now, but when I'm piloting, they glow the same color as her eyes. She's beautiful. Almost as beautiful as my wife, who I'm eager to haul ass and go see.

"Good work, Commander," a voice catches my attention. Sif Ragnulf—the ship's captain.

"Thank you," I reply, snapping her a quick salute. "A little spicier than I'd thought it would be, but nothing my team couldn't handle."

She returns the salute with an easy familiarity. "Indeed," she says with a smile. "Honestly, I'd say we waste you and your team at this post, but then again, I'm glad for you all on a day like today. A less skilled team might have either died or had to kill."

I wrinkle my nose. "Yeah. Speaking of, were there any casualties when Jax took out the engines?"

"A few engineers got caught in an explosion, but no deaths have been reported," she says.

A relieved sigh. "Good. I hate it when people die. Do you need me for anything else?" My voice betrays my impatience. *Shit.*

She smirks. "Eager to see V?"

I nod. I'm in for it now, I just know it.

"You two are trying for a kid, right?" Her smile warms.

I nod again, my face flushing. "And it's the right time for me so..."

She chuckles and shakes her head. "Give her my best and tell her thank you for... you know, never mind. There's far too much to thank her for. Just tell her she's incredible."

"Well, that's easy enough. I do it all the time."

"Commander," she says, her brows furrowed.

"Yes?"

"Dismissed, get the fuck out of here."

I really, really don't need to be told twice. "Thanks," I say with a grin on my face.

When I'm an appropriate distance away from her, I break out into a jog which turns into a sprint out of the hangar. I go up the lifts and through the long halls that make up the ship, dodging my way through people and friends, not bothering to say hello or goodbye. Time and space pass me by. Before I know it, the door to my room hisses as it opens as I step through the threshold. It closes behind me, sealing itself shut with a loud click.

And there she is—my wife. Viviana lets out a lazy whimper, the sound of the door waking her up. She doesn't even bother opening her eyes or sitting up.

"Hi," she says, her voice small and cute and adorable. She nestles herself deeper into the bed.

I love this woman, everything about her, from her tall and slender frame to her dark blue hair and especially her eccentric and always sleepy brain.

"Hi," I reply, sitting down on the bed beside her. "I think it's time to get up."

"Nooo, five more minutes," she whines, "when you make me coffee, I'll get up."

"It's midafternoon already," I tell her, a smile on my lips. Every day it's like this, our fun ritual of me coaxing her out of bed. It's like a script we play out over and over, but it never gets old. Never. "Gotta wake up, babygirl."

"Don't babygirl me," she says, turning over onto her back. She pulls the sheet up over her chest and rubs her eyes. She's just perfect. "Make me coffee and then you can sweet talk me as much as you'd like."

I laugh, lean forward, and kiss her deeply, squishing my body against hers. She wraps her arms around me as our lips dance against one another. She slides her delicate fingers down my waist, gives my ass a firm squeeze and a small slap.

I chuckle, pressing forward into the kiss. "Hey," I say, a raspy edge to my voice. "Keep doing that and I'm going to get you."

"Is that a threat?" she asks, biting her lower lip.

I grin at her, scooping her up into my arms. She squeals as she wraps her legs around me. I kiss her again and again and again, peppering her face with affection and her neck with shallow bites. If I could, I would devour her whole. Maybe I should.

"Mmmm, no fair," she whines. "You know how weak I am when you pick me up like this. Did your sortie go well?"

Some sound of acknowledgement escapes me as I just keep kissing her neck and chest. "Just a skirmish," I manage to say. "Nothing too serious."

She pushes away from me slightly, her violet eyes boring into me. "You really should open up with that in the first place, you know," she huffs. "Is everyone okay? Did Zeke handle himself well?"

"They are, and he did," I tell her. "If anything had gone wrong, I'd have said so. Maybe crawled into bed and sobbed a bit. Everything is fine."

"Okay," V says, taking a steadying breath. "I don't even know why I worry. It's not as if you're the best or anything."

I lean back in, kissing her neck and holding her tight. "I won't ever complain that you worry."

She squeezes me with her arms and thighs, clinging to me. "You'd better not. I love you."

"I love you, too," I say, griping her hips and pulling her even closer to me as I run my fingers through her silky hair. "And I have a threat I need to make good on."

She presses her hardening bulge against me, kissing me deep. "You're really, really eager, huh?"

"Of course," I growl. "Today and tomorrow are the best days for trying. I have tomorrow off and you're being... you. And you always drive me crazy."

V giggles and runs her long, slender fingers over my cheek. "Coffee first." She smiles at me but then looks away, chewing on her inner cheek.

I lift my brow as I set her down on the bed. "Yeah, of course. Is um... is everything okay? You look worried? Scared?"

She hesitates, bringing her knees up to her chest and hugging them tight. "Scared," she says. "Sorry. I got into my head. It's been six months of trying and nothing is working. I'm worried it's just never going to work. Whatever I'm doing at the lab to help my endocrine system is—"

I wrap my arms around her and squeeze her tight. It's the only way to stop her cascading thoughts and doubts. "If it doesn't work, it doesn't work," I tell her firmly. "And it's always fun to keep trying, yeah?"

She smirks and chuckles softly. "Of course. You won't be disappointed in me?"

I frown. "V, how could I ever be disappointed in you?" I bite her neck gently. "That's never going to happen. I'm going to go get you that coffee. Love you."

V shivers and her face turns flush. "Mmmph, thank you."

I go into our little kitchenette and go through the steps to make her the perfect cup of coffee, at least by that fiend's standards. Freshly ground beans, water heated to 99c, and then steep the grounds for two minutes. She's incredibly particular about this method of brewing and I, being a wonderful wife, indulge her insanity. If it were just me, I'd skip the coffee entirely and grab an energy drink. But this is how she likes her caffeine, and she gets to have whatever she wants.

I turn to look back at her; she's pulled out her datapad and is already working on the project that's been keeping her up all hours of the day and night. I watch her quietly, staring at her as her brow furrows in concentration. She brushes a lock of hair out of her face and tucks it behind her ear. I just stare.

The timer goes off.

I reluctantly pull my eyes away, give the coffee grounds floating on the surface a little stir, and wait another thirty seconds before placing the brewer over a mug. The pressure plate releases, and the coffee pours directly into the mug, leaving the grounds behind in the filter. A splash of cream and sugar and it's ready. I bring it over, a stupid smile on my face.

She's sitting naked on the bed wrapped up in the sheet, making a total mess of where we sleep. She looks up from her work, making grabby hands at the coffee.

"You're adorable," I say, handing her the mug.

She beams at me. "Why thank you. I'd say I try, but I really don't. Honestly, I don't know why you married me."

"You are such a creature."

She grins at me from behind her mug, those violet eyes of hers make my heart race. "Your creature," she says.

"Yeah." I run my fingers through her long locks and stroke her face with my thumb. "I'm going to shower and get clean before—"

"Before you have your way with me," she says, peeking up at me from behind her mug still.

My face flushes. She always manages to do this to me. My brain just goes stupid. "Yes," I manage to say. "What was I doing?"

She giggles. "Shower."

"Right." I regain my composure enough to tease her back. I stretch out, making the skintight pilot suit show off even more of my body than it already does.

She looks at me, unable to pull her eyes away from my stomach. She chews on her lip, her body quivering as she holds herself back. "No fair," she says, running her fingers along each individual muscle. "I have my coffee."

"Patience." I smirk. "I'll see you just now."

She squirms on the bed, sighing. "Okay."

"I love you." I lean forward to kiss her deeply, my tongue going into her mouth and hers in mine. It's the kind of kiss that leaves us both breathless. As I move to pull away, she yanks me down again so that the kiss can linger all the more. She releases me after a moment, her face red and her lips swollen.

I smirk at her again and saunter off to go shower. Stripping out of my pilot suit is a mission unto itself, especially with how sticky my skin gets from sweating. I turn the water on full blast and step under the raging stream. The pressure is just perfect, and the heat is soothing. Unfortunately, the interfacing system I use to pilot puts a ton of strain on my body and I am feeling it today.

V invented the method a decade ago, and it took Central by storm. A whole new way of doing cybernetic augmentation and piloting mechs opened up to people. For everything else, the system works like a charm, allowing for easy, non-invasive extra limbs or seamless implants and organs like the heart beating in my chest. For piloting, however, it's still far too much strain on most people's bodies. After a decade, I am still one of the few who can take full advantage of the method and I had to undergo major cybernetic augmentation in order to survive repeat sorties.

Steam fills the bathroom. I lift my head to let the water flow down my neck and chest. My breasts are thankful to be free of the skintight suit, though they are a bit tender today. Hormones are such a bitch. I wash up in all the important places and then my hair. I miss the length it used to be as I run the shampoo through the strands—it's regulation to keep it short. Oh well. V always tells me how much she likes me with short hair and how it drives her crazy, so it's something I can live with.

All too soon, I'm finished and clean. Without reason to linger under the water, I shut the valve off. I dry myself, put a towel around my hair, another around my body. Stepping out in the living area, I see V is pretty much right where I left her. She hasn't bothered getting dressed. I just stand there for a moment as I cool off from the shower, watching her. Her hair hangs messily around her face, a few strands linger by her neck and jaw. Her eyes stare intensely at her work, her brow doing the cute furrow it always does when she's really focused.

I love her so much it makes me stupid.

Gently, and quietly, I clear my throat so as to not startle her... a mistake I've made on more than a few occasions. She looks up at me and smiles.

"Hi," she says softly.

"Hey," I say back. "Feeling better?"

She nods. "I am."

I give my hair a quick ruffle with the towel and then toss it into a hamper nearby. The towel around me, too. V watches me with as much focus as she was putting towards her work. My face flushes. The way she looks at me makes me weak in the knees.

She stands up; the sheet falling to the floor to reveal her nudity. Her arms wrap around me, her bare skin cool against mine. I hold her tight and press my lips against hers. She's so small compared to me, small and delicate and precious. I run my fingers through her long blue hair and pepper her face with kisses.

"I love you," she whispers. "Maeve, you have no idea how much I adore you."

"Even though I'm a little stupid?" I ask, grinning widely.

She rolls her eyes. "Especially because you're stupid." She bites my lower lip.

I nuzzle her down onto the bed, kissing down her neck and chest, taking a nipple into my mouth. She groans and arches her back as I suckle on the sensitive nub. She runs her fingers through my hair, gripping tight, pulling me towards her chest. I fight back a grin as I ravish her chest, my other hand goes to cup her unattended breast. I twist and toy with the nipple, driving her wild. Her hips gently roll as she squirms under my relentless assault.

"Oh, that's perfect," she moans.

I eventually give her nipples a break, my hand sliding down her stomach, taking hold of her hard, swollen cock. She groans as I use long and tender strokes and rub the sensitive spots under the shaft, making sure every inch of her feels attended to. She rewards me with a high-pitched squeal, her hips gyrating along the same rhythm as my hand.

I pull away from her breast just so I can watch her face twist and contort into pleasure. She looks at me with those deep violet eyes.

"It drives me nuts when you look at me like that," she says to me. "You look like you want to devour me."

"Because I do," I say, kissing down her stomach, my hand still rubbing her gently. I kiss the tip of her cock, my tongue swirling around the head. I make sure to pay attention to her favorite spot, just below the tip in the space between the head and the shaft. She's leaking all over and I greedily, eagerly drink up every drop of her. I kiss down her thighs, biting and sucking on the tender flesh. She releases soft little whimpers; her breath comes out in ragged waves. When I do finally take her into my mouth she gasps and groans, her fingers digging deep into our bed.

I hold her down, making sure she can't go anywhere, placing her at my mercy. That only drives her crazier. I start off slowly, licking and worshiping every inch of her like the beautiful, divine creature she is.

"Good girl," I whisper.

She whimpers. "Yeah?"

"The best girl, Viviana." I only ever use her name when we are like this. It's the only time she likes it.

She lets out a deep, satisfied sigh and relaxes as I taste her. She lifts and spreads her legs, exposing herself to me entirely. I kiss down her shaft and just under her tiny sack. She arches her back; her moans getting louder and longer.

"Mmm, my love, I'm so close but..."

I grin and give her a few more kisses. "I can wait," I tell her.

PROLOGUE

"Nooooo," she whines. "Get on top of me and fuck me, please. The first orgasm is the best for making babies. I appreciate you wanting to eat me out though."

"Very well," I say softly as I crawl my way up to her lips. "Mmmm, you're so beautiful. How did I get so lucky with you?"

She flushes, turning to look away from me. "It's been eight years and you're still saying that to me?"

"I always feel lucky when we're together like this." I bite her ear and straddle her hips. I take my sweet time teasing her with my cunt, sliding it along the length of her shaft and getting her even more wet. Sometimes I just fuck her like this, but today I need and want her inside me.

"Mm," she whimpers, "I love it when you do that."

"I know," I whisper. I reach down between us, gripping her cock tightly in my hands, angling her just right before sliding her inside of me. It's been a while since I've had her inside of me; I can't help but let out a loud moan of my own. "Mm, fuck!"

She grins up at me, her skin flushed and glistening. "I love this."

I rock my hips up and down as I take all of her inside me. She holds her hands up above her head. I grab hold of them in one hand, riding her hard and fast. I want to tease her, to edge her with my cunt, but I can't help myself—not today. It feels too good to fuck her wildly, to rut until neither of us can move.

She bites down on her lip and struggles against my hold on her wrists as her orgasm gets closer and closer. She screams when it does, her whole body shaking and quivering as she cums. I just keep going, riding her as hard as I can, making sure her orgasm lasts as long as possible inside me. I squeeze my muscles along her shaft and start taking a slower, more deliberate rhythm that has her crying out in pleasure.

She wrests her wrist free and taps on my shoulder, unable to speak. It's our signal. I stop, moving to lie on top of her. My body almost swallows hers up completely. I kiss her neck and face, holding her tight in my arms. She pants, taking a moment to gather herself before grinning up at me.

"You make me feel so loved and cherished, you know," she says softly.

"You ask yourself how you got so lucky, but so do I, my love."

I smile and kiss her neck some more, sucking on her sensitive skin, leaving a trail of little red marks. "Maybe in another eight years we'll finally stop."

"I hope not," she says with a little laugh. "I love feeling this way."

"Me too."

"Mmm, you haven't finished yet, have you?" she asks, running her fingers down my back and spine.

I shake my head.

"Well, you know, I upgraded the strap since the last time we used it. The sensory feedback should be even better." She looks very chuffed with herself.

"Better?! Viviana, it already felt insane when I had an orgasm before! It's going to be more intense?" I ask, mildly horrified, but also very excited. "Alright."

She nods. "Mmmhm," she says. "What can I say? I'm an evil mad scientist."

"You are."

I get off her and crawl over to get into the drawer where we keep the almighty strap. I sit up on my knees, slipping on the harness. There's a little whirr and a click as it powers on and attaches to me. A nanosecond later, it connects to my nerves. The transition is seamless and easy. It simply feels like a part of my body.

I take a moment to admire it on myself, then glance over to my wife who is looking at me like a small but deadly predator. I grin at her.

"Are you sure we have time for this?" I ask, winking. "I know you have a lot of work to do today."

"We do," she says without missing a beat, a big grin on her face. "This is work—in a way."

I blink. "Come again?"

"The strap and all your other cybernetics send data to me pretty much always," she says.

"Right," I say, chuckling. "I sort of forgot about consenting to that. I've had them longer than we've been married."

She giggles. "Silly. Well, it helps you a lot," she explains. "The intensity of sex offers incredible data without putting you at risk... most of the time." She grins widely. "And I can have some work-life balance this way."

The absurdity of her logic makes me chuckle. "Fair enough," I say.

"I did ask!" she says, simpering at me. It's such an innocent look. "You and everyone who opts into testing the interfacing OS agrees to let us use that data for the sole purpose of improving it and making the system safer—It's not used for anything else."

"I know," I remark. "It's just been a while, and I didn't think about... this." I motion to the cyber-strap.

She grins at me and looks down at it with a hungry glint in her eye. "Well, that, my love, is only used to improve the Witchblade. You're the only one who can handle that level of interfacing anyhow. You're special."

I reach for her, grab her by the ankle, and drag her across the bed. She yelps. I look down at her, my eyes burning into her. She's beyond precious.

"You really are insane. Experimenting on me," I tease, reaching out to hold her hand, interlacing our fingers, giving her an affectionate squeeze.

"A little insane." She pushes herself up off the bed and kisses me.

"You're forgiven," I say softly, breaking the kiss.

"Thank you."

I grab hold of her waist and get in between her legs. She eagerly spreads her thighs for me. Her custom-made strap really is spectacular. It self-lubricates and sends little jolts of pleasure through my body even before I do anything with it. I push her legs back, exposing her cute cock. I grin hungrily at her and press the tip of the strap against her.

She's already so eager, so ready that she tries to push herself onto me, but I hold her back, rubbing myself against her, teasing her brutally until she's whining in anticipation. Then and only then do I slide into her. Fuck—she really did increase the sensitivity. I have to fight back against my orgasm just from pushing inside her. Of course, it doesn't help how aroused I already am from fucking her earlier.

"Maeve," she groans. "Fuck me."

I grin and slam my hips against hers, driving the strap inside completely. My body gets used to the overwhelming pleasure quickly enough, or at least enough for me to fuck her good and proper. She wraps her legs around my waist and pulls me close to her as I thrust my hips inside her again and again. I feel as if I am about to explode as I pound her, but I want to edge this out as long as possible.

I slow down, kissing her deeply and holding her in my arms. She kisses me back, our breasts squishing together. I bite her lip; she digs her nails into my back, dragging them down my skin. I wince, moaning in pleasure and pain.

She pulls away from the kiss, grabbing at my hair. She pulls my head to the side, her teeth sink into the soft skin, almost feeling as if she is about to draw blood. V pulls away, those magnificent eyes of hers looking me over hungrily. I belong to her. There's no denying her anything when she looks at me like that.

"Harder," she demands.

I slam the strap into her, our hips slapping together with each thrust.

"Good girl," she whispers, keeping her grip on my hair firm. "You always know just how to fuck me. Are you going to cum for me?"

"Yes."

She smirks at me, her face so smug. "Harder, Maeve. I want to see just what that strap does to you when you cum."

"As you wish." My heart races. It's not often she gets like this, but when she does, I melt entirely.

I go harder and faster, my orgasm building and building. But it doesn't matter how hard I go, how fast my thrusts are, the release of ecstasy is constantly out of reach. She smirks at me.

"Did you..."

She grins. "You're going to have to ask me nicely," she says. "Like an obedient puppy."

"V," I whimper, my heart skipping a beat. "Please? Fuck."

She bites my neck again. "I know. I can be so cruel. Keep fucking me like this and I'll let you cum as much as you want."

I can only nod and moan. I want that release so badly it hurts. "Please, V... please let me cum." Fuck, I sound so desperate and pathetic. Only she can ever make me feel owned.

She orgasms again as I pound into her, her cock squirting over the both of us. She arches her back as the feeling overpowers her and she clenches her thighs and arms around me. I groan and moan and pant, so fucking desperate to cum. She just groans, enjoying my futile effort.

"Mmmm," she whispers. "That's a good puppy. Just a little more."

I thrust again and again, my clit throbbing and aching for release. "As you wish."

"Such a good girl. Cum," she commands.

And that's all it took. Her command releases me. My whole body freezes up as the orgasm swells through me. I bite down on her shoulder, my breath coming out as strangled moans. My toes curl, my fingers dig into her skin.

I'm torn apart by bliss.

The pleasure subsides after a time, my body still shaking. We smile at one another, sharing another tender kiss.

"How did you like it?" She giggles, her eyes softening.

"It was perfect," I say, pressing my forehead against hers. "Unexpected but perfect. Used a voice command, huh?"

"Yep!"

I shudder and shiver, my orgasm still not quite over. I take a deep breath to steady myself. "Brutal."

"You love me."

"Yeah." I brush my fingers through her hair. "Yeah, I do."

**

"Here you go," V says, pushing a small device into my hands.

"Wait, has it been two weeks already?" I blink several times, wondering where the time has gone. I take it from her and set it down on the desk and get it and myself ready.

"Sure has!" She beams. "I've been counting down the minutes. Literally two weeks to the moment as of right now."

I chuckle. "You're cute."

"I know."

The thin needle pricks my finger; I wince, but only slightly—I hate needles. I pour a drop of blood into a little slot on the device, close it, and wait.

"Sooooo, what is it?!" she asks brightly. "Tell me, tell me, tell me."

"Hold on!" I tell her, my heart is in my throat, my body trembles. "It takes a few moments for the stupid machine to get the hormone readings."

"Yeah, I know," she says. "But tell meeeeee."

I sigh. "Patience."

"Fine." She sticks her tongue out at me.

The machine dings and flashes a big plus sign. I blink several times. Words don't come to me, so I just hold out the device.

She snatches it from me, squealing in delight. "WE DID IT!"

"We did," I say softly, her enthusiasm making me come back to myself. "See, you had nothing to worry about in the end."

"I knew if I kept playing around with my hormone levels, I could get them baby makers working again. Well, okay, I had some doubts. I'm not perfect." She puts her hands on her hips, looking incredibly pleased with herself. "We're going to be moms."

That makes me grin wide, elation and realization truly dawning on me. I embrace her tightly. "Yeah, yeah we are." I take a seat after a moment, just processing the news. "I'm going to miss piloting," I say softly. "Sorry, I'm not unhappy. It's just... this is happening."

V hugs me tight, her slender arms wrapping around my shoulders with surprising strength. "You don't have to get out of the cockpit right away. Baby is safe where they are and I already accounted for this. For at least the next three months, it's safe. Interfacing with the Witchblade after that will take too much out of you for it to be safe. You don't have to give it up just yet."

That makes me feel slightly better. "Well, even if it did, it was my choice to carry our baby.. Could have used an artificial womb like you suggested."

She chuckles. "I'd feel better if you did. Not too late to change your mind, either. In a few weeks, I can transfer them over to one. The zygote just needs to be more stable, but it's low risk."

"I'm considering it now that it's happening," I muse. "I'll think about it.

For now, I'm just glad we're at this stage. If we do go down that route, we should go back to Earth. I'd feel better about using one in a place with real gravity."

V shrugs and kisses the top of my head. "Whatever you want. I can drag my work anywhere and what are they going to do? Refuse my transfer request."

"As if anyone can refuse you anything." I smirk. "Would you take time off when they were born?"

She nods. "Of course. At least a year, but you know me, I'd get so bored that I'd have to do something."

I chuckle and smile softly. "Yeah, fair. Well, I'll need to let the captain know, because once I can't pilot anymore, I'm not coming back until they're off to uni."

"Now that we're here, are you happy to take such a long break?" she asks. "I know you were when we agreed to have a baby, but now?"

I take a moment to answer, running my fingers across my jaw. "Yeah. Yeah, I am. I know fighting doesn't happen all that often and I'm passionate about making sure we can keep helping people and protecting them... but I'm okay stepping away from it all. At least for a while. Not like I'll be old when they grow up."

"Very well," she says, puffing out her chest and putting her hands on her hips. "Then if you want to go back to Earth, we'll go back to Earth. I'd do anything for you except get pregnant myself." She motions to her body. "I put in a lot of effort making myself look this way and sorry kiddo, I don't want to do it over again."

I pull her close and onto my lap. "You're funny."

"I know, but I'm also serious." She leans in and kisses my neck. "I wouldn't have wanted kids on my own, but with you, I'm excited and happy. I wonder what we should name them."

The gears are already whirring in her brain, I can see it in her eyes. I kiss her nose and then her lips. She lets out a happy little hum.

"We'll sort it out," I tell her. "We don't need to get ahead of ourselves here and now."

The lights in the room flicker off and the emergency red turns on. No alarm went off and there isn't a drill scheduled for today.

"Shit."

Fight instinct kicks in. I stand up, V still in my arms. I set her down, reaching for a lockbox under my desk where I store my gun. V may not be a soldier, but she is quick to act, going into our closet to pull out two armored flexsuits and breather helmets. The suits can withstand bullet fire and the helmets vacuum seal, providing a half hour worth of air in space.

She tosses me mine and I quickly strip out of my normal pants and shirt to slip into it and then snap the helmet on. She does the same with practiced speed. This was something we trained for often in case of emergency.

"Ready?" I ask.

She nods, drawing her own gun.

I use my wristwatch communicator to attempt hailing the bridge. No response. I try to reach Captain Sif directly. Nothing.

"Comms are down," I say.

She furrows her brows. "What?" she asks. "That's not possible."

"Comms are down," I repeat.

"Fuck."

I open the door manually and very slowly spot check around the corner. At the moment it looks clear, and I hear nothing dangerous. Alex comes out of her room, looking at us with confusion. Like us, she's in her tactical gear and has her weapon drawn. I exchange a silent glance with her and step out into the hallway, motioning for her to follow. We proceed carefully, constantly on the lookout for enemies.

V is right behind me. Alex positions herself at the back and we go forward in a line, making sure not to make ourselves an easy target for potential infiltrators.

A gunshot cuts through the silence.

I peek around the corner. Armed men with assault rifles are shooting into a group of maintenance workers who hadn't had time to gear up. Outrage wells up in me, but I shove it down and focus. Under normal circumstances, we are supposed to limit enemy casualties, but when the ship is boarded like this, the top priority is keeping control of the vessel.

I hate to deal out death.

I motion for Alex to join me at the front. Taking point, I step around the corner and squeeze the trigger three times. My shots strike true, piercing their visored helmets. They die to the sounds of shattering glass. Alex hits her mark too, her targets dropping dead.

We move forward; I check the bodies of the workers. No pulse. All of them were my friends, people I've lived and worked with for years. They weren't soldiers—they weren't even armed. Fuck! Whoever is attacking us, they are entirely evil. Who guns down workers like this? For now, the best I can do for them is move them to the side so that they aren't stepped on. They deserve better than that. I'll have time to mourn later.

The dead soldiers aren't wearing any sort of uniform that I recognize. Black tactical gear, like the flexsuits we are wearing, but that's just the galactic standard. I search for any kind of emblem that might tell me who they are working for, but I find nothing. Absolutely nothing.

"They really don't want us to know who they are," Alex remarks. She removes the helmet of one of the slain soldiers and injects a retractable needle from her wrist into his neck. Her eyes flash green for a moment. "Scanning biometric data," she says, her voice almost robotic. She removes her hand. The needle retracts into her wrist with a subtle squelch. She sighs. "Their data has been scrubbed. No pings coming back from any known database."

"Someone with a lot of power is backing these guys," I remark. "You really found nothing at all, not even something small?"

Alex shakes her head. "Nothing, Commander."

Viviana furrows her brows, the gears turning in her head.

"What's going on up there?" I ask.

She frowns. "This shouldn't be possible," she says. "The ship being boarded like this without so much as the proximity klaxon going off? Comms going down? I built most of those systems and they wouldn't just fail like that."

"Well, they did," Alex says. "And enemies are here."

"Yes, I'm aware of that, you moron," she snaps. "And that's not my point."

Alex clenches her jaw but says nothing. I shoot her a glare, understanding what my wife is getting at.

"You're thinking sabotage," I say for Alex's benefit.

"Yes." V's brow furrow deepens. "It was during shift change too, when everything was chaos. We need to hurry."

Alex frowns. "Sorry," she says. "That *was* stupid of me to say just now."

"It's fine, I'm over it," V replies. "I'm not the kind of person to hold grudges. Let's get out of this alive, yeah? Sorry I called you a moron."

She nods. "Your wife has called me worse," she says with a chuckle. "I'm a pain in the ass."

Somehow, I manage a smirk. It's reflexive, an attempt to be light in a dark and shitty situation. "We'll grab a beer when this is over. Promise." It's not a promise I can keep, but it's one I make all the same. Sometimes people just need a little something to look forward to in a situation like this, to be thinking about that brighter tomorrow.

"You? Drink?" She grins. "I'd never thought I'd see the day."

"I drink sometimes," I tell her. "Not that I can right now." I pat my stomach.

Alex looks disappointed for a moment. She's been trying to get me to drink with her forever, but then what I'm saying clicks and she gasps. "No way!" She beams brightly. "Okay, well then, I'll drink double."

V smirks. "No need. I'll have her share."

"Fair," Alex says. "Congratulations. Thanks for telling me, even in the middle of this shit show."

"Of course."

I take the front again, quietly leading us down the long and narrow halls of our ship. Normally, this place is bright and filled with activity. People coming and going to their various tasks and taking time to talk to one another. We're a military ship, but we're also tight-knit and familiar with one another's lives. People have gotten married on this ship—hell, Captain Ragnulf officiated one just two months ago.

I push those thoughts out of my mind; I can't afford to have them right now. My focus needs to be on the task at hand. The objective in a situation like this is clear—eliminate the threat, secure the bridge. Charon Station isn't too far away either, and I worry about those who are still there. If pirates or mercenaries capture a capital ship like this, it will be a total disaster for those civilians.

Are they the target maybe? It's the only thing that makes sense. It would take corpo backing for this kind of operation to be successful. They have threatened war if Central kept their open border policy in place in the past. Is that what this is? Has war begun because these pieces of shit can't stand losing people to use as fuel for labor?

More soldiers. Four of them. They spot us at the same time, opening fire on us. Alex and V duck into a doorway for cover. I take position behind metal crates. A cacophony of ricochets and gunfire make it difficult to hear anything else. I signal Alex to provide cover fire and then I pop out of cover to get eyes on their position.

Projectiles hurtle past my head before I duck back into cover. The bullet fire stops. They shoot again. They favor three-second intervals. I wait for one more cycle. They shoot again. Boot steps approach. I roll out of cover. Alex does the same. Patience paid off—we catch them as they were pushing in towards us. In an instant, we cut the four of them down. Another group eliminated, but how many more?

"They must have a lot of boarders," V says. "A lot."

"What makes you say that?" Alex asks.

V furrows her brows. "Because they have poor tactics. Assuming sabotage, which I am, then they likely boarded with a large force rather than a small strike team. So far, these soldiers are hardly elites." She motions to the dead. "That means they want this to be a battle of attrition. They want to overwhelm us by hitting multiple vital parts of the ship at once. They are willing to lose many people—maybe all of them." She grimaces. "Their leaders are disgusting."

"Can you do anything to slow them down?" I ask her.

Alex lifts a brow. "Wait what? What could she even do here?" She frowns. "Sorry, I know you do a lot on the ship but—"

I don't mean to, but I laugh. "Viviana is the most brilliant woman in the galaxy. She can do whatever she wants."

Alex looks incredulous. "Commander, she's still a civvy."

"Now isn't the time for flattery, my love," V says. "I have been trying to get into the system between fights, but all the security protocols have been changed. Whoever did this was someone I trusted. Only four people, including me and Sif, even have clearance. I know it wasn't her."

She taps her chin. "Only one of the four is good enough to have done this without tripping any of my fail-safes." She hugs her arms around herself, her words faltering. "It was Cleo," she says. "She's the only one who could have done this."

What do I say? What can I say? I've known Cleo for almost as long as V. The two of them are best friends and lovers occasionally—I'm going to rip that woman's spine out for this. I reach out toward my wife, squeezing her shoulder.

"We can find out more once we've secured the bridge," I say, trying my best to put on comforting airs. It's all I know to do right now. "Keep trying to override the security and see if you can't restore comms."

She simpers, refocusing on the task at hand. "Of course."

More boot steps. We get back into cover. I see V out of the corner of my eye typing away furiously at her datapad. For now, it makes sense to hold up here and let her work. The enemy group rounds the corner, coming from the direction of the enlisted bunks and cafeteria. More people to mourn.

Like the other groups we've killed, they are armed with galactic standard assault rifles, except for one. They have some sort of weapon I've never seen before. It's heavy and has three long, thick barrels attached to a rotary. It almost looks like an ancient M134—something right out of a holovid. For the moment, it doesn't seem like this group has spotted us.

"Alpha and Orion teams aren't checking in," one soldier says.

The one holding the massive gun makes a grunt of acknowledgement. "This is Central's best," they say, their voice gravelly with a cybernetic undertone. "We knew it wouldn't be easy. Status on the captain?"

"Executed, sir. The bridge is secure," they say, sounding so pleased with themselves.

Not Sif. Not like this.

"The ship is ours," they continue, "But, we keep getting pings of someone trying to hack into security."

"The Witch," the cyber man says. "*She* warned us about that one. She's the only one who can take the ship back from us." He grunts. "The team sent to kill her must have failed. Find and eliminate her."

"Yes, sir!"

"The rest of us will proceed to the mech hangar and destroy the units inside. The fleet will move in after."

Alex looks at me for direction. I glance over at V. She is working faster than ever, the implants in her violet eyes glowing bright under the dim red lights. Static sounds in my ears as the comms come back to life. The overhead lights flicker as they turn back on properly. The klaxon goes off. My wristwatch alerts me to the emergency evacuation order. V also sent out a distress code to send reinforcements from the rest of the fifth fleet. *Damn, she's good.*

"Find that damn witch," the cyber man shouts. "Fucking distress signal is going to ruin everything."

They still haven't seen us and for now, I'm not willing to come out of cover. Better to let V just keep doing what she's doing and not drag her into a firefight. A brief look of panic comes over her face. She cries out in pain, her violet eyes turning black. A counter-hacker?

"Check out that noise," the cyber man says.

Now I pop out of cover. I can't help my wife with whatever virtual battle she's in, but I can protect her from these assholes. *She's the best. She'll be fine.* Alex follows my lead. I go for the big guy, and she takes aim at a grunt. She cuts down her target, but the man I shoot, the one with the massive gun, isn't hurt at all. My shots bounce off his armor.

I call for Alex to get down. She doesn't listen, repeatedly squeezing off useless rounds. The gun's barrels spin and let loose a painful scraping sound. It unleashes a massive violet beam. Alex dodges, somehow, and the beam flies by her, melting a hole into the wall. No cover can protect against that. I lay down cover fire to grab his attention, and hopefully let Alex take better aim. If there's a weak spot in his armor, she'll find it.

He shoots again, this time at me. I duck under the beam, cursing under my breath. Alex shoots again, and I hear glass popping. The heavily armored soldier falls to one knee and grunts in pain. She's hit him in the eye, but he isn't dead yet. I take aim at the other soldiers. I see a muzzle flash. Alex cries out in pain. I miss my shot. I take my eyes off the soldiers for one second to check on Alex. She's clutching her bleeding shoulder.

Violet light blinds me, the heat painful against my exposed face.

The beam strikes Alex square in the chest. She was there one moment, then gone the next, the bottom half of her falling to the floor in a charred heap. *Fuck! Fuck!*

Viviana screams silently, clutching her hands to her head. She's fought off whoever invaded her systems, her eyes returning to their normal color. The man grunts as his gun powers down, the long barrel smoking and cherry red. What a horrific weapon.

I dash towards him. It's my only chance, and he's going to pay for what he did to Alex. Cover will not save me from this thing. He needs to go down. Now. I see the barrels spin to life again. I hop to the left and the beam passes me by. His aim is off thanks to Alex's taking out his eye.

Another shot slips by me. I keep pressing forward, guided by pure instinct. He fires again. I roll, feeling the heat scorch me even through my armored suit. *I'm still okay.* The two soldiers behind him open fire with their assault rifles. One of them clips me in the leg. It's agonizing, but I don't stop.

My suit would have absorbed most of the impact. I know that if I stop for just one second, that's it. That massive gun will put an end to me. I need to take advantage of the opportunity Alex gave me. He shoots again; I dash to my left, out of the way. Two seconds between shots. Ten meters to go.

I can make it.

One soldier in the back gets shot, his visor shattering, and his body falls limp to the floor. Viviana must have come out of cover. I want to scream for her to get down, but I can't lose focus—I trust her. With five meters to go, I draw my knife, ready to plunge it into his neck.

The cyber man turns, point his gun at Viviana—my wife.

"Get down!"

I don't think, I just leap in the way -

PROLOGUE

***

"Maeve!" I scream until my voice is raw.

The man lets out a bloodcurdling death rattle as he falls to the floor. Dead. Maeve's knife sticks out of his neck. She must have thrown it just as he shot. I run over to her, squeezing the trigger of my gun as I move. I hit the last remaining soldier directly in the head, just like Maeve taught me to. Head shots are risky but permanent. I slide across the ground as I come to a halt, looking down at her mangled body.

She's breathing.

I inspect her, trying my best to keep my composure. She's lost her whole left arm, including her shoulder. The beam was so intense it cauterized everything it didn't destroy outright. I can fix this. I just need to get her out of here. The problem is her right leg. Stupid woman. The bullet went completely through. The suit clenches around her wound automatically, applying pressure and releasing a disinfecting gel that seals the injury. She won't bleed out. I just can't carry her.

"Oh baby, I'm so sorry I have to do this," I say, trying my best to sound cheerful even though she's out cold. I pull out my datapad, linking to it directly. Now that I've obliterated the mind of that hacker, I have access to the ship again. I just wish it had been Cleo. This guy was too sloppy, too aggressive to be Cleo.

It's not like having access at this point will do us a whole lot of good. The best I could do was hail the rest of the fifth fleet. Anything else I might do could hurt my people just as much as the enemy and Sif is already dead. Fuck.

I isolate this sector of the ship and turn off the gravity. We float. I need to hurry. Her wound in zero-g is going to get real bad, real quick. She'll lose the leg if I can't get her some place safe. I cast a glance over at Alex's remains. She saved Maeve's life with that crack shot. Damnit, she didn't deserve to be killed like that. I hope the others on Maeve's team are okay. We have already lost so many people.

I steel myself; grab hold of my wife and kick off the floor. The force sends us tumbling down the hall. I do my best to keep us steady in the air. There are chaotic sounds throughout this section on the ship. More soldiers? Friendlies? Damnit, Maeve, this is your specialty, not mine. I hear more gunshots. People die. I can't tell who. Where do I go? The medical bay is in the next section of the ship, but I hear fighting coming down there.

Sif is dead. They have taken the bridge. When I find Cleo, I'm going to strangle her. I'm going to rip out her spine and beat her until they are nothing but bloody gelatinous goo.

No time. No time. I can think about my revenge later. Okay, V, think. The escape pods are in the other direction, opposite the fighting, but they are still so far away. The way forward is filled with enemies, so that won't either.

I need to take her to the mech bay. I hold her in my arms and kick off the wall again, dashing with her back and forth as I swiftly take us down the halls. At least we cleared the way earlier. Small favors.

There's a lift not too far away. I open it up, push us both in. Someone shouts as they shoot at us. I duck, praying a ricochet doesn't hit Maeve or me. The lift door closes behind us. Normally this feels like a quick trip, but right now it feels like the moment is lasting an eternity. I tap my foot nervously over and over until the lift doors open. I shut the gravity off as I drag her out.

"Even at zero-g, you're so dense," I say, as if she's able to appreciate my humor. It makes me feel a little better in any case. "Almost there, love. Then you can get us out of here. Just a bit more."

My little stunt has pissed off some enemy soldiers already in the hangar. I hear several loud yells and slight panic. I'd smirk, but I need to get Maeve the fuck out of here. Of course, as the highest-ranking pilot on the ship, the Witchblade is all the way over by the exit hatch. The esteemed position to sortie first is now something I'm cursing. Why couldn't she suck and be right by the lifts? I look down at her leg. It's swelling even under the suit's automatic pressure. Her vitals are not looking good either. Fuck.

As much as one can in zero gravity, I sprint forward, tugging her along. Someone sees us. A friendly. Zeke. One of Maeve's team. He waves me over towards him. I shake my head. He sees Maeve and pales. He really is just a kid, just twenty years old. I try to flash him a warm and sympathetic smile, but I can't really make my lips do that right now.

"Get to your mech," I tell him. "Just get out of here. I sent the evac signal. The ship is lost."

He nods. "I lost track of Jax and Morrigan a little while ago. We said we'd meet up here but—"

I want to tell him about Alex, but what's even the point right now? He needs focus if he's going to live. "They are the best," I tell him. "They'll make it."

"She's the best," he says, looking at Maeve, his voice cracking with anxiety.

I frown. "And she's still alive. So, we need to go or she won't be. I'm sure Jax and Morrigan are behind you, and we can maybe clear the hangar for them if you can help me get Maeve into her cockpit."

"Okay," he says, sounding a little more sure of himself.

We proceed forward quickly; I've already wasted so much time. The enemy sees us. Shots ring out, the sound of bouncing bullets fills my ears. I pick up the pace frantically. The Witchblade is within sight. Zeke yells out something. Out of the corner of my eye I see blood globules floating along with the dead bodies of two soldiers.

I don't look back to see if Zeke is okay. He's a pilot. He's young, but he's still a pilot. Right now, my concern is for my wife and she is going to die if I can't get us out of here. I fight back tears of frustration and push forward. Is it right to leave and let all the others fight? What am I supposed to do? I look down at my wife and see her mangled body again. I have to save her. No matter what, I just have to. If that makes me a coward, so be it.

I get us to the Witchblade and use the mounting-lift to get us up to the cockpit in the chest. I type in Maeve's access code. The cockpit opens agonizingly slowly. I drag her inside.

"I'm going to save you," I tell her firmly. "You'd better not die. If you do, I'm going to clone you and kill your clone just to spite you. Don't think I won't." I don't even know what I'm saying, my words are just vomited out.

I put her in her chair, reaching for the neural plug and shove it into the base of her spine through the slot in her flexsuit. It connects with a subtle click. She gasps as the neural implant activates, her mind integrating into her machine. It must be awful to be forced awake like this, but I know her—she'll be fine.

The Witchblade comes to life. Maeve grabs hold of me with her arm and sits me down on her lap. I buckle us in as the hatch closes. The cockpit springs to life, showing us what's happening outside from the various optics located all over the mech.

"Thanks for getting us this far," she whispers; her voice is so weak. "I'll take us the rest of the way."

"I know you will; love you."

There are still enemies in the hangar. Maeve uses the head mounted guns to pepper them with bullets, cutting them down. Zeke has been killed, his body floating lifelessly through the air. I cling to my wife.

"I'm sorry," I say, looking down at him.

"He was a good kid," she says as she walks forward, the magnetic function of the Witchblade's feet keeping us grounded. The hangar thuds with each step she takes. "Alex and the others, too. They are all good."

She signals open the bay's airlock, but they have changed the code because nothing happens. She draws the Witchblade's massive anti-material rifle and blasts the door from the inside.

The intense beam blows a hole into space. It sucks out everything in the hangar that isn't nailed down, including the remaining enemy soldiers. The hole gets ripped open, widening, until the energy shield around the ship seals the vacuum. The Witchblade lifts off the ground, the thrusters on her legs and back propelling us forward through the gap.

I watch as we go into the deep black. Enemy mechs are waiting for us outside. They are slow to react to us. Maeve, however, is without hesitation, moving quickly into melee. She draws the weapon for which her mech is named. The massive beam sword cleaves one of the mechs in half, sending a rippling shockwave through our frame. Before I can process what's going on, she's already moving towards the other one, slicing off their head and then thrusting the sword into the mechs' chest, the cockpit. The pilot would have been vaporized instantaneously.

"Hold on," she tells me. "It's my turn to be a little insane now."

"Do what you have to do," I tell her.

The Witchblade shakes as she dances through the void, sliding between enemy shots, dodging and weaving her way towards the enemy. Swarm-bits detach from the Witchblade with a metallic clank. I watch as the blue beams of light tear through the enemy mechs, shredding them apart, leaving only pieces floating in space.

Maeve pants. She never pants when she pilots. I look down at her leg and furrow my brow. I'm not sure I can still save it. Piloting like this is going to put an even bigger strain on her whole body, especially that leg. I cling to her, tears falling down my cheek.

A bright explosion goes off, catching my attention. It's from the ship. I turn to watch in horror as the Danu goes up in flame, reduced to debris. Not even a moment later, Cerberus explodes. Chunks of rock fly off in every direction, some of the smaller pieces pelting the Witchblade as they hurtle past us.

The moon lies sundered, the celestial body once a place of hope now in lifeless ruin.

Charon Station is gone. All those people. Thousands of people just wanting a new life—on their way to a new home. People I thought of as family on the Danu. Alex and Zeke are gone; did anyone else make it? I don't know what gods to pray to, but I pray to them all. Please let some of my friends be safe. More tears well up in my eyes. I can't help but weep. How could Cleo do this? Why? How did I not see what was coming? Truly, I am pathetic.

"I'm making her pay for this, Maeve," I hiss. "I will find out who she's working for and make them all pay."

"You'll get that chance," she says, her voice steadfast and firm. "We'll make them pay."

I put my hand on her stomach and nod. "I know."

There are another three mechs blocking our way. They draw weapons. Purple beams of light hurtle towards us. She dances through them again with uncanny human movements. Her movements are so fast they threaten to throw me around the cockpit. I've never seen her pilot like this before. Usually there's a bit more separation between her and the Witchblade, but not right now. I shouldn't be surprised by this. Of all the pilots I've seen data on, my wife is the most gifted with the interface OS. She's a monster.

She'll win.

I can almost see the panic in the enemy as she dodges whatever they throw at her. Missiles, beam weapons, bullets, it doesn't matter. She's a whirlwind; a force of nature. She stabs through an enemy cockpit. The bit-swarm cuts down another, leaving behind only molten fragments. She is in complete sync with her machine. I'm awed.

Only one enemy remains. The bits come together around her anti-material rifle, snapping into place, forming an even bigger gun. She blasts them with a beam of such intensity that it reduces the entire mech into slag. That one must have been for Alex.

We fly past the wreckage—the dead. She signals the gate to activate. It comes to life, bright golden light illuminating the black quilt all around us. Nothing or no one is in our way now.

We made it. We're safe.

Gilded Cage

I scream until my voice is raw as I sink my claw deep into my enemy, rending their metallic flesh. They go limp, the frame shutting down. I rip off their head and discard the body, sending it crashing into the ground. The pilot will live to think twice before insinuating that I am his future property.

Two more opponents to go, and I've already broken four.

The first of the two enters the field a moment, a tall blue and gold mech. Another challenger for my hand in marriage, another who seeks to cage me. This is a serial battle, one suitor after another. The dueling vows already spoken. There is no pageantry or show of honor before we begin—just the raw carnage of battle.

They smash against me, attempting to knock me down, but my body, my Bansidhe, is much too strong for that. My legs grind against the ground as I'm pushed back. I bash him away, taking a swipe at him with my claw. The pilot moves well, dodging backwards and unleashing a torrent of laser fire at me. I dance through the beams, the boosters on my back and my legs igniting with each sharp movement.

An alarm blares in the mech. My reactor. It's running far hotter than it should. I often push myself to the limit, but not in this fight. Dashing forward, I move to end this quickly, spinning through a barrage of fire and grabbing hold of my enemy with all three of my arms. I rip him to pieces and throw him to the ground.

In the brief reprieve I have before my last opponent takes the field, I try to vent the heat from my core, only to find that I cannot. Someone has tampered with my mech—violated my body. A message flashes across my screen.

"If only you had listened, you could have kept your pride. You will lose even that, my dear daughter."

The message deletes itself as my next opponent appears. This one is not so quick to attack me. Do they know? Continuing would be unwise. A reactor core explosion would put the lives of everyone at the academy at risk.

That stupid, useless old man. How dare he.

"Surrendering, Highness?" my opponent asks over the open comms. "It has been a rather long battle for you. There's no shame in admitting defeat. You've done better than most, but in the end, you're still a woman."

"Silence," I seethe, integrating my mind fully into the Bansidhe. I don't know what my father has done to prevent me from venting heat, but it doesn't matter. I am the Bansidhe, and every part of my body obeys me. With a metallic hiss, I force open the panels covering my core, exposing the nuclear engine. The surrounding air becomes superheated, causing a burst of wind to rage across the field.

"You—you're insane," he says. "Absolutely mad. You'll get yourself killed like that."

"But only I would die," I say. "And that is a risk I will take. Come then, if you think victory is at hand. I am, after all, just a woman." With a thud, I step forward, pink plasma dripping out of my core and down my frame.

"No," he says, dropping to his knees. "I surrender. I—you're—"

"Pathetic." Irritated, I rush towards him, drawing my sword and removing his head in the same motion. I kick the frame violently to the ground. "You do not get to speak to me in such a way and then give up. Your pride is fragile."

VICTORY flashes across the sky along with my name—Gráinne MacAirt.

* * *

My garden is the one place I know peace. Everyone knows they are forbidden from entering. I've not had to punish someone for breaking this one rule, but they are afraid of crossing me all the same. I'm not sure what I would do if someone came into my sanctuary without my permission, but I have thankfully never had to find out. Even the guard who is attached to me like a shadow knows well enough to stay out.

Father has called for me to return to Fomoria, the capital, but I am delaying as long as possible. A few extra relative hours won't kill him. Piloting always makes me feel depressed and tired, like only a part of me is awake. Tending to my garden helps me feel hale and whole once more.

My flowers need attention, the petals are drooping and look sad. I take care to spray them with a fine mist and add some food to the soil. Pruning the trees takes a bit more effort, but it's my favorite thing to do. I do not cut them to form them into shapes, only to guide their growth and keep the trees healthy. It's hard work keeping this much greenery alive on an asteroid academy—it keeps me sane.

The travel time alone to and from the capital will be a week in real time. Some of these blooms will already be dead by the time I get back; the thought causes my heart to ache. Experiencing the progressing colors is one of the few joys I have, but this trip to hear my outraged father scold me will ruin that.

My life is a cage I long to break.

* * *

"I will not lose because you demand it." My voice is cool and even as I stare into my father's dead eyes. "I will keep my pride—it matters not how much you wish otherwise."

"Gráinne, be reasonable," mother says. "We only want what's best for you."

"No," I say, turning my back on them both, "you don't."

Father rises from his chair; I can hear the ruffling of his robe and the jingles of his gaudy finery. "Gráinne, stop acting like a child. You will marry; duels be damned."

My eye twitches. I spend a moment taking a deep breath to calm myself. "You would break your own rules?" I ask, as calmly as I can manage. If I get upset, if I show any sign of weakness, he'll use it against me.

"The loophole you found in them, yes," he says. "You've become a fine warrior and have proved your point, but this is more important than pride. Our line must continue. You are our only child."

I turn to face them. "I am the best. The strongest," I say firmly. "Only I have truly mastered the Fomorian Framework. That last battle showed it. Even sabotaged, I won unequivocally. Was that not enough for you?"

He pauses, hesitates even. "That is true," he admits, "but my point still stands, Gráinne. You must cast aside your pride and marry. If you do not, our line will fall. The houses are already biting at our heels. If we don't guarantee an heir, they will make more blatant moves against us."

I scowl. "Let me pick my spouse, then," I say. I do not want any of this but, at least if the choice is mine, then I can make the most out of my father's demands.

He scratches his chin as he contemplates my offer. "Very well," he says. "I suppose that you have earned the right, my child. If no man is great enough to overcome the future empress, then so be it."

I smirk. An opening, perhaps? "My thoughts exactly."

I look at my mother. It's a subtle glance. She flashes a quick hand sign, telling me that I'm doing well.

"You have until your twenty-fifth birthday," he says. "If you have not picked by then, then the highest-ranking duelist will be your fiancée."

"You're giving me a month?" I grimace.

"Quite generous, I think," he replies severely. "He must be of noble birth. That is my only requirement. They may all be useless, but at least your husband will come from excellent stock."

The word is a slap to my face. *Husband.* It fills me with irrational rage. I hate the idea of marrying a man; I hate their games and I hate the way they look at me. Even as I grind their pride to dust, they still look upon me as lesser; as nothing more than a trophy. I hate being owned by them. No matter how I might rage against his cage like a feral beast, my father is my keeper. Becoming a wife will only change who keeps me.

My mother flashes me another gesture. She's saying to take his deal.

"Fine," I say through my teeth. "By my birthday then."

Mother claps her hands together. "Marvelous," she says, her voice exaggerated. An act. "Thank you for seeing reason, my darling."

Father also looks overjoyed, one of the few times he ever has that look, but even now there is a coldness in those black depths. "Indeed," he says. "Now you are acting like an adult."

"You finally gave me a choice, of a sort," I say. "That is what I asked for to begin with."

"Perhaps some fault lies with me then." His tone is insincere and placating. "Finally, we see eye to eye—I am glad."

I turn on my heel to leave, saying nothing more. My only wish is to be as far from this gaudy, tactless throne room as possible. Most of all, I want to be in my garden. The guard opens the door. It makes a scraping noise that grates my ears. I step through; the door closes behind me with a heavy thud.

The palace is brightly lit this afternoon; sunlight illuminates the halls through large stained-glass windows. My handmaiden waits for me. She's dressed smartly in a long green dress, her red hair tied up into a neat bun. Her green eyes peer at me with learned perception.

"Mistress," she says, her voice light and musical. "Shall we go back to the academy?" She smiles. "I'm sure after that conversation you are eager to visit your garden."

I smile. "You know me well, Aoife. Yes, I would like that very much."

She nods. "Very well. Your ship is prepared already," she says, already beginning to walk down the long hallway. "I'm sorry for your frustrations."

I follow behind. "No need to be. I held out as long as I could. Father has given me a choice now, so at the very least, I have some control."

"But that isn't enough for you," she says, as perceptive as ever. "You want freedom."

"Yes."

Aoife has been by my side for years now. Her presence is a great comfort to me. We walk along in silence, which is usual. I'm terrible to talk to and I know it. What even is there to say? Nothing around me is mine. My future is set, the path built and carved against my will by the tradition of men.

As empress, I'll be nothing more than a tool for the man I'm forced to pick. Maybe I could just have them killed and rule on my own, or perhaps I'll pick someone exceptionally weak and easy to control.

"You're plotting," Aoife says, her tone amused. "Killing your father or your future husband?"

I laugh. "Husband today," I admit. "I am perfectly capable of ruling without one and if a child is so necessary, then I can just..." I sigh. "It is quite possible to make use of an artificial womb and a donor."

"That is not our way," Aoife says. "It goes against tradition. A child is to be born from a union of man and woman."

I grimace. "I am aware," I tell her. "But maybe some traditions should change. Central, for example, does things very differently than we do."

"That is almost heresy, Princess," she replies. "Central is the enemy who stole Earth."

"I know," I say. "I am aware that they won the war, but they are not our enemy any longer. Not officially, anyway."

"Hmm," she says, opening another door that leads out towards the car. "But it doesn't change that you're grasping for ways to be free of the burdens of your station. We all have our parts to play."

There is sadness in her voice. I know she speaks of herself, too. "We'll make the best of it, Aoife."

"Yes, Mistress."

Royal guards stand posted all over the palace entrance, armed to the teeth in power-suits and massive beam cannons that can reduce a person to ash on impact. Aoite walks out ahead of me. The guards give me a respectful nod as I'm led to the car. I step inside and relax back into the leather seat. Tension releases somewhat. One month, huh? It will take a week just to get back to the academy.

Aoife sits next to me, closing the door behind her. She gives instructions to take us to the port. I look out the window, attempting to think of something, anything, that might help me out of this.

"I have an idea," I begin, though the plan is still forming in my mind.

Aoife, calm as ever, looks over to me. "I'm listening."

I chew on my thumb in frustration. "One last tournament for the potential suitors, but it will be open it to all."

She tilts her head. "Why? Didn't your father say they had to be of noble birth?"

I smirk. "The last thing he said was I had to pick by my birthday, or the highest-ranking duelist would be my husband. If I do not pick anyone at all, but let them fight amongst themselves, I may be able to maneuver someone malleable into that position." I fold one leg over the over, sitting up straight. "It is not how I want to go about this, but if I must marry someone, I am going to make sure I can control them. I will not be under the thumb of some useless man."

Aoife chuckles.

"What?" I ask, irritated and making no attempt to mask it. "It is not as if I can marry someone I love."

"I know," she says. "I was simply musing how much better your life would have been if you were a man."

My nose wrinkles in disgust. "Do not say such things," I tell her. "Whatever my lot in life must be, I would never want to be a man. I just want my freedom."

She nods. "Of course. I meant no offense, Princess," she says softly.

Aoife only ever calls me that to soothe my temper. I am still irritated, but less so. "I know. It is this stupid idea, or I simply run away. Perhaps I can somehow hitch a ride to Central and forget these damn duels."

She reaches over, putting a hand on my knee, her soft fingers giving me a gentle squeeze. "Do not run, Princess," she says, her tone severe but still tender. "You may not believe it right now, but your people need you. Think of what you could do for them should you come into power. Marry a useless noble. Sleep with a lowborn man you like."

My cheeks burn from her touch. "I have no desire to bed any man."

Aoife pulls her hand away, chuckling. "Are you well, Princess?"

"Yes," I tell her. "Quite alright—just stressed."

* * *

Traveling at near-lightspeed for a week is a frustrating experience. Only a few hours will pass for me, but a week for everyone else in real time. I think about that often when I make brief trips like this, how time is relative and flexible. Perhaps I should just hijack my ship and spend a year of relative time at near-light and come back after seven years have passed. My garden would die with no one to tend to it; that singular thought puts a damper on my grand escape.

I sigh. My father wouldn't die in that time anyway, unless one of the other houses assassinates him. That thought amuses me somewhat, but it would also mean war, a war that would cost millions of lives. That I do not want to happen. I lean back in my seat, trying to push away the depressing thoughts. I want my freedom, but not at that cost.

When I left the palace, it was bright, during the peak hours of the afternoon. Fianna Academy, however, is in the late hours of the evening. The academy is built into a tiny dwarf planet at the edge of this solar system. I admit to feeling somewhat fond of Fianna. It's been my home for four years and is at least far away from my father and the politics of Fomoria.

Aoife remained in the capital, informing my mother of my plan. I wish her public face was not what it was, the quite demure empress who obeys her husband's every whim. She's so much stronger than that, and it's been a deep source of frustration my entire life. I would not be who I am without her, yet she does not speak up for me. I love her, but even now I feel a rising, righteous rage bubbling up from my core. As strong as even she is, even as empress, she is still stuck under my father's thumb.

That will not be my fate—I refuse.

With a soft thud, the ship pulls into the dock. Besides the pilots and one staff member, I am the only one aboard. I disembark quickly, making my way into the academy itself. The hangar is kept in constant low gravity; I float along in the air, gradually getting heavier as I leave. Even at night it's busy with many comings and goings of staff and students.

I enjoy being here, surrounded by the various mechs and ships. The people are so busy they hardly notice me, not that there is much to notice. I do not wear finery at school or make a fuss of my status. My uniform is the same as anyone else's: a smart buttoned up green tunic, black jacket, black tie, and plain slacks. I get to blend in and simply be Gráinne.

The exit door slides open with a hiss. It clicks shut behind me. A rather large, gruff man stands in my way—Renault, the bodyguard kept here to watch over me. I tolerate his presence, as I must tolerate many things in my life, but I cannot stand him in the slightest.

"Princess," he says, his voice rough and deep.

"Renault," I acknowledge him, if only barely. "Follow behind me as if you are a ghost. I do not wish to speak."

He hesitates, looking as if he is about to argue with me before stepping aside. "Understood."

"What did I say about speaking?" I walk past him without waiting for a response.

He is not Aoife; he does not make me feel safe. The way his eyes linger on me unsettles me—I often wish I could gouge them out and crush them in my hands.

The academy grounds are a massive wide-open space filled with grass and trees and people. Fianna's ceiling is a false sky far above us, currently showing the stars and the twin moons of Fomoria. It's as if I am at the palace looking up from my balcony. I wish it was any other view, any other place in the Milky Way.

My stomach growls. I turn to walk towards the dining hall near the center of campus. Even during the night, students are out and about as they please. Many are enjoying themselves with various activities, from dates to studies out in the open or simply reading under the trees. I long to join them, but they remind me I belong to a different world with their discomfort. Once I have my food, I'll withdraw to my garden.

A pair of girls walk on the opposite side of the path from me, walking away from the dining hall. Our eyes meet briefly, and I offer them a smile. Their look drifts over at Renault, who's walking behind me, and they give me, and him, a wide berth as they pass.

I sigh, fighting back the pang of loneliness that grips my chest. It's been four years since I started attending and even now, I do not have a single friend. How can I possibly make any with this lumbering idiot behind me? Tonight will be no different—another meal alone.

Perhaps I can-

Lost in thought, I smash right into someone, someone incredibly hard. I take a moment to recover my senses. The impact was enough to nearly knock me off my feet. Irritated, I look up into warm, white eyes. They are like freshly fallen snow during a winter storm. A woman—taller than me—and I am not short. Her equally white hair is long, tied back in a neat tail that reaches below her waist. It blows in the false breeze, locks of hair dangling delicately over her chiseled face. The irritation fades. My voice stuck in my throat.

Who is she?

"Sorry about that," she says. Her voice is rich, deeper than I expected, and very gentle. The corner of her eyes wrinkle, her lips forming a broad smile that draws my gaze towards the one 'imperfection' on her otherwise perfect face, a small mole just under her right eye. "Are you fine?"

"Oh, yes." Heat rushes to my face. I do my best to maintain my composure, which is difficult. I've never seen a more exquisite woman in all my life. "T'was my fault for not paying attention."

Renault reaches for his baton, rushing towards us. He is about to open his stupid mouth before I raise a hand to silence him.

"You're dismissed," I tell him firmly. "Do not speak. Just go."

His eyes burn with anger, his grip tightens on his weapon. He grunts, leaving me with the gorgeous stranger.

"Sorry," I say. "An overzealous guard. Who are you?" Gods, her white hair and snowy eyes give her a striking, uncanny beauty. I struggle to look away. "I do not recognize you."

"Dia," she says. "I'm a new transfer, so you wouldn't."

My lips pull back into as warm a smile as I can manage. I never get to talk to people like this, and I feel a bit awkward. "It's nice to meet you, Dia."

She returns the smile; kind and charming. "A pleasure. You're Princess Gráinne, right?"

A sigh escapes me. I had hoped she wouldn't recognize me. Then again, that means she has known who I am from the start—yet she is still here. *Curious.* "I am, yes."

"Well, sorry again for bumping into you. That was foolish of me," she says. "That guard of yours seemed quite keen on attacking."

I would expect her to feel some sort of fear, but I sense nothing of the sort. No, I feel that if she were to get into a fight with Renault, she would thrash him properly.

Perhaps I should call him back. The thought amuses me. "No," I say aloud. "He is a fool, but would not attack without being told, and I am not so heartless as to give the order just for running into me."

She smirks. "Good to hear," she says. "I was on my way to get something to eat. Join me?"

My heart skips a beat. *Oh, this is stupid. She's just asking me to a meal. But so easily? Who is this woman? How can she just smirk at me like this?* "I'd be happy to," I manage. My heart is racing now. Perhaps she will be my friend? She bothers to talk to me when others don't, even knowing who I am. That's a good start.

"Great," she says, winking. "My mothers will be thrilled I took a princess to dinner."

I blink. "What did you say?"

"Did I say something odd?" She tilts her head.

"Mothers? As in more than one?" I blink again.

"Yes." She furrows her brows now, a flash of anger in her eyes. "I have two mothers."

I stare at her for a long time, processing exactly what she's saying.

She folds her arms in front of her chest. "Why are you asking?" Her tone is indignant, but tinged with curiosity as if she is testing me.

I step close to her. "Keep that to yourself," I whisper forcefully. "That is a crime."

She chuckles, shaking head. "You say that like I should care."

"Shut up," I tell her firmly, taking her by the hand. I yank her behind me towards the dining hall. "Just do not speak of such things! I am going to pretend I heard nothing."

I release her hand, walking onward. To my surprise, she is still following behind. Her expression is hard to read, but I can feel the disappointment radiating off her.

"I am sorry." I sigh. "It is not something I have anything against, but the law says..."

"I know the laws here," she says, cutting me off. "Let's rather talk about something else."

"Right," I say, hanging my head as we approach the dining hall. "What would you like to eat?"

* * *

I've taken Dia back to my garden where we can eat in peace. Just going to the dining hall was a frustrating endeavor. News has, of course, reached every one of my birthday tournament, and the concentrated crowd of people in the dining hall muttering about it was exhausting. My garden is serene, far removed from the other students. Dia is looking around curiously, eyeing the flowers intently.

"You have Earth flowers," she remarks. "The lilies are beautiful. You have so many colors here, it's like being in a wild field."

"What do you know about Earth?" I ask, my brow arching.

"Quite a lot. I was born there." She smiles.

I almost drop my food. "Are you serious?" I walk up to her, getting very much into her personal space. "Tell me everything."

Dia looks quite taken aback, but she doesn't pull away from me. "Well," she begins. "Well, what is there to say? It's blue and green all over. The air is clean, and the people are kind. It's a paradise."

Earth. Gods, Earth! "Why are you here? Sorry, I am surprised that you are from Earth?"

She rubs the back of her neck. "My mother," she says, her brows furrow.

"You can talk freely here," I assure her eagerly.

"Well, my mother is a big researcher, and she travels all over the galaxy," Dia explains. "I'm here to help her with some of that while I finish off my degree. I know it's a bit hostile between Central and the Armory since the Cerberus Incident, but it is what it is."

"That is true," I say, frowning. "It very much could be worse."

She sighs, sitting under one of my tall sycamore trees. "My mothers talk about it a lot. They were there."

I sit down next to her. "I didn't think anyone survived," I admit. "At least that's not what I learned in my school days."

She shrugs. "Well, they did," Dia says. "Grew up on stories of how awful it was to see Cerberus explode and about all the refugees who died at the station." She frowns again. "The victims never got justice."

I bring my knees up to my chest. "No one knew who was responsible. Central showed remarkable restraint. Though my schoolbooks do not see it that way."

She chuckles. "Fascinating." She leans back, taking her hair and flipping it over her shoulder. It's long enough to reach the ground, though she places it in her lap, presumably to keep it clean. "I'm sure they somehow blamed Central's 'ineffectual government' or something. I don't know or care what lies they spun to be honest. Interesting that you aren't spewing the same nonsense."

"I'm privy to information others aren't," I say. "I know how large and advanced Central's military is. They would not succeed if they go to war with the entire rest of the galaxy, but they would crush any one sector-state in open war. Maybe two." I chuckle. "My father complains about that often."

"The fuck is his problem, anyway?" she asks.

I chew my lower lip, fighting back my instinct to speak very ill of him. "He believes Earth belongs to the Fomorians."

Dia laughs, a sardonic, withering sort of laugh. "It's a miracle the planet is such a paradise now. Took a whole century to clean up the state it was in.

Humanity ran it into the ground before the Secession War."

"I have always wanted to live on Earth," I say softly, staring at her. It's impossible to read her expression—her face is unnervingly stoic. Such a beautiful, fierce face. I blink, looking away to hide the red in my cheeks.

She tilts her head and begins playing with her hair. "Why? I mean, I know a lot of people do, but you're the princess. Why do *you* want to live on Earth?"

I take a moment to think. The answer I want to give is clear in my mind but fills me with dread to admit. "Freedom," I say after a few moments. "Freedom to live on my terms. I wish I hadn't been born here." That is perhaps the first time I've uttered those words aloud. Reflexive shame rises from my stomach and strangles my heart.

"You're the princess. Why can't you live on your own terms?" She continues playing with her snowy hair, twirling a long strand around her finger.

"If you grew up in this part of the galaxy, you wouldn't be asking why," I say sadly. "That you even ask tells me the difference between our worlds—how much kinder yours is."

"And this whole tournament for marriage you're hosting?"

"A compromise I made to take some control over my life." I look over at her. Gods, she feels easy to talk to. Perhaps because where she's from there are no such thing as princesses. To her, I'm just a normal woman. My heart flutters again. *Get ahold of yourself, please.* "I do not want any of this, least of all, to get married to a *man*."

"That's awful," she says, taking a bite of her sandwich. "You're really not what I expected when we ran into one another."

A chuckle erupts from within. "Oh? And what did you expect?"

"Well." She looks at me, staring at me with those almost gleaming white eyes of hers. "You're softer than I would have expected; more sincere. No offense."

I wrinkle my nose. "None taken. Everyone thinks I am stuck up or even evil, and it's not as if I can blame them. Even when I make my guards leave me alone, no one wants to talk to me—no one I want talking to me, in any case."

"Who do you want talking to you then?" She takes another bite of her food.

"Not men who want to marry me." I sigh. "Literally anyone else at this rate, but it is only them who try to approach me, to court favor rather than fight me."

Dia frowns. "I'm sorry, Princess."

I find it surprising that I am not annoyed by her calling me *princess*, though it doesn't soothe me like when Aoife says it—rather, a strange thrill travels up my spine. "My father—he told me I could pick anyone I wanted to marry because I have *earned* that much, but there is no man I would ever choose."

"Question, would you marry a woman?" she asks, a smirk on her face.

"W-what? No!" I stammer, sitting upright, backing away from her. "No! That is—"

"A crime." Her gaze pierces through me so strongly that I feel completely naked and exposed.

All I can do is nod, my words stuck in my throat.

"But you would, if the choice was yours and nothing was holding you back?"

I'm frozen in place. Never has anyone asked me such a question. My heart pounds in my chest. My hands feel cold. I look into her eyes. No matter how I might try to hide the truth, even from myself, I know I cannot hide from her.

"Yes."

Her face softens, though her eyes become sad. "You should be able to live how you want," she says, her tone a mixture of sympathy and anger. "It isn't right that you can't. Of course, it's not just you, either. Many people feel the pressure of that oppression."

"No," I say softly, averting my gaze. "It's not right. Um... how long are you here for?"

"A year," she says. "Enough for me to finish my degree. The piloting program is decent; almost as good as the one on Mars."

"Wait, Dia, are you a mech pilot?" I ask, my heart pounding again.

"Yes," she says. "I'm the best."

I smirk. "In the entire galaxy? The best in Central? Come now, you can't make that claim. I don't think you're even the best in this school."

She chuckles and leans forward, pressing her face close to mine. "The best."

I pull away, regarding her carefully. The way she looks at me, the confidence she exudes, reminds me of a wolf. Even if she is just boasting, there is an opportunity here that I would be foolish to pass up. "Fight for me in the tournament."

"No," she says, folding her arms over her chest. "I am not going to fight to be your wife, Princess."

Wife. The word sends a thrill down my spine. "You don't have to marry me so much as help me avoid marriage."

She breathes out a heavy sigh. "No," she says. "I'm not getting caught up in this."

"Dia, please." I turn to face her fully. My mind is spinning. This might be my only chance to escape this hell. I can almost feel the freedom on the tips of my fingers. My pride, my honor, my position—none of that matters to me now; I just want my freedom. "I am begging you!"

"Why should I?" she asks me, her voice now has an edge to it. "I have no interest in the sort of politics that go on in this system. As you've pointed out, it's a crime for two women to get married here, so what good would it do? Should I steal you away and cause an incident?" She smirks. "Maybe I should."

That smirk is a deadly weapon. I avert my gaze again, attempting in vain to keep hold of my composure. "The tournament," I say. "I remove myself as the highest-ranked duelist and you fight on my behalf in secret. Win and we can get married and there will not be a thing he can do." I smile at the thought. "He might be so furious he banishes me; I'll be truly free then."

"Or send assassins." She sighs again, leaning against the tree. "Would they even let me fight? I'm no Fomorlan."

That is an irksome point she's made, because no, my father wouldn't allow it. I look her up and down, my brows furrowing. Gods, she is gorgeous. I'm getting distracted. "What if we falsified your identity, and you pretended to be a man?"

"No," she says fervently. "Absolutely not. I would, truly, rather die."

"Just for entering!" I explain. "I don't want a husband, even a pretend one I know is a woman. What a loathsome word."

That gets a small chuckle out of her. She crosses her arms over her chest. "You might be as gay as me," she says.

My cheeks flush again. *What is that supposed to mean?*

"I suppose my name might throw people off, but I am not outright calling myself a man, understood?"

"Dia isn't a man's name though," I say, confused. "How do you mean?"

"It's a nickname," she says. "My name is Diarmuid."

"A good name—not a man's name on you." I chuckle, feeling my heartbeat calm. "Though I am curious, why did your mothers give you that name?" I shift closer to her, our legs nearly touching.

"They liked the name, and I was born with parts that might make one think I was a boy," she says, her tone almost amused. "Some trans people change their names to something they feel suits them better, but Diarmuid still feels like me and Dia is cute."

"It is cute, but I don't think I understand why they'd think you were a boy." I furrow my brows. "Unless—oh! Right, well, that makes sense."

Dia laughs mirthfully. "Correct," she says, chuckling still. "It's sort of cute how naïve you are."

"Shut up." I look down at my feet, trying to hide my embarrassment at my display of ignorance. I close my eyes, refocusing myself and ponder the implications of what she's just told me. "Central must be a wonderful place, to be so free to alter your body." I rest my chin on my knees. "Gods, there must be so many people like you who have wanted to do the same, but they cannot—not here." The thought makes me sick to my stomach.

"Need to," she says, her voice mournful. "It's not a want." She sighs, takes a long look at me, and turns slightly to face me more fully. "It's funny, growing up, it never occurred to me that I wasn't a girl. There came a point when my mothers had to have a talk with me because I was getting older, and my body was going to change."

She shakes her head, smiling fondly. "It was then that I realized I could be a boy at all, if I wanted, but the idea was repulsive to me. I just wasn't a boy, and I sure as fuck wasn't a *man*." Dia smiles warmly then, resting her head against the tree. "This is how I found out my mother is the same as me."

I can't help but stare at her, raking my eyes along her features. For the first time, she seems sort of vulnerable and soft. Seeing her like this gives me a feral, primal urge to bite that I quickly shove down. "I cannot even imagine anything like that happening in this sector."

"It does," she replies, lifting her head to look at me. "There are trans people among the Fomorians, too. We're everywhere."

"I feel very foolish," I admit, looking away again.

"You didn't know." She shrugs. "It makes me angry, but I'm not angry with you."

Her words offer slight relief, but I still can't help the feeling in the pit of my stomach. "There's so much I would change if I could. Before I ran into you, my best plan was to marry some impotent, useless man who I could control." I take a moment to try to keep calm, but my anxiety bubbles up to the surface despite my effort. "The other houses hold considerable sway and we're so entrenched in our traditions that they'd try to murder me if I made drastic change."

Tears form in my eyes. "I want to fix things; I know people in other sectors—especially Central—live so much better." A wave of frustration washes over me, a decade's worth I can't contain. Not even with my mother can I speak as freely as I can right now. Tears roll down my face as I choke back my sob. "I do not want to be hunted for the rest of my life—I have not even *lived* yet."

She moves right there next to me; her face is just centimeters from mine. "I'll fight for you, Princess." She reaches towards my face, wiping away my tears.

I'm taken aback; frozen in place. No one has ever touched me like that before, not a soul. I stare at her, my eyes drawn to the spot right under her eye. I feel like I could get lost in those snowy white eyes of hers—drown in them. The fear and rage in my heart seem to wash away when I look at her. "Oh?"

"Yes," she says gently, "but I want something in return."

"Anything."

"Well, it's nothing too hectic," she says, purring in my ear. "You doubted my abilities earlier. I'd like to see just how good you are in the cockpit."

I suck in a breath. My mouth feels impossibly dry; my hands shake. "Why are you changing your mind?"

She grins. "You asked me to save your life," she says. "That sort of request does something to a girl. It's like when I'm piloting; there's no room for hesitation, or else you miss your opportunity for victory."

Instinctively, I get even closer but keep my eyes fixed on hers. "You sound like me," I say. "If you agree to fight on my behalf, then we can spar one another. I want to test your skills besides. You could be a liar who is worthless to me." I simper, laughing softly under my breath.

"Taking me out for a test ride?" she says, keeping her grin. "Good. You're smart."

I blush again, sure that I look like a fool—she is relentless. "Just your skills," I say tersely. "Your skills, and that is all. Meet me at the mech launch bay at noon in three days. It will be an exhibition match to announce a new contender: you."

She thinks about this for a moment, running her fingers along her jaw—her angled, lovely jaw. "You say that like you expect to win our fight and you just want me to put on a show."

"I have never lost," I tell her. "So no, despite your boasting, I do not expect to lose. You do not need to be better than me, just better than all of them."

"I'll win," she says, standing up. Her long hair flowing behind her as she looks down at me.

I rise, meeting her gaze with narrowed eyes. "What makes you so sure of that?" I do not care for being looked down on, but, I admit, I really enjoy looking up at her.

She steps closer, her breath practically on my neck. "Because I have an enemy," she says, leaning forward so close that her lips are almost on mine. "Your gilded cage."

I feel paralyzed, unable to speak or move, trapped by her overwhelming intensity. Her hand reaches out to cup my chin.

"I always destroy my enemies, Princess."

Secrets in the Garden

She doesn't pull away from my touch, rather she looks at me defiantly with those big violet eyes of hers. The breeze catches her scent—vanilla and cherry blossoms. It's an intoxicating smell. Grudgingly, I remove my hand, pulling away entirely as straighten up.

She casts her gaze towards the ground, her raven hair falling in front of her face. "We'll see about that," she says.

I step past her. "See you tomorrow, Princess."

"Tomorrow?" she asks, looking at me over her shoulder. "Our duel is not for three days."

I smirk back at her. "Doesn't mean I don't want to see you before then." I stuff my hands into my pockets, keeping my gaze fixed on her.

"Gráinne," she says, her voice light but firm, demanding even. "You can call me Gráinne."

"I'll keep that in mind." I walk out of her garden, a smile on my face.

Step one complete.

There is a part of me that feels awful for misleading her, but I'm just not sure if I can trust her yet. I can't keep this up for too much longer, though; I hadn't expected her to be so earnest. Fuck, I really don't want to hurt her.

It isn't easy to rip down an empire.

I'm tempted to look back towards the garden—back towards her. I fight the urge and keep walking. She really is easy to talk to. How many times did I almost slip up? Too many.

Getting back to my dorm is a mission. The academy is a massive city built under the surface of a dwarf planet. Four million people are living here at any given time between the students, faculty, and the defense force. Even more will be here in the next few days, thanks to Gráinne's tournament. It's ridiculous that duels can decide a government's succession. No wonder the people of this sector suffer so much. It's rotten from the top down.

Unable to resist any longer, I look back; the garden is far out of view. My gaze lingers for a moment. It's late now and most everyone is asleep. Is this the right thing? Should I go back, tell her this was all a mistake, and go about this another way?

My enemy is your gilded cage.

I recall the touch of her skin against the tips of my fingers and the look in those eyes of hers. I recall the choked back sob; that was the moment I decided to save her. I think of the vids I've seen of her duels as I walk. She reminds me of a lot of the people I've helped across the galaxy—people stuck in situations beyond their control, desperate for a way out. Before now, I had thought she piloted for pride or to maneuver against her father. It never crossed my mind that she felt so helpless.

I'm so sick of putting worthless bandages on gaping, infected wounds. I want to save them all—I want to save her. Is her resolve stronger than her fear? Her words back in the garden, her desperate desire to just live, make my heart ache. She's not like me. She is a warrior, yes, but she fights only for herself. Will she fight for others?

My room is studio style and sparsely furnished. There is a desk to work on, a dining table with a single chair and my bed. I didn't bring any of my belongings with me just in case I get caught and have to get out quick. As I do every night, I sweep the room for bugs. There are three new ones today, and like the others I've found so far, all sloppily hidden—the security here is truly abysmal. Maybe I could have brought a few stuffed animals after all.

I sit at my desk, pulling up homework for how the princess pilots—one of her old vids. It's three vs one. Her mech, the Bansidhe, is the largest on the field, though it's slightly smaller than mine. The frame is gorgeous, platinum with pink trim, three arms, one being a massive, wicked claw, and long plantigrade legs. The face is humanoid with glowing pink eyes. Its frame maintains an elegant silhouette despite the bulk and monstrous arm.

Gráinne's Bansidhe is gorgeous.

The three mechs she is fighting are rather ugly; painted a dull gunmetal gray. Signature style of M.E.T.A Industries, the system-state near the galaxy's core. Like all M.E.T.A mechs, they have a minimalist look I just can't stand. A pilot's mech should express who they are, but these three are all uniform in appearance. Stumpy digitigrade legs with four arms that have various weapons, from blades to energy rifles. The only redeeming design choice is the singular red eye.

Several flying drones surrounding the battle arena captured this vid; I can freely swap between the various angles. Useful for studying her movements in more detail. Her enemies dash forward in unison, chainsaw energy axes revving as they close in. Those weapons are deadly, capable of slicing through armor like butter. Gráinne is quick, her movements fluid and uncanny for a mech. No doubt, the result of the Fomorian Framework allowing her to integrate directly with her mech.

The others are painfully slow compared to her, their movements mechanical and stiff. She dodges; dancing between them with effortless grace. That massive claw reaches out, sweeping across the field, pink plasma jettisoning out from exhaust vents as it clamps around one of the mechs. The arm squeezes tight, instantly crushing the enemy frame.

There is a shift in the air when that happens. I can see the fear in the movements of the other two mechs. They hadn't expected one of them to fall so quickly or easily. Not surprising, really, the difference between a pilot who integrates with their frame and one who does not is astronomical. They never really stood a chance to begin with. Maybe if she faced ten of them, they could have won.

In an instant, another has their legs and head cut off with two swift, graceful strokes from her green energy blade. The last enemy overheats their systems, electricity sparking from the reactor core, in a desperate attempt at victory. Gráinne rushes forward, her movements feral. Yet more pink plasma erupts from her back and her clawed hand as she burns with an awesome power. The mechs crash into one another, Gráinne easily overpowers the industrial mech, smashing it onto the ground, and grinding her clawed hand into the frame until it crumples.

She stops short of total destruction, but only just, sparing the pilot a grisly death. All would live to fight another day—killing is forbidden in these matches. To prevent accidents, weapons are powered down dramatically. It's not too dissimilar to the Central Arena Circuit, but those matches are purely for spectacle and entertainment. What might the Bansidhe be capable of in a proper fight, I wonder? How much more feral would she become if her life was on the line? I intend to find out.

An enlightening use of my time, in any case. I close the vid, leaning back into my chair. She's at least as aggressive as I am, capable of direct interface with her mech, and determined beyond belief to win at all costs. It won't be an easy duel to win.

Sighing, I pull out my com, select my mother and dial. She picks up almost instantly.

"Dia!" She beams at me, her face lighting up. "Maeve, come over here."

"It's a bit late to call, don't you think?" Mom asks, a teasing smile at the edge of her mouth.

"Well, I figured you'd like to know I made contact with the princess, and it's my professional opinion that I was very wrong about a few things."

"Oh?" mother asks, arching her brow. "That's surprising."

"She wants out of this place," I say. "I'm pretty sure if I suggest she just escape to Central with me, she'd take me up on the offer."

They both furrow their brows. "That is unexpected," mom says. She lifts her energy drink with her cyber-arm, tapping her metallic finger against the metal can. Tink, tink, tink, as she thinks. "You're considering bringing her on as an asset, aren't you?"

"I'm unsure right now," I say. "Her situation isn't great. She's being forced to marry a man when she's a lesbian."

My mother grimaces in disgust. "That's awful," she says, shaking her head. "Okay, so where do you fit in? Wait... Diarmuid, no!" She only ever uses my name when she's truly upset.

"She asked me to save her life," I say, holding her gaze. "I said yes. She wants me to fight in this stupid tournament, win, and legally marry her to defy her father. I have to admit, I'm taken in with her determination."

Mom sighs. "Dia, you hear how insane that is, right?" she chuckles. "The plan was to get close to the princess to see what your options were, not marry her."

"It's just a legal thing," I say, wrinkling my nose. "I want to do it because at the very least, I can get her out of this situation, and it might trigger a huge conflict among the ruling houses. The way I see it, I'd be helping her and accomplishing at least part of my goal at the same time."

Mother chews her inner lip, the gears turning in her head. "It's a lot more personal risk to take on than you intended," she muses. "I mean, it was always risky, but this puts you in a direct line of fire, even if they never discover your actual intentions."

"I know," I say. "There are already a lot of tensions if the rumors are accurate, and they are probably underselling the issues. Gráinne's refusal to marry has caused a ton of problems. I don't want to leave this place standing when I leave, and I think this will help me tear it all down."

"Are you calling her by name now?" mother asks. "Diarmuid."

"I like her name," I say defensively. "Anyway, I think this is the best idea for now. I have three weeks to really feel out the situation, and if I think it won't work, I'll just refuse."

"Will you?" mother asks, her eyes giving me their all-knowing piercing look. "Will you really?"

"Yes," I say, "if I think it won't work."

She squints at me. "You need to get out."

"Not happening." I fold my leg over the other and lean forward. As much as my mother is squinting at me, I squint right back. "I will do what I have said I will do; we're not getting into a fight about it."

Mom looks over. "V," she says. "Give her a chance?"

"Look at her, Maeve," mother says, pointing right at me. "Diarmuid is the definition of a hopeless lesbian. She's going to do something insanely rash because there is a girl involved, and she needs to be saved."

"A girl who is a good fucking pilot," I retort. "Well, she looked good on vid.

I'll find out for sure in three days when we have our match."

"See?! She's already planning on a date with this woman." Mother shakes her head.

"V, my darling..."

"Don't you 'my darling' me," mother says firmly, sighing at us both. "Damnit, you wouldn't even be here if I could find that bitch. The Fomorians are the only lead I have on where she ran off to. Twenty-five years and I'm nowhere close to her."

"Mother," I say, keeping my tone even but firm. "I am here because I want to be, because I'm so sick of being a merc running around the galaxy like a chicken with my head cut off, helping people but solving nothing."

I grip my fist tight, struggling to keep my emotions down. "You just so happen to be helping me. Don't act like this isn't my choice." I take a deep breath, relaxing my jaw and letting the tension out. "Also, I am *not* hopeless."

They exchange long glances with one another. Mother finally smiles, subtly, but I know her expressions. "Okay," she says. "Consider me convinced."

"Moving on, I have some news regarding Cleo," I say. "The Fomorians are using an adapted form of the Tuatha OS, but it's not as clean as what you built. From what I've been able to gather, it involved a lot of unethical human experiments. I'll send you my notes—it's disgusting."

"Well, they sure as shit didn't do *that* all on their own," she mutters. "I still can't believe she sold the Fomorians the OS, not that I can believe anything she's done."

Mother seethes, and my mom wraps her arm around her. She leans into the embrace, the fire in her eyes calming somewhat.

"Alright," mother says, her tone much softer and more relaxed. "Check in once a week. If I think you've become stupid and fallen in love with this woman, I'm going to bitch and moan until you come home."

"Don't worry," I say. "I will not fall in love with someone in three weeks."

* * *

There she is. Her soft black hair neatly tied and pinned to the back of her head. Class begins shortly; she's sitting by herself, the other students avoiding her like she's down with a plague. She looks lonely. The bodyguard fellow is in the corner of the room just watching her. It's disturbing, really. I go to sit next to her.

She looks surprised that anyone has approached her at all; her face brightening up considerably when she recognizes me. The bodyguard makes a move toward us, and using some sort of sixth sense, Gráinne turns to glare at him. He's cowed by the look alone, and he steps back into his corner. I smile at her.

"Morning," I say.

"Dia." Her voice is stiff and formal. "It is good to see you again."

"Likewise." My smile turns into a smirk. I'm acutely aware now of all the eyes on the two of us, but that somehow just makes this whole game of mine a lot more fun. It's difficult not to be amused by these people, and I enjoy shattering their sense of ceremony. "Are you well this morning?"

"Perfectly well," she says. "Perhaps even better than that now. I did not realize you took this class."

I smile. "Well, you wouldn't. You've only just come back to the academy. Frankly, I'm surprised you're even in class, what with the big tournament for your birthday that needs planning."

She narrows her eyes at me. Others around us murmur among themselves. "The tournament is being arranged as we speak. How my birthday is to be celebrated is up in the air."

"Hopefully, you will have cause for genuine celebration. Marrying some idiot wouldn't be ideal." My lips pull back into a teasing grin.

She glares at me. It's the kind of glare that makes me grin wider—it's adorable.

"Watch yourself."

"I'm not like the rest of them," I say, pointing at our class. "You don't and can't scare me, Princess. I'm only teasing you anyhow. You'll have something good to celebrate. I promise."

She narrows her eyes, staring hard at me until her façade breaks. Her smile is subtle as she turns away.

Unfortunately for me, several people in the room are muttering angrily, looking at me with twisted snarls. It's a price I am more than willing to pay, and besides, maybe a few of the others here will learn a thing or two if they can keep their nonsense in check.

"Watch your mouth when you speak to her," a man says, approaching me and putting his leg up on the desk. "Filthy commoner."

"Bres!" Gráinne snaps. "Leave her be."

"I'm not a commoner," I say, my voice relaxed. I watch him closely in case he decides to get violent. "Just not from around here, and I don't care that she's the imperial princess. She's just Gráinne to me."

Out of the corner of my eye, I see her cheeks turning slightly red. The man, however, pulls away, a look of abject horror in his eyes.

"How dare you!"

"Where I'm from, people are treated like people—not tools or trophies. Which is what she is to you, right? All the dueling for her hand in marriage. You're disgusting. The whole thing is disgusting."

That gets him to take a swing at me. The movement is so wide and over-exaggerated he's almost in slow motion. I duck out of the way, slip around to his side, and slam my fist into his ribs. He crumples. Gráinne has almost no reaction besides gripping the desk in front of her so tightly I wonder if the wood will break.

Maybe I'm pushing this a little too far, but I just can't stand any of this—it makes my blood boil. "You're too slow," I tell the man who is currently writhing on the floor in pain. "Go to a doctor. I think one of your ribs cracked."

"Dia," Gráinne says. "I do not need or want you to speak for me; I am perfectly capable of doing so on my own."

"Fair," I say as I sit back down. "It's just the more I think about what's going on around here, the angrier I get. Should I rather not care at all?"

The man's friends come to collect him. Unlike him, they leave us alone. The bodyguard guy looks a bit disappointed, but has otherwise stayed in his corner. Gráinne looks at me. She chews on her lower lip.

"I am not saying that," she says. "I am merely of the opinion that none of these men are worthy of me. Not even one has proven their worth." She looks over to Bres. "I have seen nothing to change my mind."

The man's rage evaporates, shame overtakes his face. He shoves his friends away and stomps off, clutching his side as he does so. I turn to look back at her with an arched brow.

"You do not understand our ways," she says pointedly. "You are an outsider, so I will forgive you the way you speak to me. I am not easily offended by a lack of formality." She stands. "This is my friend, Dia, from Central."

More murmurs and looks of surprise from the people in class. I lift my brow, curious as to what she's up to.

"As a guest here, you will all treat her with the utmost respect and show her your best face. If she speaks of how things are where she is from, do not be fragile. Are you ashamed of our ways?"

They shake their heads.

"Good," she says. "Now, I believe the class bell has already rung. Please, professor, begin."

The older man looks quite shocked that she addressed him. "Right, of course!"

She sits down, looks at me and leans in close, her violet eyes burning with wild rage. "Never do that again." Her voice is a quiet dagger.

I knit my brows together, whispering back just loud enough for her to hear. "If you win our duel, I'll do exactly as you say, but not before." I pull away, turning to pay attention to the professor.

Gráinne fumes in silence.

Sorry, Princess, but I'm not the type to be frightened by this insanity.

Destroying something like this isn't just something one does with acts of violence. It starts by standing in defiance of what is wrong. She wields her power and authority over the others, that much I've seen, but she's still a prisoner. She knows it too.

If you can't break your cage, Princess, then I will.

Class goes by in a blur, the bell sounding once it's over. The students stand

and file out in an orderly fashion. I move to stand, but Gráinne grabs my sleeve. I turn to look; those big violet eyes stare up at me again. They seem to look right through me, defiance on the surface but deep vulnerability underneath.

"Eat lunch with me," she says softly.

I smirk, quirking a brow.

"Please?"

"That would be nice," I say. "Dining hall or your garden?"

"Garden." She lets go of my sleeve, her eyes flitting over to her bodyguard still hanging about.

I smile warmly at her. "Shall we then?" I reach out a hand towards her.

She looks surprised, but gingerly takes hold of me. It's difficult to tell, but I see the hint of a smile as she helps herself up. We walk together out of class, going down the long, stark halls. Fianna Academy is a beautiful place 'outside' with the grass and trees, but the buildings are sterile and lifeless.

The architecture here is straight and angular, nothing of the more organic and circular designs that have become popular in Central Space. There is no color or joy in these buildings. A pang of homesickness hits me. How many years has it been now since I was on Earth? I miss home.

Gráinne walks next to me, her back straight, pride in each stride. She's a far cry away from the woman I saw in the garden last night—an act. Seeing it fills me with even more rage. Everything about this place makes me angry. I link my arm with hers. She glances up at me, confused, but doesn't pull away. Immediately, others glance in our direction and whisper. I can't quite make out what they are saying, but the tone indicates they think this is something scandalous.

We make our way outside into the courtyard. Several stone paths branch out from here. She takes the lead, pulling me behind. I smile—I don't mind being dragged around a bit. She visibly relaxes with each step, the act melting away the longer we talk together.

I order a simple noodle soup and bread today. The food at the station is not very flavorful, but it is nutritious, I suppose. It's a bit irritating, really. The Fomorians spent so much money and resources on making this place *look* nice to live in, but living here exposes the cracks. The academy is all flash, and no substance.

Gráinne leads us out after we've gotten our food. It's the same path as last night. I frown, almost wanting to encourage her to stay in the hall instead. She's never going to make friends this way. A pair of girls I recognize from seeing in passing approach us, stopping us along the path. Now that I think about it, I have seen them a lot over the past week.

"Sorry," one of them says, taking a step closer to us. "I had a question for you." She looks at me.

"Sure," I say. "What's up?"

They exchange nervous glances. "Right, yeah. I'm Layla and this is Quinn. We're from engineering, and I couldn't help but notice you didn't have anyone listed to be on your mechanic team."

"I don't really know anyone yet to have asked." I beam at them.

Layla grins. "Would you let us be on your team, then? No one else wants to consider us."

"Oh?" Gráinne asks, a brow arched. "Do they doubt you?"

"Yes," they both say.

Quinn casts an unsure look over at Gráinne before looking back towards me. "We're top of our class, but none of the other pilots want us to touch their mechs. So, we thought maybe since you're the only other woman who pilots, and who also doesn't have a team, that you would be interested in having us."

"Have you two been following me?" I ask. "I feel like I've seen you two tailing me."

They nod awkwardly.

"Sure," I say, grinning. "I could use the help, truth be told. I'm going to be in the tournament, after all."

Gráinne has a panicked look, but seems to fight back her urge to scold me. The two girls look at one another in delight, not really paying attention to the implications of what I said.

"Amazing! I'm glad we finally had the nerve to come up to you," Layla says. "When we saw what you did earlier, it made us think maybe you were really nice."

"Cracking a guy's rib?" I furrow my brows. "That's sort of the opposite of nice, no?"

Quinn chuckles. "We're here on scholarship," she says, "and they... well, some of the rich students have threatened to get them revoked before. It's hard feeling like we can't ever speak out. But you just... you just did. It was awesome."

"I see," I say. "Well, then I'm glad. I'll send you both the specs of the Phantom Queen later."

They smile broadly, exchanging triumphant glances at one another.

"You won't regret it," Layla says.

They are about to leave, but then Gráinne clears her throat. Layla and Quinn freeze in place, looking as if the princess is about to order their execution.

"Would you like to have lunch with us?" Gráinne asks softly.

They blink in surprise, exchange another nervous look before nodding. "Um... sure?"

"You can say no," she replies. "Your refusal will not hurt me."

They both shake their heads rather fervently. "No! It's just surprising, is all," Layla says. "We just always see you alone. We'd love to, right Quinn?"

She looks a bit more unsure of the situation. "Y-yeah!"

"Okay," Gráinne says, her voice gentle and vulnerable. "Let's sit then. I know Dia is hungry."

"How thoughtful." I grin, taking the lead back from Gráinne, heading back into the dining hall.

The four of us sit together at a table in the back. More glances from various people but significantly less hostile overall. I turn to look at Gráinne, only to see an actual smile on the princess' face.

Good. She deserves to smile.

Looking at her now, like this, I realize I would do anything to make sure she keeps on having reasons to be happy—to feel joy. My mothers were right, I didn't come here for this, but Gráinne has become even more reason to smash this place to dust. Her pain, her cage, her loneliness; it all eats at me.

I'm going to make sure she gets to *live* every day for the rest of her life.

"Dia?" Gráinne asks. "Are you alright? You look lost."

"Of course," I tell her, coming out of my head. "Just thinking about a few things is all."

"Oh? Like what?"

"It's difficult to articulate," I say. "But it comes down to being happy that I met you."

She smiles, a subtle flush in her cheeks. "Me too."

* * *

Dia has become a fixture in my life over the last two days. I roll over in bed, reveling in how she is consuming my every thought. She is in every one of my classes, eats lunch with me, and spends the evenings with me in my garden. I have dismissed Renault from protecting me, not that he ever did much of that, nor do I really need much protection to begin with. Besides, if I really need protection, Dia is more than enough.

It's as if I'm just any other student who goes to Fianna—I almost feel normal. I've even made two new friends in Quinn and Layla. This is the happiest I have ever been in my life; I wonder if I have ever been happy. With certain people, like Aoife, I have felt safe. I'm content in the sense that my needs are met, but I cannot recall a time in my life where I was eager to fall asleep and just as eager to get out of bed at the break of day.

Not until her.

I wonder as I lay here, just how does she make me feel? Joyful, yes. Safe? No. Being honest with myself, that woman does not make me feel safe. Her words contain hidden intentions and there is something behind her eyes that I cannot discern. Her eyes burn like a star, but I worry that her light is blinding me to some darker truth—in truth, she frightens me.

The words she spoke in my garden have been swimming in my mind since she uttered them. What did she mean? Why would she say that? I sigh, exasperated. That woman is so stubborn, too, and she takes any and all chances to annoy me and poke fun at my position in public. Then again, that's why I have friends at all. Layla and Quinn shared with me how they thought I was terrifying before, but not anymore.

Not since her.

She's a whirlwind. An all-consuming tornado in my life that has pulled me in completely. Maybe that's what she meant. Maybe that's why she insists on treating me like normal, even at the expense of the honor my station demands. Is that a way of fighting for me? Maybe. I want to believe that, but there is just something about her I cannot trust. Perhaps I should just confront her. I was so quick to ask for her help that I never bothered to really interrogate her about her intentions.

That night I felt so safe, so secure as we spoke. It only changed when I convinced her to fight for me... no, that's not true... it's when she challenged me. When she stood up and put her hand on my chin. A shiver goes up my spine, recalling the way she looked at me. The way she spoke to me, the way her lips almost touched mine. The way she wiped away my tears. That is when I knew something had changed, when I felt both joy and fear.

Tomorrow is the exhibition match, though only Layla and Quinn know Dia is the one I'm to fight. Rumors have spread of a new challenger. The others have just assumed it is some man I wish to put in his place.

I suppose I have built up something of a reputation for doing that.

A smirk crosses my face. I want to throw caution to the wind, but first I need to see what Dia is made of. I desperately need her to be as powerful as I am. By myself, as strong as I am, I cannot change anything. If she is as I hope, then perhaps I do not have to flee my home. Perhaps I can convince her to stay at my side, to fight with me. She makes her distaste for how things are quite clear. Perhaps our strength together will be enough to bring change.

Hope fills my heart. Hope. How long has it been? Perhaps, like joy, it's never been something in my life. Joy. Hope. Friendship. Those are the things she has brought into my life. I sigh. I need to confront her, that much is clear. Tomorrow. The stakes for the duel. That is what I will put on the line for if I win. To know her intentions.

To know her.

Yes, that is what I will do. If I win, I'll demand she tell me everything about her. After all, she said she'd do what I told her if I won. I close my eyes, a smile on my lips.

Sunlight pours into my room. Birds chirp outside my window. I slowly lift my head and rub the sleep from my eyes. I'm surprised I could sleep at all. Forcing myself out of bed, I head to my closet. At least picking out my outfit for the day is easy. I slip into the underclothes of my flightsuit and then the suit itself. It seals to me automatically, gently compressing my muscles. I tie up my hair, pinning it back.

I've never really considered how revealing the flightsuit is, but right now, as I stare down at myself, I am intensely aware of how the skintight, white nanocarbon material leaves little to the imagination. It's hard for me not to wonder what she might think of me. Heat rushes to my face.

How am I going to respond to seeing her in one of these? Oh no.

I just won't look at her. I'll go right to my mech, get inside, and finish the final calibrations before the match. From there, I'll go right to the dueling arena, and I just won't have to see her at all. Perfection.

There's a knock at my door.

The sound makes me jump out of my skin. I sigh, calming myself down. Who would call on me at this hour of the morning? "Yes?"

"I brought breakfast!" Comes Dia's voice. "Can't have a duel on an empty stomach."

"Dia?! What are you doing here?"

"Didn't I just say?" She laughs. "Can I come in?"

"Fine."

The door opens at my vocal command. My breath catches in my throat looking at her. She has also pinned her hair back like mine, and like me, she's in a flightsuit. Hers is black, a striking appearance against her snow-white hair and eyes.

My mouth goes dry as I stare at her. I don't know where to look. At her hard, chiseled stomach? Or her arms that look like they could fold me in half? Her incredible breasts?

I turn around, unable to bear the sight of her—she is simply too beautiful to look at.

"Cute," she says through a smirk.

"I am not cute," I tell her.

A chuckle, rich and joyful. "Of course you are." She steps inside, the door closing shut with an audible click. "In fact, you're adorable."

"Shut up." I fold my arms over my chest, turning back to look at her. I focus very, very hard to only look at her face, but even that feels overwhelming. That little mole under her right eye in particular drives me insane. I turn around again. "I cannot look at you."

She laughs. "Cute," she says again. "Very cute."

"Did anyone see you come here?" I ask, desperately trying to change the subject.

"Not sure. I didn't really care to pay attention." She shrugs. "Let people see me come up."

"Dia! I don't want people to see you in a suit and know you're the one I'm to duel today." *Stubborn woman!*

"Speaking of that," she says, setting down the breakfast. "I've been thinking about your question. The stakes of the match. I know what I want."

"Me too," I say, "But you go first."

She's silent for a moment. "No. You first. I want to hear what you have to say."

"Very well." I turn to look at her—it's easier now. "If I win, I want you to tell me everything about you. I'm not a fool; I know you're hiding something."

She rubs the back of her neck, frowning. "I am."

Her words sting. Did I want her to deny it? No. I'm just surprised by her bold honesty. The moment passes, and appreciation takes hold. "Good. I will get your secrets after I win."

"Well," she says as she begins plating up the food—pancakes with fresh berries. "I am going to tell you now. I think I can trust you, and I think we may want similar things."

There's that hope again, deep in my chest. "That sort of cheapens my victory, but I will allow an early surrender."

She rolls her eyes. "Here," she says, handing me the plate. "I cooked these."

"Thank you," I say softly. I take a bite with a bit of syrup, whipped cream, and a strawberry. It's light, fluffy, rich, and altogether delicious. "Amazing, Dia. You can cook."

She smirks. "I know. I can't stand what's being served here, and we both need actual food for a proper duel." She takes a bite and lets out a sigh of contentment.

"Okay, stop stalling," I say, taking a seat on a chair in the living area of my quarters. "What are you going to tell me that you can trust me with now?"

Dia hesitates. She looks frightened and unsure. I wasn't sure anything could frighten her. What could she possibly have to say that makes her feel like this?

She takes a deep breath. "Gráinne," she says my name sweetly, which makes me all the more concerned. "I am going to burn this entire empire to the ground."

I laugh. "Dia, be serious." I wave a dismissive hand. "What do you want?"

She steps closer to me, her body eclipsing my own. She cups my face, just like that night in the garden, lifting my gaze to meet hers.

"Your help, if you're willing," she says, her tone deadly serious. "I want to free people like Layla and Quinn. I want to shatter your cage."

Oh gods, she means it.

I try to pull away, fear and horror gripping tight at my chest, but she holds my face so gently with the tips of her fingers. Her touch is so light, yet I feel unable to escape her all-consuming gaze. I'm not sure I even want to.

"It's okay, Gráinne," she whispers. "I won't ask anything of you that you can't do, but you deserve to know my plans. If you want to join me, the choice is entirely yours."

I swallow hard. I want to say yes; so badly, I want to scream out the word and throw myself into her arms. "You are insane, Dia. Stop this sort of talk."

Her response is a growl, low in her throat, as she puts her lips are on mine. Her arms pull me in close, and I push myself into her. I take hold of her hair, grasping at it like a lifeline. This is my first kiss; what a glorious, nightmarish kiss it is. I shove her against a counter. She looks surprised, but before she can say anything, I smash my lips back against hers until we're both bruised. She picks me up, and I wrap my legs around her, keeping my lips locked against hers until I'm left breathless. In a twisted way, this is all I was dreaming of—everything I wanted.

Not like this.

"Dia," I say, pulling my face away from hers. "Put me down."

She does so. I gulp as I try to gather my senses. "What do you mean burn this empire down?"

"Was I unclear?" she asks, wiping away a bit of blood from her lip. "No more noble houses, no more princesses. You will witness the Fomorian Armory cease to exist, replaced with something better. Is that more clear?"

I pinch the bridge of my nose, trying to wrap my mind around what she is saying. "Even if you could, which you can't, do you know how many people would die in the process? How can you say this?"

"People are already dying," she retorts, brushing her hair out of her face. "I've paid close attention to you these past few days, listened to your dreams of the future, how you might fix things. I wonder if you are you considering that this empire has already murdered more people than you could possibly imagine?"

"No," I say. I fidget in place, my hands have gone cold, and my stomach feels as if it's doing somersaults. "I have, admittedly, not thought of it that way."

"In the last decade alone," she says, her voice on the verge of rage. "Thanks to your father agreeing to relax safety measures for profit, five million people per year have died in mines and factories. That's more than all the people on this station every single year."

She laughs then, but it's not her mirthful laugh I love so much. It's a dark laugh, filled with righteous indignation. "Nobles are paying 'pirates' to kill workers attempting to take collective action. I exposed a few even, and it did fuck all to make a difference."

I shake my head. My hands go numb. I know she is right, but I am just one person in a sea of monsters.

"Trillions of people live in this sector and the scale of death is unimaginable. I've seen the suffering up close. I'll do whatever it takes to put a stop to it."

She pauses, taking a deep breath to calm down. "None of us are free until all of us are free; help me protect the least among us."

"I don't need to be convinced to fight for them," I say, practically hissing at Dia. "But there's fighting for them and then there is this insanity. Open revolution would be a devastating, catastrophic loss of life." I turn my back towards her. "Though I cannot deny what you have said, either; I do not know what to say, Dia."

"Look," she says, her voice earnest, almost pleading. "No matter what, I will save you, and take you to Central—to Earth—but I cannot join you in living a normal life. Not while I am so painfully aware of how things are. Somehow, I will put a stop to this; with or without you."

"Do you care about me, Dia?" I hold my hands in front of my chest, pressing the tips of my fingers against one another. The pressure soothes me, if only a little. "I mean genuinely care about me?"

"Yes." She puts a hand on my shoulder. "For what it's worth, it was never my plan to care about you, or make you care about me. I thought the struggle of succession would suit my goals, so I got close to you."

Her tone is so gentle, I find it impossible to summon up any rage. My chest aches less, but I dare not turn around to look at her.

"Princess," she says, her voice thick with emotion. "No matter what, I will save you, too."

I lean back against her, still unable to meet her eyes. Her words bring me a measure of comfort, along with a dozen other feelings that terrify me to consider. "I believe you."

Now I feel safe—mostly.

Her arms coil around me, pulling me back into her chest. When was the last time someone simply held me? I try to reach back into my memories for such a moment, but only very early memories of my mother come to mind. No one has ever just held me—not like this. I fall back into her embrace, tears falling down my cheeks.

"Well, I am the best," she says. "Though I am not so powerful that I can do this all on my own. I need your help. I need allies. Help me, and I am sure we can do this, Princess."

"Show me that power," I tell her, the strength returning to my voice. "Then and only then will I consider your proposal. I will not entertain this if you cannot, at the very least, match me in battle." I reluctantly pull away from her, my heart aching from the distance.

"Dia, you must win. I will not hold back. Bring your all to bear against me, for that's what it will take. If you do not…" I turn to face her, finally able to look her in the eyes, tears still streaming down my face. "If you cannot, I will have no choice but to kill you."

"I'm to treat you as my enemy?" Her tone is like ice, her eyes sharp and cold.

"Yes," I say, lifting my chin up to gaze into her wintery eyes.

Her jaw sets, her eyes narrow. "I'm going to destroy you, Princess—completely."

Please.

Phantom vs Bansidhe

I stop in the doorway, casting my glance behind me towards Gráinne. Our eyes meet; she's glaring at me, but I'm not sure if it's rage that I sense or unbridled determination.

"I'll see you out there," I say, my voice stiff and choked with emotion.

"Just remember what I said." She looks away, turning her back towards me.

"You too." I step out into the hall. My gaze lingers until the door seals itself shut with a hiss.

I walk, I walk, and I walk like a ghost through the halls of the dorm. My heart is heavy and aches in my chest. Our kiss left my lips cut—pain still lingers from the intensity. Any chance I had of walking away from this is now gone; I'm fully committed. Mother will be incredibly upset with me when she hears.

Three weeks? I couldn't even last three days.

Campus is quiet this morning. It's the weekend; people spent the night partying, unable to contain their excitement for blood sport. There is an air of eagerness when the princess duels, everyone waiting on bated breath to see if *this time* she is conquered in battle and who her husband might be. It's beyond vile. Under different circumstances, mech duels are fun to watch or take part in, but there is no joy to be had in this.

Especially not today.

The hangar bay is quite different from the rest of the campus. Staff and engineering students are here working, some just getting off their overnight shifts. Layla and Quinn are standing by the Phantom Queen, finishing up their last-minute inspection of her. Despite telling them they really didn't need to do this, they insisted. I think they mostly wanted a chance to take a look at the Phantom up close—can't fault them for taste.

I take a moment just to admire her, standing there in twenty-two meters of glory. Truly, I am a very simple creature with colors and designs. Though I suppose that is my mom's fault. It was difficult growing up around the Witchblade and not having that style reflected in my machine. The jet-black frame and silver trim along the thighs, chest and arms are almost identical. Her face is more angular and detailed, her long legs end in a traditional boot style instead of hooves like the Witchblade. Instead of indigo paneling on the eyes, chest and thighs, the Phantom Queen's is white.

She is me; I am her—my mantra every time I get into the cockpit.

Layla and Quinn spot me and wave me over, both with bright eyes, though Quinn looks awkward as per usual. Seeing their smiles instantly puts me in a better mood.

"Dia!" Layla exclaims. "You did not tell us how incredibly amazing this machine is. Is this just how they build mechs in Central?"

"No, not even slightly," I say, chuckling. "I've had to do a lot of solo sorties in rough conditions, so I've tinkered with her a lot. She's unique."

Quinn whistles. "Well, she's gorgeous and that OS she has is really something else. Her ability to do that much parallel processing while you're integrated is insane. How are you not cooked alive?"

It's nice to see Quinn come out of her shell when she talks about mechs. I can't help but grin. "That's a secret. Is it really so different from the Fomorian Framework? I know you all do something with integrated pilots."

"It is," Layla says, "very different. I can see some similar DNA between the two, but the FF's function is to reduce higher brain function to enhance a pilot's instincts. It makes them fearless in battle."

"It turns pilots into berserkers then?" I furrow my brow.

"Yes." Layla says. "I'd say especially the men, but there are very few examples of women who pilot, so there's no real data. What I can say: Gráinne has showed remarkable resistance to that effect of the Framework." She points back towards the Phantom Queen. "This though? I don't know how a human has the brainpower to operate this. The swarm-bits alone would generate an astronomical amount of body heat."

"I'm augmented," I say, "extensively—but Central has ethics surrounding the practice. It's also freely available to get cybernetics. Mine are all specifically designed to pilot the Phantom."

I think back to the fights of Gráinne's I've seen. The one recent fight where she ground that M.E.T.A mech into scrap was telling. If I hadn't seen it with my own eyes and known it was her, I wouldn't believe the same woman I've gotten to know would be capable of fighting that way. I hum in thought, scratching my chin.

"Is there anything else you can tell me about the FF? Doesn't sound like pilot safety was a big concern." I cross my arms over my chest, my foot tapping anxiously.

Quinn shakes her head. "Not more than what we've said. It's a recent inclusion into mechs and not a lot of pilots can even make use of it. A lot of cybernetics are required, too, and that's expensive." She shrugs.

"Someone has to be very rich or be in the military to get that kind of augmentation. It's also very dangerous—a lot of student pilots have died because it's so important to the high houses to have one of theirs marry Gráinne."

"Fuck," I say. "The Princess sure is fucking determined to have gotten that shit done to her, despite the risks."

"Yes," Layla says. "Gods, I thought she was so cool the first time she stepped out into the arena. The way she thrashed everyone who stood in her path." She smirks, her voice rising in her excitement.

"I was rooting for her to stick it to the emperor, truth be told, but not even a tricked-out princess can stand up to that kind of power." She chuckles sardonically, rubbing the back of her neck. "Never thought she'd be so kind, though. I think this might be the first fight she's ever had just for fun."

"Not entirely for fun," I say with a smirk. "I fully intend to marry that woman—if she wants. I need to win first."

The pair of them look at one another and then burst out laughing. "Really?"

Quinn asks, her eyes burning with intensity. "But you're both girls." She glances over at Layla briefly, her cheeks darkening before she pulls her eyes away. "I guess it's different in Central. Will the two of you have to leave?"

"No," I tell her. "No, it's not my intention to leave with her. There's a lot we want to accomplish if I win today. Do you two trust me?"

They both nod without hesitating. "Of course," Layla says. "Without a doubt."

"Okay." I step forward, putting a hand on each of their shoulders. "I'll see you both after the match. Thank you for all your help. You two make a great team, and I'm better for having you both on my side."

Quinn glances over at Layla, then at me. She smiles faintly. "Go get her."

* * *

"XF01-Phantom Queen, Diarmuid Mirren, launching." I surge forward, pressed back into my seat by the force of the sling. I'm launched out at the end of a tunnel and onto a massive, rocky battlefield. There's cover behind small hills littered over the terrain. A drone flies past me, one of hundreds flitting about, broadcasting the duel live to the local cluster.

Gráinne emerges from her own tunnel on the far side of the arena. A communication screen pops up in my cockpit, revealing the princess. Her helmet obscures her features—except her eyes—her violet eyes shine through the tinted glass visor.

"Are you both ready?" asks a rather amused sounding voice. Another screen blinks into existence. A woman with long braided pink hair is grinning widely through the screen.

"Yes," Gráinne and I say in unison.

"Then I, Brigid of House Áine, shall bear witness to this duel." Her tone is rather dramatic, almost mocking. She grins, clapping her hands together. "Duelists, you both agree to honor the terms of the stakes you levied against the other?"

"Yes," we say in unison again.

"Marvelous," she says, "Recite your vows and then you may begin!"

"For honor, for pride, I swear to bring my all to bear against my opponent, to leave nothing on the field of battle," Gráinne says, her tone fierce and powerful.

"For glory, for dignity, I swear to cover my opponent in my radiance, to conquer the battlefield by force of will."

"Oh, my goodness." Brigid chuckles. "This is all, dare I say it, very romantic."

"Brigid," Gráinne says, making no effort to hide her irritation. "Focus."

"Of course, your highness." Brigid looks at me. "By the by, you have such a pleasant voice, Diarmuid. You are no man."

"Is it that obvious?" I ask, chuckling. "I thought I could keep my secret a bit longer."

"Not with that voice; it's delicious," she says. "This will be quite the scandal if you win."

"Focus," Gráinne repeats, practically seething. "I would like to start, Brigid."

"You've *never* this eager, your highness." She cackles. "Very well then. As always, the one to take the head of the other first wins. Aces, begin!"

The false sky above shifts at her proclamation, becoming like the void of space. Both Gráinne and I move simultaneously, hurtling towards one another at full speed. She draws her sword, slashing at my head, immediately aiming for victory. The thirteen swarm-bits pop off my body, creating an energy barrier around me that parries her blade.

I lock the bits together, forming a proper shield as I draw the long, red lance—Gáe Dearg—from my back. I thrust it forward. She deftly swipes it aside with her blade, striking again in the same motion. I catch her attack with my shield, push her back, attempting once more to thrust my spear, aiming for her mech's head. She dodges, leaping away, and draws an energy rifle, shooting with except precision.

I detach the bits from themselves, forming a barrier around me again. The plasma from the shot strikes the wall of energy, dispersing harmlessly around me.

"You really are good," she says over comms. "I wasn't sure what I was expecting, but those drones of yours are incredibly annoying."

I smirk. "If you marry me, I'll be your annoying wife forever, Princess."

"This isn't a game, Dia," she snaps. She rushes forward, stowing her weapons and activating her massive, clawed arm. Pink plasma courses through the entire frame, causing her mech to glow brightly. She holds out that arm, the clawed hand launching forward, synthetic muscles exposed as it detaches at the joints to extend far beyond normal reach.

I dash to the side, dodging it completely. I don't think even the bit-barrier can stand up to that thing. If she grapples me with that arm, the fight will be over in an instant. I draw my second lance—Gáe Buidhe—a short yellow one that emits an electric overload when it strikes true. Flourishing both weapons, I drop back into a ready stance for her next attack.

"I never joke about romance, Princess," I tell her. "Either way, I am going to keep my promise and destroy you."

I dodge a second swipe of her hand, just barely, and plunge the yellow spear into one of her joints. A burst of electricity courses through the tip, overloading the arm and causing it to go limp.

"What did you do to me?" she hisses, trying to retract the arm. It lies inert on the ground, totally disabled.

"That arm of yours was scaring me," I say, not hiding my cheek. "So, I took it from you." I take a ready stance again, circling around her like a hunter would. "You're an exceptional warrior, Princess, but I have my tricks."

"You are insufferable," she says. "Do you think you will beat me with tricks?"

I furrow my brow, taking a deep breath. "You were the one who said to bear my all against you, Princess. I intend to do just that."

She boosts forward, plasma jettisoning out from behind her. Even with the massive claw hand rendered unusable, she twists her frame around rapidly, turning the limp arm into a flail. I shake my head, engaging the swarm. Bursts of green light pour out of the weapons, shredding the arm in midair, severing it from her frame. I push forward, attacking her from all angles.

She dodges and weaves through the blasts but one catches her leg, cutting out a chunk, and causing her mech to fall to the ground. Another beam severs an arm, leaving her with just one remaining. I hear her grunting in pain and frustration over the comms. I'm sure the neural feedback from losing her limbs was agonizing, even with the safety measures put in place.

Through sheer will, she stands up on her good leg. Sparks flare from her reactor core. Panels burst open, exposing the core itself. She lets out an unholy scream as the pink plasma erupts from the frame, dripping molten slag onto the ground.

"Gráinne, what the fuck are you doing?" I step back into a stance again, ready for anything.

"Bearing *my* all!" She runs towards me, picking up the remains of her clawed arm along the way. She throws it at me. "I will not lose quietly, Dia—not to anyone, not even to you."

The bits reform into a shield, and I attach at my wrist. I parry the thrown arm away from me. She is right behind, moving at a blistering speed I wouldn't have thought was possible in her condition. She draws her sword, slashing at my head with feral intensity.

I catch the sword with the red spear, holding my ground against her incredible strength. Even being bigger than her, she pushes me back, shouting in rage. She overpowers and disarms me, sending my spear clattering across the battlefield. She discards her sword, reaching for my head with her bare hand.

I shove her away, but she is quick to rotate her body, kicking at me with the damaged leg. I barely raise my shield in time, her leg shattering against me. The impact makes stumble back, falling onto the ground with a thunderous clang of grinding steel. She growls over the comms, using her propulsion systems to keep balance on one leg. She jumps on top of me, smashing my head with her remaining arm.

There's nowhere to go. Her hand grips my faceplate, attempting to crush me. Without her other leg to keep steady, I'm able to shove her off me with a solid punch that sends her reeling. Her frame skitters across the ground. She recovers, using her jets to fly in the air, righting herself before charging back in recklessly.

I dodge her attempt to kick my head off, dashing to the side. Each attack of hers goes for victory. She doesn't bother trying to hit me anywhere else. It makes her predictable despite her great speed. I thrust the short energy spear towards her face. She slips her head past the spear, but the energy tip impales her shoulder. Another burst of electricity renders her attached arm worthless. She growls in frustration, spinning her body to slam the limp arm into me.

"Sorry, Princess," I say, raising my shield to block the blow.

She floats in the sky for a moment, thinking about what to do next. The once pristine looking platinum frame is turning black because of the dripping slag pouring out of her reactor core.

"Gráinne," I say, trying to keep my concern in check. "You're going to melt down if you keep this up—then what good will any of this have been?"

"Dia, you..." she says, her breath comes out in ragged heaves as she struggles to talk. "You are still holding back. You said you would blind me with your radiance, that you'd show me your will. So, where is it? Show me!"

Hesitation grips at my chest. "I've already won, but, very well, if you want to see my final trick, then so be it," I say, taking a deep breath to prepare myself. "Moralltach Protocol: Engage." My breath is stolen from my lungs. My vision splits as my mind shatters into a thousand pieces, only to be reformed again in an instant.

The Phantom Queen overheats, hissing and creaking as the cooling system catches up to keep me stable. The thirteen swarm-bits snap together, forming into a massive blade I need both arms to use. With the integration is complete, my senses are not just restored, they are honed into a perfect edge.

I am the Phantom Queen.

"Yes!" she cries out. "This is what I want—show me all of you."

The engines on my back and legs ignite. I float above the ground a moment before blasting off towards her. Even without the use of her arms, she still tries to lash out at me with her leg. I slip past the kick, spinning away in the air and swinging the Moralltach in a blindingly quick arc. It slices through her leg easily. She tries again to slam to the limp arm into me, spinning in the air to create enough momentum to get it to move. I catch it at the elbow, crushing it into scrap with the overloaded strength coursing through me.

Like this, she stands no chance against me, and she knows it too. I can see it in the desperation of her movements. She still tries to fight, armless and legless now, only able to move because she can fly. Still, there is something about her that sets my nerves on edge—she is still dangerous.

This cannot go on any longer.

I slip to her side, moving faster than she can react, slashing my sword up diagonally across my body. My blade cleaves the head from the Bansidhe, the lump of metal crashing into the ground. The sky above us turns into a cloudy day, my name flashing across the sky with VICTORY written underneath. I detach the bits from themselves, directing them back onto me with a heavy metallic clang. The protocol ends, my mind returning to normal levels of integration.

I catch her broken, beautiful frame in my arms, taking us to the ground gently. I cradle her close; she is precious to me. My cockpit opens, I detach myself completely from the Phantom Queen, my body becoming flesh once more. I step out, walking across our mechs. Gráinne opens her cockpit, too, and I step into it. She's lying back in her seat, tears streaming down her face.

"Thank you," she says, her voice thick with emotion as she sobs. "Thank you, Dia."

"Of course," I say, my voice dropping low as I take off my helmet. "I told you I'd win, and I never go back on my word."

She sniffles, chuckling a bit. "I am annoyed by how long it took you to finish me after all that boasting."

I return the chuckle, my cheeks turning a touch of red. "Sorry," I say gently. "You really are an excellent pilot. It's been ages since anyone pushed me that hard, and that's impressive—I do this for a living."

"What, save princesses in over their heads?" She laughs. "What are your rates?"

"In your case? I'll call it even with marriage." I reach out to her. "If you'll have me, that is."

She takes my hand, pulling herself up. Her fingers interlace with mine. She removes her helmet with her free hand, smiling at me once it's off. I do the same.

"I will," she says. "Of course I will."

I pull her close to me, her chest pressing into mine. I tip her back, kissing her deeply. She wraps her arms around my neck to hold herself steady. We linger like this for a long moment, drinking in one another, only to be interrupted by the sounds and heat from thrusters. A squad of four pale blue humanoid mechs drop in from above, each with a singular ominous red eye.

I pull away and step in front of Gráinne, staring down the four mechs that have surrounded us.

They train their guns on us but don't yet fire. "Cease dueling immediately," one of them says.

"It's already over," I shout back.

"Diarmuid Mirren, you're under arrest; the results of this duel have been nullified."

"Like hell I am," I say, glaring at them. I glance over at the Phantom Queen. I can control the bits remotely if I need to, but I would really rather not with the princess in my arms. *Fuck.*

"You are not taking her!" Gráinne shouts. "She is *my* champion."

"Your father has ordered her arrest, your highness," the same voice replies. "His orders supersede yours."

The princess seethes, her eyes blazing with fury. "That useless old bastard!" She moves to be in front of me, spreading her arms out to block me as much as she can. "You will have to kill me—I am not letting you take her."

"Princess," I say. "You don't need to do this."

"Well, I am going to anyway," she hisses.

A viewscreen blinks into existence in the sky above us. Brigid is looking down on us, her lips pulled back into a smug expression. "That's enough," she says, her voice haughty and indignant. "This Academy is under the jurisdiction of House Áine."

"The high houses agreed to his terms of how the princess is to be betrothed, and he wants to change his mind now? After a champion has earned the title? I think not." She snaps her fingers.

Dozens of high-powered turrets rise from hidden compartments all over the battlefield. All of them point towards the four mechs.

"This is treason!" one of them shouts.

"Is that so?" she asks mockingly. "Shut up, grunt. If Emperor Cormac wishes to make a fuss over this, he's welcome to take it up with House Áine, but right now, I am the one with the power here. Go away, or I *will* kill you."

They consider their choice for a moment, obeying Brigid in the end. Their boosters ignite, the four of them lifting off the ground as they retreat. The emperor must have been desperate to pull a patrol off duty to come arrest little old me.

I breathe a sigh of relief. The viewscreen vanishes from sight.

"You owe me, Miss Mirren," Brigid says over the comms, sounding very pleased with herself. "You and Princess Gráinne should meet me in the dueling office—tomorrow. We have much to discuss."

The line clicks off before I can respond. I look at the princess, her eyes filled with pure, unfiltered hatred.

"I wish every curse upon my father," she says.

"At least we're okay," I tell her. "You really didn't need to step in front of me like that; I still had some tricks. Thank you."

Her nose wrinkles in disgust as she fumes. She lets out a sigh after a moment, her expression softening considerably. "Of course," she says, smiling up at me. "We are to be brides. Protecting you is only natural." She lifts her hand to touch my cheek, running her thumb across my skin before kissing me. "Will you give me a ride back?"

I grin widely. "Of course, Princess. You can sit in my lap."

I scoop her up bridal style. She lets out a small, surprised yelp, wrapping her arms around my neck as I carry her over the cockpit's threshold into the Phantom Queen. I sit, the hatch automatically closing. For such a simple trip, I don't need to integrate into the mech, so I don't. I want my flesh body to be focused as much as possible on Gráinne.

She smiles as we walk, her face slightly flushed. "What are our next steps?" She brushes her fingers through my hair. The anger in her eyes is gone now, replaced with a calm joy as she looks at me.

"Well, I know we got engaged first," I say, smirking. "So, call me crazy, but I think we should go out on a date now."

She blinks a few times; her face is becoming several shades redder. "Right—a date—I would love to."

* * *

The Fianna sky is gold and orange and pink as it shifts into evening. There's a knock on my door. I smile, knowing who it is and why she's here.

"Come in."

The door slides open with a hiss as I turn my attention towards it. My breath catches in my throat, again, for the thousandth time even. Dia is wearing a short purple jacket with a matching crop top, tight pants, and knee-high boots. The outfit looks stunning on her, her muscular stomach on full display—I must fight back the urge to drag my tongue along her skin. Tattoos peek out from under her top, but I can't make out what they are, despite staring very hard at her exposed skin.

I gulp, intense heat rushing through my body. "Good evening," I say, trying very, very hard to keep my composure.

"Ready?" she asks, a smirk on her face. That deadly, dangerous smirk. "You look good tonight."

"Yes," I say, running my hands down the length of my dress, smoothing out imaginary wrinkles. "You are the gorgeous one tonight. It is difficult to look at you—again."

"You're cute," she says, holding out her hand to me. "Come on, let's go have dinner."

A date.

The thought forces a broad smile on my face. I walk over to her, taking her hand in mine. I can't take my eyes off her as we walk out of the building. Until, that is, I see a motorcycle parked outside the dorm. It's not at all like the transit vehicles students can use. Its design is much sleeker and far more aerodynamic. It looks like it's built for racing, not transport.

"How did you get this into the school?" I ask, walking up to it to run my fingers along the cool chrome.

"I can store her on the Phantom," she says. "She can compress when needed, so I get good use out of her when I'm in the field."

"How fast does she go?" I look at her, a smirk on my face. "Can I drive?"

She chuckles at me. "Fast." Her eyes glance back and forth between me and her bike. She nods. "You can. I have a surprise set up in your garden."

I arch a brow. "Not one of the extravagant restaurants?"

"I cooked," she says. "Let's see what you can do with her." She motions towards the bike.

I can't help but grin as I pull up the hem of my dress to mount the motorcycle. The bike whirrs to life when I touch the handlebars. I feel it's a part of me, quite like when I'm piloting, but not nearly as intense. I remove my hands; the sensation fades away. "Remarkable. Is this is the same system your mech uses?"

She mounts the bike behind me, wrapping her arms around my waist. "Sort of. You can think of the two systems like siblings."

I place my hands back on the handlebars, the bike once again whirring to life. It responds to my thoughts, my body knowing exactly what to do. The only problem, of course, is being very distracted by Dia's chest pressed up against my back.

I don't drive nearly as fast as I want to; we are at school after all. More than that, I want to go slow and savor the ride and her body pressed against mine. She's holding me far tighter than she needs to, not that I'd dream of complaining—her touch thrills me.

As slowly as I go, the drive is still over far too soon. I pull into the garden over the stone path, carefully parking it so as to not damage any grass or flowers. Dia gets off first, walking over to a crate underneath a sycamore. It opens at the touch of her palm. A delicious scent wafts over, making my mouth instantly water. She pulls out a blanket, a few plates along with cutlery, a bottle of bubbling liquid, and a wicker basket with steam rising from the top. She lies the blanket on the grass, motioning for me to come over.

I sit, watching her do final preparations on the food, plating it delicately before sitting down. The food makes me lick my lips; I am unable to help myself at the sight of fluffy mashed potatoes, caramelized on the top, and layered with meat and fresh vegetables.

"You made shepherd's pie," I say, eagerly taking hold of my plate, breathing in the scent.

"Like my mom taught me," she says. "But I couldn't get a hold of lamb, so it's not really shepherd's pie."

I giggle. "Well, it's shepherd's pie to me. Thank you."

"Try it before you thank me too much," she remarks, almost pouting. Dia scoots next to me, her legs outstretched. She watches me, clearly waiting for my opinion.

I smile at her before taking a bite. The flavors are explosive, fresh herbs and spices igniting my tastebuds. I let out a little moan at the taste, going back in for another three bites. Not even the royal chef could have done better. I look up to see Dia smiling at me, a look of relief etched on her features. I blush slightly, taking one more bite before talking.

"Beyond delicious," I tell her. "You are an excellent cook. I look forward to many more meals from you."

Her cheeks flush. "I'm glad." She takes a few bites of her food as well, eating in silence.

I watch her curiously while I eat. "Something is on your mind," I say. "Tell me."

Dia sighs. "Things are happening faster than I had planned. I'm dealing with powerful feelings. Concerns. Anxiety. You name it, I'm feeling it." She sets her food down, looking over at me. Her piercing white eyes stare at me, unblinking. "About us. I don't want to feel taken for granted; I don't care about the duels."

I blink several times, my face turning red. "I already said yes?" I ask, confused. "Are you asking me again?"

Dia's face turns redder. She looks away. "Well, yes," she says. "I wanted to ask away from a fight, when we were both level-headed. It's foolish—never mind."

"It is not foolish," I say quickly, reaching out to put a hand on her leg. "Unexpected, yes, but very sweet. Do you want me to say no?"

"Wait, what?" She takes my hand in hers, interlacing her fingers with mine. "You can if you want to, but I'd really rather you didn't—I do like you, Princess."

I stifle a giggle, but only just. "Well, I should hope so. There is a lot that comes with this, and your goals, but I knew that when we went into that fight." I look down at our hands, stroking my thumb over her skin.

"I fought as hard as I could, even though I desperately wanted you to win. Truth be told, I am the one who should feel foolish, Dia, but I had to have it settled like that. My feelings were complicated."

"And now?"

"Now I feel safe." I laugh. "Which is idiotic of me; you want to go to war against the Armory." I look back at her, taking a deep breath. "Yet, I feel like I am *living,* finally. Moments like this. A kiss. Spending time with friends. I am *alive.*"

I lift her hand to my lips, placing a gentle kiss on the tips of her fingers. "Even if that ends abruptly in the fires of battle, I will be happy because now I can *live.*" I pull away, shifting my legs to be more comfortable and wrapping my arms around myself. "It is all I have ever wanted, you know—to be *alive.*"

She gets very close to me, her body radiating glorious warmth. Her arms embrace me tight, and she presses her lips to the top of my head. "You'll live, Gráinne. I promise you. For a long, long time, you will get to live."

Her long fingers cup my chin, tilting my face towards her. I gladly turn to look her in those gorgeous white eyes, my attention drawn to her little mole. I lean in for a kiss, pressing my lips against hers. She squeezes me, making me feel swallowed up and overwhelmed.

I push her down. She chuckles, seeming to not expect this from me. I bite at her lips, my fingers digging into her jacket. My breath comes out in ragged, passionate waves. Whatever shock I put her through, she recovers quickly, pulling me on top of her. I grin, keeping our lips together. My heart pounds in my chest so hard I fear it might burst.

I feel alive. Gods, I feel so alive.

My datapad sings a song—it sings a very specific song that rips me from my heavenly thoughts—my mother is calling me.

"Fuck."

Dia looks quite confused. She arches her brow. "What?"

"I need to take this. I am so sorry." Pulling away from her to fetch my bag is agonizing. I reach inside to grab the datapad, clipping my nail against something within. My nail folds back on itself, excruciating pain shoots up my arm. I hiss, trying not to let out a string of profanities.

I take one extra moment to gather myself as the song drones on. "Mother," I say, keeping my voice steady.

"Gráinne," she says, her tone like a sharpened sword. "We need to talk."

Forged Bonds

My emotions are a storm. The conversation with my mother last night was brief, but left me feeling numb. Even now, as I sit in the office of the Dueling Council, I can hardly pay attention to my surroundings. Dia's at my side, her presence a great comfort to me. Six days. Mother will be here in six days. I feel the minutes clawing at my mind, each one passing by both too fast and far too slow. I hate this. Not even a single night to just enjoy my life.

Dia held me in the night while I cried, soothing me until I slept. If not for her, I'm not sure how I could even function today. I glance over at her, admiring her features and allowing myself a moment to dream about the future.

"Move in with me," I tell her.

"What?" She blinks.

"Move your things into my dorm." I squeeze her hand. "I don't want to waste more time. When we're finished here, I want you to move in."

She smiles at me, squeezing my hand in return. "Alright."

The door behind us hisses open.

Brigid steps into the office, crossing the room to stand in front of us. She is not a woman to be trifled with. Her expression is curious, like a cat looking at prey. She sits lazily on the couch, crossing one leg over the other. Her long pink hair cascades down her shoulders and around her face. She's beautiful and a bit terrifying.

"Quite the mess you stirred up, Your Highness," she says. "What were you thinking?"

"A lot," I retort. "Why did you get in the way of my father's men?"

Dia folds her arms behind her head as she listens. She looks quite calm, a subtle smirk resting on her face.

Brigid looks towards her. "Well, I see what the fuss is about," she says, chuckling. "Rumor had it, your highness, that the emperor granted you the right to pick a husband. A better deal than most. Yet, here she sits, your bride to be." Her smile is sickeningly sweet, setting my nerves on edge. "Looking at her, I can understand why you'd throw caution to the wind—an exquisite woman."

"I am," Dia replies, sitting up and returning a grin. "But I'm more than a pretty face, I'm afraid. Let's get down to business. What do you want, Brigid?"

I smirk. Her experience in battle is showing itself in other ways. She does not flinch from the power struggle at play here and has the air of someone who has all the cards. If that is true or not, is immaterial, that she can so easily convince others she does is the key to her strength in this arena.

"Now, now, we'll get there," Brigid says. "No rush."

Dia shakes her head. "There sort of is." She furrows her brows. "Might be my last few days of peace before I need to wage a one-woman war against the Fomorians if you all try to kill me."

"You wouldn't be just one woman," I remind her.

She smiles at me. "A two-woman war."

This takes Brigid by surprise. She's silent for a moment—she's never rendered speechless. "You are very bold to just openly admit that." She furrows her brows. "Your stupidity is as remarkable as your piloting."

Dia shrugs. "You underestimate how fragile empires are," she says. "Throw the right stone, and the glasshouse shatters."

Brigid frowns. This is clearly not how she was expecting this conversation to go. Knowing Fomorian politics, she was likely expecting threats of blackmail, or a back and forth of self-serving deals—not talk of revolution. "What, pray tell, is the right stone?"

"Me," I reply calmly. "The houses want to end my father's immortal reign." I reach over towards Dia, taking her hand into mine. I'd rather reserve handholding for a private moment, but it feels pertinent to show off such affection in this negotiation. "Refusing to get married destabilized my father's rule—openly marrying a woman will ruin it."

"That's true," she admits. "My house has been quite thrilled by your willfulness, truth be told." She looks at us for a moment, her face looking quite serious, or at least more serious than I am used to seeing. "You asked what I wanted: the Empire. I will rule instead if you are so keen to give up your throne, your highness."

"No," Dia says flatly. "There won't be an empire when I am done with this place."

"You're not serious," Brigid says, for the first time looking truly unnerved.

"Oh, I am serious, Brigid." Her tone is firm. She pulls her hand away from mine, sitting upright, and straightening her shoulders. She stares hard at Brigid, her eyes like swords. "I didn't come here to play politics or games. I came here to destroy the whole thing. You can help me, or not, but don't get in my way."

The lady of House Áine looks perturbed, confused, even outraged. "You're ridiculous." Her flamboyant pretense is gone entirely now. "And I should have you killed. Destroy the Fomorian Armory? Do you have some kind of death wish?"

"Why would you want this rotten corpse?" She stands up to her full height, towering over us both.

Gods, she is tall.

"Think you can run it your way, maybe obtain some semblance of control? Perhaps you want to fix a few things, even?" Her tone is cold and biting, harsher than she's ever been with me. "Or perhaps you're worse than Cormac?"

There's a threat in her question that sends a chill down my spine. Brigid can sense it too; I can see it in her eyes. She crosses her arms in front of her chest, sitting up.

"It's just foolish," she says, frowning deeply. "What would you replace it with? Would Central come in and sweep up the mess you make of things?" She shakes her head. "The people wouldn't stand for that. They would see it as an occupation and resist. It would be generations of conflict."

"I'll tell you the same thing I told her." Dia glances over at me. "There already is conflict. People are already dying. More than you and I can count." She sits back down, her easygoing smile returning.

"I'm not so reckless, though, as to do what you suggest. I came here to explore options, formulate a plan, and gather allies. So, what are you going to be, ally or enemy?"

"You really are insane." Brigid's lips draw back in a smile. "But I think I like it. I had expected you to be far more emotionally driven. I underestimated what you were really after." She looks at me. "I assume this was part of the stakes agreed upon prior to the duel, but why did you accept them to begin with? Are you not afraid she's using you?"

I smile, shaking my head. "She wanted to break my cage." My heart races, recalling the way she looked at me that first night in my garden, the thrill that went up my spine. "Truly, I am the one using her—she is my champion, after all."

Dia looks over at me, her cheeks tinted slightly red. I smirk at her, fluttering my eyelashes. She chuckles low in her chest, shaking her head.

"I sure am."

Brigid laughs, for once sounding genuinely pleased. "You sure are something, Miss Mirren. I'll consider this nonsense. Turning you over to the emperor doesn't benefit me, and I get the impression trying to blackmail you or otherwise force you to do anything wouldn't work, anyway." She sighs. "For what it is worth, I don't want to be your enemy."

Dia flashes her a wolfish smirk. "I was thinking the same thing. If there's nothing else, I have moving in to do." She turns back to me, winking.

I flush, averting my gaze. "Yes," I say. "Thank you, Brigid. For your intervention, I mean. I would not have expected that." I stand up then, straightening out my uniform. "A shame we have avoided one another before this. I would like to think we could be friends." I extend a hand towards her.

She hesitates, glances between Dia and me, and then finally stands up to take my hand in hers. "You've changed, Your Highness." She tilts her head. "Truth be told, I am unsure what to think. For now, I assure you House Áine supports you, and your champion."

"Before I forget, will the two of you be attending the masquerade? I've never had to mark you down with a plus one, Princess Gráinne."

I glance at Dia; she looks rather pleased with herself. I take my hand back from Brigid, stepping towards Dia and linking our arms together. To my surprise, she flushes quite red.

I'm glad I'm not the only one who becomes a bit of a mess in this situation of ours.

"Yes," I say. "We will. I plan to enjoy every moment of peace we have left to the absolute fullest."

* * *

"This room is a lot bigger than mine," I say, setting a box of my things down. I don't have a lot to move into Gráinne's room, and yet it's still somehow more than I initially thought. "Suppose it's nice to be the princess."

She sticks her tongue out at me. "You don't have to rub it in." She takes some of my clothes out from a box and begins neatly putting them into her wardrobe. "Well, if you really want to, I suppose it is fine. You are not wrong." She sighs.

"Sorry," I say gently. "It's more so that I'm giving it a proper look. You have a full kitchen and an extra room."

"A nice bathtub, too," she says, looking over at me. "We should take one later."

"I'd like that." I smirk at her, looking her up and down until she flushes and averts her gaze.

"This is fun," she says, going back to putting away my clothes. "Thank you."

"For what, moving in?" I chuckle. "Did you think I'd not want to?"

She frowns. "I don't know. I sort of just demanded it earlier. Everything is moving too fast while also being too slow." Gráinne brushes her hair behind her ear. "Hmmm, you have great fashion sense." She holds up a black dress of mine, along with my frilly pajamas. "After seeing you in that jacket, it's difficult to imagine you in these."

"I look good in anything," I say. "From a three-piece suit to that dress you're holding. The jacket and pants are my default style, admittedly."

"Well, you looked so stunning in your uniform that you took my breath away the day we met," she says, beaming. "You know, I have always thought women were beautiful, but it is like staring at art when I look at you."

I giggle, my face turning red, and a smirk forms on my face. "You're getting much better at this."

"At what?" she blinks. "What am I getting better at?"

"Flirting."

She turns a deep shade of crimson. "Am I flirting? I am just telling you what I think."

"That's precious." I place the one nicknack I brought with me, a mech figurine I built and painted as a kid with my mom, on top of the dresser. "That you aren't intentionally flirting—truly adorable."

"Well, we *are* engaged," she says sheepishly. "I want to tell you all the things I think and feel. I have put my life in your hands, after all. There is so much I love about you, from your charm, your looks, and your unflinching intensity. You are incredible, Dia."

"Sounds like you've fallen in love with me," I say, leaning back on the dresser with a big grin on my face that shows off my fangs.

She stammers for a moment; her face is the reddest I've ever seen. "I..." she pauses. "Yes, I think so. I have little in the way of a frame of reference for what love feels like, but I know I feel better being around you. You make me feel safe. I could listen to you talk for hours about anything at all. The way your mind works fascinates me, even when you frustrate me." She runs her fingers through her hair, pushing her raven locks back, looking up at me.

"It is lovely, the way you play with the lock of hair that hangs down in front of your face. Gods, your cooking is truly divine." She approaches me, placing her hand on my chest. "I especially like how you make me feel normal, that I am not a princess at all. I even like that you call me that." She keeps her gaze locked with mine, her face beginning to go back to normal. "Sorry, I am rambling now, but if this is not love, then I know not what is." She takes a deep breath. "I love you."

My heart quickens as I drink in her words, her raw depth of feeling. "You really are good at this," I say softly. "I..."

"Only say it if you mean it," she says, cutting me off. She turns her back to me, taking in a shaky breath. "Don't you dare say it to me if it's not the absolute truth. I could not bear that, Dia."

I walk over to her, wrapping my arms around her waist, and lean in to kiss her neck. She tilts her head to the side; I run my fangs across her skin. The princess shudders in my arms, leans back into my chest, and whimpers softly as my fangs dig deeper into her skin.

"Princess," I whisper in her ear. "Truth is, I fell in love with you that first night in the garden. I had all these plans when I came here, my mission, but one conversation with you and I was yours." I squeeze her tightly in my arms, kissing the top of her head. "My mothers, they told me not to fall in love with you. I promised I wouldn't, but I was already lying."

She turns around and pushes me back onto the bed roughly, practically leaping on top of me. She kisses me, clenching her fingers into the fabric of my uniform with desperate fervor.

"No one can interrupt us now," she whispers in my ear. "Would you like to finish what we started last night?"

I roll us over, locking our lips again. "Yes," I hiss, beginning to take off her clothes. I fumble with the buttons for a moment before just ripping the front of her uniform open completely.

She gasps as I devour her neck, sinking my fangs into her, and dragging my nails along her exposed sides. Gráinne grips my hair, pulling me tight against her body, her legs wrapping around my waist. I pull off the rest of her top, tossing it to the side. I kiss down her chest, taking her breast into my mouth. She cries out, her fingers tugging at my hair.

"Oh fuck," she whimpers.

Taking off her pants is easier; they slide easily down her hips along with her panties. My fingers brush along her inner thighs; I avoid her most sensitive spots quite on purpose. She groans louder, her hips lifting off the bed. I bite at her lower lip.

"Patience," I whisper in her ear. "I will make you feel such ecstasy that for the briefest of moments, you'll die right here in my arms—I'll bring you back with a kiss."

She squirms under me, releasing a breathy moan. "Do whatever you want to me."

I grin. "As you wish," I say, kissing down her chest and stomach, licking at her well-muscled body.

There's not an inch of her that isn't built for combat. She is just like me, a living weapon both in and out of the mech. I worship her skin, my tongue dragging along her, tasting every inch. I sink my fangs into her thigh, hovering just on the edge of ripping her apart, longing to drink and consume her.

"Harder," she hisses. "Don't be gentle with me, Dia, don't you dare."

My fangs pierce flesh, droplets of blood touch my tongue, and I drink from her. Gráinne screams in pleasure, her body shaking as she cums. I pull away from her thigh, wrapping my lips around her clit. She only screams more, digging her fingers into the bed so roughly her knuckles must be bone white. I drown in the taste of her like she's the water of life.

Her thighs squeeze around my head as she orgasms again. Her back arches, her entire body spasming with pleasure. I lick, and lick, and lick, unrelenting in my assault on her cunt. She taps my shoulder, unable to form coherent words. I stop, looking up at her as I lick her arousal from my lips. She's a ruined mess on the bed, panting and clutching her head. Her whole body is flushed, delightfully tinted red and glistening in bliss.

"Fuck, Dia," she says after gathering a little composure. "I have never felt so good in all my life."

I grin, flashing my fangs at her. "Would you like me to be inside you?"

She lifts her head, looking me in the eye. "Yes. I want nothing more."

I stand up, taking off this annoying uniform. She watches me, rubbing her legs together and biting her lip. Before I can take my pants off, she sits up, putting a hand on my breast.

"Wait," she says softly, wrapping her lips around my nipple and her arms around my waist.

She sucks on my breast, her tongue bringing me to a moan as her nails dig into my back and rake across my skin. She takes my other breast in her mouth, her touches needy and desperate. My knees become weak; it's a struggle to even stand. She nibbles me gently at first, but then becomes bolder and bites into my nipple. A sharp pang of pleasurable pain sends shivers up my spine.

She throws me onto the bed, crawling on top of me. "I love your body and your tattoos." She smiles, running her fingers along the designs. "I was so curious about them on our date. They're everywhere."

"I like ink," I say, a smirk on my face. "My body is my canvas for me to do as I please. There isn't a single thing about me that isn't of my choosing."

"Mmm," she says, licking up my stomach and sides. "Then I should take my time to enjoy you. As much as I want you inside me. Gods, you have no idea how badly I want that." Her hands hook into my pants, gently tugging them down. "First, I need to carve every inch of your body into my mind. I want to recognize you in the dark by touch alone."

My cock giving a little twitch as she pulls my pants over my hips. Gráinne grins down at me, licking her lips. I can't help blushing a little as she spreads my legs.

"You are perfect," she growls. "I do not know what I am doing, but I am going to show you just how much I love everything about you."

She licks along the shaft, taking the head of my cock into her mouth. I let out a breathy moan, my hips arching up. The sounds I make encourage her to keep exploring, her hands touching my thighs, and squeezing my hips. It's as if she wants to be everywhere, all at once, and it drives me wild. Her licks become bolder as her confidence grows. Her hands knead my breasts and pinch at my nipples. I'm a mess on the bed, writhing against the sheets.

"Just like that," I say. I run my fingers through her silky hair and across her face.

Gráinne moans on my cock as she licks and sucks, looking up into my eyes with a mischievous glint in her expression. "It is nice to see you like this," she says, her voice low. She gets up and crawls on top of me. "At my mercy for once. You always unnerve me, and it is time to get you back." She kisses my neck, biting me gently.

"I'm just taking it easy on you because it's your first time," I tell her, tilting my head to the side. "I'm considerate."

She giggles, beginning to grind her hips on me. She slides her slick cunt over my cock, back and forth, causing us both to let out whimpering groans. "Never hold back," she says in my ear. "I always want you to bear your all to me."

I grab her shoulders, turning us over and press my lips to hers as I slide my body against her. Our breasts squeeze together as we cling to one another. She lets out a groan as I press against her clit, sliding my length along the sensitive flesh.

"I'll always give you everything," I say as I slide inside her. She's wet and relaxed, taking me inside easier than I expected. Still, I go slowly at first. I bite at her neck, my fangs brushing against her pulsing carotid.

She wraps her legs around my hips, holding me inside of her. She arches her back, letting out a long moan of pleasure. "My love," she whispers, her nails digging into my shoulders. "Fuck me."

I growl, slamming my hips against her as hard as I can. The room fills with the sound of our gasping moans. She cries out, drawing blood from my back with how roughly she clings to me. The bed rocks back and forth, the wooden frame straining under the weight of my thrusts.

"Harder!" She bites into my shoulder, her teeth sinking into me to keep from screaming.

I grunt in pain, and in pleasure. I thrust harder, deeper, driving my cock into her relentlessly. The bed rocks back and forth, the foundation creaking. The frame's legs break under us, the bed landing on the floor with a loud thump. Neither of us pays any mind, we are too in the moment of our blissful release.

"Inside," she whispers, wrapping her legs tightly around me. "Finish inside."

The softness of the request is more than I can bear. I hold her tight as I cum; my toes curl, the intensity takes my breath away, leaving me a mess on top of her. This goes on for several long, perfect moments, waves of pleasure coursing through my entire body. I rest my forehead against Gráinne's, my cock trembling gently inside her.

"Sorry about the bed," I say, chuckling.

"I will just get a new bed." She giggles, brushing her fingers through my hair. "That was perfect for my first time. Better than our duel even."

I furrow my brows. "Well, I should hope so. This time, we both won." I kiss her, gently nibbling on her lips. "I'm surprised how rough you wanted me to be."

"Mmm," she groans. "I do not know what to say. I am just an all-or-nothing kind of princess."

"You're my princess now," I tell her, peppering her neck with affectionate kisses.

"Promise?" She kisses my jaw, running her fingers along my sides.

I kiss her, my tongue dances with hers. As we break pull apart, I whisper into her ear, "Yes, Princess, I promise."

Dancing Wolf

Three duels in as many days. I worry about Dia's stamina, but she doesn't seem to show any signs of wear. At the very least, it's the masquerade tonight, and that means she gets to rest today, and likely tomorrow as well.

"Everything is fine, Princess," Dia says, her arms folded back behind her head as she lies under the willow. "Don't look so concerned."

"Easy for you to say," I mutter. "I am used to fighting my own battles. It is novel to have a champion, but I would just as soon be done with all of this."

"Soon," she says. "A little over two weeks until your birthday."

I cross my arms over my chest, sighing. "Two endless weeks," I say. "At least the ball will be fun for once—the benefit of having a date I quite like."

"Have I been downgraded? I'm only *liked* now." She looks up at me, smirking.

"Not dignifying that," I tell her. "Have you decided what to wear tonight?"

"One of my dresses," she says. "I think you'll *like* it."

I roll my eyes, smiling despite my irritation. "Of that, I have no doubt." I sigh. The lunch hour is coming to an end, and I do not look forward to going back. "I suppose we shouldn't miss class."

She grunts as she sits up. "Can't skip the regularly scheduled propaganda."

"Do you have another suggestion?" I look at her, my brow arched.

She shakes her head, standing up. "Nope," she says, offering a hand to help me up—a sweet but unnecessary gesture. "We may as well behave normally."

I take her hand in mine, am hoisted up and brought right into her arms. Heat rises to my face. "Oh," I say, fighting back my disappointment. "If you have no alternative to suggest, then, yes, we should go pretend to listen to the propaganda."

She grins as she walks out of my garden, taking me along with her by the hand. It still makes me nervous to be seen out in public like this with her—the hateful glares sting more than I expected. Still, I'd rather deal with a thousand hateful glares from the worst people than not be as close to her as possible. I ignore them as we head to class, keeping my eyes fixed on her long white hair and broad back.

The propaganda truly is insufferable. Our professor drones on and on. Dia makes sitting in lectures far more pleasant, even with the occasional murmur that our relationship is not real, it is a trick, or that we are disgusting. More than once in the past few days, I have gotten nearly irritated enough to proclaim how wonderful it is to have a woman's face between your thighs at night. I have refrained from doing so for the sake of propriety, but only just. Dia, at least, does not care in the slightest, which seems to bother our peers most of all. With me, they can see how their words hurt, but Dia has an air of superiority, returning pity in response to their derision.

Class comes and goes; thankfully, it is the last class of the day. I retain nothing of note, too distracted by the stress in my life—particularly my mother's arrival in four days.

"Don't think about stressful things tonight," Dia says, gently patting my thigh.

"How could you tell what I was thinking?"

She smiles. "The way your brow furrows," she says. "Your mother is on her way and your father likely wants me dead. There is nothing you can do about either of those things right now. What we *can* do, however, is have a delightful time at the ball."

"You are correct," I say, leaning back. "Okay, let us go get ready—I look forward to seeing you in that dress."

Bres steps in our way as we exit, using his mass to block the door. Dia clicks her tongue, glaring at him.

"There a reason you're in my way?" She steps in front of me, fully putting herself between Bres and me.

"I know what you are," he says, a sick, twisted smile on face and venom in his voice.

My heart rate spikes. What could he mean by that? Has he somehow heard of Dia's plan? Has Brigid betrayed us?

Dia flicks her wrist out, grabbing Bres by his uniform and marches out of the room. He yells for her to unhand him as she drags him along the floor. The sight is quite comical in truth; I find myself wanting to laugh.

She drops him to the floor with a thump. "Yes, I'm a woman with somewhere to be. Later."

I follow behind her, linking my arm with hers. "You enjoy humiliating him."

"He makes it very easy," she says. "Blocking a doorway like that, as if he's owed my time, attention, or respect. I'm used to men like him. They are all over the galaxy—entitled and pathetic."

"Yes," I say, frowning as we walk. "What do you think he meant?"

"I have a good idea," she says. "It's not the first time someone has put that together and decided to be cruel."

"Oh." I squeeze her arm tighter. "How could tell it was that, and not about your plans?"

She stops, turning to look at me. It's the first time I have seen her genuinely hurt. "It's the look," she says. "I can always tell when someone finds out about me, because they look at me like I'm not human."

I wrap my arms around her, pulling her tight against me. "Oh, my love." I squeeze her tighter. "I am sorry that people can be so vicious."

"It's okay, Princess," she says, kissing the top of my head. "It really shouldn't bother me. I grew up in a place where this is *almost* non-existent, and it's extremely condemned when it happens. Just takes me off guard how common this bullshit is away from home."

My thoughts drift to the cold, pitying looks Dia has been giving the others. I realize how very foolish I have been to think none of this has bothered her. I squeeze her harder, burying my face in her chest, not caring who might be looking. "One day it won't be."

* * *

I arrive at the ball alone, casting my eyes above. There is beauty in the false Milky Way of Fianna's sky, but it only makes my heart yearn to be back in space or home on Earth. I adjust my mask, a wolf's face, as I walk up the stairs into the ballroom. Nearly the entire student body and most of the faculty have packed into this room. There is space enough to move and mingle, but I hate being around this many people.

Heads turn as I enter, eyes following my every moment. My black dress makes a rather loud statement, I admit. Slits go up both sides of the dress, exposing my thighs; cloth drapes down the center, flowing side to side with each step. The bodice covers my neck, obscuring my chest completely, and the diamonds that adorn the front resemble Earth's night sky. The back of the dress is open, showing off my tattoos and muscles.

"Miss Mirren."

"Couldn't you have pretended not to know me, Brigid?" I turn to look at her. She wears a golden dress embroidered with multicolored gemstones, each one catching the light from overhead and gleaming brilliantly.

"Well, I'd have looked rather foolish trying," she says. "Your hair and height, especially in those heels, give you away. You're gorgeous."

I smirk. "Have you just come to flatter me?"

"No," she says, her tone turning serious. "To warn you. Bres is planning to make trouble tonight. I wanted you to be prepared for it."

"Ah," I say, "it makes no difference to me—I have a princess to hunt."

She chuckles. "I'm sure she will be thrilled when you catch her. Have a good night, Miss Mirren."

I bow my head as we part ways. As I glide between people, my eyes scanning for my prey, I spot Layla and Quinn standing off to the side. Both wear masks of animals I don't recognize; something from their homeworld no doubt. Layla's dress is dark green, Quinn's is a rich blue—both with matching vinelike gold trim that sprawls across their bust and down their sides. The pair stand centimeters apart, looking as if they want to cling to one another amidst the chaos.

Adorable.

I find her, my princess, by the sound of her laugh. She's distracted by conversation, her back turned towards me. Her lavender dress clings to the contours of her body like liquid silk. I keep just out of her field of vision, approaching her blind spot.

"Princess." I whisper the word in her ear, my hands gently taking hold of her shoulders.

She relaxes into my touch, turning to look at me, her violet eyes peeking through the slits of her cat mask. "I was just talking about you," she says.

I grin, flashing my fangs at her. "Oh?"

Her smile makes my knees weak. "Yes, about how terrifying you are in a mech." She turns her attention back to her companion, a woman with soft amber hair tied up in a loose bun and adorned with flowers. She wears a serpent mask; her dress is an earthy brown and rather plain in design.

Motioning for me to step forward, Gráinne says, "Lady Airmid, this is Lady Diarmuid—my champion."

"We've met," I say.

"Wolf." She takes a sip of wine from a long flute, smiling behind the rim.

"Pirates give you any trouble lately?" I ask, linking my arm with Gráinne's.

"None," she says. "You did excellent work."

Gráinne looks between us, her brows furrowed behind her mask. "I suppose this is the least surprising development."

"She gets around," Airmid says. "I had to see this for myself after that match."

"See what?" Gráinne's grip on my arm tightens.

"If this was real—your feelings for one another." Airmid looks between the two of us, her smile thinning. "Foolish in hindsight; I'm not sure you know how to do anything without excessive sincerity. That's your best and worst trait."

"Well, now you've seen," I say. "What next?"

She shifts to the side, her eyes glancing about the room. "When the time comes, I will support you, Wolf. This isn't how I would have done things, but…" She looks between Gráinne and me again, her eyes softening. "The sparks have caught flame, and the people will need a balm once this fire has consumed the empire."

"I'm glad we're finally on the same page."

Her eyes roll. "Princess Gráinne, a word of wisdom," she says. "Do not be afraid to tease this one relentlessly, lest her head will get too large and she becomes insufferable."

Gráinne laughs then, the tension in the air snapping and giving way to a lighter mood. "I will do so, though it is difficult. I rather like my wolf as she is."

My cheeks burn behind my mask. "I am right here."

Airmid smirks. "Yes, you are," she says. "Have a good night, the both of you."

"And you," Gráinne says.

"Stay safe, Airmid—secret, too."

The lady curtsies to us both. "Don't worry about me, Wolf," she says. "Keep yourself out of any snares." She departs without another word, not bothering to look back at us as she exits the ballroom.

Gráinne turns to me, her distress visible even behind her mask. "What was *that* all about?"

"We can talk and walk," I say, taking her by the hand, leading us to the dance floor. "She's an old flame. She leveraged her position to aid workers and the company owner, Lord Conaing, had her kidnapped."

"I did not know Conaing was behind that," Gráinne says as we walk. "I take it you were responsible for his *accident?*"

"Naturally."

We find a suitable spot with enough space; I place my hand around her waist, taking the lead as we dance. Her expression relaxes, her shoulders dropping as we find our rhythm in the sound, though I can see her worry lingering over her like a black cloud.

"Airmid and I didn't work out," I tell her, pulling her close to me. "Both of us decided we were better allies than lovers."

The princess nods, clinging to me tighter. "I have never seen her so informal," she says. "It is like she was a different person around you—

though I am the same." Her face brightens into a smile, her grip on me relaxes. "Why did she call only call you Wolf?"

"It took me a long time to trust her with my name." I guide Gráinne into a spin, the tempo of the music around us picking up. "She got into the habit of using Wolf as a nickname, and I rather liked it, truth be told." I pull her back to my chest, wrapping my hand around her waist, resting it on her stomach, my lips almost on her neck. "You look gorgeous, Princess."

"Thank you," she says, her cheeks darkening. "You were right, earlier—I really do like your dress."

We resume our dance, picking up the pace and intensity. Our heels clack against the ground, our dresses flair out with each spin as we seamlessly alternate who leads the other. As we get swept up in one another, we capture the attention of those present; murmurs spread like wildfire.

I tip her over as the music fades, her leg hooks around my waist. I lift her mask off, pressing my lips to hers. We linger for a moment, our passion displayed in this kiss for all to see. There is a stunned, uncomfortable silence hanging in the air. I pull away from her, casting my gaze around the room. Not surprisingly, the men are most outraged, their anger almost palpable. A few women step forward and begin applauding, calling our dance a great show—there are more than a few red faces among them.

I'm grabbed from behind, yanked back by my hair. Bres looms over me, his face twisted up in rage. I grab his hand, twisting it at the wrist until his grip breaks.

"Don't touch me." I step away from Bres, his two cronies lingering behind him like a malaise.

"You're filth," he says. "A disgusting man parading around as a woman. I should kill you where you stand, you freak."

I bellow out a laugh, pressing my palm to my head. The others in the room glance around at one another, the whispers spreading that Bres has lost his mind.

Gráinne steps next to me, her face stone cold but for the rage in her eyes. "Tomorrow, you shall duel Lady Diarmuid." Her voice is ice, commanding absolute respect. "The terms are this: should you lose or refuse, you will be stripped of your ranks and titles. You will live as a common man."

His expression turns from one of anger to frantic desperation. "Princess, Plea…"

"You have disrespected my lover," she snaps. "The woman who earned the title of champion from my hands in honorable combat and has kept it ever since. With all here as my witness, I deem this offense intolerable."

"If I win, the punishment you have judged me worthy of gets passed to *them* instead," he says, glaring at me. "Those are my stakes."

"Deal," I say. "Though I have one thing to add."

"What?" he spits.

"After I win—which I will—I want you to know I will kill you if I ever have the displeasure of hearing your voice again."

* * *

"You cannot lose," I say, pressing my hand to Dia's chest. "Not ever, but especially not to him. Do you understand?"

She runs her fingers along my face. "I won't lose," she says, gently cupping my chin. "Not to anyone."

I press my lips to hers, stepping away after a moment that passes far too quickly. "See you when you get back."

Dia winks, lazily saluting with two fingers as she steps into the Phantom Queen. Layla and Quinn surround me on both sides, their presence comforting my rising anxiety. The Phantom disappears into a loading container that moves along a conveyor belt to be taken to the battlefield.

"Usual watching spot?" Layla takes my hand in hers.

"I would like that," I say. "Walking will distract me."

The 'usual spot' is a café not too far away from this mechbay. It has become a place of comfort, a time to spend with my friends while we watch my girlfriend fight to protect me. There is a small part of me that enjoys having someone fight my battles for me—I've never had that before. The larger part of me hates all of this—I am not property. I remind myself that this is temporary, a convenient mask until we can take our next steps. Keeping a cool exterior is something I am used to; I can manage this façade a little longer.

We take our seat at our habitual table outside the café. There are trees decorating the seating area, along with indigo flowers. Other students are here as well, presumably to watch the duel. Projectors in the center of the table display the battlefield. It is mountainous terrain today, with large rocks to take cover and deep crevasses to fall into.

So far, neither mech has taken their position, and the pilots have not exchanged their dueling vows. I'm not sure what I was thinking last night, insisting on this duel. Rage overtook me, clouded my judgement.

I am a fool.

"Dia will be fine," Layla says.

"Yeah," Quinn says, scooting closer to Layla. "Everything will be okay. It always is."

My heart pounds in my chest as I turn on the projector. "It's different this time," I say. "Bres, for all his disgusting faults, is an excellent pilot. At least he was when I beat him."

The pair exchange glances. "I've never really paid attention to the duels," Quinn says. "Never saw much point."

"I remember it." Layla frowns, resting her chin on her palm. "You lost one of your arms, I think."

"Sacrificed it to save my head," I say. "Rationally, I know Dia will be fine, but Bres would be the worst person to lose to." My anxiety is high, my pulse throbbing so intensely I can hear my blood. "I hate that man. I hate him with every fiber of my being."

The screen flickers, drawing our attention to the battlefield. I'm grateful for the distraction, as I'm not keen to share the misery of the time I thought I'd have to marry that man. The Sétante, Bres' mech, stands slightly taller than the Phantom Queen. The frame is deep blue with white detailing along the chest and shoulders. Spikes protrude out from along its arms and out from its head, the face of it is twisted and demonic.

The two frames could not be any more different. The Phantom is elegant and beautiful, the black and white a striking display under the lights of Fianna.

Only in their weapons of choice is there any similarity, the Phantom with her twin lances and the Sétante with a single, but much longer spear.

I recall the thrill of fighting her; our weapons clashing, the infuriating swarm-bits that seemed to always know what I would do next. She pushed me to my limit in a way no other pilot ever has, and I don't even think she went as hard as she could have. I long to fight her again, to feel that thrill as we struggle to overcome each other.

"Are you okay?" Quinn asks. "Your face is red."

"Ah," I say. "I was recalling my fight with Dia and how ferocious she is. There really is no worry she'll lose."

Layla smirks. "Ferocious, huh?"

I purse my lips, my face somehow becoming even more red. "Yes."

Brigid's face appears in the screen's corner, her smile broad as she addresses the pilots. "Good morning," she says. "Are the two of you prepared?"

"Yes," Bres says quickly, his voice strained.

"Always." Dia sounds calm, but I can make out the edge in her voice—the wrath that threatens to bubble up.

"Excellent. You have both agreed to the stakes?" Brigid glances between them; her face and voice are giddy as she always is when officiating a duel.

"Yes," they both say.

"Then exchange your dueling vows."

"Just for the sake of it, I am going to utterly humiliate and destroy my opponent," Dia says, her rage now barely contained. "Only his cockpit will remain unscathed."

Bres hesitates, his voice shaking as he says. "We'll see about that, you freak."

"That is not a vow," Brigid interjects. "Address your opponent, the champion, with the proper respect due to *her*."

"On my honor, I will take what is mine and cast you into the abyss." Bres seethes. "You will never see Gráinne again."

Brigid's face sours considerably—it's rare to see her upset. "The first one to take the other's head is the victor," she says lazily. "Begin."

The Phantom glows white, the paneling along the frame igniting. Bres is the first to move, thrusting his spear towards Dia's cockpit. She retreats with a quick step backwards, deflecting the blow as she moves. He keeps attacking, sinking his mind deeper and deeper into his mech. Bres was never one who could truly harness the Fomorian Framework, he too easily gives into the frenzy. His rage shows in his attacks. His movements are wild and undisciplined.

Dia moves gracefully across the battlefield, parrying and deflecting with ease. She is toying with him, drawing out his rage. He overextends, dashing past her harmlessly. The yellow lance is driven into his arm, a burst of energy rending the limb immobile. The massive spear is unwieldy with a single arm, but he tries nonetheless, stabbing and thrusting haphazardly.

Dust is kicked up as Dia seems to skate across the ground, her movements quick and sharp. The panels along her body glow brighter, the swarm-bits detach from her, and she unleashes a barrage of deadly plasma. Bres stands no chance; the Sétante is sliced into molten pieces that scatter across the battlefield, only his head remains attached to his core.

The fight is not technically over, but Dia has won. It's a humiliating loss for Bres. Even I am surprised by how quickly she dispatched him. I wonder if Dia simply went easy on me, though she claims she didn't. Only another spar will clear my lingering doubts, not that I need or want more reason to cross blades with my lover beyond the simple pleasure of it.

The swarm-bits reattach to her body as she walks over to him, taking her time, dragging out his disgrace. He squirms helplessly as she presses her foot to his head, crushing it under her heel. The victory emblem flashes in the sky, displaying her name boldly. She walks away without embellishment or flourish. It's unusual. She looks exhausted and upset, her steps lacking their customary spring after winning.

Disgrace is far too good for the likes of Bres.

I wonder, how many times has she had to fight to assert her humanity while traveling away from home? It's a shock she does not simply stay in Central and leave the rest of us to rot. Of course, she doesn't fight for herself, she fights for others—even the people who might hate her for who she is. A tear forms in my eye, and then another and another until they are streaming down my face.

It is not fair; the dehumanizing looks, the cruel whispers, the violence received for going against the expectations set by *tradition*, but also the violence received for living up to them. She sees these things clearly; it drives her forward, no matter the cost.

"Princess?" Quinn asks, her voice tender. "What's wrong? She won."

I nod, wiping the tears from my face. "Yes," I say. "I am relieved, of course, that Dia won, glad that Bres is to be banished. However, I just cannot overcome the heartlessness in his words towards her—it makes me indignant to think about. There was weight behind his words; the voice within the twisted core of this empire."

"It's why our personhood can be stripped from us at any moment," I say, glancing between my friends. "It's why you could never touch a mech despite your brilliance. Me, forced to marry against my will, to spend a lifetime as an ornament—good only to produce an heir. It's how that bastard treated Dia, as if she is a monster. It is a twisted, rotten *tradition* that we Fomorians live and die by."

Layla takes Quinn's hand in hers, the pair of them looking at me. "We aren't fools," Layla says. "You and Dia are planning something, and we want to help. We trust you both."

Quinn looks at me, her eyes filled with determination. "Whatever you need, just say the word."

"The two of you are wonderful friends," I say, my tearful face giving way to a smile. "Thank you."

I would like to speak more openly, but it's not safe to do so here. It's also not relevant now, anyway. Any proper planning will happen away from Fianna—on Earth. There are tools and resources there. Most importantly, there will be freedom from prying eyes. For now, we bide our time until my birthday passes; despite my protests at marriage, I really would rather like to get married to her.

Dia appears at the café wearing her unassuming uniform, her beautiful white hair hanging down around her waist. "Yo," she says. "Told you I'd win."

I walk over to her, throwing my arms around her as I press my lips to hers. "Splendid victory," I say as I pull my face away. Our eyes meet, her cheeks slightly flushed from the sudden affection. "Let us celebrate."

Her smile reaches her eyes. "Whatever you want, Princess."

"I will hold you to that," I tell her, brushing my fingers through her silken hair. "For now, I want very little besides eating lunch. I think I will even have some wine."

Mothers in Law

The low gravity of the shuttle bay makes it impossible to stay grounded—I wait for my mother floating in the air. Her ship is due in the next few moments. I dread seeing her; the time went by too quickly. Still, I'd rather be here to greet her directly than make her come find me on her own. Dia offered to join me, but I insisted I meet and prepare my mother for meeting with my girlfriend, my fiancée, on my own beforehand. If that proves to be wisdom or not remains to be seen.

Mother's ship docks smoothly, the clamps fastening themselves to the hull. The boarding ramp stretches out as the hatch opens. When I return from the capital, I always try to be subtle. Mother, on the other hand, is all about her fanfare. Several servants file out of the ship, playing the Fomorian Anthem, capturing the attention of all eyes in the shuttle bay.

Aoife appears before my mother, her job to check for any danger. Naturally, there is none—this is a school. She smiles at me when our eyes meet.

Mother descends from her shuttle, her chin held up high as she floats down toward me. As usual, her icy expression is impossible to read. She has her hair tied up, lacing her jeweled crown through her raven strands. Her royal gown ripples as she walks imperiously towards me. She is slightly shorter than I am, but usually her presence is enough to fill the room, but today she does not quite feel so larger-than-life.

"Where is your guard?" she asks sharply.

"Dismissed and sent back to the capital," I say. "I despised his presence."

"Gráinne," she says in exasperation. "You cannot go around without an escort."

"I would kill any assassin sent after me, mother," I tell her. "Besides, I have my champion, and she is more than enough protection."

She sighs. "Let us go someplace private. I do not wish to speak here—especially not about your *champion*."

"Very well." I hold out my arm to link with hers. "You can see how my garden is coming along."

She takes the offered arm; her face softening slightly. "Very well."

We walk into the campus, the gravity slowly becoming normal. There is an awkward, deafening silence between us. Normally, mother is not quite so cold with me. Though, I suppose finding out your daughter is a lesbian after seeing her kiss another woman on a live broadcast has a way of souring one's disposition.

I find myself not caring at all. I thought I'd be more nervous to face her, but seeing her here and now, I only feel determination to help free her, too. For all her faults, of which she has many, I still love her. She raised me to be as strong as I am. Perhaps with that strength, I can save her from my father.

Royal guards trail behind us, a respectful distance away. There is not a single eye that is not drawn to us as our entourage moves across the campus. Layla and Quinn are on the grounds; they see me but shrink back. I wave them over to us. They exchange nervous glances, as is their wont, and then approach us. Mother blinks in surprise.

"Who are they?" she asks, her tone genuinely curious.

"Friends of mine. This is Layla and Quinn," I say, pointing at each of them. "They are here on scholarship. Truly brilliant engineers. The top of their class."

"I see," mother says, her smile warm. "You do your empire proud, young ladies. Your empress wishes you the best in your studies."

They beam brightly at her. "Thank you!" Layla says. "We'll always do our best. It's, um, really nice to meet you."

Mother chuckles, a very rare sound coming from her. "The pleasure is mine. If you will excuse us, however. I have precious little time and much to do."

They nod, stepping out of the way. I flash them both a warm smile before moving on. As we arrive in the garden, I look back towards the guards. "They must stay outside," I say firmly. "You and Aoife can join me here, but I will not have them in my sanctum."

"Of course," mother says.

I step beyond the arch that leads into my garden, making my way to a bench so that I may sit. Mother joins me, gathering up the train of her dress before sitting. Aoife stands off to the side, watching us and our surroundings.

"What a fine mess you have made, my darling." Mother wraps an arm around me, pulling me into a hug. "Your father is furious, and now we are nearly at war with House Áine."

"I am aware." I lean into the hug. "It is not my fault things are the way they are."

"What do you mean?" she asks, pulling away. "Gráinne, this is entirely your fault. I want to know why you have done such things!"

"No," I say, moving away so that I might face her. "I am not the one who made our laws or traditions. I am not the one who forced their daughter into a position she begged and pleaded not to be in to begin with." My rage is difficult to contain; my fists are clenched so tightly I draw blood from my palm.

"The only blame that lies with me is that I took steps to obtain power. Father was all too happy to indulge that, for it benefited him and our house that I be in a cockpit—that I could humiliate his enemies." I shake my head. "No, mother, none of this is my fault."

She looks at me, stunned, her mouth agape. Her eyes flit over to Aoife. They exchange a furtive glance with one another. Aoife looks troubled but nods. It's not a good look.

"Mother, what are you scheming?" I ask, looking between the two of them.

"Your fiancée," she says. "She is from Central?"

"What does that matter?" I ask, my voice cold.

She sighs. "I wish to know more about the woman who has made my daughter so incredibly reckless. Is that forbidden?"

I glance away, chewing on my inner cheek. "No," I say. "I had considered her being here when we met, but I did not want to overwhelm you."

"I see," she says. "Your duel with her—I will admit, she is an incredible pilot. I am not sure even our elite could defeat her in a duel like the ones done here. It is unfair, really."

My brows furrow. "Your point, mother?"

"That when she is piloting, it may take a small army to kill her," she says, her voice detached, like she is guilty.

I stand up, barely able to constrain my fury. "If you are even thinking of harming her..."

"She is," Dia says, slinking into the garden. Her uniform is tattered, like it has been slashed several times. Blood leaks from a cut over her eye, though she wears her characteristic smirk and looks nonplused she is bleeding.

Mother's eyes go wide in shock. She snaps her fingers. Aoife pulls a knife from her sleeve, rushing at Dia and slicing at her with it. My fiancée slips one, two, three slashes before pivoting on her heel and sweeping Aoife's legs out from under her. Mother shouts for Aoife to kill Dia. The royal guards standing outside rush into the garden, their heavy boots trampling over my flowers—my lilies.

Aoife is a well-trained handmaiden, one of the best, but she's still no match for my lover. She's disarmed, the knife clattering to the ground. Dia kicks it over to me. Without hesitating, I pick it up and grab at my mother, pressing the edge of the knife into her neck.

"Enough!" Uncontrollable fury courses through me. How dare my mother do this, and here of all places. "I will kill her."

The guards freeze. Dia presses her knee into Aoife's back, pinning her to the ground. My mother, my dear mother's face is contorted in confusion and fear.

"Gráinne..."

"Silence," I say, pushing the knife harder to her skin. "Not a word." I turn my glare to the guards. "Get out of my garden."

Mother waves them away, desperation in her eyes. They comply, unwilling as they are, filing out of my sanctuary. I keep myself under control, but only just.

"My love," I say coldly, "please get off my handmaiden."

She does so, standing up and casually brushing herself off as if this is just an ordinary day.

I remove the knife from my mother's throat, taking a step back to get a better look at Dia. "Where is the one who did that to you?" I motion to her eye.

"Knocked out," Dia says. "She'll wake up with a wicked headache, but she's fine."

Mother pales considerably. "I don't believe this," she says, shrinking back until she nearly stumbles over the bench. She sits down, trying to regain her composure. "You are much harder to kill than I thought. That was my second-best assassin." She glances at Aoife. "Not that my best did any better."

"You're not the first one to make that mistake," Dia says, leaning against a tree. "You're lucky Gráinne made you send the guards away. It would've been a bloodbath." She folds her arms over her chest. "If you remotely value their lives, don't summon them back. I will kill them all if I must."

"What even are you?"

"Your future daughter-in-law." She grins.

"You are not," mother replies. "Not in this life or the next."

"That's her choice," Dia says, glancing at me, "there isn't a power in this universe, or any other that can stop me from marrying your daughter except for *her* word." Her voice is calm, collected, and forceful. "If you would like to test that, Ceridwen, you do so at your own peril."

My heart throbs in my chest, my face flushing as I just stare at her. Mother is much less impressed, her expression one of shock and rage.

"You impudent little witch," she spits. "Do not call me by name. You know not what you've done with your selfishness. I know you people from Central live as you will, but we have a way of doing things here."

Dia tilts her head, the look in her eyes like that of a predator about to launch herself at her prey. "I am aware of how things are done here—I just don't care. Why should I? Because your houses will kill one another if your daughter isn't sold off like a broodmare?" She narrows her eyes. "Gráinne has told me about you, the face you wear in public. You operate under the delusion that if you're smart enough, you can eke out a bit of freedom or power."

Her words are like a slap to my mother's face. She looks away, unable to speak for a moment. "Gráinne," she says, looking me in the eye. "What are you trying to do?"

I've seen my mother with many expressions in my life, but fear has never been one of them. Today she looks terrified. She's on the verge of tears. I approach her cautiously, sitting down next to her calmly, doing my best to keep my own raging emotions under control. Despite having held a knife to her throat a moment ago, I wrap an arm around her, pulling her into a tight hug. She accepts the embrace.

"I am living," I say softly, taking in a shuddering breath. "Did you see the way we kissed?" I glance over at Dia, just watching her stand there with a curious look on her face.

Mother frowns. "Yes," she says.

"Did you see how happy I looked before father's men tried to arrest her?" I pull away slightly, sitting up straight. "I love her, mother."

Mother pinches the bridge of her nose. "You always have been a willful child," she says, her tone gentle. "I did not know." She sighs, rubbing her hands to her upper arms as if to soothe herself. "Your father is so angry. He thinks this is all some game." She looks over towards Dia, her eyes soften. "What are your intentions with my daughter?"

Dia gets off her tree. Aoife watches her warily, standing a healthy distance away, rubbing at her wrist. Dia, my beautiful Dia, walks towards us and takes my hand into hers.

"My intentions are to love her and to marry her." Her voice cascades with warmth. "It's my hope that at the very least, you accept that much."

"Accept it?" Mother asks, scoffing. "It's not about accepting anything. If it was as easy as accepting that my daughter loves another woman, this wouldn't even be a conversation. However, the situation isn't so simple." She shakes her head, as if to push away the storm that must be raging within. "This is a scandal that might trigger a devastating civil war. Is that really something you are both willing to cause?"

"*I* am not starting a war," I say firmly. "This is not *my* fault." I squeeze Dia's hand. "Call me selfish if you will, but I mean to live my life, and love who I wish." I let go of Dia's hand, fully facing my mother. "This is a basic right, one our laws deny to our people—not only me. This is justice, not war, for all the people who have their humanity stripped from them."

Mother shudders. She says nothing for a moment, simply glancing between us as the full gravity of the situation dawns on her. "I understand," she says. "There is nothing I say that will dissuade you, is there?"

"No, mother," I reply. "Nothing at all."

"Are those guards loyal to you and you alone?" Dia asks.

Mother looks up at her, surprised. "Yes."

Dia looks to Aoife. "And her, and the one you sent to kill me?"

"Them, too," mother says. "Why?"

"I have a plan." Dia runs her hand through her hair, flipping it over her shoulder so that it rests in front of her chest. It's something she only does when she's anxious. She taps her chin rhythmically, as if to find the right words. "Announce publicly that you support our marriage. It will buy us all a bit of time. Your men and very competent assassins will keep you safe here." She toys with her hair. "I mean to destroy the Armory, freeing you, and your daughter and all the other women who get subjected by the whims of men. So, you decide, are *you* going to stand with us or not?"

I look at my mother, my breath stuck in my chest. She has always stood by me in her own way, but never like this; never like I have needed her to.

She chortles, looking away. "Forgive me," she says after a moment of laughter. "I understand now, I think. Miss Mirren, you have an infectious confidence that makes even me want to cast my lot in with you." She sighs, placing her hands in her lap. "I do not appreciate the way you spoke to me, but I cannot ignore the truth in your words. More to the point, what kind of mother would I be to deny my daughter this?"

She looks at me then, reaching out to hold my hand. "Everything I have ever done has been to protect you, to guide you to be strong. I just never imagined how much you would outgrow me."

I squeeze her hand, tears forming in my eyes. "Thank you." What else can

I say but that? There are a million words that swirl in my mind, too many to articulate. I squeeze tighter, lean forward, and embrace my mother. "This is worth fighting for, mother."

"What will you both do next?" she asks, returning the embrace. "Surely you do not intend to stay locked away here at Fianna."

"Well, the secret is out," Dia says. "I think we should just go to Earth. Your mech needs repairs, and leaving will sow chaos that suits us."

"Earth," I say, rolling the word over my tongue. "I agree; we should leave before my birthday."

"I know you just agreed," she says, "but one other reason to leave sooner rather than later—fuck all these duels."

I chuckle, nodding at her words. "Yes, quite," I say. "I am rather sick of wearing this mask."

"And then?" mother asks. "How do you plan to use the chaos you are sowing?"

"Before I answer that," Dia says, furrowing her brow. "Something about all of this has been bothering me from the start. The emperor is pushing eight hundred and was ruling during the Secession War. Losing that didn't get him deposed; what's important about an heir now? Is his health failing?"

Mother shakes her head. "No, nothing like that. The houses do not want an immortal emperor any longer—he's made too many enemies."

"No longer powerful enough to stop them from taking over outright, is he?" Dia asks.

"Correct," she says. "His rule has been waning for decades. Central keeps growing. We lose more and more people as he tightens his grip on industry and commerce. He won't admit it, but the Fomorian Armory is dying."

Hearing this spoken by my mother is quite shocking. I've never heard her outright disparage father and his rulership. "Mother, did he marry you specifically for an heir?" I ask an unspoken question I already know the answer to.

She nods.

"But you did not give him a son." I look down. "And for whatever reason, you never had more children."

"I could not," she says. "My pregnancy with you was a difficult one; it nearly killed me. I refused to bear another child." She grimaces, her face contorting into disgust. "He has let me live because I have proven myself a useful tool, and I convinced him that having a daughter was advantageous in other ways."

"Because he could sell me off," I say. "He never cared about me as his child. Not even for a moment, did he?"

"No," she says. "I am sorry, my child. You deserved better parents."

"I did," I say, retreating to my personal space. I hug my arms around my chest. "Dia, I want to leave as soon as possible."

It sickens me to think that they have always seen me as a tool or property. I have always known these things in my heart, but hearing them stated so clearly by my mother cuts deep. I want to hate her as much as I hate my father, but I cannot bring myself to summon the same hatred. She did her best, even if her best was abysmal. I can find it in myself to forgive her—eventually.

"If Quinn and Layla would agree, I would like them to come with us." I look to Aoife then, her face impassive, but her eyes speak of a terrible sadness deep within. "Please keep mother safe."

"Of course, Princess," she says softly. "Your betrothed bested me easily enough, but that will not happen with another. I'd say to stay safe, but you've never needed protection."

I walk over to her, throwing my arms around her. In all my years, this was the one person who has been with me through all my troubles. "I will come back for you, Aoife," I whisper in her ear.

She hugs me back tightly. "I know. I'll keep your mother safe until you return." She pulls away, looking me in the eye. "Stay safe, Gráinne."

* * *

"Oh baby," I say, putting my face in my hands. "Dia, my child, my darling girl. You are insane."

"Mother, it's fine." She grins at me.

I hate her stupid grins; they always mean trouble. "Even your mom, who supports all your insanity, is going to freak out when she hears what you've done—probably."

"Everything is going well," she says calmly. "In fact, I was thinking the two of you should come get us so we can all go to Earth. If you're up for the trip, anyway."

"No, we're going to leave you to rot," I say, my voice dripping with what I hope is the appropriate amount of sarcasm. "We'll be there, Dia. We have a daughter-in-law to meet, and we miss you. Don't cause any more trouble."

Another of her stupid, aggravating grins. "Love you, mother."

"Yes, yes, I know," I say. "We're close and we'll see you tomorrow."

"Perfection."

She hangs up the call. I sit there for a moment, gathering myself and my nerves. My daughter did not need to inherit both my brains and her mom's temperament; she's an utter monster. Maeve comes into the room, dropping off my perfectly made coffee. I take it from her gratefully, tugging her down to sit next to me on the sofa.

"We're meeting with Dia and her fiancée tomorrow," I inform her. "They're traveling to Earth."

Maeve chuckles as she sits. "She really didn't make it three weeks." She leans close to me, swallowing me up in her larger frame. "We can leave after your coffee. It's a real time day from here, right?"

"Mmm," I say behind my mug. "Can't say I'll complain about getting off this station. I'm just worried Dia is biting off more than she can chew." I take a long, long sip of the delicious elixir of wakefulness. "She's always taken after you with how she is so free with her affections, but this is something else, and the stakes are ridiculous."

Maeve taps her metal finger to the aluminum can. "They always were," she says softly. "You know, I thought she'd give it up once she realized how monumental of a task it is. If it were so easy to tear down a system-state, Central would have done it already." She laughs a rancorous laugh.

"Yet, the entire thing is in shambles, and not because she destabilized the economy or assassinated a leader, but because she fell in love with the princess. My darling, it's actually hysterical when I think about it. Lesbians, am I right?"

I can't help but chuckle along with her. My wife is right. "It has been insane since their duel," I muse. "And what a duel. I understand their connection, seeing them in that fight. She's our baby, though, and I just can't help but worry." I sigh, pinching the bridge of my nose. I take another sip of my coffee. "But worrying overmuch is useless."

"Exactly," Maeve says, running her fingers through my hair. "Look, we finally have a lead on *her*. Our daughter is getting out of this sector, at least for a while, and we get to meet her partner—all-in-all, things aren't so bad right now, my love."

"You always focus on the positives," I say fondly, leaning on her. "You're right." I down the rest of my coffee in three big gulps. I stand up, run my fingers through my hair, and let out a sigh to steady my increasing anxiety. "Let's go; no time like the present."

* * *

The Danu Mk. II is my home away from home. Memories of my childhood come flooding back to me as Gráinne and I get on board. It's a relatively small cruiser-class vessel that's well-armed and even better shielded. The mechbay is modestly sized, capable of fitting three mechs with a bit of effort. It's always comfortably fit the Witchblade and the Phantom Queen, but it's cramped with the remains of the Bansidhe, the pieces taking up a surprising amount of room.

Quinn and Layla walk behind us. I cast a glance back at them. Quinn is nervous, as usual, but Layla is infectiously enthused. Her eyes dart around every which way, as if she is reverse engineering the ship in her mind.

"Excited?" I ask.

"Gods, yes," she says. "First of all, this is a gorgeous ship. I love the curves and color she has. Nothing at all like the eldritch, gray nightmares the Armory produces. Also, we're going to see Central. If it's half as awful as the propaganda makes it out to be, we might never leave."

That gets a chuckle out of me. Gráinne looks back at our friends, her eyes screaming out how much she agrees.

"You'd be welcome to," I tell her. "You won't even need to do paperwork."

"Maybe we will," Layla says, her smile dampening. "We have our families to think about. It's not a choice to be made now, in any case."

Gráinne squeezes my arm. The door of the ship seals itself behind us as we enter. I show them to the common area. In it, there is a small kitchen, a round table with chairs tucked in under it, and a sofa in front of a large viewing screen.

Mom is in the kitchen already, gathering ingredients for lunch. "Dia!" She beams at me and the others. As always, she radiates joy and warmth. "Girl, it's been ages. Get your ass over here."

Despite being an adult, a very competent one at that, I can't help cringing a bit at her greeting. I suppose some things never change. "Hey mom," I say. "Let me introduce you to my friends and fiancée first. Where's mother?"

"Doing last minute checks on the autopilot. You know how she is with the details. She'll be out in a moment." She grins at us, crossing her arms over her chest.

"On a scale of one to ten, how is she taking all this?" I ask. "With ten being great and a one being she'll try to ground me until I'm sixty."

"Negative one hundred," mother says, appearing from the hall that leads to the bridge.

Instinctively, I flinch at her tone, fighting the urge to retreat into myself. "Hello, mother."

"Hello, my sweet," she says warmly. She puts a hand on her hip, looks at me up and down, and then sighs. "Lucky for you, you're not a child anymore. I have no power to do such things these days." She smiles as she scans over me and the rest of my group. "I'm here to support you. Introduce us properly?"

"Of course." I beam, motioning to my fiancée. "First, the princess you warned me not to fall in love with, and I did it anyway."

"Hello," Gráinne says, her voice rather calm under the circumstances. "It is lovely to meet you."

"Likewise," mother replies.

"This is Layla, and Quinn," I say, pointing at the pair. "Two of our friends we've made at the academy. Truly brilliant engineers, the both of them."

Mother cocks an eyebrow. "That so? Wonderful to meet you both."

Layla beams brightly, looking unphased and cheerful. Quinn is warming up; her cheeks have a touch of red but even so, she grins.

"Well, it's a two-hour trip to the gate and another five to Earth. Let's have lunch," mother says. "You can regale me with how the four of you got yourselves into this, and I can share embarrassing photos of Diarmuid as a child. That's the proper tradition, right?"

"Mother!"

She snickers, lifting a hand to her mouth delicately.

I sigh, kiss Gráinne on the cheek, and head into the kitchen. "I'll make lunch."

"You will not," my mom says, shaking her head.

"Why not?" I frown. "You came to get us. It's the least I can do."

"Because you always try to take care of everyone else before yourself." She puts a hand on my shoulder, giving it a comforting squeeze. "You've been through a lot recently and I don't care how impossibly strong you are. I'm your mom. I'm going to make you lunch. Sit."

My nostrils flare. I turn to see mother laughing. Layla and Quinn exchange smirks. Gráinne is looking at me, her expression so tender. I am utterly defeated.

I pinch the bridge of my nose and sigh. "Well, I suppose if you're all going to bully me, I may as well take it with some grace."

Everyone laughs. I do too, unable to help myself in the face of such joy.

* * *

There is a peaceful air on the ship. People are talking and laughing, exchanging looks of joy and comfort. Dia is considerably more at ease, more than I've ever seen her.

Is this how family is supposed to be?

I watch as Quinn blossoms, eagerly asking Dia's mother questions about this concept or that theory.

"Wait, wait, wait," Layla interrupts. "Hold on, how many papers have you written?"

Dia's mother taps her chin. "You know, I never bothered to count—I've lived a long life."

Layla blinks. "How long is long?"

She shrugs. "Well, I was born before the founding of Central, so a fairly long time. To be honest, I've stopped counting the years, but I do always celebrate my birthday." She preens. "It is *my* day, after all."

Layla furrows her brow. "Mrs. Mirren, forgive me for asking this, but who are you? Besides my friend's mother, I mean."

She chuckles. "Just call me Viviana or V if you feel comfortable enough."

Quinn nearly drops her food, a delightfully toasted ham sandwich with fresh greens and melted cheese. "Viviana Mirren?" she asks. "How did I not put that together before?"

"The one and only."

The girls lean back into their seats. Quinn puts her hand on Layla's and gives it a squeeze. I take a sip of my tea, smirking at them from behind the cup.

"You're famous," Layla says. "Well, infamous is perhaps the better word. You've been holding out on us, Dia."

"In my defense, she really is infamous," Dia replies. She wraps her arm around me, pulling me into her chest. "Broadcasting who my parents are isn't exactly safe."

I nestle in close to her; she is comfortable and radiates warmth. A sigh of contentment escapes me. This is a good day. I look down at my datapad, checking the time. We should leave near-lightspeed in about half an hour. Leaving Fianna was easy enough as house Áine controls that space, but I suspect we may run into trouble once we reach the Slip Gate.

"That explains so much of how the Phantom Queen operates, and why it's so close to the Framework," Layla says. "I mean, you invented the Tuatha OS! They built the Framework on the foundations you laid. This is like meeting my hero—not that I could ever say that in public."

Viviana laughs mirthfully. "Well, I appreciate your good judgement. I imagine that I'm public enemy number one amongst Armory scholars and engineers."

"Completely reviled," Quinn says, her voice betraying her eagerness. "In part because you're a woman, I think. Getting a hold of your theorems is very difficult, and even when we could, they were all heavily redacted."

"I'll send you my full body of work," Viviana says through a smile. "And make sure to check out the Grand Library while we're on Earth. I'm not the only brilliant mind you can learn from."

The girls nod eagerly. Quinn in particular looks bright-eyed and bushy tailed, a look I've not seen on her. Perhaps, like me, she is feeling a weight lift off her shoulders.

"Gods, that would be incredible! Thank you," Quinn says.

"We'll definitely visit the library." Layla beams.

"It's my pleasure," Viviana replies. "Libraries also make for lovely dates."

I look over towards my friends, their faces are cherry red. Quinn holds Layla's hand tighter. Layla recovers first, her lips pulled back into a wide grin.

"It will be," she says.

Dia chuckles softly before kissing the top of my head. She gently lifts me off her shoulder. "Excuse me everyone," she says, rising to her feet. "I'm going to get into the Phantom before we drop out of NLS."

I try not to pout, but it's difficult not to—she was just so comfortable to lean on. Dia sees this, smirks at me as she always does, and leans down to kiss me. It's a quick kiss, leaving me hungering for more.

"I'll be back soon." Dia folds her arms over her chest. "I'm sure it will be fine. We have clearance to leave, and unless Brigid has betrayed us, no one followed us from Fianna."

"I'll come with you," Maeve says, getting up as well and stretching out her arms and shoulders. "You and I haven't had a sortie together in ages. Even if nothing happens, it'll be fun."

Dia grins. "Right."

"Can we also come?" Layla asks. "I mean, we want to take any opportunity to prepare the Phantom and we'd love to see the Witchblade up close, too."

"You two really love mechs, huh?" Maeve asks, her brow arched. "Alright, let's go."

Layla and Quinn rise to their feet quickly, following behind Dia and Maeve. I watch Dia closely, unable to help myself—she's exquisite. Each stride she makes has an easygoing confidence; she's a woman who knows she is powerful beyond measure.

"You really love her," Viviana says, interrupting my thoughts. "Not that I doubted it, but as a mother it's good to see first-hand."

My flush creeps up my neck into my cheeks. "Yes." I straighten up in my chair, folding my arms in my lap. "She's taken on all my selfish desires on top of her own goals." I look down at my hands, pressing my fingers against one another nervously. "She means everything to me."

Viviana smiles. She crosses one leg over the other, her piercing gaze studying me closely. "For what it's worth, she's strong enough. I fuss because I am a mother, but I know what she's capable of. In fact, that brings up something I'd like to talk to you about."

"Oh?" I ask, my brows furrowed.

"The way you pilot and the Fomorian Framework." She pauses, pursing her lips. "How attached are you to that?" She tilts her head to the side, her tone even and calm.

I take a moment to answer, weighing the question carefully. "I feel like an animal in a cage most of the time, but when I am in the Bansidhe, I feel like I can break free. Though I suppose I could not even manage that in the end—Dia had to do that for me. What are you thinking?"

She nods. It's a curt, sharp gesture. "Well, this may interest you," she says. "Whoever designed the Framework did so poorly off the back of my work. However, I can see the merit in the concept even if the execution is awful." She sighs. "Dia sent me the reports. The experiments..." She shakes her head in disgust. "I don't even want to think about those."

"I confess, I was not aware of how it was developed," I say, frowning.

"Not sure anyone was, except maybe your father and a few researchers." She furrows her brow. "But it is grizzly, and as a result, it's deeply flawed.

Ethics in research and development aren't just about doing the right thing, they also ensure your ultimate results are the best they can be."

She sighs, barely able to restrain the offense in her voice. "My point is: you are being held back. From the way the Framework functions, to the way your mech is built, along with a few other small things, you simply can not pilot at your best. After seeing you fight my daughter, I'm inclined to think you are as good as she is—she agrees."

"That's flattering to hear, but I think you both overestimate me." I shake my head. "I would have been crushed even if we were on equal footing," I say. "After our battle, I feel rather foolish that I ever thought I could win."

Viviana smirks. "Her experience would have won out for her in the end, but you weren't even close to being on equal footing. Trust me, with some adjustments, you will see a massive performance boost."

"What did you have in mind?" I ask. "If what you say is true, then I will need these improvements to not be a burden in our upcoming struggle." I frown then, wrapping my arms around my chest. "I refuse to be a burden."

"Well, I suggest you let me modify the Framework," she says, "improve your flightsuit, and design you a new mech that can better handle the berserker integration. The remains of the Bansidhe will be used as the basis for its rebirth; ideally, the transition should feel smooth."

"Why would you do all this for me?" I can't help but ask, overwhelmed by the generosity and the willingness to expend so much effort on my behalf. "I am a stranger to you, and no small part of the reason for Dia's current predicament."

"No, child," she says softly. "She's done that to herself." Viviana gets out of her seat and embraces me tightly.

I'm stunned, unable to move at first. Eventually, I wrap my arms around her, pressing my face into her shoulder.

"You're my future daughter-in-law," she says. Her tone is so calm yet decisive it brings tears to my eyes, as if showing me love is the easiest thing in the world for her to do.

"Thank you."

Battle Stations

"Wow, I love her," Layla says, running her fingers delicately over the Witchblade's paneling. "So similar and yet different from the Phantom Queen, too. Does Central mass produce mechs at all?"

Mom grins. "Nope! Your mech should be a genuine expression of yourself. In my military days, you could have more expression with your frame than yourself. Though that's been relaxed in the last two decades."

"We're not at the same level as M.E.T.A regarding uniformity, but in comparison, it almost feels that way." Layla sighs, stepping onto the lift that will take us down to the ground level. "Costs are kept lower that way, but you really lose so much personality. These frames are so modular and customizable."

"Correct," I say, joining her on the lift. "Designers in Central have all agreed to make mech fittings universal, intentionally to allow for greater customization—think of it as our lifeblood. We're standardized in some ways to be highly innovative in others."

Mom joins us as we descend to the ground. Quinn is finishing up her final pre-flight checks, tapping her fingers along a datapad that is taking readings from the Phantom.

"One of the first things Central did when it got its independence was to standardize charging ports on datapads." Mom shakes her head, taking no effort to hide her disgust. "They all used to be different. What an annoying time. Oh, and basic tools like screwdrivers."

"Did you fight in the war?" Quinn asks, looking up from her checklist.

"Nope. I was only nine when it started," she says. "*Our* side didn't use child soldiers, and it was over by the time I was of age."

Quinn and Layla both visibly recoil at the implication. It's not a time either of my mothers talk about very often and I've never pressed them on the issue.

"What's it like, living for so long?" Quinn asks meekly. "It's not something most of us get to even dream about. I'm curious."

Mom rubs the back of her neck. "To be honest, I don't really think about it all that often. I'm a very in the moment kind of woman. Even after three hundred years, I still feel like I haven't really lived long enough."

"Shit, I met my wife less than forty years ago, and I'd like to be married to her for more years than I haven't been, you know?" She grins widely and her eyes practically light up—she always has that look when talking about mother.

Quinn glances at Layla, her cheeks turning red. Layla does the same. They make eye contact briefly before turning away. I exchange a look with my mom, both of us grin.

"Five minutes before we drop—"

The klaxon blares loudly, interrupting me. A spike of adrenaline courses through me, my muscles flex instinctively, my fight response kicking into high gear.

"Alert: Unknown IFF tags detected. Proceed with caution," the ship's computer says. "All hands, level 2 battle stations."

"W-what does that mean?" Layla asks.

"It means get up to the bridge," I say. "Mother is going to take direct control of the ship, and she'll need you both up with her. Level 2 means we're on high alert. Level 1 means we're engaging. Quickly, go."

They take off, holding one another's hand as they run.

"Dia, Maeve," mother's voice sounds in our ears. "The ship's scanners picked up something else. Something I recognize. These are the same people from twenty-five years ago."

"Fuck," Mom says, setting her jaw firmly. "They've got to be here for us, right?"

"I'm going to assume they attack us as soon as we drop out of NLS," mother replies. "I'm also not picking up any of the Fomorian IFF tags, and there should be a small contingent guarding the gate. It's possible whoever is waiting for us killed them all."

I'm already climbing into the Phantom Queen, strapping myself in and engaging the neural integration. "Nothing is ever easy," I say.

"No, it... Gráinne, wait!"

I disconnect my vision from the Phantom, sitting up in my chair only to see Gráinne racing into the hangar. She rides the lift to the cockpit and just stands there looking at me with a pale face.

"What are..."

"We cannot fight them," she says, cutting her off, her voice frantic. "We have to run."

"Why are you so afraid?" I furrow my brows. I only have a general idea of who they are. Neither of my parents have ever gone into detail on the attackers of the original Danu with me—too traumatic.

"I'll tell you when we are safe, but we can't drop out of NLS and take them on. They will kill us all." She clutches her hand to her chest. "Please, just trust me."

"We're not going to run, Princess," I tell her firmly. "First of all, we have nowhere to even run to. They'd chase us, right?"

Gráinne hesitates, then says, "Yes."

"Then we can't run." I purse my lips, reaching out for her to take my hand. She takes it, interlacing her fingers with mine.

"We'd have to stop, turn around and then jump again," I say, keeping my tone even and calm. Whoever these people are, they have her spooked; I've never seen her like this before. "If mom and I can't handle these people, at least we can hold them off. The best option is to go through the gate and get to Sol. SDF reinforcements are on standby there."

"One minute, you two!" Mom calls out.

"Promise me you will come back," she says, glaring at me with stormy violet eyes. She squeezes my hand tightly, like she'll never let me go. "You are not allowed to die."

My instinct is to reassure her, to promise her I'll come back on the wings of victory, but I can't. No pilot ever goes out on a sortie knowing they will come back. "I will do my best, Princess. I always do."

"That's not good enough," she says, stepping into the cockpit.

"Oi! What..."

"Thirty seconds!"

She sits down on my lap, clinging to me. "I know you would die to save everyone else; more than that, I know you won't let me die. You had better win, Dia."

There isn't time to argue. I close the cockpit and step into position on the launch sling. "You're insane."

"I know." She kisses my lips gently.

Dropping out of near-lightspeed is a rather gentle affair. The ship's engines decrease power gradually and reverse thrusters are engaged to help the deceleration. Time dilation ceases as we settle back into real time—that is where the danger lies. At NLS, it's impossible to attack an object moving that fast. The most dangerous time when enemies are lurking about is at that moment a ship returns to normal but is still moving too quickly to take any sort of evasive action. Even a ship as well built as the Danu would sheer itself in half in the attempt.

"All hands, Level 1 battle stations," mother says over the comms. "Brace for impact."

The ship rattles and shakes. Either missiles or perhaps a high energy weapon struck the powerful energy barrier surrounding the ship. For a ship of its class, the Danu has a remarkable shield generator that can take a hell of beating before it falters. Several more attacks strike the ship. From the feel of them, it seems the nose of the ship is taking the brunt of the attack. The enemy must be right in front of the gate.

"Pilots, you're cleared to launch." Mother's tone is severe. "Your objective is to clear the way to the Slip Gate, hold them off while the gate opens and ensure the ship's safe passage. I will tolerate no clever heroics."

"Yes, Ma'am," Mom and I say in unison.

The Danu comes equipped with two launch tubes. I step into the launch-sling of tube number two while mom steps into the other.

"X10Z-Witchblade, Maeve Mirren, launching."

"XF01-Phantom Queen, Diarmuid Mirren, launching." Clamps engage around my feet; the sling hurtles me into space. Into battle.

The Danu's shields protect me only briefly, but it's enough time to gather my bearings. This is no duel, there is no exchange of vows or pageantry, just the cold hard reality that people are about to die. If I'm not careful, Gráinne and I will be among them. I can only barely feel her clinging to me now, my senses fully integrated into the Phantom.

As soon as I pass through the shield, I dance through enemy lasers. It's easy at first, but as I rapidly approach their location, the firepower becomes denser and more difficult to dodge. I detach the swarm-bits from my body with a clang, surrounding myself with them. Laser fire pounds against the barrier, each one straining my brain.

"There are so many of them," Gráinne says. "Dia..."

"We'll be okay, Princess. Just hold on tight." I spin my body rapidly, turning myself into a mass projectile, deflecting attacks with the barrier as I race towards the enemy.

My scanners pick up three dozen enemy mechs. They are black frames that don't quite catch light the way they should; slim and humanoid, with glowing red eyes. It's not a design I recognize, even in all my travels I've never seen something like them before. From visuals alone, they look incredibly well made—uncanny, even.

Mom destroys two of them, their IFF tags going dark. I arrive in the middle of the fray just behind her. The red lance is in one hand, the yellow in the other. I thrust the red lance forward. The enemy dodges deftly, but not the follow up. The swarm-bits slice through their mech, reducing the core to slag. I move onto the next, thrusting the yellow lance at my target. It strikes true, a burst of electricity overloads the frame's internal systems. I kill them while they're immobile. In a fight like this, one cannot afford to show mercy or hesitation—you kill quickly and move on.

I'm kicked from behind, the force of the blow sending me reeling and off-balance. The Phantom rattles and shakes as I attempt to get myself under control. Gráinne lets out a grunt but otherwise keeps her calm, her head buried in my chest. I form the bits into a shield, catching one of their swords in mid motion. Deflect. Thrust. Dead. I kick them off my weapon, engage my thrusters, and press forward.

"The Danu has engaged with the Slip Gate. Encrypted codes uploading now," Mother says, her tone betraying the slightest bit of desperation. "Five more minutes, you two."

"Acknowledged."

Mom's voice sounds strained. I can't waste a moment to check in on her. I must trust that she'll be fine. Three mechs, smaller than my own, ram into me. The impact is enough to take my breath away. They grapple my arms and legs. I try to shake them off, but they are stubborn. Suddenly, a fourth mech appears; their gun aimed directly at my core.

I roar aloud, twisting myself frantically against the three mechs that are holding me down. With everything I have, with more than I have, I'm able to move just enough so that the shot slices through my arm instead. The dismemberment wracks my body with neural feedback. It's overwhelming; the price I pay for this level of integration.

Implants activate to prevent pain, spiking my adrenaline as high as my body can take it, but then I push even past that. The Moralltach Protocol triggers, subsuming my consciousness fully into the Phantom Queen. The bits first slice through the enemies grappling me, freeing my remaining arm and leg. Without my other arm, I can't use the Moralltach; it's too massive. I do, however, have even greater control over the swarm. They dance around me, simultaneously deflecting shots and cutting down nearby enemies. I thrust the red spear into the frame that took my arm, the superheated plasma tip utterly melting the core and the pilot within.

"Gate activating. Danu's shields are at 60%" Mother launches the retreat flairs.

The unknown frames stop suddenly, becoming frozen. Their weapons and engines are all turned off, according to my scanners. A trap?

"Running off, are we?" a chilling voice asks over the comms. "Such a shame. The fun was just beginning."

"*You*," mother hisses. "Where are you hiding, you prissy little bitch?"

"Far away from you, hound. Give my best to Viviana." the woman says. "It's a shame my mutts didn't fare very well today. Half dead already—pitiful."

There is a cry over the comms, the enemy frames exploding in sequence. Their deaths are swift, but I hear each and every pilot screaming as they die.

"What the fuck?" I fight back my disgust. "Did..."

"I have no use for worthless mutts," she says. "Besides, I've found something much more interesting to play with." She speaks through a smirk, as if she is fighting back a laugh. "We'll be seeing one another again—especially you, Miss Mirren." She chuckles then. "Your daughter is exquisite, hound. Congratulations."

"You know I'm going to rip out your spine and beat you to death with it, right, Cleo?" Mom says. "We will find you."

"I'm counting on it." The comm goes dead.

"Damnit!" Mom takes a moment to breathe and calm her rage. "Come on, the Gate is open. Let's go home."

* * *

Dia can hardly walk when we get out of the Phantom. Her body is dripping with sweat and her breathing comes out in ragged waves. Maeve looks slightly better off, but the strain of the fight is clear on her as well. Viviana orders them both to their rooms for the remainder of the journey.

"I-I'm fine," Dia stammers out. "It's been... been a while since I hard to push that hard. I'll be okay in a few hours."

"Okay," I say softly, doing my best to help her stay upright. "I will help you to your room."

"Thank you," she says, leaning on me as we walk.

She is very dense—literally. Between her cybernetics and sheer muscle mass, she is heavy. I support almost her full weight as I help her back to her room. If not for my own augmented strength, I am not sure I could support her like this. The door to her room hisses open, greeting us with a most surprising sight: a veritable mountain of varied stuffed animals.

"Cute." It's hard to imagine the woman I just saw mercilessly kill having a bed full of stuffed animals, from wolves to cats, to rabbits and even dragons. "Very cute."

"Thanks," she says, getting off me and stumbling her way over to the bed. She collapses with a loud thunk.

"Are you sure you are okay, Dia?" I ask. "You were not like this after our fight or any of the other duels."

"Fianna's regulations," she says. "A real fight has significantly more neural feedback, and those weren't pirates in junk. I'm…" She turns over to look at me. "Just a lot of adrenaline, for a lot of reasons."

"Are you upset that I got into the cockpit with you?" I fold my arms over my chest, fighting the urge to glare.

"Annoyed is a better word," she says, shivering on the bed. "You almost died."

"But I did not," I tell her. "You protected me."

"I wouldn't have needed to protect you like that, if you had stayed on the ship," she says. She tries to peel off her flightsuit, but her fingers won't work properly.

I walk over to her, shooing her hands away so that I can do it for her. "I needed to ensure you would survive." Slowly, I remove her suit layers, kissing her neck and chest. "Your fault for not promising to come back."

"I can't make that kind of promise, Princess," she says, leaning into my kisses. "I'm not the kind of girl to make stupid promises I can't keep."

She's right, and I know that. "That is true," I say softly. "I know that—I appreciate it even. It was a panic moment. Those mercenaries are like ghosts. No one knows where they come from, but I have not heard of a single person surviving an encounter with them."

She tries to lift her hand; it shakes from the effort and falls limply onto the bed. "Fuck. I forgot how intense post-sortie drop could be. We can talk about this later… sorry."

"Of course," I say, kissing along her collarbone. "When you truly fight, you are utterly breathtaking. Did you know that?"

She chuckles. "Are you seducing me so that I feel better?" she asks, turning her head to look at me.

"Is it working?" I ask.

"It helps," she says in a trembling voice. "The touching, and the kissing, I mean."

"Good." I grab her wrist, pinning it above her head. "You were brutal and efficient. I couldn't take my eyes off of you."

She struggles playfully against me, but in the state she's in, I'm the stronger one. "You know I killed people today, right?"

"I am aware." I take off the rest of her suit, leaving her naked on the bed before me. "But I am not naïve. It was us or them. Do you feel bad about it?"

"No, but it's not the first time I've killed," she admits. "Nor the last. I'm just a little surprised at you, is all."

I kiss a trail up her thighs. "Maybe I will be horrified later, but I chose to get into that cockpit with you and I saw exactly what I expected to see. Now hush and let me take care of you."

"Make me, Princess," she says, a challenge in her tone.

A dark urge bubbles up in me when she says that—an urge I didn't even know I had. "Very well." I remove my shirt and tear a long strip of cloth before straddling her. "It seems I'll have to put a muzzle on you." I wrap the cloth around her head several times, tying it in between her lips, gagging her.

Her white eyes burn passionately, drool pools on the cloth. I grin as I hold her down on the bed firmly.

"Something is missing." I rip off another piece of cloth from my shirt and tie it around her neck, turning it into a short leash. I take care not to tie it too tight around her neck, but just enough that when I pull, she feels it. "There," I say, grinning, my heart pounding in my chest. "Now look at you; my perfect, pretty wolf."

She squirms under my touch as I run my hand along her thighs; I watch her with delight. Leaning forward, I kiss along her hypersensitive skin. She moans through the cloth, pushing her body towards mine as best she's able.

"My Dia," I purr, leaving little bites along her flesh. "Always working so hard, always thinking of others. You are precious and kind, but, most importantly—right now—you are *mine*." I sink my teeth into her thigh.

She mewls under her gag, moaning and groaning as my teeth gently sink into her. I kiss up her thigh again and along her cock. Lavishing her with my tongue is something I've become quite fond of in our time together. I've learned so many ways to pleasure and tease her, but never have I just had her under my control like this.

I lick along the tip and shaft lovingly as I squeeze her thighs with my nails. She lifts her arms above her head as if I had them bound.

"Good girl."

She groans; I smirk.

Her skin arouses all my senses as I lick and kiss her. It's easy to get lost in the woman I love so very much. I lift her legs up, pushing her knees to the side so that I might have my way with her fully, lick anywhere I want on her, do whatever I want with her. Each lick, kiss and bite earn me loud moans of bliss. When I take her into my mouth, she arches her back, pushing herself deep into my throat—I eagerly accept.

Her arousal is intoxicating, making my mind buzz and swim. I long for her to touch me, but I'll have to wait until she recovers. For now, I focus on her, drawing out her stress with every touch. I reach up to take her breasts into my hands, pinching and rolling her nipples between my fingers while I suck on her. She holds her legs open for me, spreading herself so that I might keep having my way with her.

"Such a good girl," I purr, kissing along her cock, nuzzling my face into her shaft. "Mmm, I have an idea. Did you bring it with you?"

She nods, pointing to her yet unpacked traveling case. Her eyes are hungry and desperate. I hurry over to it, digging through the case to find what I want. The cybernetic strap she introduced me to. I've only used it on her once before—well, she used it on herself while it was attached to me. It drove me completely feral, and she did not relent, no matter how many times she made me cum.

Now, I get to be the one using it on her. I grin as I strip and attach it to myself, my nerve endings syncing to the metal shaft. Red paneling along the side igniting as it hums to life.

Climbing on top of her, I kiss her body, her neck, and her gagged mouth. She's panting through her gag. I can't help but smile at the state she's in.

"Such a puppy," I whisper in her ear.

She moans, wrapping her arms around me. I smile as I press the self-lubricating shaft against her, slowly sinking myself inside her. Dia lifts her arms above her head again, arching her back.

"I am going to fuck you now, my love," I hum. "I am going to use you until you cannot think straight, and the only thoughts in that brilliant little head of yours are about me. Just a puppy for her princess."

Dia can only emphatically whimper in agreement, her snow-white eyes glazing over with pleasure as I slowly push the strap in and out of her. I never imagined speaking to her like this; that she'd so eagerly allow or even want me to. I think she needs it from me right now. With each thrust I take, I can't help but think how she's always the one looking after *me*, thinking of *me*, putting so much of her passion towards saving *me*.

It's time to return the favor.

I fuck Dia, my nails digging into her back and shoulders, slamming the strap into her roughly. I pour every ounce of augmented strength into my thrusts. She wraps her legs around me, keeping her arms up above her head. I slide my body against hers as I fuck her, our breasts rubbing against the other's with each motion. She and I fill the room with our moans. Orgasm after orgasm wracks my body and I can feel hers coating our skin.

I fuck her into the mattress while she screams into the pillow, her ass high in the air. I fuck her against the wall, gripping her hips for dear life, her legs wrapped around me. We go until I am spent, until the muscles in my thighs threaten to lock up and my nerves can take no more.

We lie on the bed in the glorious aftermath, clinging to one another. The strap and gag are discarded off to the side. She slides her cock into me like this, gently moving her hips. I moan as I'm filled, overstimulated, but I don't care. If she needs more, if she wants more, then I am hers. She makes love to me, her cum pouring into me as I gasp and cry out her name.

When she is done, I gently brush her white hair out of her face, kissing her forehead. "I love you," I whisper.

"Thank you," she says, clinging to me. "You understood what I couldn't put into words."

Pressing my lips to hers, I smile as we kiss. "I admit, I did not think I had that in me, but it was fun." A small giggle erupts from me. "Was I believable?"

She chuckles and nods, her eyes watering up. "I enjoyed being called a perfect, pretty wolf. It was nice to just trust you—I don't get to just trust people, Gráinne. Not with myself."

My arms wrap around her tightly. I massage her flesh with my hands. "Oh, darling," I whisper. "I am glad that I could be the one to take care of you this time. It was foolish of me to get in the cockpit with you. I am sure I only made you stress out more."

She shrugs. "Who knows? Maybe those four would have gotten the better of me if I were alone. You were right. I could have handled dying. It's something you expect when you go out on a sortie like that, but I couldn't allow you to die." She presses her head to mine, releasing a relaxed sigh. "I'm alive and so are you; from where I am, that's all that matters."

"Okay," I say, taking a deep breath and kissing along her cheek and jaw. "Can we do this again sometime? I think you would look beautiful with a leash attached to a collar."

Dia chuckles, pulls me close, and runs her fangs along my ear. "Yes, but be careful, Princess, I'm not a dog and I might just snap that leash."

I shudder, nodding my head. My loins aching as my heart skips a beat. "Mmm, that sounds perfect."

Futch for Breakfast

"All hands—report to the bridge for re-entry," the ship's computer says loudly.

The noise wakes me up from the deepest sleep of my life. My body feels sluggish—heavy. Even my fingers resist my attempts to move them. I sigh. It really has been too long since I had to push myself if that fight was enough to put me into a state like this. To be fair to myself, however, Fianna's restrictions also dampen neural strain considerably, even for basic sorties. It's only natural that being in that environment was going to dull my edge.

Gráinne isn't in bed with me, her presence sorely missed. I grab one of my stuffed animals, a white wolf, and cuddle it to my chest. I can't help wondering how it even stayed on the bed after what Gráinne and I got up to a few hours ago. As my brain slowly catches up, I realize I feel remarkably clean, which isn't a feeling I should have. I run my fingers along my stomach—no trace of bodily fluids.

She must have cleaned me up.

The thought makes my eyes water; I choke back a sob. My fingers grip the stuffed wolf tight. I lift it to my eyes and cry into it. It's not the first time this stuffed animal has caught my tears. My thoughts run away from me. Flashes of what Gráinne did to me, did for me, race across my mind; her breath on my neck, her hands on my hips. There was someone else, once, who made me feel that safe. I push those thoughts away. That's ancient history—she hates me now.

There is a terrible emptiness in me—sorrow that feels impossible to articulate. Why? It was perfect. She was perfect. So why do I feel this hole in my chest? I reach between my thighs, running my fingers along my shaft and burst into uncontrollable sobs.

Right, this shit again.

Bottom augmentation has crossed my mind before, but I've never felt such intense emotions until now. I've never broken down into a mess of sobs because I don't have a pussy. The opposite, in fact. I've always liked my cock, and thought it was pretty, and it feels good using it, too. Yet, I can't help but feel that as perfect as being fucked by Gráinne was, I would have preferred to have a cunt; to experience sex like that with someone I trust.

"All hands—report to the bridge for re-entry."

A few deep breaths to clear my head before I drag myself out of bed. I'm annoyed by this post sex, post sortie revelation, but I suppose it's better to know. We're going to Earth, and this is something I can get done while we're there. I missed out on that this time, but it's not as if it's going to be the only occasion that I'd let Gráinne put a leash around my neck and rail me into the mattress. That thought makes me smile.

Everything is fine—for me, and for people in Central. For too many others across this shithole of a galaxy, life is needlessly cruel and difficult. One day I will make it fine for all of them, too. Even if it takes me ten thousand years, I will not rest until people like me can live the lives they deserve.

Somehow, through the soreness of my muscles, the stiffness in my joints, I get dressed. My choice in outfit more like pajamas than actual clothes. Very cute, very short black shorts, black socks with white stripes that come up just above my knee, and the biggest, poofiest black hoodie I own. I don't bother tying my hair back. I simply brush out the tangles and part it to the side. The strands fall to my knees. My hair is, truthfully, at a ridiculous length, but it makes me happy.

"All hands—report to the bridge for re-entry."

"Yeah, yeah," I grumble. "Calm your tits."

The comm buzzes. "We can orbit if you need longer to rest," mother says. "I don't think anyone minds."

"No, no. I'm dressed," I say. "Thank you, though."

"Of course." Mother pauses. "Are you alright, Dia? Besides the exhaustion."

"We can talk about it when I come up," I reply.

"See you soon."

Walking to the bridge helps, the movement loosening my muscles and relaxing my nerves. By the time I arrive, I feel much better than when I woke up. Gráinne, Layla, and Quinn are talking with one another, sharing a laugh at a joke I didn't hear. It's wonderful to see them smile.

"Yo," I say, offering a lazy wave.

Gráinne looks up, her smile broadening. "You look cute like this," she says, her violet eyes raking across me.

I grin. "Thanks. These are my lazy clothes." I take a seat, strapping myself in to prepare for the re-entry to Earth's atmosphere.

"Everyone ready?" mom asks, sitting at the helm.

"Yes," we all say.

It takes only a few minutes to get past the worst of the upper atmosphere, but the energy shield around the ship protects us from the spike in heat. The ship also comes with state-of-the-art stabilizers, making the descent smooth.

"It's safe to get up now," mother says after we have breached the troposphere. "You won't be able to see much until we get below the clouds, but there will be a lot to see as we come into port."

I'm too tired to get up, but Layla and Quinn are quick to rush to the windows to look as we pass over snowcapped peaks. Gráinne stands but comes over to me instead, resting a hand on my shoulder.

"Thank you," I whisper.

She smiles, leans down, and presses her lips to my forehead. "It is my privilege. Are you sure you are okay?"

"Yeah." I squeeze her hand. "By the time we get to Central City, I'll be fine. I'm excited for you to see my home—I miss my apartment." I pull her hand to my lips, kissing her fingers softly. "We should ride on the trains while we're here, too. You can take them around the globe from Central Station."

"Trains that go around the globe?" She's incredulous, her brow knitting together. "Even over oceans? That cannot be."

I can't help but chuckle. "You'll see, Princess. There are a lot of things on Earth that'll shock you. Go look with the others and you'll see some on our way in."

"I love trains," she says softly. "For your sake, this had better not be a prank—I would be very disappointed."

"Go look outside!" I swat at her ass, smiling brightly at her. "You're missing so many things, my love."

Her cheeks turn red, she bites her lip. "Hmph." She turns away without another word, swaying her hips more than usual as she walks over to the window.

I sense eyes on me. Mother is staring at me with her brow arched. Mom chuckles but says nothing, keeping most of her attention on flying the ship.

"The two of you are cute," she says. "Do you want to talk about what you were upset about earlier?"

"I wasn't..." I sigh; there was no use in lying. "I thought about bottom augmentation again, but it was really intense today." I glance at Gráinne, a simper forming on my lips.

"Ah," mother says. "That happens. Sorry, my dear. Are you going to pursue it?"

"Yes." Sighing, I gather my hair up and run my fingers through it. "But it's complicated. I don't hate what I have now."

"You don't have to for it to be right for you," she says. "Just feeling more comfortable is enough, you know? Besides, there are options to preserve your current... um... bits. Have you done research?"

"No," I say. "It's not something I've given that much thought, but now you've got me curious." I have always been able to appreciate how I can just have these matter-of-fact conversations with my parents, especially my mother.

She pulls out her datapad, taps at the screen a few times. It makes a soft beep, and then she puts it away. "I sent you some information about a recently developed procedure. Of the options I know of, it's the one I think will suit you best. If not, there are a lot of methods." She stands up, walks over to me, and wraps her arms around my shoulders. "I am sorry it caused you distress. It happens to me sometimes, too, and I'm ancient. Dysphoria is awful."

I roll my eyes as I embrace my mother. "Shut up." I cling tight to her for a moment. "You're not old."

She chuckles aloud. "I am very old, in fact, but thank you. You'll be okay, and as always, your mom and I are here for you."

Releasing her, I wipe my watering eyes and nod. "I know, I just thought I had everything sorted out, and then..." I glance over at Gráinne. "Things change."

"I can relate to that," she says, brushing my hair out of my face. "A new situation can make us reevaluate our relationship to our own bodies or reveal something hidden. Just make sure that whatever you do to deal with the dysphoria is what you want; what makes you feel most at home with yourself."

Those are familiar words—words she's said to me all my life. "I will. Thank you."

She kisses the top of my head before turning to go sit in Mom's lap at the helm. They share a kiss and exchange a few words. Mom looks back at me, flashing me a sympathetic smile. I return the smile, feeling a wave of exhaustion hit me again.

I shut my eyes for what only feels like a moment before I'm gently shaken. "Hm?"

"We're here," Gráinne says sweetly. "You fell asleep."

* * *

Dia holds my hand as we disembark the Danu. We exit to the outside world, a short path in front of us leads into the massive space port. It's overwhelming, being on Earth. I've dreamed of this moment most of my life and now my feet are touching solid ground on the birthplace of humanity.

"I'm here," I whisper. "Gods, I'm finally here."

"Welcome," she says through a brilliant grin. "Seeing your face right now is priceless."

I don't bother to hide my blush. "I'm glad you think so."

"So, here's the plan," Maeve says, loudly enough to get the attention of everyone. "V and I are going to stay behind and finalize transporting the mechs to the workshop. I suggest you all get some rest before exploring the city or riding any trains."

Dia chuckles. "I'll play tour guide and host. My home has two rooms, if the two of you don't mind sharing a bed." She looks at Layla and Quinn.

"Nope!" Quinn exclaims rather quickly. "Not a problem at all."

Layla looks a bit surprised. Her cheeks flush, and a subtle smile appears on her face. "That's perfect," she says.

"Wonderful." Dia squeezes my hand. "Let's head out. I'm sure everyone is tired."

We exchange goodbyes with her parents for now, and Dia guides us through the port. The building is far bigger than even the biggest space port on Fomoria. The inside is colorful and well lit. I also notice a remarkable lack of stairs, instead there are ramps.

What really takes me aback, however, are the people. Smiles on every one of their faces. Joy abounds. A woman with a tail... "Dia! Why does she have a tail?" I ask, pointing rather rudely. "And... are those cat ears on her head?"

Layla and Quinn share in my surprise, but Dia laughs good-naturedly. I feel mortified by my behavior, sheepishly shifting from side to side.

"Ah, sorry," I say. "I am just surprised."

"Body modifications, including animal ears, tails and even fur, are... well, I won't say extremely common, but they are rather normal." Dia smirks. "My fangs, for example."

"And... you can just go to a surgeon and have this done?" I ask, knitting my brows together. I touch the top of my head, running my fingers through my hair. "That's incredible. H-how long is the wait for something like that?" I look up at Dia, trying not to get my hopes up.

"People have the right to augment their body however they wish," she says, smiling warmly. "And there are a lot of excellent surgeons who make sure people can. The wait isn't too long at all."

I glance at the woman, who thankfully did not see my outburst. She's with her partner, grinning and laughing. Her tail sways behind her and her ears wiggle when she laughs. Her partner likewise has modifications done to his body. Neither of them gets any ill looks from those who pass them by. My eyes flit around the terminal. I notice many others now that I know what to look for. As Dia said, it's not anywhere near the majority of the people surrounding us, but there is a noticeable amount of people with animal ears, tails, and even eyes.

Truly, I am on a different planet with an entirely different culture. That this exists fills me with relief, joy, and a touch of rage. None of this has ever been possible for me, for my people. It isn't fair or right. I look back at Dia, gazing into her snow-white eyes—truly, she has saved me in ways I cannot even begin to articulate.

"Do you want to become a catgirl?" Dia asks. "It can be reversed if you don't like it."

"Yes," I say, coming out of my thoughts. I blush, looking down at my feet. "Though it does not feel like a decision I should make lightly." I press the tips of my fingers together, struggling to gather my words. "I have always feared going under the knife, despite my already extensive augmentation."

"We could get it done together," she offers. "There's something I want to get done anyhow and I would like to complete my wolfish look. Especially after..." she trails off, her cheeks turning a touch of red. "Anyway. I'd get it done with you."

"I think you'd look adorable," Layla chimes in. "If my opinion matters at all. Can't say I want them for me, but I think you would look great."

I look at Quinn, my brows furrowed. She senses my unasked question, tilting her head. She walks over to me and makes a box around my head with her hands as if she is taking measurements.

"It would look very... you," she says finally. "Especially nice, pointy cat ears. Plus, and this is maybe a petty reason to suggest it, but it would be an amazing act of defiance for the imperial princess to do illegal aesthetic body augmentation."

Dia nods several times at this. "Quinn, you've really broken out of your shell, do you know that?"

"It's nice having friends that listen to me," she says, "And who encourage me to take up space."

I pull her into a hug. "I am glad," I say to her, "and thank you for the advice. You are right; it would be an act of defiance." I step away from Quinn, glancing back at Dia. "Alright. Let us do it. What else did you want done?"

Dia winks at me and flashes me one of her dangerous smirks, the one that makes my knees feel weak. "It's a surprise I think you'll *like*."

"You are never going to let me live that down, are you?"

* * *

I sit on a barstool in Dia's kitchen, resting my elbows on the countertop, in nothing but panties and one of her shirts. On me, the shirt may as well be a dress; it smells like her, too—understated blackberry and lily. I sip at my cup of coffee, which she made perfectly to my tastes, and watch with rapt attention as she flips pancakes in a skillet.

Just to torture me; she has decided to be topless and is wearing only the tiniest of shorts. Her long white hair is tied up in a tight bun, exposing her back. Should I focus on her taut muscles, her years of accumulated scars, or the tattoos that spread out like vines across her body? Unable to decide, I look everywhere, devouring her with my eyes.

Gods, she is the most incredible creature to exist.

"Should you really be naked?" I ask behind my cup, doing my best to use it to hide my flushed cheeks. "You could get burned."

"It's a risk that I'm willing to take, Princess." She turns to peek at me, that damn smirk on her face. "It's your first morning on Earth; I'm duty bound to make it as perfect as possible."

I giggle, biting at my lip. "You really are my perfect, pretty wolf."

She blushes deeply; her face going through several shades of red at once. *Victory!*

"Careful, Princess—I might skip breakfast and eat you." She flashes her fangs at me, able to cook skillfully even while her eyes are on me.

It is not fair how attractive she is. "I think you would lack the energy without a proper meal, Wolf."

"Keep that up and you'll find out."

I bite my lip harder. If I were not so hungry, I would bait her more, drive her feral with irritation and earn myself a smack on my rear. She has only spanked me once, albeit it was a light, playful smack. Being very honest with myself, I would like her to do it again—definitely while I am naked.

She pulls the skillet off the heat, sliding three pancakes out onto a plate. They are thick, fluffy, and smell delightful. She tops them with sweet syrup and a slice of butter. She hands the plate to me, along with cutlery. Her breasts are on full display, practically in my face.

"Princess?" She smirks.

I've forgotten to breathe and am just staring at her.

"Right." My face feels hot, as if it will combust at any moment. Doing my utmost to calm myself, I take a bite of the pancake. It's divine—delicious enough to distract me from her radiance. "Mm. You were right; this is far better than what you could cook at Fianna. I can understand your frustrations now."

"I'm glad I can cook for you properly." She kisses my forehead, lingering for a moment while her fingers brush through my hair.

I take another blissful bite, the syrup and butter mixing along with the subtle sweetness of the pancake. I moan, in part at the taste and texture of the food, and in part to tease my wolf. "Mmm. Cook for me forever?"

"Of course."

I grab at her, pulling her in for a kiss. It's awkward with the countertop in the way, but we manage, our lips pressed firmly together. I open my mouth, sticking my tongue into hers so that she can taste her cooking on me. She groans softly.

"Hmph," she says. "I can see you're already embracing your inner catgirl." She pats my head.

Heat rises to my cheeks. I smirk and take another bite.

Her datapad makes a chirping noise. The sound draws her attention away. She pulls it over to her while I eat, tapping her long fingers across the touchscreen.

"No way," she says, her tone betraying shock and eagerness.

"What?" I tilt my head curiously, waiting for her to divulge whatever is causing her to smile.

"My doctor, Tessa—she's told me she has room for us if we can make it today."

"That's amazing," I say. "You said it wouldn't take long, but this is quite remarkable."

"It really is," she says. "I would have expected a week at least, but apparently someone canceled and she has nothing booked."

I drum my fingers along the countertop. "Layla and Quinn already left for the library, and they have the codes to get back in?"

"They do," she says. "The only thing we need to do is eat quickly, catch the next train, and fill out the paperwork on the way. You're spared from me devouring you this morning."

I look at her through hooded eyes. "Maybe," I say, batting my eyelashes at her. "How long is the train ride? Does it have a private booth?"

"Yes."

***

Gráinne and I wait in silence for Tessa. The paperwork somehow got done on the way here. How we managed that and fooling around on the train is beyond me, but here we are. Gráinne reaches for my hand, giving it a tight squeeze.

"Nervous?" I ask.

"A little," she says. "But also, I am happy. This is the first time I am augmenting myself for the sake of it. Not for survival or power, but just because it brings me joy. Forgive me, I am still getting used to how wonderful Earth is." She lifts my hand to her lips and gives my fingertips a lingering kiss. "Thank you for doing this with me."

I give her hand a squeeze. "Of course. Anyway, don't apologize," I say. "This is what I am fighting for, you know? This should be normal for everyone."

The door slides open, Tessa steps through. She takes a long look between the two of us. "I had a feeling you'd come back to me for ears one day," Tessa says, smirking. "Didn't think you'd bring a fiancée, that's incredible truth be told."

The two of us have always had a rather close bond, an easy-going familiarity. She's cut her hair since last I saw her. It's shoulder length now, but still very purple.

I chuckle. "It's nice to see you again too, Tessa. I like the hair."

"Thank you," she says. She has a seat in front of us. "So, the two of you are here about augmenting your ears and adding on tails. Cat for Miss MacAirt and wolf for you."

"Yes," Gráinne says brightly. "It's nice to meet you."

"Likewise," she says. "A pleasure, really. You're in expert hands." Tessa smiles, folding her hands in her lap. "Oh, and Diarmuid, I arranged your other operation. Your surgery will take a few hours longer and you'll need to spend an extra eight hours in the tank."

"The tank?" Gráinne asks, tilting her head to the side.

"The recovery tank," Tessa says. "You get submerged in a vat of liquid that speeds up external healing and helps the body accept cybernetics. There's always a slight risk of rejection and this minimizes that."

"Oh," Gráinne says softly. "That's not a common practice where I am from."

Tessa furrows her brows. "I see." She shakes her head. "Well, it is here. Anyway, I always meet my patients beforehand to make sure they are comfortable and to answer any last-minute questions. When we're done here, you'll be taken to theater."

"None for me, doc," I say. "I read through the literature and I'm sure about it."

"Well, I didn't think you would," she replies warmly. She turns to look at Gráinne, folding one leg over the other.

"I am sure," Gráinne says, her tone somewhat nervous. "Most of my organs have been replaced, and I am at least as much machine as human. I have just never had something done that is visible." She chuckles. "I suppose

I may miss having human ears."

Tessa quickly scribbles down some notes. "You might. Body dysmorphia after an operation is common. You go from seeing yourself one way to another all at once and it can take a bit for the brain to adjust to the new self-image." She smiles reassuringly.

"If that causes you serious distress, you come back, and we reverse the whole procedure. Visually, you won't notice anything different from how you are now, should it come to that. I take exact measurements, and note every detail, even little scars you might not know you have."

Gráinne smiles then. "I feel even better about going through with this."

"Perfect," Tessa says. "I'll go over the operation briefly. I know you've both read, but I have to do this. For the ears, I'll use a variation on synth-skin, including synthetic muscles. Texturally, they feel like the animal ear of choice. In case you're wondering, they will be quite sensitive to being rubbed—I'm told this is a bonus."

She displays an anatomical diagram to us on her datapad, showing us a woman with a shaved head and feline ears attached at the parietal bone. Her acoustic meatus is gone, giving her skull an eerie appearance with no hair. The diagram shows that new ear canals are made, running through the parietal bone, and intersecting with a human's natal auditory anatomy.

"Do you fill the entrance of the old ear canal so that it doesn't cause issues?" I ask, already knowing the answer, but I'm curious about the process.

"Exactly. It'll be like it doesn't exist. The way you hear as a result will be different, the additional muscles in the ear along with the structure of it, and the new eardrum will make your hearing far more sensitive than your natal ears. This has its benefits and drawbacks, as one might expect."

"That makes sense," Gráinne says with an excited smile. "It is odd to look at, but I'm sure with hair it will be fine."

"Quite right," Tessa says. "Here." She flips to an image now—one without the anatomy and shows us the same woman but with hair. She flips through several images, showcasing different hairstyles from long hair to pixie cuts that strategically hide where the former ears would have been. "Look good?" she asks.

"Definitely," I say.

Gráinne nods eagerly. "Extremely cute."

She adjusts in her seat, glancing between the two of us. "Like I said, it'll take some getting used to, but most patients are happy with how much more expressive they feel they can be because of the extra ear muscles; the superior hearing is a bonus."

"Useful as pilots, too," Gráinne says. "Well, maybe not when we're in the mech where it doesn't matter, but in other combat situations."

"Like an angry future mother-in-law sending a very good assassin after you," I say, rubbing my head.

"You know what... I won't ask," Tessa says, giving us both wary look. She flips to a new image, showing us the same woman with a cat tail attached at the tailbone.

"Moving on—the tail will be fully cybernetic. You will be able to move it freely and expressively. It'll be covered by synth-skin, also very sensitive to touch, and capable of growing fur. Reportedly it's quite pleasant to brush. Just be careful with bumping it."

"The fur will grow and shed continuously, and I will connect the synth-skin to your body's blood supply. It's a part of you. Your balance will improve once you've gotten used to it, but you may notice you're clumsy at first."

As Tessa talks, I can see Gráinne's eyes get wider and wider. She taps her foot rapidly as she takes all this in; her smile broadens. When the time comes for Tessa to give me the details on my bottom augmentation, I ask Gráinne to leave the room. I was nervous she'd be upset that I am being so tight-lipped about the surgery, but she isn't—not in the slightest. We share a kiss; she ruffles my hair as she leaves.

"See you soon," she says. "Love you."

When she is gone, I turn my gaze towards Tessa, who has the biggest shit-eating grin on her face.

"Well, well, well. Diarmuid Mirren is getting domestic," she says.

I fold my arms over my chest, staring at her. "And?"

"I mean it as a good thing," she says. "I've known you most of your life, and you are the wildest woman I've ever met." She chuckles. "Though, I suppose you still are. That girl's mother tried to kill you? That's very... Dia."

"Whatever," I reply, narrowing my eyes. "Do we really need to go over all the details for the operation?"

She smirks. "Afraid so. I know being ethical can be tedious for people so used to flying by the seat of their pants, but it is what it is." She scoots her chair back and dims the lights in the room. A projector comes on from the ceiling, and a diagram of my body appears on the wall. "First things first, this is a very new technique. Creating interchangeable cybernetic genitals is a new frontier."

"I know," I say, crossing my right leg over the left. "Sorry, I know you have to do the thing."

"Yes," she says, taking a laser pointer and highlighting the affected areas. "Essentially, we hollow out the pubic region, create an insert that attaches to your nerves and allows you to slot in your desired bits. There will be a small seam."

She shows me a projected after image of what I'll look like once the surgery is complete. I stand up to take a closer look. Side-by-side images of me with a vulva and penis are displayed, and like she said, there is a faint but noticeable seam where the genitalia slot into the body.

I smirk. "Is it odd that I find that sort of attractive and affirming in and of itself? Can we make it more pronounced? I feel trying to hide it makes it worse, but we can stylize it a bit and it'll be cute."

Tessa grins. "It's not odd at all. A few of my patients have said the same thing. Especially you mech pilots." She shakes her head. "I can make the seam more pronounced and stylized; that's not a problem."

She clears her throat. "One more thing—this is becoming increasingly popular: exotic penises are being made to fit this augmentation. I, however, will make you bits that match your current configuration. If you want something else, you'll have to procure it yourself. As far as your neo-vagina is concerned, however, you have some options for aesthetic, depth, etcetera." She showcases some examples.

It only takes me a few moments to choose what I'd like. I've never let myself really give this much thought. It feels surreal to actually be here, sorting through the various options. Tessa's easygoing nature makes it easy—it's why she's the best.

"Perfect," she says once we're done, and having taken copious amounts of notes. "Just wait until you feel fully healed before having sex. Between your augmented healing factor and the tank, you should walk out of here just fine, but you know yourself best. Don't rush."

"Will I need to dilate?" I quirk a brow.

"It wouldn't hurt," she says. "I would take it easy your first time having penetrative sex, as it'll be an entirely novel sensation, but the synth-muscles make it easier." Tessa smiles warmly, taking a deep breath.

"Something else relevant to you and your fiancée; this form of augmentation can make it much easier for trans people to impregnate a partner. These testicles don't rely on hormones to produce viable gametes. Is that..."

"No," I say firmly. "I do not want that. I have no intention of having children in any capacity. None."

Tessa makes another note. "I'll turn that setting off. That is everything you need to know. Any last questions?"

"No," I say. "Thank you, Tessa."

"I'll come get you when the theater is ready," she says. "See you soon."

I thank her again for seeing so quickly as I walk out of her office and into the waiting room. There aren't many people here, but one sticks out immediately to me—She's got medium length blue hair, shaved close on her left side, and blue eyes to match. She's talking with Gráinne, sharing a laugh. She looks vaguely familiar to me, but I'm blanking on where I've seen her before. That's unusual; I never forget a face.

"Yo," I say, leaning against the wall nearby.

Gráinne looks at me, instantly reaching out to take my hand in hers. "Hey." She looks towards her talking companion. "Dia, this is Sif. We just met."

"I know who she is," Sif replies. "We were in the same pilot program together back in the day, and she always kicked my ass."

I snap my fingers with my free hand. "I thought I recognized you," I say, grinning widely at her. "Glad to see your egg finally hatched. Exploded even. You look great."

"Egg?" Gráinne asks, her face betraying how confused she is.

"It's a joke," Sif replies. "I'm not really sure where it originated from, but it's just always been what's been said about people like Dia and me before we figure things out."

"Oh!" Gráinne says brightly. "That makes sense. When did you two last see one another?"

"Five years ago," I say. "She was still chasing after my top score back then."

Sif folds her arms over her chest, scrunching up her face. "Don't get smug."

"You know me." I chuckle softly. "I can't resist ribbing on you. It really is good to see you again, Sif. I knew you'd make a gorgeous, gorgeous girl."

She rolls her eyes. "Whatever," she says. "What are you two here for?" Sif lifts a brow.

"Cat ears and a tail for me," Gráinne says, not quite able to hold back her enthusiasm. Her eyes are practically sparkling.

"Wolf for me, and bottom augmentation. It's time," I say.

Gráinne turns to look at me, her face soft. "That's the surprise?"

"Yeah," I say. "I didn't want to say until it was happening, in case I changed my mind after hearing what Tessa had to say."

She squeezes my hand. "Happy for you."

Sif regards the two of us for a moment, her brow knit together. "When's the wedding?"

"We haven't actually booked a venue or set a date," Gráinne says. "It is my first time on Earth—to Central at all, even. I want to take it all in for a while."

"Makes perfect sense to me," Sif replies. "Well, I hope to get an invite."

"Of course. Send me your new details," I tell her. "Come around for dinner soon. There's an idea I have that I want to pitch. I know you would be a good fit. This is serendipitous."

She keeps her arms folded in front of her chest for a moment; the gears turning in her head. "It's something insane, isn't it?"

"Always."

Sif scoffs. "Alright, I'll come around soon then. Take care, you two," she says, giving us a small wave. "Suppose it is fortuitous I just had some augmentation done myself if you're up to old tricks. See you around."

"Yeah," I say. "Be seeing you."

"Miss Mirren, Miss MacAirt," Tessa's assistant calls for us. "We're ready for you now."

Cradle of Humanity

I hate being on an operating table, even one so nice as this. The overhead lights are blinding and hot. I almost want to run away; it takes all I have to keep myself still on the bed. No matter how many times I have been under the knife, it is always the same.

Like all the others, I will get through this—most importantly, this augmentation is just for me. That thought helps relax me a little. This is not something I feel forced to do in order to survive and overcome the men in my life who would have had me in chains. This is because I have already broken my chains; I am free to do whatever I want with my body.

Tessa enters the room; her eyes look bright and cheerful. "You feeling okay?"

"I am," I tell her. "Or at least I will be. How is Dia?"

"Perfect," she says. "She's off to the tank. The two of you will wake up around the same time."

"That is a relief," I say, trying to relax. "I am ready."

She relays some orders to her staff, and they get to work making final preparations. The anesthesiologist talks me through the process, her calming voice putting me at ease.

"Count down from ten," she says.

"Ten...Nine...eigh..."

I wake up in a new bed, the room dimly lit. It takes a few moments to adjust. My vision is blurry, and my body feels heavy, as if someone is lying on top of me. I manage to get up, my feet pressing against the cold tiles on the floor. It sends a little shock through me that helps get my brain out of its fog.

The lights turn on automatically as I move about the room. There's a mirror against the length of the wall, just next to the door that leads into a bathroom.

Ears!

I hurry off the bed, eager to look at myself. In my haste, my tail swings and knocks against the footboard of the bed. There is a loud clang and immense pain shoots through me.

"Fuck!"

I had totally forgotten about the tail. Instinctively, I coil it up and stroke the spot that had banged against the bed. The fur is remarkably soft, and it is quite soothing to rub my fingers along its length. Like my hair, the fur of my tail is black, its sheen glowing under the lights. The pain fades away, replaced with joy and giddiness.

I hold my tail high behind me, curling the tip down towards my back. Lesson learned—don't forget about it when you're in a hurry. I'm in a sterile hospital gown; I take it off and stand naked in front of the mirror. My tail sways it side to side, I curl it in various ways, testing the limits of my control over it. After a few moments of practice, I can even make the tip of my tail look like half a heart.

My face is an entirely different matter. It occurs to me as I study myself, that I often used my hair to cover my ears. New hair covers that area completely, hiding where my ears once were and giving my face a pleasing profile. I practice moving them around, folding them back or forward—I suppose I must look a bit like a kitten seeing their reflection for the first time. The thought makes me giggle, my ears perk up unconsciously. Tessa was quite right—the ears really do add ways to be more expressive.

Oh, how far I have come since the day I quite literally ran into the woman who would change my life. It scares me, at times, to think about how much has changed in such a short time. For my entire life, I have railed against my cage to no avail, only to throw myself wholeheartedly at this woman with long white hair and piercing cold eyes. In my darkest moments, I wonder if I didn't trade one cage for another. A ridiculous thought, really, Dia has given me many outs from this relationship—in all likelihood, she will offer more.

I look at myself in the mirror one last time—eyes and tail that would have been unthinkable to have mere months ago—proof that finally I am free. There is one week left until my birthday, and not too long ago I was scheming and plotting to retain even a grain of agency. Never in my life did I imagine I could smile as I have, feel such deep joy, and make such stalwart friends.

Not until she arrived on her mission, sweeping me up in her cosmic winds. Now—now I can look forward to my birthday, my future. I even look forward to my marriage, which I want to delay for a while, but now the thought no longer fills me with dread. Now, I only feel excitement and eagerness to give my body, my very soul, over to this woman. My cheeks burn red at the thought of her, my heart pounds in my chest.

I gather myself and go put on clothes. Nothing dramatic, just one of Dia's hoodies and a pair of form fitting leggings. I realized rather quickly when we arrived on Earth that I did not own casual clothes. I have formal wear and my academy uniform, none of which is particularly comfortable for going out. Dia, being a gracious fiancée, however, has given me free rein over her wardrobe. I admit, I rather like how baggy all her tops are on me.

Gods, she really is so much bigger than I am.

I push down the increasingly lewd thoughts of her as I walk out of the hospital room. The door hisses open, bright light stings my eyes. There she is, talking with a nurse who is sitting behind a desk, a fluffy tail gently swaying behind her. Dia looks towards the sound of the door—directly at me.

"Look at you, Princess," she says, walking towards me with a grin on her face. "Being a catgirl suits you perfectly."

I link my arm with hers, a shy flush in my face. "Thank you," I say, looking up at her, studying the changes her augmentation made. Her lupine ears match her snow-white hair except for the tips, which are black as night. She somehow looks both adorable and ferocious, especially when she flashes her fangs at me. "You look perfect, as always."

"Oh good, you're awake," Tessa says, stepping out of another room. "I was coming to check on you again. You were out longer than I expected."

I turn to face her. "Is that bad?"

She shakes her head. "Not necessarily. It was your first time in the tank," she says. "If you feel fine, then you're both free to go. So long as you promise to call me if you notice any pain or discomfort in your ears or tail—that can be a sign of rejection."

"Of course," I tell her. "I will not be foolish."

"Good, good." She gives me a once over, checking the ears and tail for responsiveness. Satisfied, she steps back and hands me her datapad that has a form displayed on the screen. "Sign here."

I do so. "Thank you again," I say. "You did remarkable work."

She bows slightly at both of us and then walks off to go check on her other patients. Busy woman.

Dia puts her hand on my shoulder, giving me a loving squeeze. "I have some news for you," she says. "You'll like it."

"Oh?" I take her hand in mine, interlacing my fingers with hers.

"The Bansidhe has made it to the workshop," she says, lifting my hand to her lips to place gentle kisses along the back of my hand. "It's being worked on, and I thought we could go see her on your birthday—if you're fine with being on the transpacific train the whole day."

"A train that goes across the ocean on my birthday?" I ask, my ears perking upright. If I were not in a public space, I would leap onto Dia and wrap my legs around her. Seeing as I am, however, I wrap my arms around her instead and bury my face in her chest. "That sounds like a perfect birthday to me."

* * *

Three days have passed since the operation, and it's been quite an adjustment getting used to how I fit in pants now. Namely, that I can fit into the tightest leggings and feel absolutely comfortable. I never cared if bulge showed in other pants, but I was always aware of it. Sometimes I enjoyed that, but mostly I was ambivalent about it or wore pants that made it less pronounced. Now, I look at myself in the mirror and I'm flat where my cock used to be—I feel elation.

It's early hours still. Gráinne is sleeping, cuddling one of my stuffed animals to her chest. She's kicked the covers off and has somehow turned herself so that she lies diagonally across the entire bed. I pull the covers back over her and kiss the side of her head. I specifically make sure to kiss her new ear. Perhaps because the ears and tail are novel to us, but both of us have made every effort to pay special attention to the other's augmentations. It was a struggle to even get out of bed just now because her tail was wrapped around mine as we slept.

She whimpers softly as she wakes up, turning over to half-look at me through sleepy eyelids. "Mmmorning," she says. "Why are you so awake and out of bed so early?"

"Shopping," I tell her. "We're having dinner with Sif tonight."

Gráinne rubs the sleep out of her eye, her ears twitching side to side. "Right, I forgot. I will come with you. Just give me a moment to get dressed."

"You can just sleep if you want." I stroke her hair gently, brushing a few stray locks out of her eyes. "It's just to the market."

"No," she says firmly. "I want to see as much of Earth as possible. Do not laugh but, I have never gone to a market before—I was never allowed."

She sits upright; the covers falling off her. I stare at her nude body, drinking her in as I always do. She catches me staring; her face flushes as she beams at me.

"I thought we were waiting until my birthday?" she sits back on her hands, pushing her chest out. "Or are you just admiring what's yours?"

"We are and I am." I lean down, press my lips to hers and cup one of her breasts. "Though you are exceptionally tempting."

She sucks in a breath, holding back a moan. "Good. I want you to ravage me when you feel fully healed. The waiting is torture for me."

I nuzzle her cheek with mine before kissing her again. "For me, too. Trust me, I am just as eager to ride your face with my cunt as you are to be ridden."

"Dia, stop!" She giggles, her face red as a tomato. "You cannot tease me like that while you are off limits." She pulls her lip into a pout. "Not fair."

"Alright, alright," I say, patting her head. "I'll go make coffee while you get dressed."

Gráinne beams up at me. "Thank you," she says softly. "It is—difficult to articulate how much something as mundane as a trip to the market means to me, Dia. In so many ways was my life a cage. Gods, I feel so free now. I don't want to waste any of it now that I can finally *live.*"

I scoop her up into my arms. She yelps as she wraps her arms around my neck. Tenderly, I kiss her, letting out some of my pent-up passions. Gráinne kisses me back, desperately holding herself back.

"No matter what, my love, I will make sure that you never feel caged again." I press my forehead to hers, taking in a deep breath.

"A princess has never been so fortunate as I am," she whispers, "to have such a perfect, pretty wolf as her champion." Her tail wraps around my leg as she clings tightly to my chest. "I am truly blessed."

"Flatterer," I tell her, fighting back the heat creeping into my cheeks. As I stare into her eyes, I can't help but think back to those first few days after we met. I still have that burning feeling in my chest, that feeling that I would do anything—fight anyone for this woman.

"I can't say that I believe in blessings or fate, but I know that for a long time, all I had was my crusade. Now I have more than just my next battle. I..." The words get caught in my throat, choked back by a singular anxiety I have not yet been brave enough to give voice to.

"What is it?" she asks, her voice gentle and soothing. She brushes her hand along my cheek, her thumb over my lips. "You can tell me anything." Her eyes gaze into mine, rich pools of warmth and love.

I am undone by her eyes; the walls harboring my thought crumble away like ash. "I don't want you to feel bound to my private war against the galaxy. If you want to just stay here and live your life, I..."

Gráinne presses her finger to my lips, her eyes narrowed, and her jaw clenched. Her expression is furious, but her eyes—her eyes are still soft. "Banish that thought," she says, slipping back into her imperious ways. "Banish it and do not think of it again. Your war is no longer private, my love. My eyes were not opened by you, only for me to close them now that I have freedom and peace."

"Others deserve the same. You and I will succeed together or die together. Either way, to me, that is a life worth living. Now set me down so that I can get dressed. We have a life to live."

Relief washes over me; I can feel my heart rate coming down. Another deep breath. I kiss her forehead and set her down gracefully. She pats my face wordlessly—such tenderness in her touch.

"As you wish, Princess."

* * *

The warm, late morning sun shines down on my face. The smell of street food fills my soul with bliss as I walk hand in hand with Dia. A gentle breeze ruffles my sundress, which my wolf got for me just yesterday, and my hair as I peer around at the various stalls. It's almost overwhelming how many options there are, and I'm thankful that I'm not here to decide about what we're eating tonight. I leave that for my fiancée who knows what she is doing in the kitchen.

Occasionally, I slip my hand from hers to investigate something of interest—clothes or jewelry or even toys. Miniaturized mechs catch my eye; I recognize several here from Dia's collection. They need to be built, rather like a puzzle, and seem quite poseable if the packaging is to be believed. They have incredibly detailed internal engineering—for toys.

"Should we get a couple?" Dia asks me, peeking over my shoulder.

"It seems rather silly, no?" My brows furrow, a flush rising up my neck. "We pilot the real thing which are not toys, they are weapons."

"You didn't answer my question, Princess," she says, kissing my cheek.

My blush deepens. I'm not sure what's sillier, wanting the toy or being embarrassed that I want one. It's not as if Dia will judge me. "Y-yes," I admit. "I think they could be very fun to build with you."

"They are fun," she says. "These are from the arena line. Professional mech athletes that do honor matches for sport. It's all a spectacle, but the fights can be really fun to watch."

"No one is hurt?" I ask, turning to look at her. "The Fomorians also have an arena circuit, but there are *accidents,* you know?"

"Very, very rarely," she says. "There are a ton of safety measures and strict safety rules. It's just a game and everyone knows it. The last death in the arena happened before I was born."

"That does sound fun," I say, turning to browse the selection. I pick out a white and blue mech that has lovely red accents on the shoulders, the chest, and the waist. "I like this one. The fin and the head antennas are really striking. The face is cute, too."

"Very popular," Dia says through a grin. "She's the current champion of the ring and she uses swarm-bits just like I do." She chuckles then, inspecting the box closely. "It's been ages since I fought with her, long before she was champion. I wonder who'd win these days."

It doesn't at all shock me that my wolf would know a mech celebrity, or that her instinct is to wonder who would win in a fight. It's wildly attractive how competitive she is; I'm reminded of how she was with me prior to our duel. My cheeks darken. "Is she another schoolmate?"

"Yeah." Dia hesitates, reaching up at her hair and plays with her ponytail. "We dated for a while, but our paths diverged. She's thriving as Central's Arena Sweetheart though."

"Why are you nervous about saying that?" I look at her. "You're playing with your hair, which you only do when you're anxious."

"Ah," she says. "I was just thinking that I have a lot of ex-girlfriends."

I pat her on the cheek, brushing my thumb along her face. "Well, you are very charming. I am glad your life led you to me." With a warm smile, I return to looking at the model mechs. I take the box from Dia, giving it a close look.

The mech is the Seraph. On the back there is a picture of the pilot, Evangeline. She has short, untamed red hair, and stunning blue-green eyes. "Ah, she's gorgeous. You have excellent taste."

Dia looks away, her cheeks flushed. "Thanks," she says. "I'll get this one." She reaches past me and picks up another model, the Caliburn. It looks rather like the Seraph, but it is white with gold and black accents. "I've been meaning to get this one, too. It's her current mech, as far as I know."

"I look forward to building them with you," I tell her, wrapping my arms around her waist.

The rest of the shopping trip is rather uneventful. Though I am sure I add at least an extra hour or two to this trip with my curiosity. Dia never once gets impatient with me. Several times, in fact, she encourages us to stay out longer so that I might look around to my heart's content. I only feel bad agreeing the first two times she does so. After that, I finally believe her when she says that being out with me brings her joy.

The oddest thing to me on the trip is the lack of money. Dia would scan the items at a kiosk at each stall which would account for the goods we were taking, but there wasn't an exchange of currency. According to Dia, Central long ago abandoned the use of money. It's difficult for me to wrap my mind around how any of this functions, and yet I see the fruits of Central society all around me.

There is abundance for all, and very little is wasted. A society built on the principles of taking care of one another, of making life easy and accessible to all. Dia once told me, *"No one can call themselves free until the least among us are free."* The more time I spend here, the more I understand her unquenchable thirst for justice.

When we're done with the shopping, we return to Dia's apartment. Layla and Quinn stayed in today. Their faces are locked against one another, the sound of kissing filling the room while a romantic drama is playing on the viewscreen. They don't notice us coming in at first and pull away from one another rapidly when they do.

"Hi," Layla says sheepishly, her face exceptionally red.

"Yo," Dia says. "Don't mind us. I'm going to the kitchen to get started on dinner."

"Sorry," I say, chuckling. "Didn't mean to interrupt."

Quinn chuckles, shaking her head. "Nothing we can't resume tonight," she says, her voice rather smug.

"Hey!" Layla says, the red in her face deepening. "I... okay, that's true."

I grin at them both as I take a seat in a comfortable chair in the room's corner. "Is this new, or have you just been private?"

Layla takes Quinn's hand in hers. "Maybe a bit of both? It wasn't exactly a secret, but so much has happened that I supposed it slipped our mind to mention it. We confessed to one another during the attack on the Danu-II."

My eyes turn to Quinn, who looks rather pleased with herself. "You know, that really does explain why you were so exuberant after the attack."

"Yeah!" She leans on Layla's shoulder, her lips turned up into a warm smile. "I thought we might die, and then we didn't and suddenly it just didn't make sense to go through life so scared anymore. You're always talking about just wanting to live—I feel the same."

"Good," I tell them. "You know what, I am going to rather join Dia in the kitchen and see what I can learn about cooking."

* * *

"Damn, Dia," Sif says, patting her stomach. She leans back in her chair, looking rather content. "When did you learn to cook? Last time I tried something of yours, you made charcoal."

"Hatsuko," I tell her. "She taught me."

Sif furrows her brows. "Seriously? Well, I suppose you were always her favorite."

"Not anymore."

An awkward silence falls over the table. The mood which had been good a moment before gets a shade darker as no one is sure what to say next. Sif shoots me an apologetic look.

"Sorry," she says. "I heard what happened between you two. That wasn't kind of me to say in light of the history."

I shrug. "It's fine. We just didn't see eye to eye anymore, and she wasn't the only one who didn't agree with me."

"Can I ask what happened?" Gráinne reaches over to me and takes my hand in hers. "You have never mentioned her."

I take a moment to answer. Painful memories push down my words. "She was our teacher," I say. "Hatsuko didn't approve of me waging a one-woman crusade against the corporations that run the rest of the galaxy into the ground."

"To be fair, it's idiotic," Sif replies. "What Central does works. Every year we grow as more and more systems defect. You're just impatient and would have gotten many people killed."

"Central can pretend to keep their hands clean that way if they want to," I say harshly. "It's so fucking easy to say stupid shit like that when you get to be who you want, Sif." I furrow my brow, trying my best to keep my temper in check.

"And you only figured that out recently under the best of circumstances." I squeeze Gráinne's hand, struggling to keep my cool. "So yes, I'm impatient, because I see the rivers of blood already flowing and just can't handle how many more people are going to die. Rather blood on my hands for doing something than on my conscience because I did nothing."

Quinn looks down at her lap. She clenches her jaw tightly. "Sometimes we can't defect either," she says. "My family comes from a farming world deep in Fomorian space, nowhere near the border. People who talk about wanting to leave... well, they don't last long before they vanish."

Sif looks taken aback, her mouth agape for a moment as she tries to gather herself. "I didn't know ya'll were from the Armory," she says. "I'm sorry."

"It's not really a one-woman crusade anymore anyhow," Gráinne says. "Not when the imperial princess, powerful Armory nobles, and regular working-class folk are backing the cause. People desperately want freedom, and sometimes all they need is to be shown a bit of hope—that it's possible to obtain at all."

"Wait, you went through with your plans?" Sif asks, her tone incredulous. "That's where you've been all this time?"

"Of course," I tell her. "What, you thought Hatsuko's disapproval of my actions was going to stop me? That I really wasn't willing to do it alone? I love that woman to death, like a third mother, but I've done what I've had to do."

She takes a moment to process that. "Fucking hell, this could incite a war. You know that, right? How the hell have you not been grounded?"

"I'm a simple mercenary," I say with a shrug. "Nothing wrong with being a merc."

"Consorting with imperial princesses and nobles isn't being a merc, Dia," Sif hisses.

Gráinne laughs then, a dainty and controlled laugh. She looks perfectly calm except that her tail twitches behind her. "Oh my, I suppose I could call you my consort." She looks at me, winking. "Though I much prefer champion."

Despite my irritation, my cheeks go a shade red. "Really, Princess?"

Layla and Quinn both chuckle. Gráinne smiles warmly at me as she lifts my hand to her lips so that she can kiss my fingertips.

"Wait..." Sif blinks several times, the gears in her head turning over several times before she speaks. "You're the princess? I suppose I should have put that together; except for one problem—I can be very stupid."

Gráinne smirks wickedly. "Just so," she says, "but do please go on about how she is *consorting*." The princess shakes her head. "The Armory is rotting and the people are suffering. I, for one, am glad for Dia."

"Me too," Quinn says. "Being a woman there feels so impossible. You can't do anything, and when you try, you get mocked. Every inch you gain is fought for tooth and nail. It's awful."

Layla frowns. "That, and knowing everything could be taken from you on a whim," she says. "Gods, and the expectations to be perfect for the sake of men. I can't count the number of times I was told that being an engineer was stupid because a man wouldn't want to marry me." She looks at Quinn, then at me. "So, I'm glad for you, too. I never would have had the courage to accept my feelings for Quinn."

"Same," Quinn says, taking Layla by the hand. "I don't even want to think about how long we'd have danced around one another. Seeing you two kiss and dance was life changing, but what really made the difference was how you stood up to all the people who hated you for it."

Sif falls silent, her cheeks and neck several shades of red all at once. After a moment, she looks over at me. "And to think this started because I asked you about the food."

"It happens." I sigh, my ears twitching. "Believe it or not, I had it in mind to ask you to join me. There was a whole evening planned to catch up after we ate and then I'd bring it up for you to sleep on."

She clears her throat. "Why me?"

"Because the list of S-Tier pilots is very short," I tell her. "I need and want the best, and you're the best sniper alive."

Sif folds her arms over her chest. She looks at me, then at Gráinne and finally at Layla and Quinn, who are both giving her a hopeful glance. I sit and wait patiently for her to answer, hoping that by meeting the people I care about, she would care about them, too.

"Two pilots, Dia?" she asks mournfully.

"Three," Gráinne corrects.

"Three pilots is better," Sif says. She pinches the bridge of her nose. "But if you're really looking for the best, that's not you... well, I'm not really the girl to be calling on. Sure, I'm a great sniper like you said, but I was never really in *ya'll's* league."

I let out a sharp breath. "I don't think *she* wants anything to do with me, and I can't really blame her for that."

"Evangeline?" Gráinne asks, looking down at the floor. "Is that who you mean?"

"Yes."

Gráinne wraps her tail around mine and squeezes my hand. "If it is to liberate my people, I think we should reach out to all the best assets we can. You said so yourself, to Brigid, that you needed allies."

"Whose Brigid?" Sif asks, her brow lifted curiously.

"Heir to House Áine. She is a pragmatic and ruthless woman when she needs to be. She saw the value of liberation rather than the throne—I count her among our allies." Gráinne puts on her dignitary voice, sounding almost the way she did that day in Brigid's office.

"Sounds like my kind of woman." Sif grins. "Alright, Dia, I'll join you on your hairbrained scheme, but only on one condition."

I cross one leg over the other, looking at her intently, trying to restrain my bitterness. "What *condition*, Sif?"

"You gotta talk to Eva," she says. "If you talk to her like you talked to me and she gets on board, then I will too. Even with a pragmatic, ruthless politician, *and* a pilot-princess on your side, I don't feel good about this. If somehow you manage to convince Eva of all people, then I'll join up with no complaints."

"Fuck you, Sif," I say irritably before I let out a deep sigh. "Fine."

She lets out an unholy cackle. "It'll be just like old times."

"Well, not totally," I say, motioning towards her chest. "You have tits now."

Sif bites her lip and looks away, her face the reddest it's been all night. "Touché."

* * *

My wolf paces back and forth in our room, chewing on her thumb anxiously. She stops, goes to the bed and flops over, looking utterly exhausted.

"Oh, my love," I whisper, stroking her hair. "Does the idea of speaking with Evangeline really fill you with such stress?"

"Yes," she groans. "That woman is a bloody nightmare. Literally. She won't listen to anything I have to say, I can promise you that much. At best, she's just going to demand that we fight, then tell me to fuck off forever."

She chuckles darkly, her ears flattening back. "If, by some miracle, she agrees to be a part of this, we're going to have to talk about *us*, and I just don't have it in me to deal with all those feelings—they are buried for good reason."

"You still love her," I whisper, stroking her hair and ears. "How did it end?"

Dia opens her mouth, her offended expression screaming even if no words come out. I press my finger to her lips, shaking my head.

"Do not deny it," I tell her. "You would not be this stressed otherwise, and you need not hide your feelings on my behalf."

She furrows her brows, rolls over onto her side, and puts her head in my lap. "She begged me not to leave," she says. "And this is not a woman who begs for anything. She bared her entire heart to me, and I told her I couldn't stay and live a happily ever after."

"I see." I continue stroking her hair, brushing stray strands out of her eyes. "That must have been agony for you both."

Dia nods silently, tears forming in her eyes. "Yeah, and I'm afraid of reopening old wounds for nothing. She's already refused to join me once, and there is even less reason to join me now."

"Is that all you are worried about?" I ask, gazing into her snowy eyes. "Or are you worried that you will make new wounds because of me?"

She purses her lips tightly. "Not exactly," she says. "That's part of it, but I also worry about us, too. This relationship is still so new—I am not sure where the boundaries are. We haven't had much of a chance to talk about them."

I smile, running my fingers across her lips. "Let us talk about them then," I say. "I suppose I am a bit of a blank slate to be fair. I have fully rejected what was instilled in me, such as it being wrong to desire women at all." A wide grin forms on my lips as I look down at her. "I very much do desire women. In fact, I ache for this one woman in particular. She has eyes like freshly fallen snow—she stole my heart at first glance."

Her cheeks turn a subtle shade of red. "My love, be serious," she says through a hint of a smile. "So, are you saying it's all up to me? That you trust me that much?"

"That is one way of putting it," I say, rubbing her ear between my fingers. "I would tell you if something bothered me, so rather just go about things as you normally would."

She looks up at me, leaning into my touch. "And if I told you it's not unheard of for me to have more than one partner at a time? Is that something that bothers you?"

"No," I say with an ease that surprises me. "I would like to know of them, of course, but I do not own you as much as I tease you about being *my* champion."

"Consort, too," she reminds me through a smirk.

I chuckle as I run my hands through her hair and then down her neck. I massage her gently, pressing my fingers into the muscles on her chest and shoulders until I feel her relax. "If there is a chance for you and Evangeline to reconcile, are you going to want to take it?"

"Maybe," she says. "It depends on if you two get on. You are my main partner and she and I have a troubled history—I will not risk us, Gráinne. At the very least, if I meet with her at all, I want to patch things up and become amicable."

"Then do not let your mind be troubled, my perfect, pretty wolf," I murmur. "I will follow you unto the ends of the universe and beyond. If you are putting us first, then I have no cause for worry, nor do you over our bond. Be yourself—I support you."

"Alright, Princess," she says, closing her eyes. "Let's get some sleep. We have another two days before our trip, and we won't have much of a vacation once we get to the workshop."

"True," I say. "I admit, however, that I very much look forward to testing the new Bansidhe on you."

Lesbians on a Train

Central Station is one of the most gorgeous buildings I have ever laid eyes on, and I have traveled to many worlds across the Milky Way. The ceiling is a tall dome made of fine marble; pillars covered in vines line the walls and various forms of art from mosaics to murals dot the interior.

It is the beating heart of Earth.

One could get on a train here and be anywhere on the planet within three days. I lead Layla, Quinn, and Gráinne through the station towards our train. It's on an off day for travel, but even so, there are thousands of people walking about. We take about an hour to get through the various checkpoints within the station and get to our train. It's an overnight trip—the four of us could have shared a sleeping compartment, but Layla and Quinn have opted for their own.

The five of us share a single compartment for now. In 'travel' mode, the room has two plush wall-to-wall benches for us to sit on and a collapsible table in the center to take our meals on. When we want to use it as a bedroom, the entire compartment can reconfigure itself into a bedroom.

"Alright," I say, finally able to relax now that we are settled in. I check the time on my datapad. "About an hour and we'll be off. Sorry I made us get here so early, but I'm paranoid about getting to places on time. Especially today." I smile over at Gráinne. "So, what do you think, birthday girl?"

Gráinne leans on me, wrapping her tail around my wrist.

"I think you should not be sorry," she says. "Rather early than late." She kisses under my jaw. "I am impressed with the train." She smiles, her violet eyes peering up at me. "Truly, it seems impossible. A project like this would never get approved in the Armory."

"Wait until we're moving. You can see even more of her." I put an arm around her, kissing an ear. "We'll get up and walk around, and we can have dinner in the restaurant car. A famous chef runs it."

Her eyes light up, her smile broadens. "A restaurant? On the train? Is it as wonderful as your cooking?"

I roll my eyes. "Princess, what kind of question is that? I'm not a proper chef."

"Hmmmm," she says, chuckling. "I will be the judge of that. Either way, my birthday has become considerably better. My friends. My fiancée. A train that travels over the sea." She sighs wistfully, snuggling up against me tightly. "Perfect."

"You know," Layla says, "I feel very silly that I was ever scared of you now that we're friends."

Quinn frowns. "The bodyguard didn't help," she says. "But really, it's the whole of Fomorian society that's broken."

"It is," Gráinne says. "From top to bottom."

"We'll build something better once we tear it down," I say. "That said, we're relaxing and celebrating." I squeeze Gráinne's knee, kissing the top of her head. "The road ahead is long. Let's relax while we can."

"You are right," she says, sitting up straight. "I wonder what your mother ended up doing with the Bansidhe."

"No idea," I say. "There is no telling what she might come up with."

Despite my own words, it's difficult to keep my thoughts of the future at bay. The Fomorian Armory is just one of many corporate empires to dismantle. There is also whatever agenda Cleo has, though I am leaving her to my mothers—she is their enemy. Then there is speaking with Eva, and I am still not ready to handle that conversation despite the princess' reassurance.

Yet, I need allies, there's no escaping that fact. Gráinne and her feral tenacity, while exceptional, is not enough to make meaningful and strategic strikes at our enemies. We need a team.

Like a cat, she seems to sense my growing anxiety and rests her head on my shoulder, wrapping her tail around mine. I take in a deep breath, pushing aside my thoughts for now. There's nothing I can do to solve any of these problems right now. The next best step is getting the Phantom and Bansidhe up and running. Most importantly, I owe it to the princess to be present on her birthday; not thinking of battles.

"I think we're going to set up our cabin," Layla says. "I want to take a nap before the train leaves."

"A nap sounds wonderful," Gráinne agrees. "I had an awful dream that woke me up in the middle of the night. Horrid."

"What sort of nightmare?" Quinn furrows her brow.

"That I was back at the palace and had not met any of you," she says. "I was in a wedding dress, too, and I think my groom was Bres." She shudders. "Like I said, it was awful."

"Oh yeah, I remember that asshole—broke his ribs and banished him." I take Gráinne's hand in mine.

"The very same," she says. "He was reigning champion, once. I learned to pilot and augmented my flesh to defeat him. The way he looked at me—treated me while he was champion. It was vile."

"I should have just killed him, honestly." I shift in my seat, pulling her to my chest and wrapping my arm around her shoulder. "Would have been worth the murder charge."

She hums contentedly. "A pleasant thought," she says. "He learned I am not to be trifled with, and he stayed away from me after I beat him. In fact, that day in class, and the ball were the only times he so much as looked at me. I think he was jealous." She makes a gagging sound. "As if he thought I would pick him in the end. Truly, he deserved far worse than humiliation."

"It was really satisfying to see that though," Quinn says. "Man was a terror to people like us."

"Him and all his stupid friends," Layla says. "I'm glad we're all away from that. Coming to Earth has been an incredible breath of fresh air—literally."

Gráinne sits up and stretches. "Me too," she says, smiling warmly, and wiggling her ears with joy. "Present reality is far preferable."

SUNDERED MOON

* * *

The mag rails below us make the train feel motionless as it races across the continent. The only way to know we're moving at all would be to look out the window and see the world pass us by. That will have to wait, however, as Gráinne's catnap has turned into a three-hour sleep from which she hasn't woken from.

I hold her tight in my arms, kissing her forehead as she sleeps. She stirs, yet remains fast asleep. It would perhaps be kind to wake her so that she can enjoy more of this trip. I pepper her face with more kisses, each one slowly rousing her from sleep.

She smiles, fluttering her eyes as she wakes, and hides her face in my chest. "Mmm, how long have I been out for?"

"Three hours," I say. "Shame, you fell asleep almost as soon as your head hit the pillow."

"Three hours?" She whimpers, digging her fingers into me as if to pull herself even closer. "Well, at least it is a rather long trip. Thank you for staying with me the whole time."

I kiss the top of her head, my hands idly stroking down her naked back. "Of course," I whisper.

"Did you nap, too?" She crawls on top of me, resting her head in the crook of my neck.

"No." The weight of her body on mine is pleasant, her warmth radiating into me. I keep stroking her hair, occasionally running my fingers across her ears. "My mind was on our next steps. Stressing that our mechs won't be ready if the situation takes a turn for the worse suddenly. Worried about what Cleo is up to. Sleep isn't coming easily to me these days, but that's okay. I don't need as much sleep as normal people."

She kisses under my jaw, her hands cup one of my breasts. "Your mind needs sleep even if your body does not."

I suck in a breath as her dexterous fingers massage my nipple. "Are you trying to encourage me to sleep, or are you claiming your birthday present?"

Gráinne giggles as she adjusts her body, pressing her thigh right up against my clit. "Well, I know you sleep after I wear you out," she teases. "So, a bit of both. Gods, I am hungry for you." Her mouth latches to my nipple, her fingers playing with the other.

My hips roll as I grind myself against her thigh; pulses of pleasure race through my body, overwhelming my senses. Groans and moans escape me as she teases, suckles, and toys with me. "Whatever my birthday girl wants," I say, struggling to keep a steady voice.

Teeth clamp down on my breast, nails drag down my sides and hips like claws. I arch my back, hissing in painful rapture. Her long, beautiful fingers find my clit, stroking it gently. My eyes roll to the back of my head. The concentrated bundle of nerves instantly becomes overstimulated. I open my mouth to talk, but only a whimper comes out.

"Mmm, you will get used to it," she says softly. "I will go easy on you."

"Thanks," I say hoarsely. "It's very new."

"I know." She kisses my neck. "Tell me if it is too much, or if it hurts."

She rubs around the sensitive nub instead, avoiding direct contact. The almost painful amount of pleasure subsides. I press my hips into her hand, grinding myself against the tips of her fingers. She grins, kissing me deeply. Her tongue is in my mouth, my breath stolen from my lungs.

I wrap my arms around her, pulling her tight to my chest as we kiss. She grinds herself needily into my knee, moaning as she edges herself. Gráinne pulls away from me, her violet eyes burning with hunger and passion. She sits up and gets between my thighs, pressing her cunt to mine.

I bite my lip, reaching out to squeeze her breast as she rolls her hips against me. Her taut abs flex as she fucks me, her head thrown back. Long black locks tumble down around her face and back, her mouth slightly agape.

I match her pace as we press ourselves against one another, both trying to make the other scream out in pleasure. My orgasm comes first, but only just. My toes curl. I grip the bed and bite into the pillow to keep myself from making too much noise. She bites into me when she cums, her whole body shaking with pleasure.

We lie there in bliss for a moment, gathering our bearings.

"Fuck," I say, my chest heaving up and down. "That was—I wasn't sure what to expect, but that was amazing."

"Mmm, quite," she replies, stifling a laugh. "I read about how to do that, and it was much better in practice."

I kiss her neck and face, my hands idly stroking both her tail and her ears. She shudders and whines. "You're adorable for doing that. Is there anything else my princess wants to try on her birthday?" My tone is light and teasing. "Your wish is my command."

She clings tightly to me, pressing her face to my ear. "Sit on my face and use me, Dia. I have been thinking about that for days. I want us to consume one another until we can't walk."

Wordlessly, I flip us over. Gráinne yelps and giggles as I straddle her. She looks up at me, her tongue dragging across her lips. I pin her down on the bed and tease her by keeping myself just out of reach. She whines, her eyes pleading with me to release her. I grab her by the hair, taking a fistful of her raven locks between my fingers. I stuff her face between my thighs and rock my hips back and forth.

Her moans and whimpers are muffled as she digs her tongue inside me. I toss my head back as I ride her. She eagerly laps me up, drinking her fill of me like she is stranded in the desert. With her arms pinned under my knees, she lies there helplessly as I grind myself into her, reveling in the primal urge to rut.

I cum but do not stop my hips, my body now used to the overwhelming pleasure. A gush of warm fluid squirts into her mouth and on her face, only making my lover moan and cry out. I edge myself on the precipice of another orgasm, panting and touching my own breasts as I enjoy my princesses' mouth.

But I am hungry, too. I lift myself from her so that I can turn around and mount her again—this time burying my face in her. She is soaked, leaking nectar down her thighs and onto the bed. I take long licks, raking my tongue across her folds, drinking my fill of her.

Our feral passion eventually gives way to a desire to simply be close to one another.

"How was your first time?" she asks.

"It was my first time, wasn't it?" I chuckle. "Euphoric in more ways than one. I'm glad I got the surgery where I can swap whenever I'd like, but that was incredible."

She kisses my neck and runs her fingers along my sides and back. "Good," she says, "I am glad. You deserve…"

The door to our room bursts. I yank myself away, looking up to see the barrel of a rifle pointed down at me, a soldier dressed in all black with a featureless helmet. The muzzle flashes, there is a deafening crack as the bullet rips across the compartment.

Blood pours down over my eyes, my vision goes black.

"Dia!"

* * *

Snow white hair runs crimson as my wolf's very life flows out of her.

I snarl, leaping off the bed towards her attacker, crossing the compartment in an instant. The soldier reacts slow, barely able to register that I am now about to kill them. I take the rifle from them just as another shot goes off; the bullet ricocheting off the wall. I smash my fist into their head, shattering their helmet.

They crumple to the floor as I take the butt of the rifle and slam into them again and again. The man's face becomes visible, his face bloody and broken. I discard the gun and wrap my hand around his neck. He tries to fight me off, but it is no use. It takes only a second to rip his throat out. Spurts of blood gush as he falls lifelessly to the floor.

I stand there panting, my fingers covered in blood.

"Fuck, that hurts," Dia growls, a bullet lodged in her forehead. With a grunt, she yanks it out and tosses the metal lump to the to the ground with a thump—her skin already beginning to heal over the wound.

I rush over to her, throwing my arms around her waist. "Thank the gods you are okay."

"Yeah, of course," she says. "Takes a lot more than that to get through my skull. Just stunned me for a moment."

"Okay," I say, taking only a moment to feel relief. I go to our luggage, taking out fresh clothes for us both—leggings and crop tops will be easy enough to move around in. We silently don our clothes; our bodies will have to be our armor.

After getting dressed, Dia takes the rifle and tosses me the dead soldier's sidearm. "We need to check on Layla and Quinn, then find out who the fuck these people are."

I flip the pistol's safety off and ready it. "I know who they are," I tell her. "They belong to the same group as the pilots you killed."

"Ah, so Cleo's people." She grits her teeth. "Well, they are going to pay for shooting me in the head and ruining your birthday."

"The day is still young," I say. "So long as our friends are alive at the end of it, this will still be my best birthday."

"Princess," Dia says, her voice soft and slightly amused, "that is absolutely tragic."

We make our way down the train. No other soldiers are in sight. Layla and Quinn's compartment is adjacent to ours, so we need not walk far. We find them hiding behind their bed.

"We heard shooting," Quinn says, her voice quivering. "Dia, holy shit your hair."

"It'll wash out," she says. "You two just stay here. Gráinne and are going to see if it was just the one, or if there are more. It's unlikely they were working alone."

"Is there anything we can do?" Layla asks, trying to sound far braver than she must be feeling.

"No," I tell her. "Things may get even bloodier than they already have. Stay here and stay safe. We will manage this."

They nod at us and go back to taking cover. Dia and I exit their compartment, sealing it shut behind us. It dawns on me only now that I have taken my first life. It was a rather trivial task in the end—his flesh tore so easily.

Movement in the corner of my eye. I duck as a bullet buzzes overhead. Three more soldiers came from the train car in front of us, another four from the car behind. Dia takes aim at the group coming from our rear, squeezing off several rounds. I rush forward towards the group of three. The cacophony of gunfire is deafening. I use my arms to cover my vitals as I approach. Their bullets tear into my skin, ripping flesh from bone. Adrenaline and neural implants blunt the searing pain. Flesh will heal, my augmented body is durable enough to survive this much.

I strike a soldier with an elbow, shattering their helmet in a single blow. One of them grabs me. I kick off the wall, smashing them into the side of the train. Like me, they are most likely cybernetically enhanced and difficult to kill. Still, there are still weaknesses to the human body that can be exploited—soft tissue, organs, and arteries make for deadly targets.

My hand becomes the edge of a sword, slashing through a soldier's throat. Blood gushes in spurts as my fingers slice through the sinew. The hemoglobin is quite beautiful when it's fresh, but I have no time to admire my wet work. The soldiers have realized that their guns are not effective against me. They draw knives. One thrusts their blade, aiming for my stomach. I parry, the knife slicing through my forearm instead. More pain to be ignored as I shove my knee into the soldier's side. There is a loud crack as their bones break.

I rip the knife from their hand, thrusting it in between their ribs. I twist the blade, widening the gap between their bones and drag the knife along their body, slicing through vital organs. Two are dead. The third, whom I stunned just a moment ago, has now recovered. They are undaunted, unnaturally so. One would think seeing your friends dead would give you pause, but they attack with me the ferocity and fearlessness of someone who knows they are already dead.

They lash out at me, each strike aimed at with a precision that could easily kill me. I parry and block with my arms, taking care to protect my weak points. Being the last one alive, they attack desperately—recklessly. They step a hair too far forward as they try to grab me, their balance only slightly thrown off. It's all I need. I throw them to the ground and press my knee to their carotid. They feebly try to throw me off, but already the lack of blood flowing to their brain makes them impotent. I hold firm, choking the life from them. They gurgle a death rattle; fingers that are scratching at my leg fall limp.

I whip around, looking behind me, and see that Dia has killed three of the four assailants. She looks no worse for the wear as she tosses the rifle to the ground.

Dia steps on the last soldier, her heel right on his neck. "Are you going to talk?" she asks him.

"Fuck you," he spits. "Just kill me."

"But if I kill you, then I don't get an answer, and I really, really want an answer," she says, digging her heel into his neck. "And your boss' trick will not work this time. I scrambled all your external communications. You're cut off."

The soldier's eyes widen with panic. He opens his mouth and tries to bite down, but before he can, Dia's fingers are in his mouth, her movements a blur. She grunts in pain and curses under her breath.

"Ow," she says, ripping her fingers out from between his teeth, a molar in hand. "Damn, that's old school, but very thorough." She tosses the tooth to the ground nearby. "Now, be a good boy and talk. You'll get a whole new life if you do you know? Must be better than working for a psychopathic bitch that'll pop your brain if you fail."

"I'm already dead," he says. "There is nothing you can do for me. I'm dead. Her arm is longer than you can imagine. Please, just kill me."

Dia tilts her head, her brows furrowing. "You are really afraid," she remarks. "Any more of you on the train?"

He shakes his head. "No, it was just the eight of us."

"Mission?"

The soldier hesitates a moment. "You," he says. "The mission was to bring you in. The boss is obsessed with the idea of studying you."

"At least she has taste," Dia says, the sardonic edge to her tone as sharp as any blade. She sits down on her haunches, holding the man down with an outstretched hand. "Here's the score, friend. I don't really want to kill you unless I have no choice. Now, I'm not really all that afraid of Cleo—Cleopatra, whatever she wants to call herself."

"Sure, sure, she has a long reach but see, she's made the big mistake of pissing me off. There's not a place in this universe or the next that she can hide from me." Dia grimaces. "But that's between me and her. So, what's it going to be? Do I need to put you down like a dog, or do you want to try living?"

The soldier reaches for his sidearm in a flash of motion, but Dia is faster still. She takes hold of his gun, twists it out of his hand and presses the barrel to his eye before shooting thrice. She stands up, tossing the gun aside.

"Like a dog it is."

* * *

Naturally, with eight people dead, Dia and I are questioned by the staff of the train. Security footage was reviewed, and we were told they had no cause to hold us—defending oneself is no crime. Dia, being an officer of Central's navy, helped our case considerably; that information is news to me.

We were given a new compartment; our luggage was moved there for us by the staff. Layla and Quinn are shaken by the fighting, but otherwise unharmed. My flesh wounds have healed already, as have Dia's. Almost everything is as it was, except for one undeniable truth: there is a new danger in our path, and it can strike at us even in places we think are safe. I mull that over in my mind as Dia and I sit, looking out the window as the train passes over the ocean below.

"I have wanted to ask what you know about these people," Dia says after a long silence, "but I wanted to give you a chance to just enjoy Earth. Now, I really need to know. Sorry, Princess."

I take her hand in mine, putting it in my lap. "I've only seen them a few times. A private military company I don't even know the name of. As far as I was aware, they worked directly for my father. They were his personal shadow ops."

Dia frowns then. "I see," she says. "Well, I have a feeling that may not be the case. I just don't see Cleo working for your father—she must have her reasons." She runs her fingers through her still bloodied hair. "What's really concerning is that despite Central's open nature, it's not a simple place to infiltrate—Earth, especially. The people who protect Central are incredibly dedicated and highly trained to make sure things like this don't happen."

"Who *is* Cleo?" I ask. "I have never seen or heard of her before all this. What is her history with your mothers?"

She casts her gaze out the window for a moment, collecting her thoughts and perhaps even her composure. "Cleo," she says, taking in a deep breath, "betrayed my mother twenty-five years ago. She is the reason the Cerberus Incident happened at all."

Dia looks back at me, her gaze somewhat distant. "As far as I'm aware, they were lovers at one point. My mother trusted her the same way she trusts mom—implicitly. Cleo, for whatever reason, turned on everyone she knew for reasons no one understands. My mothers have been hunting her down ever since."

My grip around her hand tightens as I lean on her shoulder. "Now she's set her sights on you."

"Right." Dia shifts to lean back on me. "It's just a problem I wasn't anticipating. My focus has been on the Fomorian Armory and the other system-states. I wasn't expecting Cleo to have amassed an army of indeterminate size with the ability to hit me on Earth. Sooner or later, she's going to have to be dealt with. Though, I guess if I am her target, she'll come to me eventually."

"I will not let her take you." My fingers interlace with Dia's as I lift her hand to my lips. "And we will deal with what comes together, as have everything else thus far."

She smiles then, her free hand ruffling the top of my head. "I know," she says. "I've never doubted that."

"Good," I tell her. "Can I ask you something?"

"Of course," she says. "What do you want to know?"

I take a deep breath. "I am wondering why you never told me that you were formally part of Central's Navy."

She chuckles. "Oh, that." She rubs the back of her neck sheepishly. "Truth be told, I just forgot. I've been on 'extended leave' since I left Central space and it's not something I think about very often."

Her red cheeks cause a giggle to escape from my lips. "My perfect, pretty wolf. You really are just a creature who lives entirely in the moment. I love that about you."

Dia smirks at me, the smirk that makes my knees weak and my heart skip several beats. "What can I say, Princess?" she asks, leaning in close. "I am who I am."

Our lips meet, my arms wrapping around her neck, pulling her tight against me. I know now that my wolf was never in any danger, but I can still vividly recall that void-filled rage I felt when I thought they had killed her. I kiss her furiously, as if I may never kiss her again. It doesn't take long for me to end up in her lap, straddling her and running my fingers along her back. Her tail wags behind her as we kiss.

"Mm," she says, pulling away to take a breath. "What was that for?"

My cheeks flush, my heart pounds in my chest. "Because you are still here with me." I kiss her again before she can talk, my fingers digging into her skin.

Even when my lips are swollen and chafed raw, I don't stop kissing her. She kisses me back, pulling me so close I feel I might become part of her. There are no more words for me to say, only affection and desire to show her. This foolish, foolish woman barged into my life and tore it apart with her gravity, and so I cling to her now, like a planet orbiting a star. I pour my very being into my touch, into my kiss.

She is my reason—my purpose. I will protect her unto the end of time.

Ordinary Day

"It's going to be okay."

Gráinne nods into my chest as I stroke her hair. We both take a moment to breathe as the sun disappears beyond the horizon. Golds and reds reflect off the surface of the ocean, making a brilliant display of color that washes over us.

"It's going to be okay," I say again, kissing the top of her head. "Like you said, I'm still here with you... because of you, you know? You saved my life back there."

She looks up at me, her brows furrowed. "I know," she says. "Well, me and your exceptionally hard head. Not much I could have done without that."

I chuckle, wrinkling my nose at her. "We'll call that foresight on my part; augmenting my bones was painful, but worth it." I brush my fingers along her face. "We made a great team, not that I ever doubted that we would."

I sigh. "Are you okay, Princess? That was the first time you had to fight in a life-or-death situation."

Her face softens as she nuzzles into my hand. "I am," she says. "My training and instincts served me well. I do not feel any sort of remorse for taking their lives. My emotional energy is better spent on being glad we are alive, and my time better spent planning for future engagements with our growing list of enemies."

"You're right." I lean my head back against the comfortable bench, sinking into the plush upholstery. I push my worry out of my mind. What she said may as well have come out of my mouth, and I appreciate the pragmatism in her way of thinking. "Speaking of our enemies—I have been conflicted about contacting Eva, but now I am certain that we need to. I will just have to get over my issues."

"I think that is wisdom." She kisses the tips of my fingers. "When will you reach out?"

I cast my glance out the window as I gather my thoughts. There is a part of me that wants to call Eva right here and now, but I know that is foolish—I'm not in a state to face her. "Tomorrow morning," I say. "After we get off the train and we're on our way to the workshop. I can work up the courage by then."

Gráinne kisses my cheek gently, running her fingers through my hair. "I will support you," she says. "Tell me about her? If I understand the two of you better, perhaps I can help."

The very last thing I want to do is talk about my past with Eva, even though I see the logic in what Gráinne is offering. I want to keep the past buried, to keep up my barriers—they keep me safe. Or do they? I turn to look at my lover, staring into her rich violet eyes. Was I not safest when my walls came crashing down? Did I not discover new things about myself because I allowed myself to dig deep into agonizing emotions?

"Alright, I may as well," I say, forcing the words out. "Eva and I were friends ever since we were kids. We were always competing, but in a way that made us better people as well as pilots. People sometimes thought we hated one another—our fights were intense."

The words get easier to say as I talk, as my walls come crumbling down around me. "But that was just how we were with one another. Sometimes we communicated more with our fists or our mechs than our words."

Gráinne chuckles softly. "Adorable. I am a little jealous she has gotten to spar with you so much, though. You will just have to make that up to me." Her smile is playful, her eyes warm and loving. "What happened in the end?"

A deep frown creases my face. "I had just turned twenty and went out on a mission to a Titan Tech controlled sector. There was a guerrilla insurgency fighting, trying to free their world out from under Titan control, and they reached out to us for humanitarian aid." I take a deep, steadying breath.

"When we got there, Hatsu... Admiral Tatewaki ordered us to go beyond the scope of our mission. We provided military aid as well—the conditions on the planet were disgusting. The insurgents won because of our intervention; We freed the planet for a little while."

"That sounds ominous." Gráinne furrows her brows as she studies me. "What happened?"

The memory is painful, and I fight against the instinct to shove it down, to run away from it. "The new planetary government did not want further aid from Central, as is their right. We left. Within two years, Titan forces reclaimed the world."

I grip my seat so hard my knuckles turn white. "It just didn't matter in the end. Titan Tech still existed, and these corporate empires don't give a fuck about worlds that just want to govern themselves. They just see resources to be exploited." I take another breath, trying to regain a shred of composure. "It doesn't have to be Central, but until something else takes the places of these corps, no one is ever really free. Not even in Central."

I press my forehead into Gráinne's, trying to contain my bitterness. "So, I went to Eva with this frustration. I told her I was tired of watching the rest of the galaxy burn. She didn't agree with me when I suggested we do something about it. Like Sif, she believed in Central's policy of *slow growth*." I practically spit out the phrase, it fills me with such contempt.

"I made the choice to pursue my goals anyway, even though it meant abandoning her. It was agonizing, my love. I loved this woman with everything I had, but even so, it wasn't enough for me to stay." Tears roll down my face, my body beginning to shake. "And her love wasn't enough to come with me, either. I don't know how either of us is going to face the other."

My princess holds my head to her chest, kissing the top of my head. Her fingers gently soothe my ears, stroking the sensitive skin. "My wolf," she whispers. "I understand a bit better now. Let us get some rest, and tomorrow I will be at your side. Neither of you is going to face the other alone."

* * *

It's a perfectly ordinary day.

The sun shines in through my window. Coffee is brewing in the kitchen, filling the air with its pleasant fragrance. Just the smell of it makes me feel more awake. I have nothing to do today except do chores around my flat, which I'll get to when I get to.

It's a perfectly ordinary day.

Then my datapad flashes a name across the screen—a name that I've not seen for three years: Diarmuid Mirren. My heart instantly pounds in my chest, my heckles rising as I stare at the name. What could she want after all this time? What in the world could she possibly have to say after what she did to me?

Against my better judgement, I accept the call as I sit down on my couch. I keep the video off—I can't handle seeing her face. "What do you want, Dia?" I hiss, not even attempting to hide my contempt.

"To talk," she says, calm as ever. "I wouldn't be calling if it wasn't important."

"Are you dying?" I furrow my brows, my tail slapping against the sofa. "That would be a little funny."

She sighs. "I'm not dying, Eva."

The irritation in her voice amuses me; I smirk. "Well, I'm not sure there is anything important enough to be calling me about then."

"I need your help," she says softly. "And I'm on Earth. Will you please think about visiting me at the workshop so we can do this face to face?"

"The last time you asked me for help, I said no, and then you left me," I say, biting back the stream of profanity I want to unleash on her. "What reason would I have to drop what I'm doing to come listen to you, Dia? You burned that bridge."

I hear her sigh and can imagine her pinching the bridge of her nose in frustration. No less than she deserves. A voice I don't recognize asks her a question. I can't make out the muffled conversation, but I hear a brief crackle over the line as someone new connects to the call.

"Hello," says the unfamiliar voice. "My name is Gráinne, and it is my fault that Dia is asking anything of you."

Her voice is smooth as silk, easy to listen to. I really should hang up, but curiosity gets the better of me. "And who are you to Dia?"

"Ah, that is not... I am her fiancée," she says cautiously.

Great. Just great. "You should run," I tell her bitterly. "Dia doesn't care about anyone but Dia and her plans. She's a real bitch."

"Correct," she says, her tone even despite my insult. "Dia is still carrying out those plans. She is fighting for my sake, and for many others. Please, Miss Evangeline, this is not a call made lightly given the history the two of you have. It is a matter of life or death."

I want to scream into the line, but the earnestness of the plea makes it difficult to summon any of my rage. "Gráinne, right?"

"Yes."

"If Dia is fighting on your behalf, that means you're not from Central?" I ask, my tail swaying in annoyance behind me. "How are you involved besides being her fiancée? What do you want?"

"I am the heir of the Fomorian Armory, Miss Evangeline," she says. "And it is my deepest desire to free my people from the tyranny of my father's empire."

I let out a sharp whistle. "No shit, you seduced a princess, Dia?"

"Eva..."

"Correct again," Gráinne interjects. "While a crude way of putting it, yes. I do not need or even want you to forgive Dia for what she has done to you, but I am desperate, Miss Evangeline."

I lift my hand to my chin, tapping my fingers along my jaw as I think. A part of me, a huge part of me, wants to be angry, to mock her or better yet, just end this call. Gráinne's continued sincerity gives me pause. More than that, I admit there is a part of me that doubts my rage. I refused to get involved because I was sure we'd just end up dead. *What could we do against a galaxy? It was too much. Too big.*

Yet here is this girl, this *princess*, asking for my help. It's not an entire galaxy anymore, it's just one person. Dia made progress—she made progress by herself.

Fuck.

"It takes a lot of balls to ring up your fiancée's ex like this," I say. "I like you, Gráinne. I can appreciate the gravity of what you're asking of me." A sigh escapes me. "Dia, I'll come meet with the two of you. I'm not even all that far, so I'll be there in a few hours."

"Thank you, Eva," Dia says. "Really."

"Yeah, yeah."

"It means the world to me, Miss Evangeline," Gráinne says. "We shall see you soon."

I chuckle softly. "You know, you can just call me Eva, Princess."

"Ah," she says. "I will remember that."

"She's cute, Dia," I say before hanging up the line.

I stand up, walking into my kitchen to pour my coffee into a travel container. My chores around the flat are going to have to wait. The sun doesn't seem so bright anymore in the sky. I sigh, taking a sip of my coffee—at least it tastes as good as ever.

It *was* a perfectly ordinary day.

* * *

The air is heavy. My gaze lingers on my wolf, watching her face as she processes a thousand emotions all at once. Just as well, for I have my own thoughts to gather. Eva seemed kind enough in our conversation, though somewhat bitter. I worry for Dia and how the two of them might wound one another further in this awkward dance around their trauma.

I will do whatever I can to ensure her happiness, that much I have decided.

Wordlessly, I lean on her, pressing my body against hers. We have the transport to ourselves as we make our way to the workshop, Layla and Quinn having agreed to take a separate one to give us the space we needed to call Eva. Dia leans back on me, her face displaying a quiet, troubled storm.

"Princess," she says, the word like honey on her voice. "Thank you for stepping in. You got through to her when I couldn't have."

I squeeze her arm, laying a few kisses on her shoulder. "I am glad," I say. "It will be okay, Dia; I will support you both. The two of you will need it."

"Thank you," she says. "Maybe with you between us, we can have a productive conversation for once."

A teasing smile forms on my lips. "I think the two of you are far too alike," I say. "I understand now why you two communicated more with fists and machines rather than your words."

She exhales. "Yeah," she says, shaking her head from side to side. Her ears droop, a frown forming on her face. "We *are* too alike—stubborn beyond fault." Her voice drops low, a note of anguish in her.

I smile softly, pressing my hand to her face. "Hey." I brush my hand down her neck, softly tracing my fingers across her collarbone. "I like that about you. You never back down from anything. Gods, you are so strong it takes my breath away."

Dia simpers, her face softening considerably. "My concern is that I'm dragging you along because of my stubbornness, and you don't deserve to be put in this position if it isn't fully your choice."

"Okay," I say softly, "I am going to say this one *last* time to you, my perfect, pretty wolf. If you care for her, then I care for her as well. I will be there to help you both, and whatever happens between the two of you is what happens. I am fully here, with you, because I want to be. Understand?" I narrow my eyes, glaring at her sharply, but with love.

"Yes, Princess," she says, her cheeks slightly flushed. "I believe you."

"Good," I say, leaning forward to kiss Dia's collarbone gently, my lips lingering on her skin. "Now stop asking me if I am fully committed to all this. I love you."

Dia takes in a sharp breath, squirming under my touch. "I love you, too." She wraps her arms around me tightly, pulling me close.

I lick along her neck before pulling away, leaving her shuddering and red. Now that I know her spots, she is quite easy to tease, a far cry from how she was when we first met. "We just take it one step at a time. Are you feeling better?"

"I am," she says. "You have both distracted me with your kisses and assuaged my concerns with your wisdom. Truly, you are perfect."

"Hmph." I glance away, a flush creeping into my cheeks. "Do not forget it."

* * *

Mother sits across from me, wearing an expression somewhere between concern and unfathomable rage. She runs her fingers through her dark blue hair, her jaw muscles twitching as she restrains herself from screaming. The two of us are alone as she fumes—the others are inspecting the new Bansidhe.

"Cleo is again, several steps ahead of me," she says, her voice exhausted despite her anger. "I thought I had some leads on her, but every time I think I am getting closer, she slips away. I thought she was allies with the Fomorians even, but she clearly has no issues killing them either." She sighs. "Now, I don't know what to think."

"At the very least, we know I am her target," I say. "A minor consolation, but it's something."

She narrows her eyes at me. "Daughter, that offers me no comfort. You underestimate how dangerous she is. Don't jest like that."

"It's not supposed to be comforting, Mother," I say. "It means we have information we didn't have before. You've never known her goals or intentions and now, in part, you do. We can work with that."

"Hmm," she says, turning to look out the window. "Despite my misgivings, that is true."

I lean over the table, giving her a soothing pat on her shoulder. "What about me would make her so obsessed, do you think? That's the part I am struggling to understand."

"Really?" she asks, a hint of a smile on her lips. "I thought that part would be the most obvious."

My brows furrow. "No," I say. "I'm just a pilot."

Mother chuckles then, the tension in her face breaking. "No, my darling, you are my masterpiece—the best." She looks back at me, her eyes soft. "You were so fragile after what happened to your mom, your life hung on by only a thread."

"I didn't think you'd survive long enough to be transferred to the artificial womb, but you were a survivor, even then. The things I did to ensure you'd live birth have shaped you in ways I couldn't have imagined."

"Masterpiece, mother?" I raise a brow. It's never been a secret to me that she altered and enhanced me, but referring to me as such is new. "What did you do?"

She smiles. "I don't mean it poorly—you are a remarkable achievement. In part, because the things I did were as a mother desperately trying to save her child. Though my motives were driven by selfishness and love, it would be true to say I crossed several ethical lines." Mother closes her eyes for a moment, taking several deep breaths. "If you really want to know, I will send you my notes."

"It doesn't matter." I stand up from my chair. "Like you said, you were being my mother. The way you raised me had a much bigger impact on me than whatever you did to save my life."

Another chuckle as she rises. "I'm glad you feel that way. Let's go check on the others. I hope your fiancée is thrilled with the Bansidhe."

My communications implant alerts me to a new call—flagged as urgent, and it's from Brigid. I motion for mother to go on without me, answering the call when I am alone.

"Yo."

"Miss Mirren," she says, her tone haggard. "We need to talk."

"You have my attention," I say. "What's happening?"

"To put it mildly, all hell has broken loose," she says. "The other noble houses were about to make a move against the emperor, but then workers started unionizing across the empire. The emperor has declared martial law and deployed the fleets to suppress the *uprisings*." She spits out the last word. "People are going to die."

"Very convenient," I mutter. "The timing I mean."

"Yes, very," she remarks. "There's more. Fianna was sacked. The empress and I escaped and are on our way to Earth. The princess' handmaiden is with us as well, though injured badly."

"Fuck. Where are you now?"

"We made it through the Slip Gate to Sol. We'll be jumping to NLS soon," she says. "The empress would like to know how Princess Gráinne is."

"She's hale and whole," I tell her. "We were hoping our preparations would be done before something like this happened, but the Bansidhe needed an overhaul. When you arrive, we should talk strategy. In the meantime, there are still arrangements to make."

"Very well," she says. "See you soon, Miss Mirren."

* * *

"You're gawking," Maeve says, a wide grin on her face. "Does that mean you like her?"

"Like her?" I turn to look at her. "Maeve, this is incredible! I hardly recognize her, but I say that in a good way. Does she have a tail?"

"Sure does."

I walk around the rebuilt Bansidhe, admiring what they have done to her. Her colors are the same, brilliant platinum with pink trimming around the frame. The tubes that house the superheated plasma are dormant for now, but when I'm piloting, they will ignite brilliantly. Her arms, now reduced to only two, are symmetrical and her silhouette is much sleeker. Her head is more humanoid, and —

"Cat ears, too? Seriously?" I turn back to look at Maeve, furrowing my brow, my own ears twitching against my will. "A bit on the nose, do you not think so?"

She chuckles at me, Layla and Quinn joining her with small giggles of their own.

Her grin grows all the wider as she says, "When Dia told us what you two got up to, I thought it would be a cute addition. They are only cosmetic, but they will look fantastic when you take her into all-four mode."

"It can transform?" I look back at the Bansidhe, my heart racing with delight. "Tell me more."

"Allow me," Viviana says, joining us. Her conversation with Dia must be over, though there is no sign of my wolf. "I took into consideration that you channel a berserker mode when you pilot for long periods of time. If the need arises, you can alter the Bansidhe's form in such a way that will suit your inclinations."

"The hands will exude plasmaclaws that can be extended to a range of about fifteen meters. The tail is bladed. You can wield it as you desire in both forms—it is sharp enough to cut through anything, I guarantee it."

"The risk," Maeve says, "is that in all-four mode, you have no weapons to use at range besides the claws—fifteen meters close quarters combat still. On the other paw, you'll destroy anything you can touch."

"Mom," Dia says, standing above us on the catwalk. "How long have you been waiting to say that?"

Maeve lets out a deep laugh, rubbing the back of her neck, as my wolf also does when feeling sheepish. "Don't give me shit, young one. As your mom, it's my right to tell awful jokes. My duty, even."

"It was a good joke, Maeve," I tell her. "Pawsomely adorable even." I look up to Dia to see her eyes roll, a faint trace of a smile on her mouth.

"Thank you, Gráinne." Maeve winks at me. "I know it's quite different from what you were piloting before, but she flies, and she fights like you wouldn't believe."

Dia joins the rest of us, stepping next to me. With Dia this close to me, I realize she is troubled. A heavy cloud of anxiety clings to her.

"Before we jump into testing, I have some news for everyone." She pauses, making sure she has all of our attention. "The Fomorians have declared martial law and are sending their fleets to quash nascent unions. Fianna has been attacked—your mother and Brigid are safely on their way here."

My heart feels as if gravity is about to rip it out of my chest. Hearing that my mother is safe is a slight comfort I cling to. "Aoife?" I ask.

"Hurt." She frowns deeply, placing a comforting hand on my shoulder. "We'll know more in three days."

I nod curtly. There is nothing I can do for my oldest friend now but wait. "Gods, martial law," I say. "Unionizing is illegal; the fleets will use deadly force." The thought disgusts me to my core, fills me with rage. "And there is nothing we can do to stop it, is there? There's not enough time."

Dia's grip on my shoulder tightens, her jaw set, her eyes ice cold. "We'll do what we can."

"You will have enough time," Viviana declares. "Come with me." Her expression is stoic, unreadable, and yet I can see fire in her eyes. She hastens through the mechbay into an adjacent building—a massive hangar.

There is a ship in the center of the room, as large as a Fomorian Destroyer—large enough for a thirty-person crew, at least just from looking at the outside.

"She doesn't have a name yet," Viviana says, looking back at me and Dia. "You said three days?"

"Yes, but how does this solve our issue of time?" She folds her arms over her chest. "She'd—no. Mother, don't tell me this is what I think it is."

Viviana smiles. "Yes. She's equipped with a Slip Drive, and I've almost perfected the shields to protect from the radiation. In three days, I'll see that she's ready."

"Do you mean to suggest that this ship can go into Slip Space on its own and the crew can survive?" I ask, my mouth slightly agape with awe. "That is not possible."

"If my wife says it'll work, it'll work," Maeve says, sounding wildly optimistic. "With the Drive Engine she has equipped, she'll go several times faster than light, and in real time—no time dilation. Honestly, we aren't sure how that works, only that it does."

It is common knowledge that Slip Space is deadly to humans, no matter what augmentations they might have. The Gates provide us with the means to go instantaneously from one point to the next. The deadly radiation of that ethereal plane has no time to harm you. This is altogether different—revolutionary.

"We could reach the Gates faster than anyone else," I say, piecing together a plan. "But even if we could intercept a fleet, how are we to fight or evacuate the people?"

"How many mechs can she hold?" Dia asks. "At least four?"

"It has seven docks in its mechbay," Viviana answers, her face troubled. "And it's equipped with a capital-class railcannon—it will pierce shields and hulls without trouble. Once every few minutes anyway, so make the shots count."

Dia steps out ahead of me. "Mother, I know you didn't just start this project," she says, her tone betraying a hint of rage. "Why would you make a ship like this and for who?"

Viviana stiffens, hesitates. Even Maeve and her usual boisterous nature is subdued. I glance between the three of them.

"To prevent what happened at Cerberus," Viviana says, looking away from her daughter and back to the ship. "I still remember seeing the moon sundered, the remains of Charon Station and all those people—dead in an instant. I still don't know what kind of bomb was used to cause that much destruction. All our friends on the Danu, too—so many ghosts who received no justice."

She takes a steady breath before continuing. "Time was our enemy; our closest allies were hours away instead of mere seconds. So, I built this ship—this weapon. And now, when time is your greatest enemy, I want you to take it and fulfill its purpose: to save the lives of those who do not deserve to have them cut short."

"Alright." Dia takes a step back, her face still troubled. "I can do that, but you didn't answer the second question."

"Ah." Viviana frowns. "I was hoping you'd forget; Admiral Tatewaki is the intended captain of this ship, but your need is greater."

Another shade of my wolf's past coming back to haunt her. I can practically taste her discomfort as my own, the intense unease is palpable.

"That may be, but I can't steal a ship right out from under her either," Dia says, releasing a long sigh. "Another person to talk to and the hours are ticking down. Where even *is* Hatsuko?"

Maeve walks over to her daughter—she is slightly shorter than Dia, I now realize, but only just. "I'll talk to her. You focus on the mechs and putting together your crew."

"Right," she says. "Thank you."

* * *

The workshop is the same as it ever was; high walls, and massive in scale. Nostalgia strikes me like a hammer. Many of my younger years were spent here with Dia and her family, listening to Maeve go on and on about mechs, or Viviana come up with some brilliant new idea I never dreamed could exist. I didn't totally lose contact with them when Dia left me. Viviana and Maeve are the only mech designers I trust, but this is the first time I have been back *here* since our schism.

A drone comes over to me as I step inside. I go through the process of stating my name, why I am here, all that bullshit. The drone leads me through to the living area of the building, the old family home. Not much has changed in all these years. The potted plants are bigger than they used to be, but it's the same color on the walls, the same paintings and marble statues.

Voices sound in the distance. I recognize Viviana's lyrical voice instantly, along with Maeve's gruff bluster. Two voices I don't recognize at all. The princess is unmistakable, calm, and calculating but with an earnest passion. Then I hear *her* and my heart stops in my chest, my breath taken right out of me. The urge that I have to run, to summon another transport and go back to my flat, is unbearable.

I want to go back to my perfectly ordinary day.

My feet carry me to the door despite my emotional protests. It slides open, the group of six turn to look at me. My eyes make contact with Dia's. Rage and grief bubble up in my chest, threatening to burst forth. She looks as soft and kind as ever, which only makes me all the more incensed.

Fuck her and her stupid, gentle face.

"Yo," she says, her new ears folding back against her head as she gives me her usual, ridiculous two fingered wave. "I like the tail and the ears."

I hate her.

"Got them about a year ago," I say. "You too, I see."

Her long fluffy tail sways behind her, the motion stiff and agitated. "Can we have the room?" she asks the others.

All but Gráinne go, leaving just the three of us to stand in deafening silence.

"I..." the words get caught in my throat. *What am I supposed to say? Fuck, what am I supposed to say?*

"Do you still take your tea the same way?" Dia asks. "Heavy on the honey, no cream, right?"

"Yeah," I say, my voice choking out the word. "Yeah, I do. Thanks."

The princess looks relieved when Dia goes off to put the kettle on. She's still within earshot of us, but the tension is less. I do my best to offer a warm smile, inspecting her. Her raven hair is long, tumbling down her back. Her violet eyes draw me in, making it easy to stare at her. Between the ears and the O-ring on her choker, she truly looks the part of a cat—adorable, but with claws that I'm sure can rend steel if need be.

"Hello," she says, holding out a hand. "It is a pleasure to meet in person."

I take her hand in mine. It's petty of me, but I give a much firmer handshake than is necessary. She only smiles at me as she returns it, her grip tightening. "Likewise." I take my hand back, flashing her a grin. "You're much cuter in person."

Her cheeks flush slightly, but she holds her gaze to mine. "Thank you. I was not expecting you to look as you do now, just from the pictures I have seen on the back of the model mechs I have of yours."

"You got those? Which?" I lean against the wall, crossing my arms in front of my chest.

"The Seraph, and the Caliburn," she says. "They are back at our flat. I had quite a lot of fun building them."

"That would be why," I say. "The pictures of me on those are old. New me, new mech."

Dia hands me the cup of tea, and another for Gráinne. We both accept, offering thanks. It's strange, looking down into the cup—I never thought she'd make me tea again. Grief and joy are in this black liquid.

"What are you flying now?" She speaks as if we're just old friends catching up.

I can't stand to look her in the eyes; her expression is too gentle. "The Morningstar." Lifting the cup to my lips, I first take in the tea's fragrance—citrus and spice. The warmth offers some comfort to my nerves as I drink.

"Right, look," Dia says, "why don't we talk about why you're here? Unless you want more small talk."

My ears twitch, my nose wrinkles. "No," I say. "I hate small talk. Tell me what you've gotten yourself into."

So, they do just that, alternating between the two of them to relay the events that have unfolded over the past month. Their duel, their engagement, the attack on the way to Earth and on the train. Gráinne spends a significant amount of time sharing her story with me, her desire for freedom from her station, and that Dia was her salvation. Each thing she says makes me furious; I had no idea how people were treated in the Armory. I was ignorant — I chose to be ignorant, to look away.

Dia tells me about her time working alone, the state of the Armory's 'common' people, and how she fought off 'pirates' or had an occasional skirmish with the Fomorian Navy. It's much to catch up on, and I do my best to take in every word. Jealousy mixes with anger, which mixes with shame, leaving me standing there with a pit where my heart should be.

All I can think is that I should have been there with her, that I shouldn't be hearing about these events as an outsider. It becomes clear as they speak that the bond they share with one another is deep and intense. A part of me had wondered how genuine they were. Seeing them like this, the ease of their words with one another, the glances back and forth, and how they both lean towards one another fills me with agony. I wonder how it would have turned out had I joined Dia on her crusade; the thought gnaws at my marrow.

After they finish, I take a moment to consider my words. I suppose I knew my answer all along; I wouldn't be here if I had intended to refuse them. Even if I wanted to, the ship Viviana has created changes everything about this plan. It's no longer just the right thing to do — it can actually be done.

My eyes lock with Gráinne's, and I manage a small smile. "Alright, Princess, I'll show you what a real champion can do." I wink.

Dia rolls her eyes, which very much amuses me to see. "The Phantom is ready to go if you really want to find out that I'm still better than you."

"No need to show off, Wolf," I tell her. "I'm sure she knows how good of a puppy you can be."

Gráinne's cheeks turn slightly pink, her chin raises. "Ladies," she says firmly. "That is quite enough about that."

"Fine," Dia says, a seething look in her eye.

It was a cheap shot, I admit, but it's easier this way, to joke and tease—better to keep myself at a distance.

"Can I ask why?" Gráinne says tenderly. "Why are you deciding to throw your lot in with us?"

"Does it matter?" My brows furrow, my grip tightens on my cup. "I said I would help, and that's really all there is to it."

"It matters to me," she says. "Please, Evangeline."

Her tone and gaze cut through my carefully constructed walls; I don't know how I can refuse to answer such a genuine question. "Because I don't want to make the same mistake again. Looking at you, Princess, hearing your story... listening to you and Dia... how can I refuse?

"It was wrong of me to run away. I'm still pissed that you couldn't somehow convince me. I know that isn't fair or rational, and so right now I just want to make the choice I wish I had made then."

"Okay," Dia says. "For what it's worth, I'm also angry at myself for not being able to convince you. I am sorry, Eva."

"I know," I tell her, feeling the knot in my stomach relax. "It's in the past now. Let's just focus on the future."

"Thank you, Evangeline." Gráinne reaches out, taking my hand in hers. "I believe that together, we can shatter the very stars. It will not just be the people of the Fomorian Armory that we free, but all others. No one is free until the least of us are."

It's my turn to feel heat rise up my neck and into my cheeks. "R-right," I say. "I look forward to fighting alongside you, Princess... and you can just call me Eva."

She grins at me, her eyes staring right through me. "Very well."

I take my hand back, handing Dia the empty cup before turning my back on them. "I'm going to bring the Morningstar here," I tell them. "Your mom can help me get her combat ready in the bit of downtime we have left. I'll be back soon."

"I have a thought, Eva," Gráinne begins. "When you get back, help me test out the new Bansidhe. I have already tested Dia's might, and I am most eager to test yours."

"Careful what you wish for, Princess," I tell her. "I don't take prisoners in a match, not even a friendly one."

"I would have it no other way," she says, flashing me a feral grin.

"Sif can fly in later today, too," Dia says. "Now that I can tell her you're on board."

"Was that her condition?" I arch my brow.

Dia nods. "She was a real shit about it, too."

I let out a cackle. "Hell yeah," I say. "Well, that'll be real fun. I haven't seen that girl since her egg shattered."

Battle of the S-Tiers

Viviana orders us to get into a line. Sif falls in on the far left, Layla and Quinn next to her. Dia stands next to me on one side, Eva on the other. The red-haired woman is shorter than I am, but her bulk and untamed mass of hair makes her appear far larger than she is. The problem, of course, is that being between the two of them fills my mind with thoughts I have no business having while Viviana relays important information. Eva looks over at me, winking at me and flashing a grin. My cheeks flush as I turn away.

Dia notices me, and the way Eva is looking at me and furrows her brow. "Oi," she hisses. "Don't do that to her, Eva."

"She's just fun to tease." Eva chuckles, looking past me at Dia. "Her face is cute when it gets red."

I glare at her. "Is teasing me just a game to you?" I ask. "Because if so, I would rather you not."

"And what if it's not a game, Princess?" She tilts her head, her ears standing upright, and her tail curled up behind her. "What then?"

Irritation bubbles up in my chest, my tail twitching behind me. Eva's laugh becomes louder, her smirk broader. Without a word, I grab her by the hair, pulling her head back slightly and smashing my mouth against hers. She squeaks, yelps even, as I kiss her. She kisses me back, her hands gripping and twisting at my blouse.

Our lips are locked only for a moment before I pull away from her, releasing her hair and leaving her face a ruby shade.

"That is what, Evangeline," I tell her firmly. "Only keep pushing my buttons if you know what you are getting yourself into."

She presses her fingers to her lips. "Damn, Princess," she says, recovering quite quickly. "I'll keep that in mind." Her smirk returns in full force, taunting me.

"Good," I say, looking away from her—she's unbearable to look at for the moment. My gaze instead goes to my fiancée, who is smiling warmly as she looks between Eva and me. "What?" I ask.

"Impressed," she says. "You got her to shut up and blush."

It is my turn to smirk now. I do not look to see what Eva's reaction might be, or anyone else's for that matter; instead, I refocus on what Viviana has to say to us.

"Right, if we're done messing about," she says. "Before any testing of your mechs happens, I need the six of you to swallow these." She walks down the line, handing each of us a capsule.

Sif is the one who looks most distrustful, her brows furrowed deeply. "What is it?"

"Nanomachines," Viviana says. "They will disseminate into your body over the next hour, and when called upon, they function as a flightsuit, or do so automatically if the situation requires it. For those of you with cybernetics they will seamlessly integrate with your systems. You'll all be unaware of them when they are dormant."

My brow quirks up. "This seems a bit excessive, Viviana," I say. "For what purpose?"

She casts her gaze on me, a sly smirk on her face. "Well, some of you have decided to get animal ears and tails, and these are better suited for a vacuum. The truer purpose is that they will protect you *briefly* in Slip Space should the ship's shielding fail—long enough to return to normal space and avoid death, anyway."

I nod curtly, rolling the capsule in my hand before swallowing it. It goes down easily enough, and the expected discomfort doesn't manifest. My fellow pilots are the first to swallow. Layla and Quinn, however, show hesitation.

"What if we want to remove them?" Quinn asks, her tone hesitant and suspicious. "Once the mission is over, I mean."

"I'll teach you how to set up voice commands," Viviana replies. "When you want to remove them, you'll speak the codephrase, and they will pass out of your body over the course of a week. They are as temporary or permanent as you desire."

Quinn's face visibly relaxes. "Oh, that's fine then," she says, swallowing the capsule.

Layla does as well, similarly looking relieved, though a bit more eager. Of the two, I think she's the one who would seek ways to alter her body. For me, this is yet another augmentation to my flesh. I find some measure of comfort that I am yet again doing something that pushes me beyond my limits. For my friends, who have never sought such things, I can understand their hesitation and am glad for them that this is not an irreversible choice.

"Now, for the next step," Maeve says, stepping in front of the line. "You're leaving soon, and in the meantime, it's essential that the six of you are in sync with one another. Layla and Quinn, your role will be vital in the field."

She casts her gaze towards the pair of engineers. "The ship is equipped with a mass-printer, but it takes considerable resources to reprint a mech, so only do that if you have absolutely no choice. It will come down to you two to know each of your pilot's machines intimately—to know exactly what they need for field repairs."

"Understood," Layla says. "We look forward to it."

Maeve grins. "Good," she says. "For you lot." She taps her metallic arm to her chin, her jaw clenched. "You're going to need to learn teamwork. Dia, you're used to being a lone wolf. Gráinne, you've never been in a proper battle. Eva, as much as I love watching you fight in the arena, it's not the same as war. Sif, your sniping abilities are incredible; the best I have ever seen. Your sister would have been proud of you."

Sif looks down at her feet. "I don't know if I would go that far," she says. "I still haven't broken Alexandria's record for longest shot."

"You'll get that chance," Maeve says. "Of the four pilots here, you're the one who needs the most support, so you get first pick."

"Rules of engagement?" Eva asks. "How hard can we go?"

"Hard as you want," Maeve says. "The designs for all your mechs are in the printer, and we have ample resources. I trust you not to kill one another." She smirks then, her eyes scanning over us. "Sif, go ahead and pick your partner."

She grins, rubbing her hands together gleefully. "Well," she says, "I have worked with these two monsters before, so I'd like to see what the princess has got."

I lift my chin, my ears twitching. "Very well then," I say. "A rematch with Dia, and I can finally see what you're capable of, Evangeline. I cannot think of a better outcome."

Maeve claps her hands together. "Wonderful! Oh, and just one more thing. This is a teamwork exercise. It's not about just winning, but also watching out for your partner." She looks over to Dia, then to Eva, her gaze deliberately lingering on the pair. "The first team to lose a member loses the match; you don't get to avenge them on your own."

* * *

Slipping into the cockpit of the Bansidhe is like putting my skin back on, like being wrapped tightly in my lover's embrace. She is home—she is me. I am taken into her, my mind joining with chrome and metal, my flesh abandoned.

I rise, taking the field of battle once more. My eyes are fixed on my wolf; the Phantom Queen is as breathtaking as Dia is—powerful, sleek, and altogether deadly. It's difficult not to be distracted by the obsidian frame's sharp angular face and white-hot eyes. The creeping flush that washes over my skin is all that reminds me that I have a body of flesh, too.

The Morningstar is another stunning frame to behold—crimson and black with magnificent angelic wings. A golden crown floats atop her head. Strength defines her; thick shoulders and powerful arms that could crush the Bansidhe in an instant. She rests a battleaxe of ludicrous size on one of her shoulders, her hand resting on the haft of her weapon.

I can feel Evangeline's smug smirk as her eyes flash green.

Sif, in the Valkyrie, is taking position before the spar officially begins.

Unlike the other frames, the Valkyrie has no set color palette. She can camouflage to match the environment completely, not that there is much for that here. We're on a literal field. Trees are forty meters behind us. Her frame is slighter of build than the rest of us, designed for agility and evading her enemies entirely. Her true strength is the massive anti-material rifle she wields—the Gungnir. If I can protect her well enough, she may be the most dangerous combatant on the field.

"Ready?" Maeve says over the comms.

"Yes," we all say, the tension in our voices thick and palpable.

"You will be out if you lose your head, just remember that," she says. "Three... two... one. Begin!"

Thrusters at my back launch me forward. My best chance for victory is to engage with both of them, preventing them from reaching Sif at all. There is a risk that they could overpower me and take my head—I will just have to trust my partner.

The 'feathers' of the Morningstar's wings detach, turning into swarm-bits that fire at me from all directions. I wave between the deadly light, approaching her with my sword drawn. The Phantom Queen appears in the corner of my eye, a foot smashing into my side. I tumble and roll across the ground, tearing up chunks of earth.

My wolf doesn't hesitate to strike, aiming her lance at my head. A shot from the Valkyrie, perfectly aimed, nearly takes the Phantom's head. The bits form a barrier around her, keeping her safe. It's enough time for me to get to my feet and boost away to put distance between us.

"Don't take them on at once," Sif says to me, "I don't care how good you are. The two of them know one another's movements like the back of their own hands. Doesn't matter if they are exes—once they are in the cockpit, they never lose focus."

"Right."

My sword collides with the Phantom's crimson spear, sending a shockwave reverberating through me. I step to the side, twisting my body to use my tail to slice at her arm. Only at the last moment do I see her yellow spear thrusting towards it. I jump upwards, coiling my tail towards my body to prevent it from being struck. I recall all too well what that fiendish weapon did to me the last time we dueled.

The Morningstar is soaring, her wings creating bursts of wind as she flies across the field. She is heading straight towards the Valkyrie. I pursue from behind—the Morningstar is fast, but I am faster still. We collide in the air, our frames shuddering from the impact. Wrapping my arms around her waist, I spin midair, hurtling her to the ground with a crash that sends chunks of rock and dirt into the air.

"Keep her right there!" Sif says. "I'll line up a shot."

My left hand igniting into plasmaclaws. I rake them across the Morningstar, ripping through her metal flesh. She kicks me away before I can do more serious damage. With claws, blade, and tail, I press my attack relentlessly, not giving her a moment to gather her wits. Still, she parries or dodges my blows with frustrating deftness.

A piercing shot tears through the Morningstar's wing, severing it from her body. "Damn," Sif says. "That'll slow her down, at least."

There's no time to respond. I keep up my assault, bringing my sword down on my enemy. The Phantom is there in front of me once again. Our weapons smash into one another. The swarm of bits surrounds me, beams of light attempt to cut me down. It takes all my focus to avoid the barrage of attacks, everything I have not to get sliced to pieces. She pauses her attack to form a barrier again, deflecting another shot from the Valkyrie.

It's clear that between my two opponents, the Phantom is the one with more control over the swam-bits. Her awareness is uncanny—monstrous even. I am unsure if the Valkyrie's rifle will ever strike true so long as it is just me to occupy the Phantom's attention. She suddenly leaps away, tracking the shot back to my partner; the Morningstar slams into me in the same moment, knocking me off my feet. Their movements are in near perfect synch with one another.

Frustration and rage boil up, my reactor core pumping superheated plasma throughout my body. Without realizing, I am sprinting towards the Morningstar on all fours. I leap into the air, flipping my body forward, using my extended claws like a whip. She creates a barrier with the bits, but

I smash through it, slicing through several of them. It was a sacrifice for her to reposition. Her speed and reflexes are keen, and she moves without hesitation.

I dodge a slash from her axe, spinning around to cleave at her arm with my tail. She catches it and lifts me high into the air, only to smash back down against the ground. Her foot comes crashing down onto my chest, pinning me. She raises her massive battleaxe above her head, meaning to bring it down upon me. In a frenzy, I wiggle just enough to get use of my tail, the bladed tip slicing through the haft of her axe as she swings. The collision between tail and axe pushes her back a step, just enough for me to get free out from under her foot.

Leaping through the air, I catch her with my claws, digging them into her shoulders. She falls back, slamming into the ground—it's now my turn to be on top. I press my advantage without hesitation, my tail aimed like a spear at her head.

"Winner!" Maeve shouts into the comms, "Morningstar and Phantom Queen."

The blade stops just short of slicing through her head. I look over to the Valkyrie and see that the Phantom has claimed her head. Biting back my bitterness is difficult, if only I had a moment more—if only I had protected Sif better.

"Hell of a fight, Princess," Eva says to me. "No one has given me a thrashing like that since your girl over there."

Her praise is genuine, I can tell by the softness of her tone. It does somewhat soothe the pain of defeat. "Thank you," I say. "I have much to learn still."

"We all do," she replies. "Let's go get a drink to unwind from that."

Indeed, as the passion from battle wanes, I can feel that my body is coming down from the high of piloting. It was not as intense as a proper fight would have been, but a drink would not be unwelcome. "Gladly. I would like to get to know you better anyhow."

She chuckles over the line.

"What?" I ask suspiciously.

"I'm just thinking it's funny that you kissed and pinned me down first, you know?" She speaks through a smile, a broad one by the inflection of her voice. "Usually, that happens on a second or third date."

Heat rushes through me; I am thankful that my chrome body obfuscates my reaction. "Ah. Yes," I say, trying to gather my composure. "Is this a subtle way of suggesting we go out on a date, Eva?"

"I'm suggesting we should go on a *second* date."

"Oh," I say, my blush deepening.

* * *

Hot water cascades down my skin. I stand there for a moment, letting the heat relieve the tension and aches from my muscles. Piloting is hard on the body, especially when you have a feral princess who won't relent. If Dia hadn't taken Sif's head when she did, that would have been it for me. It was exhilarating—how long has it been since I was that thrilled in a fight? Not since Dia, not really; even my life in the arena pales in comparison. I had forgotten what a proper grudge match is like.

There is a knock on the bathroom door. My ears swivel towards the sound. "Come in," I say.

The door behind me hisses open. Dia stands there, looking at me with those icy eyes of hers. I never could cope when she glared at me just right.

"Just going to watch?" I ask, turning so that she can get a good view of my back. "I don't mind, but I didn't know you developed a voyeur kink."

To my surprise, she disrobes and steps into the shower with me, her arms wrapping around me. "Shut up," she says, her fangs sinking into my shoulder.

I lean into the embrace and moan. "Okay, fuck." From my toes to my tail, everything feels alive and on fire, my cock hardening in an instant. "Where is this coming from?"

"I missed you, brat," she says. "Fighting with you made me feel like no time passed at all—I remember what we used to do after a fight."

"Yeah," I say, turning around to wrap my arms around her neck. Our bodies press up against one another in blissful comfort. "Fuck, I missed you, too." I put my head on her shoulder, squeezing her tight to me. "I don't know what I want right now, but this is nice. Just stay here with me."

"Alright," she says, her fingers gliding up and down my back. "Eva, for what it's worth, I never got over you. Not for one minute."

Stupid, irrational tears form in my eyes—at least we're in the shower and the evidence will be washed away. "I know," I say. "What does your cat princess have to say about you showering with a lion, hm?"

"Well, she doesn't know I'm showering with you, but she knows I'm here. Given that she kissed you, I'm going to assume she'll be okay with this." Dia pets my hair for a moment more, pressing her lips to my forehead softly. "She says 'yes' to a date, just by the way."

That brings a smile to my face, and more relief to my heart. I cling to Dia, my lips peppering her collar bone with lingering kisses. "Did it make you a little jealous she kissed me?"

"No," she says. "It made me happy; made me think that there's a way forward for all of us. I came here to talk about that."

"Instead, you found me naked in the shower." I grin, looking up at her. "And just couldn't help yourself to a mouthful, eh?"

She squeezes my ass, lifting me up to kiss me. I crumble under the weight of her passion—like I always have, like I always will. My nails dig into her back as I return the kiss. She pushes me back against the wall, pinning me under the stream of hot water. I grin.

"Mmm." My hand slides down her body, in between her legs. "Oh... oh!" I grin wider. "This is new," I say, rubbing her clit.

She gasps, resting an arm above my head as I touch her. "Still getting used to it."

"Would it be cruel of me to make you wait before I let you fuck me?" I ask, smirking up at her as I keep teasing the sensitive nub. I slip a finger inside, gleefully watching her struggle to maintain her poise. "Because, as much as I want to do this, I want to ask your fiancée to be my girlfriend *first*. That feels more proper—she is a princess, after all."

Her hand grips my wrist, lifting it until my fingers are in my mouth. I suck eagerly, cleaning up her arousal, groaning at the taste.

"It wouldn't be cruel," she says. "I think she would like that."

I take a deep breath to calm myself from my aroused high. "Okay," I say. "But more seriously, I just want to sit with this for a while, you know? Post battle-drop isn't the time to make a life-changing decision." I stroke her hair, rubbing her ear between my fingers. "Dinner. Tonight. A date for the three of us. I'll ask her then if I feel it's right for me—for all of us."

Dia brushes her hand over my face. "Perfect," she says through a smile. "Now, turn around—I'm going to wash your hair."

I do as she says. It's hard not to when she uses that gentle and commanding voice on me. The shampoo is fragrant and delightful. Her fingers knead my scalp firmly. I try very hard to hold back a moan, lest I be tempted to change my mind about letting her fuck me. She saturates my hair, ensuring that she cleans every strand.

We go through the motions of tending to one another. I wash and condition her hair, too, running my fingers through her silvery locks. It feels normal, like time has unfrozen and can finally move forward. Finding the recent scars on her body is a stark reminder that time has always been marching onward—for her. I am the one who has been stuck.

Fuck me; I don't want to be stuck anymore.

She kisses me tenderly, cupping my chin in palm as her tongue dances between my lips.

"It scared me to talk with you again," she tells me, her brows furrowed. "Caught up in more anxiety than I'd like to admit. Gráinne helped me through that, and I'm glad she did."

Her expression is pained, her eyes watering at the edges. "I was going to leave the past in the past, to respect your wishes and never speak to you again. Fuck, I am glad that circumstances threw us together again. Really, I am."

All I can do to not burst into tears is bury my face in her chest. It's like it used to be, the way she holds me. She was always my rock when I lost control of my emotions, which is often. I have always been a sensitive creature, prone to irrational outbursts and hysterics. When she was gone, I had to be my own rock—I didn't trust anyone else to hold me like this. That time with myself made me better. It strengthened me. I was just so incredibly lonely, desperate for touch, yet too afraid to seek it out.

She squeezes her arms around my shoulders and back, kissing the top of my head, stroking my hair and ears. I lean into her touch, nearly collapsing in her arms. For once, it's nice to have a little breakdown under scalding hot water while being held.

"Me too," I say, my voice coming on in a choked whisper. "I was fine, I really was. You know, I was doing what I loved—fighting and having a lot of fun. I was fine, but I was never *good*, Dia. You were always the one who made life *good*. I won't lose sight of how important that is again."

Dia lifts my chin, pressing her lips to mine. "If you do, I'll drag you along by force this time. Deal?"

Laughter bursts forth, cutting through the building tension in my chest. "Hmm." I smirk, putting my hand on her face. I stare into her eyes, drinking in the sight of her.

She's so tall.

I stand on my tiptoes, kissing her again and again and again. "Not a deal—a promise."

* * *

My last night on earth and I am on a date with two women. Truly, I am blessed. Impending battle aside, I intended to enjoy tonight. The only thought that dampers my spirits is facing my mother tomorrow. I knew, of course, that she would see me as I am now eventually, but not this soon. Will she accept me? It is a thought that weighs heavily on my mind and one I do my utmost to shove down. If I do not, the anxiety threatens to overwhelm me; my night will *not* be robbed of joy. I remind myself to focus on where I am, and where I am is with my fiancée and—well, I don't know what Eva is to me yet.

Dia has cooked for us a simple meal of garlic roasted potatoes, steak, and a medley of sauteed vegetables. Everything is cooked and seasoned to perfection, the vegetables are appropriately crunchy; the meat falls apart in my mouth and the potatoes excite my taste buds in heretofore unheard-of ways.

It is quite amusing to watch the two of them eat. Dia is so refined it would put even those on the highest rungs of Fomorian society to shame. Every movement is intentional—controlled. Eva, on the other hand, is like a ravenous lion, tearing into her meat with indifferent savagery. I am most certain she would give mother a heart attack should the two of them ever have dinner in the same room.

"What are you smirking at, Princess?" Eva asks, her brow arched.

I chuckle fondly. "You," I say. "Do not mind me. I am lost in my own thoughts this evening."

"Good thoughts?" Dia asks, reaching over to squeeze my hand.

"Yes," I say. "I am thinking of the two of you, and those are very good thoughts."

Eva tilts her head, her ears folding back as a grin spreads across her face. "Maybe now is a good time to talk to you about something."

"Oh?" I quirk a brow. "And what might that be?"

She leans back, spreading her legs and folds her hands behind her head; a bold, feral way of sitting. I can't take my eyes off her and blush involuntarily.

"I want to date the both of you," she says. "Not to put pressure on the situation, but considering the imminent danger we're about to rush off to, I wanted to say something tonight."

My brow furrows. I knew this was coming, as Dia had told me what had happened between the two of them in the shower. It's even an exciting prospect, to be entangled with these two as we carry on with our life. Yet, like with Dia, there is a part of me still that has gnawing doubt, an unsafety that gives me pause.

She is lovely to gaze upon, with sharp features and musculature that begs for my fingers to touch, for my lips to kiss. Her wild, untamed nature is a delight even though, or perhaps because, she enjoys getting under my skin. The thought of a life with these two, to drown in them, makes my pulse race. Yet, I cannot bring myself to take the leap.

"Why, Eva?" I frown, crossing one leg over the other as I lean forward to look her directly in the eyes. "Tell me the reason, or I will have to politely decline." I look at Dia, then back at Eva, smiling warmly. "If the two of you wish to reignite your passions, I will support you both. Why involve me at all?"

Her bravado falters, her sly smirk giving way to a somber expression. "Because you enchant me," she says. "I am here at all because you earnestly asked for help—it sure as shit wasn't for Dia's sake." Eva adjusts herself, leans forward and takes my hands in hers. "I'm asking to be your girlfriend apart from, but also alongside with Dia. I'm greedy, and I want you both for wildly different reasons."

Her touch is welcome. We intertwine our fingers and gaze into each other's eyes. The fluttering of my heart comes back, the unease in my stomach relaxes. I sense no deception from her. Her intensity dispels my doubts. In that, Eva very much has the same effect on me as my wolf—her muscles, too.

I certainly have a type, don't I?

"Okay," I say, breaking through the silence. "My fear is that you see me as a trophy or an addendum to Dia. If you hope to be *with me, for me,* then I accept." I smirk then, taking one hand to place on her face, stroking my thumb across her cheek. "I am also quite greedy."

Eva's face darkens considerably. She leans into my touch. "I want you for you," she says softly. "I'm a simple girl, with simple tastes. All I want is for my partner to be able to kick my ass a little, and um... yeah, you sure did."

"Well, you annoyed me," I say, smirking. "But I like the way you annoy me."

She preens, her face wearing a smug smile. "I look forward to annoying you for a long time."

"You know, Dia said something very similar once," I tell her, chuckling softly as I lift my hand to stroke through her hair. We kiss deeply, our lips pressed against one another with tender passion. Out of the corner of my eye, I see Dia watching us, a smile on her face. I reach over and grab her, pulling her towards us.

She lets out a surprised, but very cute, yelp. Quickly, I find myself alternating between them—my lion, and my wolf—tongues, lips, and hands becoming a tangled mess of desire. A hand touches my breast, I don't know whose, and I moan. My fingers grab at hair and clothes, pulling these two towards me so tightly I fear we might fuse into a singular being of pure ecstasy.

I pull away from them, breathless, my heart pounding in my chest. "Dia, our bed had better be able to fit three."

The bed can very much fit three. In a flurry of crazed activity, the three of us are laid bare, mouths and hands all over one another. My lips latch to Eva's breasts; a hand on her cock, stroking her until she moans my name. Dia's tongue laps at my cunt. Every neuron fires intensely, my body overwhelmed from touching and being touched. Fingers dig deep inside me until my wolf is fist deep in me, my insides squeezing and pulsing until I cum again and again.

Dia mounts my face, grinding her hips as I desperately lick and drink as much of her as I can. Above me, I see Eva's cock buried in my wolf's mouth. Guttural moans fill the room, my lovers saying one another's names. I would join the chorus if not for my mouth being occupied by my dripping fiancée.

Eva is thrown to the bed, Dia mounting her and grinding herself against Eva's swollen cock. She teases as she grinds, frottribing until our lion cums over her stomach and chest. Only then does she take her inside herself, hands on Eva's breasts as she grinds her hips back and forth. I straddle Eva's head, squeezing my thighs around her face. Dia's mouth is on mine as we use our lover's body until we're satisfied. Tongues dance with one another, our hands touching and kneading each other's breasts.

Before long, I'm on my back, Eva deep inside me, her hips driving her cock inside me so hard the bed threatens to break. I see Dia wearing the strap, glowing red lines igniting along the shaft as it connects to her brain. She thrusts herself into Eva, fucking her as she fucks me. We form a rhythmic waltz of sex and ecstasy; I scream and moan into my lion's mouth. This goes on, this simultaneous chain of rutting, until Eva's cum pours inside me, her seed driven deeper and deeper as she rolls her hips.

Spent, exhausted, and well fucked, we collapse into a tangled mess on the bed. I grapple an arm to my chest; a leg covers me. I fall asleep entwined with them, lovingly in the middle. My last thought as I drift into peaceful slumber is that being between the two of them—my lion and my wolf—was far better in reality than anything I could have imagined.

* * *

There are few things better than waking up with the women you love in various positions over and under one another. Gráinne and Eva are still asleep when I'm roused; I watch them fondly until I feel forced to gently wake them. If not for our regenerative capabilities, none of us would be able to move after last night. It's tragic that we can't linger in this mass cuddle as I am wont to do. Too many things to take care of—to prepare for war. Reluctantly, the three of us get up, exchange kisses, and hurry through our morning.

The ship is ready; supplies are being packed, and the mechs are loaded. The morning sky is clear. That's always a good sign on the day one sets out on a journey, or so they say. All that remains is to say goodbyes. Gráinne isn't quite ready to face her mother, who I've been told has arrived with Brigid in toe. Aoife is at a nearby hospital; her condition is critical.

"Dia," she says to me, her tone barely above a whisper. "Will my mother hate me, do you think?"

I wrap my arms around her shoulders, squeezing her tight. "No," I say. "I think becoming a catgirl might take her by surprise to be sure, but no, she won't hate you."

She nods into my chest. I hold her for a moment longer as she steadies herself. When she's ready, she pulls away and marches out of the room, a look of sheer determination on her face. I follow wordlessly behind, supporting her as best I can with my presence.

Almost everyone is in the hangar, doing final preparations on the ship before we set off. Layla and Quinn are missing, most likely inside doing system checks. It's a scramble of activity all around except for my mother and Ceridwen, who are talking on the catwalk overlooking the hangar itself.

At our approach, Ceridwen turns to look at us, her eyes immediately drawn to her daughter. She rushes towards Gráinne and embraces her tightly.

"You look well," she says finally, pulling away to get a good look at her. "You look happy."

Gráinne smiles faintly. "I am," she says. "I am very happy, and most glad that you are hale and whole. Will... will Aoife make it?"

Ceridwen grimaces. "I believe so," she says, "but it will be quite the recovery. She saved our lives—Saoirse too, but..."

"I see," Gráinne says, turning to look at me. "Saoirse was the one who tried to kill you."

My heart goes out to both of them, though I didn't know the woman besides the aforementioned assassination attempt. She really was very good. "I'm sorry," I say. "We'll add her to the list of people who deserve justice."

Gráinne sets her jaw tightly, nodding at me. "Yes." She turns to look back at her mother. "Would that I could, I would wait for Aoife to wake up, but we need to leave as soon as possible—to save as many as we still can."

Ceridwen stiffens her lip and raises her chin. A thousand distressed emotions cross over her eyes, but she keeps control over all of them in a way only an empress could. "Then go with my blessing, and my love. Viviana has been kind enough to let me know what you plan to do." She turns to look at my mother, wearing something of a fond expression. "Promise you will come back, Gráinne."

"We will, but I need something from you." She steps away from her mother, her gaze passing over each of us. "I am going to kill father." Her voice is filled with icy rage, like a blizzard in the mountains. "The heads of the noble houses will have one chance to surrender the entire Fomorian Armory to me—any who live will face severe tribunals."

"Did you know about this?" Mother asks me, her brows furrowed.

"Of course," I tell her, smirking. "I am her champion, after all."

Mother rolls her eyes. "Right, well, I don't expect either of you to reign as empress and consort. So, what happens after?"

"I plan to meet with the union leaders who are already rising against the Armory," Gráinne says. "When it's over, I will dissolve the empire completely and give it to them. Under the condition that whatever rises from the ashes adopts the values of empathy and egalitarianism—no exceptions."

Ceridwen sighs, her face relaxing into a soft expression. "You have never wanted the throne. Now you'll take it only to destroy it. I am proud of you." She takes her daughter's hands in hers, closing her eyes.

When she opens them next, her eyes emit a green hue, data passing between her and her heiress. It takes only a moment, the light fading as her eyes return to their normal hazel. "You are now Empress of the Fomorian Armory, Gráinne MacAirt—all my authority is now with you."

Last goodbyes are said between them as I excuse myself to go help with the preparations. I find Eva speaking with Brigid and Sif near the ship's open cargo ramp. Helper drones are loading even more supplies onto the ship, enough to last a year. It's an over precaution, but it's always better to have more than you need when traveling in space.

"Nice to see you again, Miss Mirren," Brigid says, bowing her head formally. She notes my ears and tail, a small smirk on her lips. "You always struck me as rather wolfish. Are all worlds in Central as eccentric as Earth?"

"Yes," I say. "I encourage you to see as much of Earth as possible. It's early summer in the Northern Hemisphere."

She blinks several times, shaking her head. "Oh, no. I'm coming with you, of course."

"Your choice," I say, furrowing my brow. "I didn't think you would want to throw yourself into danger so soon after the attack on Fianna. Tell me about your skills."

Her lips curl up into an easy-going smile as she brushes her pink braids back over her shoulder. "It *was* my fate to take over House Áine's fleet—moot now that the emperor seized it. I will be your tactician, your overwatch, while you and the other pilots engage directly."

Sif clears her throat. "I need a spotter, too," she says. "You and the others can't really help with that, and there are certain things she'd be able to help me with. Long-range shots that would be impossible otherwise, for example."

Brigid looks over at Sif, her eyes looking the sniper up and down; her gaze lingering overlong. "Marvelous. I look forward to it."

"Welcome to the team," I tell her. "I'm glad that we're firmly on the same side now."

She chuckles, grinning widely as she crosses her arms over her chest. "As am I, Miss Mirren."

"Dia," I say. "No need to be formal anymore."

"Very well." Brigid smirks, her eyes going back to gaze upon Sif.

Eva claps her hands together. "Fuck yes," she says. "I am so ready to kick some ass, but there is one thing that we *have* to do before we set out or everything's fucked."

It feels good to see Eva so enthused about this. I can't help but draw the comparison to the day we tore ourselves apart; the tears, the anger, the bitterness we both felt. "What do we have to do?" I ask, smirking at her.

"You gotta name her, Dia," she says, pointing with her thumb over her shoulder at the ship. "It's her maiden voyage and so she needs a name! It's bad luck otherwise. You wouldn't want us to die because of a stupid engine malfunction or something, would you?"

It's also good to see that she's back to her old self, the way she was with me before. It's almost like our breakup didn't happen—almost. "I know that, brat," I say, rolling my eyes. "There's a name I have in mind for her. I just want everyone here. Her name isn't my choice alone."

Without a word, Eva dashes off to gather everyone with all the grace and speed of an actual lion. It only takes her a few moments to bring everyone around me. Their eyes are on me, mine on them. What started off as a crusade I was fully prepared to go alone has now grown beyond my wildest expectations.

"Hi," I say, somewhat awkwardly. I'm not used to *this* many people bearing down on me. I much prefer to act unseen or unheard. "Suppose I should give something of a speech, shouldn't I?"

"For good luck!" Eva flashes me a shit-eating grin—she's enjoying my discomfort.

Gráinne smiles softly at me, her head slightly tilted to the side. "I would hear what my champion has to say, yes," she says, exchanging a glance with Eva.

They are *both* enjoying my discomfort—*fuck me.*

"When I look at all of you, I think that we've already achieved the impossible. The Fomorian Armory is on the cusp of cannibalizing itself. The most advanced ship in human history is ready to carry us to victory. All we have to do is finish the job." I look up at the ship, at our ship. "The name I had in mind for her is the Banféinní."

"That's a perfect name," Gráinne says. "I second it."

"Me three," Layla adds. "A pretty, powerful name for an incredible ship."

The others offer their agreement, sounding off one by one. Despite what our mission entails, the mood is upbeat and optimistic. I look outside; the skies are still clear. The sun hangs high in the sky, blanketing the surface with gentle warmth.

It's a good day to set out on a journey.

Slip Space

There is a special kind of fear a parent gets when worrying about their child. It eats at your mind, stripping away rational thought. That my daughter is perhaps the best pilot in the galaxy, that a capable crew surrounds her, and that she has two women who love her does nothing to assuage that fear. I have always struggled with this anxiety over her, since before she was even born.

I vividly recall the panic in my chest the day I woke up in the hospital after Cerberus. At first, I didn't know where I was, my mind disoriented from my injuries. Through the haze of pain, though, I remember being terrified for my daughter. She very nearly died, too. Losing two of my limbs had put such strain on my body that I nearly miscarried. The doctors had no hope she'd survive the week.

Viviana, of course, did not agree. We could have tried again, we knew that. Looking back on that time, we felt so strongly about saving Dia because we lost everyone else. All our friends, our colleagues, the people we considered family died on the first Danu. Everyone. We couldn't let Cleo take Dia, too.

V ended up inventing at least two new techniques and performed the earliest transfer to an artificial womb in history. As far as I'm aware, it's still the earliest that procedure has ever been done. That she was successful is a testament to my wife's skill and her love. It was nothing short of miraculous.

My Diarmuid—my proper miracle.

Watching my daughter as she boards a ship, off to battle, off to change the face of the galaxy as we know it—or die trying—is painful in a way that is difficult to articulate. All I can see is the day she was born; how delicate she felt in my arms. I can only see the first day of school; her eyes red from crying, her voice hoarse from begging me not to leave her alone. Now I am the one who is on the verge of weeping, the one who wants to plead with her to stay and live a peaceful life.

"It's going to be okay," my wife says, her arms coiling around my waist. "Worry not, my love."

The hug pulls me from my thoughts. I wipe away the tears gathering in the corner of my eyes. "Yeah," I say, hugging her close to me. "Just having a moment. I'm usually the one who tells you not to stress about her."

Viviana chuckles. "I think we will stress about her for the rest of our life." She leans on me, watching as the ship's engines burst into life. "We do what we've always done: support her however we can."

"I don't know how either of you do it," Ceridwen speaks up. "Even now, I selfishly want to put a stop to this. I know I can't." She clutches her hand to her chest, twisting the fabric of her dress. "I know I shouldn't. She deserves to walk her own path; I have spent too much of her life trying to shield her."

"That's how we do it," I tell her. "And sometimes, there is a little drinking involved."

The Banféinní lifts off the ground, its engines creating pulsing gusts of wind as it takes to the skies. I watch it for as long as I can, my heart sinking into my stomach as the ship disappears. My wife touches my cheek tenderly, reassuring me once more.

"Come, you two," she says to us. "Let us be cliché and lament over wine. Do you favor white or red, Ceridwen?"

The former empress smiles wryly, glancing between the two of us. "Wet rosé is my wine of choice."

Viviana smirks, her fingers interlacing with mine. "A woman after my own heart. I have an excellent vintage I've been too busy to break into. Shall we?"

* * *

To be among the stars is to feel at home. My time resting on Earth was good—

necessary. I recharged and recovered in ways I didn't think I needed. Now, looking out through the optical viewscreens, I see only an ocean of stars out in front of me. If not for the mission that lies in front of us, I would feel totally at ease. I take a moment to just bask at the sight, pushing away my troubles for just a few seconds.

"Prepare to engage the Slip Drive," I say. "I suggest everyone has a seat. We'll be at the Gate in just under an hour."

Eva whistles sharply. "Damn, this girl really can fly."

Despite myself, I smile as I angle the Banféinní. Piloting a ship isn't completely unlike piloting a mech, but the massive size makes maneuvering feel sluggish by comparison.

I make sure my crew is all seated and strapped in. Eva, cheekily, is not. She flashes me a bratty grin as I glare at her. She snaps herself in, winking at me. None of us really knows what it will be like when I activate the Slip Drive—the nervous energy in the air is palpable.

"Right, here we go," I say as I activate the system.

Entering Slip Space is not something done with fanfare or a burst of speed. One moment we are not there, and the next we are. It's an eerie, alien place. A place of purples and greens that dance before our eyes. Static radiation rages everywhere and nowhere at the same time. Nothing resembling material reality is here. My brain fills in the gaps to form vaguely recognizable shapes—clouds, specifically.

Being here is decidedly uncomfortable. Even through the ship's shielding and the nanomachines in my system, I feel a chill running through my bones. More than that, I think I'd go mad if I stare out into the celestial shroud too long.

This is not a place for mortals to tread.

"I can see why humans cannot survive here," Gráinne says softly. "Would you mind changing the viewscreen to something more pleasant?"

I do so, turning off the external optics and instead have the ship's computer track our location in real space, displaying the Sol system as we travel through this extra-dimensional ocean. It's a benefit of having a ship with no windows—mother doesn't believe in them for structural integrity reasons.

"Thank you," the princess says, relaxing somewhat, though her eyes reveal her anxiousness. "I suppose now is as good a time as any to finalize our strategy."

Brigid clears her throat, our attention drawn to her. "There are three major fleets being sent to quell nascent uprisings," she says. "They will crush the unions brutally and swiftly, hoping it makes the others fall in line. It's worked for them in the past. If, however, we can stop the largest of the fleets, I may be able to convince House Áine loyalists to mutiny."

Eva cackles. "You make it sound so easy," she says. "One ship against the largest fleet. How do you suppose we do that?"

"The railcannon can destroy a capital ship easily enough," Brigid says., shrugging her shoulders. "If you're comfortable killing a few thousand in an instant, give or take."

Gráinne stiffens, her fist clenched so tightly that her knuckles turn white. "I would like to give them all a chance to surrender," she says. "I know they will not. No sane admiral would surrender to just one ship, not even one that carries their empress, but I want to announce to my father that I am coming for him."

"That's smart." I cross my arms over my chest, my brow furrowing. "Not that I like the idea of playing nice with soldiers who are more than willing to kill their own. We broadcast it across the Armory; we'll show the people you won't tolerate your father abusing and killing them."

"That could spark a widespread revolution," Brigid says, "if the people knew their empress stood beside them." She turns to look at Gráinne, a sly smile forming. "You may even convince not just those from my house to join, but others, too. For better or worse, we're a people who respect strength above all else."

"Why don't we just go right to the capital and kill the emperor?" Sif asks. "I mean, it would be a lot easier than playing political games, and it's not like they can stop us with their fleets spread so thin."

Eva nods in agreement, looking as if she is about to speak.

"Don't abandon the people!" Layla shouts, her eyes wide with near panic. "Please, whatever we decide, do not let the people fend for themselves. Our families..."

Gráinne lifts her chin. "I swear to you both that we will not," she says firmly, settling the matter. "We can and should do both." She turns to stare at Sif and Eva, her intense gaze threatening to set them aflame. "It will take us precious hours to battle through the capital's defenses to get to my father. That is time for fleets to turn whole worlds into glass."

"Right," Sif says, her face contorting into a deep frown. "Sniper brain, sorry."

"With our speed, it won't matter if we 'play political games' first," Gráinne says, her tone like a blade. "We're going to stop that fleet, and I'm going to convince the union leaders they need to prepare for leading the people into a new, better future."

* * *

Magh Meall is on fire, ships raining hell from the safety of orbit. It's a vile, disgusting act, even by the standards of the Armory. Father must truly be desperate to keep control if he is resorting to such cowardly methods. My blood boils. I look forward to tearing out his throat, though he doesn't have nearly enough blood to pay for his atrocities.

"I've changed my mind," I say, white knuckling my fist, nails cutting into my skin. "Destroy the flagship. Don't bother opening communications."

Sif gets into position, her skills as a sniper are as good for aiming a railcannon as the Gungnir. The ship rattles as the superheated projectile launches into space. It strikes the cuttlefish monstrosity, tearing through energy barrier and hull alike. Sif hit something particularly volatile, causing a chain reaction of explosions along the remaining fragments of the ship. A brilliant shot.

The bombardment stops, our presence announced. It will take several precious moments to prepare another shot, but they don't know that.

"This is Empress Gráinne," I say, opening all frequency communications, broadcasting this not only to the surrounding ships but to the Armory itself. This is a declaration of war. "Surrender immediately, and I will spare your lives."

"Em-empress?" The captain speaks with a shaken and uncertain voice. He stammers, "Why did..."

"Because I am taking my father's throne and you are killing my people," I say firmly. "Don't ask me stupid questions. A new dawn for the Armory is here, Captain. Be a part of it or die now. You have ten minutes to decide."

I close communications, sitting back down and finally taking a proper breath. It's a gamble to bluff like this. Could we win in an open conflict? Perhaps we could, but it would be a bloody and long fight. At least Sif can get off another shot before we sortie.

"Well, you certainly sounded the part of an empress," Dia says.

"It is how I was raised, after all." I manage a weak smile, my heart pounding in my chest. "I hope this works. We need to get aid to the surface."

The minutes drag, time seems to stand still. Dia seems as calm as ever, her eyes fixed on the enemy fleet. I can see she's already planning how to win should it come to a proper fight. Eva likewise looks quite calm, relaxing back into her chair as if nothing is wrong. Layla and Quinn are the ones who look most worried, of course, but even so they keep their cool.

"Empress Gráinne," the captain says over the comms a touch earlier than I had demanded. "I spoke with the emperor just now. We have been ordered to destroy you."

"Are you going to listen to a living ghost?" I ask coldly. "Because you can die along with him, I will not hesitate to destroy your entire fleet."

"No," he says, taking a deep breath. "He's gone completely mad. You said there was a new dawn approaching. What is your command, Empress?"

I drum my fingers along my knee, gathering my thoughts. Even now, my actions will set the stage for what is coming. I do not want to make the transition more difficult than it needs to be by being bullheaded. "Atonement," I say. "My orders are for you and this fleet to provide aid to the people you just slaughtered. They can decide what to do with you when they are finished burying their dead."

"Yes, Empress," he says, the comms going dead again.

I look at Brigid. "Thoughts?"

"I think you did exceptionally well," she says, idly stroking her fingers along her pink braids. "It's almost a shame you have no plans to keep the throne."

There is an urge to smile that I fight down. It doesn't feel appropriate under the circumstances. "Let's head to the surface and take stock of the situation."

The descent to the surface is somber. None of us speak, unable to tear our eyes away from the scorched surface. The city is in ruins—the loss of life is devastating. Unfathomable rage courses through my chest. It's difficult not to scream until my voice is raw.

Dia reaches the survivors over the comms and spreads the news that the bombardment is over. They do not trust us at first, especially in light of the fact that the fleet that just bombed them is coming to offer aid. After a few moments, we settle on a place to meet.

Angry survivors greet us on the outskirts of the city, drawing their weapons as we step out of the Banféinní.

"Empress Gráinne." An older woman with short black hair approaches me, her face haggard and sunken in. "Forgive the mistrust, but I'd really like to know what your intentions are."

"Freedom for all of us," I tell her stiffly. "For what it is worth, I would ask that you not call me Empress. It is not a title I intend to keep overlong."

"Just Gráinne then. Call me Laoise." She grimaces, extending her hand out for me to grasp.

I do so, giving her a firm shake. "Laoise, we have a lot of work to do."

* * *

We sit in the ruins of an underground bunker; the walls cracked and crumbling. Above us, relief efforts are underway. Tensions are high, but no one is eager for further bloodshed. Gráinne's face is expressionless, like she used to be in the weeks when we first met. Sebille, the union leader of Magh Meall, is across from us. Her face is stoney, and there is rage in her eyes. She brushes her brown hair back, tucking it behind her ear as she takes a deep sigh.

"I admit," she says, "that the last person I expected to stop the bombardment would be you. I know you and your father have never gotten along, but to think you'd move against him so openly... it belies belief."

Gráinne purses her lips. "I needed more courage." She folds her hands in her lap, sitting upright, making herself look more regal—a habit for when she's uncomfortable. "The courage you have showed, the kind that will be needed in the days ahead."

Sebille crosses her arms in front of her chest, her brows knit tightly together. "Over the broadcast, you said there was a new dawn coming. What did you mean by that?"

"The empire is going be dismantled and turned over to the people," she says. "I have been to Central, to Earth, and have seen how people live—how they work together for the benefit of all. I would like that for us, too."

The grizzled woman relaxes somewhat, her weariness showing. "And how do you intend to go about that, Gráinne? Killing your father and even the nobles won't be enough, though it's a start."

I put my hand on Gráinne's shoulder, silently telling her I'd like to speak. She nods and motions for me to do so. "This is my Champion, Lady Diarmuid."

"Yo." I stand, looking round the room. Besides Sebille and Laoise, there are a few soldiers on duty. The rest of my crew, too. "I have an offer: when the dust settles, when the emperor and the ones who empower him are dead, Central will provide whatever you need and leave as soon as you ask."

That causes a murmur of discontent. Laoise looks behind her, silencing the soldiers with a glare. "We will not bow to you either."

"Wouldn't dream of asking," I say. "But you're going to need help to fend off remnants of the empire, and vultures from the other system-states. You don't have to take the offer, but I think it's wisdom to take it."

I pause, turning my gaze towards Sebille. "The most dangerous time after winning your freedom is keeping it. Many of the people who helped found Central in the aftermath of the Secession War are alive and well. I implore you to lean on their experience."

"That's a fair point," Sebille says softly.

"You can't..."

Sebille lifts her hand, Laoise goes quiet, her face betraying her outrage. "I studied what I could of the Secession War, tried to model it even, but I didn't think the emperor would destroy his empire so recklessly."

"We'll make him pay for what he's done and end everything he's built," I say. "In the end, taking Central's aid or not is entirely up to you all, but we're going to destroy the Armory either way."

Sebille laughs then, a rowdy and hoarse laugh. "Gods, kid, you sound insane. You know, I never wanted to overthrow the emperor. I didn't think we could, but I thought we could make things better and we were ready to fight for it." She smiles viciously. "We got nothing to lose anymore, so let's kill the bastard."

"We will," Gráinne says firmly. "From here we are going to directly to Fomoria. Brigid of House Áine is coordinating with her people to mutiny against the fleets to spare other worlds your fate."

Brigid stands, bowing her head slightly. "My people are very loyal to me," she says, "and are already securing ships as we speak. With the Banféinní's speed, we can capitalize on the in-fighting."

"We will cut through the forces protecting my father and the nobles," Gráinne says. "We will rip out the beating heart of the empire."

"Good," Sebille says. "The two of us are coming with you. I want to watch you live up to your word or die alongside you."

Laoise lifts a brow, letting out a huff. "Well, at least now you're talking some sense. I don't trust them. Lieutenant Elatha!"

A young soldier snaps a salute, then approaches. She looks younger than I am, certainly younger than the students at Fianna. Her golden hair tied back into a neat ponytail. "Ma'am," she says.

"You're in charge while we're away." Laoise's face remains stoic, difficult to read, but she speaks with a voice filled with trust. "Keep the boys in line and coordinate the relief. Understood?"

"Yes, Ma'am," Elatha replies. "Good hunting."

*　*　*

For as long as I live, I will never forget walking among the rubble and the death of Magh Meall. It is one thing to hear and know of other's pain, but another to see it—to see the depths of human cruelty. I will never forget how Dia only flinched at the sight, a burning but quiet hatred in her eyes. She always was the warrior, the soldier, the mercenary.

I was only ever a fool.

The Banféinní rumbles as we exit the planet's atmosphere. I'm pulled from my thoughts, my gaze refocusing on the two women I care about most. Gráinne catches my glance, her face softening as she walks over to me. I'm pulled into a tight embrace; her lips press gently to my neck.

"You okay, Eva?" Dia asks, embracing both Gráinne and me.

What do I say? What can I say? "I don't know what I feel." I lean into my lovers, as if to absorb them into me. "Or rather, I'm feeling too many things, and I can't pin anything down." I take a deep breath. "Shame. Stupidity. Horrified."

I shut my eyes as they squeeze me, kiss me, and hold me. When I've put myself together, I look up, kiss them both and step out of their embrace. "I'm okay," I tell them. "I'm not used to death and horror like that, and I'm hit with the guilt again for not having joined this fight sooner. Feels impossible to get those thoughts out of my head."

"You are in it now," Gráinne says, putting her hand on my cheek. "That matters more to me, to Layla and Quinn, to the people you're helping. Stop dwelling in the past, Eva."

"Right."

Dia ruffles my hair, kisses my forehead, and then goes off to take the ship into Slip Space. It's only now that I realize we've made quite the spectacle for the others. My cheeks darken.

"I hadn't realized it was romantic," Sebille says, fixing her eyes on Gráinne. "It makes a lot more sense now that Diarmuid would fight so hard for you—why you'd all fight so hard for one another. Are all of you involved?"

"She literally shattered my bonds, yes," Gráinne replies, linking her arm with mine. "And no, just the three of us. You do not sound too terribly shocked or outraged."

Laoise huffs. "There are a lot of us lesbians out and about," she says, shaking her head. "Just because we're illegal don't mean we don't exist."

"Honestly, I can't imagine what that kind of life must be like," I say. "Where I'm from, we hack our biology freely and love whomever we choose. We protect that fiercely, too."

"We didn't just become that way by accident, to be fair," Dia says as the ship once again goes into that otherworldly plane of existence. "It started with liberating the weakest among us, the queer, the destitute, and the outcasts. That's what triggered the Secession War in the first place."

Sebille frowns. "How did you get that far even?" she asks, her exhaustion seeping into her voice. "Because I'm at a loss. Mostly all people care about is labor rights, which was already hard enough to rally people around."

"Violence." I shrug. "There came a point where all the theory in the world was doing no good. It didn't matter how well anyone broke down the problems or isolated root causes. It was all an appeal to power in the end, and it never worked."

Dia leans on the console, her arms crossed over her chest. "A small group of lesbians, who called themselves the Vipers of Eden, formed a resistance and support network when no one else would. They picked targets, from powerful people to vital infrastructure, and destroyed them without hesitation."

Everyone is looking at her now, a common occurrence when she starts in with one of her passionate speeches—she's just so good at them. She flushes slightly as she realizes we're all staring.

"Small, but impactful acts of resistance galvanized the apathetic and the nihilists," she continues. "The foundations of the system cascaded out of control until war broke out." Dia gathers her thoughts, her eyes flitting between everyone in the room. "I think that the secret was that they didn't ask permission to make changes—they just did. When the dust settled, we had a new society, a better one."

"We were never taught that part," Gráinne says. "The entire war was obfuscated—the motives and circumstances. They sound remarkable. It is almost unbelievable that it started off with such a small group."

Dia grins wide. "I never thought about it quite like this, but it dawns on me now that we're carrying that legacy. It's the same fight, just a different battleground."

The mood on the ship shifts, the somber tension dissipating. "You're right," I say, "and we're going to win. Whatever it takes, we're going to win."

"You damn right." Laoise walks over to Gráinne, looks at her, then me and finally at Dia. "I misjudged the whole lot of you and came because I didn't trust you—especially you." Her gaze fixed on Gráinne. "You're really going to just give it all up when you kill your father?"

The princess nods. "I swear on my love of these two that I will," she says, glancing at Dia and me. "Liberation is what I desire, not power."

"Then I'm with you until the end," Laoise says.

"I'm glad my instincts were right." Sebille steps next to Laoise, kissing her on the cheek. "Let's get some rest, love. We haven't in a while and gods know we need it."

Laoise leans into the touch, nodding. "Of course. We'll see you all soon... thanks for putting up with the hostility."

"Eh, don't worry about it," I tell her. "They put up with me, and I'm way worse."

"It's true," Dia says, shaking her head. "I think everyone getting rest is a good idea. Tomorrow, we change the galaxy."

* * *

The hours we have left are too few, and so I revel in the flesh of my lovers. The pair of them graciously indulged my request to lie in our bed, completely in the nude. We three agreed it was best not to fuck one another so soon before the battle, as tempting as it might be—we need rest. Gods, I want them. To take one or perhaps inside me, to have my body wrapped around theirs.

I squirm on the bed despite myself, doing my best to shove the thoughts down. Dia's face on my breast, and Eva with her leg over my hips is, of course, not helping in the slightest. Almost worse than the physical contact is their scent, fragrant vanilla mixed with spices and subtle sweetness. Lucky for me, the two of them are already asleep, leaving me to my incessant imaginings.

I am going to live. I will make sure they live, too. We will go home together.

I repeat the thought again, and again, and again like a determined mantra. Eva snores softly, rubbing at her face in her sleep. Dia looks so peaceful, her face so much softer now compared to when she's awake. My wolf and my lion. They are precious to me. They are my joy.

We will live.

All too soon, the alarm goes off, signaling the end to the rest. There's very little time to dwell on anything when we wake up. We pushed our nap to the last possible moment and are paying for it by having to rush into our mechs.

I miss their skin.

"We're dropping out of Slip Space behind enemy lines," Dia says. "Mechs are launching immediately. Laoise and Sebille will go down in the dropship once we've secured the palace courtyard."

My flesh gives way to chrome and wires as my mind is pulled away from my body. The impact of reentering reality is harsh. The ship shakes violently as the atmosphere of Fomoria clashes with the hull of the Banféinní. With metal clamps snapping to our feet, the four of us are positioned into the launch tubes.

"XF01-Phantom Queen, Diarmuid Mirren, launching."

"S3X9-Morning Star, Evangeline Lilith, launching."

"OX77-Valkyrie, Sif Sigyn, launching."

"L50X-Bansidhe, Gráinne MacAirt, launching."

The skies of my homeworld smash into me, my chrome flesh becoming superheated as I descend to the surface. Fomorian ships are too slow to realize we've already gotten behind them. Their shots go wide. It's nearly impossible to accurately hit such small targets moving at these speeds. The only threat we're likely to face in the air is mechs scrambled from the surface that will attempt to intercept us.

Indeed, a group of mechs approaches, my alerts buzzing with each new enemy. Dia and Eva are quick to respond, their swarm-bits cutting down our enemies as they approach. We do not stop to fight them, instead we rush through them with brutal efficiency. The blade at the end of my tail is particularly effective at sweeping through the small aerial horde. Getting stuck in the air means death, and so we keep pushing forward even at risk of leaving our back exposed.

The Amory mechs struggle to keep up with us. Within moments, we outpace them entirely, leaving them in our wake. The palace, the place of my birth, comes into view—I urge to dismantle it piece by piece. My boosters work double to slow me down, my feet crashing onto the surface, cracking the ground under my feet.

It's a flurry of fire the moment we land. Royal guard mechs greeting us with a barrage of attacks. I once admired these machines. Grouped together, their uniform color, purple and black, and identical design is quite striking. Today, they only fill me with rage, my years of captivity coming to the surface.

To say we caught them off-guard isn't quite accurate, but they are still slow to respond, having had hardly any time at all to prepare for our arrival. Sif takes the head of a mech with her rifle instantly, the mech falling to its knees. Dia slices through it, moving towards her next target without stopping.

Eva joins me back-to-back, our enemies beginning to surround us. "Sif, find a place to perch and cover us," she says.

"Way ahead of you."

I dash forward, my blade clashing against a guard's shield. It takes little effort to overwhelm them with a flurry of strikes. Before long, I stab the beam saber into the cockpit. I kick them off, moving onto my next opponent. This is not like the duels at school, not at all. This is a battlefield of survival and to survive, I must deal out death with brutal and efficient grace.

I strike at another guard. They parry and repost. I spin, avoiding their thrust, my tail slicing through their core. The mech explodes as it falls to the ground. Two more appear before me. Sif shoots one down almost as soon as it moves, the other I crush myself, slamming my body into theirs. I throw them to the ground, shoving my foot through metal and flesh.

An alert goes off. A mech somehow manages to sneak behind me. It's unlike the others—a custom designed white and green machine with a wicked face. Our blades catch one another in the air.

"Not letting you go any further, *Princess.*" The voice is familiar: Bres.

Dia appears suddenly, her foot smashing into Bres' mech, sending him hurtling into the wall. "I got this one," she says.

"If you're so inclined, love," I tell her, dashing away to support Eva.

"You!" Bres yells. "Oh, I've waited for this. I'm going to take pleas—"

I turn back to see my wolf reducing Bres' mech to slag with the full fury of her swarm-bits, seeming to take delight in reducing him to parts. To see one of my tormentors slain with such swift and elegant violence by a woman I love fills me with joy.

I smirk.

"Well," Dia says, "I told him that if ever had the displeasure of hearing his stupid fucking voice again, I'd kill him. I am a woman of my word."

Eva is taking on three enemies by herself, holding two of them off with her wings, smashing into another with her massive axe. I enter the fray, ramming into one and knocking them over. Eva follows my movements, taking advantage of our enemy writhing on the ground. Her axe seers through the chrome flesh. Sif takes down the third with another perfect shot from her Gungnir.

We support one another as we fight, our bonds synching our movements together. It doesn't take us much longer to secure the courtyard. The royal guard mechs lie in ruins, their pilots dead or fleeing. The path inside is now open to us. Laoise and Sebille join us not too long after. We load the mechs onto the drop ship; they have now served their purpose in getting us this far. The ship's AI flies back to the Banféinní.

From here, we take the palace on foot. There is still a veritable army in our way. My father will have gathered all his men to him in a last-ditch effort to save himself. It matters not. I know every secret pathway in the palace, and we will weather any trap he might set.

He cannot escape me; I will take off his head with my bare hands.

Promises

The opulent courtyard lies in ruins. Fire engulfs the manicured rosebushes along the walkways. Walls and pillars crumble and collapse. Remains of mechs litter the ground, smoke bellowing out from their reactors.

Laoise's grip tightens around her gun as she scans over the destruction. "This doesn't bring back our dead," she says, "but fuck does it feel good to avenge them."

Sebille steps next to her, the two taking a moment for themselves amidst the carnage. Eva watches them closely, seeming to handle this destruction much better than Magh Meall's.

"We will do more than that," Gráinne says. "Father will be in his bunker by now, an army between us and him. He will have either collapsed most of the emergency tunnels that lead directly to his haven or filled them with soldiers."

"What do you suggest?" I turn to look at her. "It's all narrow, cramped halls to me anyhow, so I'm not exactly picky."

"There is a tunnel system he's not aware of," she says. "I used to hide there as a child. It should be the clearest path."

Eva furrows her brows. "How do you feel, Princess? About what we're going to do?"

Gráinne turns to look at Eva, the softness in her eyes a stark contrast to the death that surrounds us. "It has been a long time coming. That man sired me, nothing more. I may feel differently once the deed is done, but we are not there yet." She brushes her hand along Eva's face. "Thank you—for checking on me."

"Always."

They share a quick, warm kiss before Gráinne's eyes harden, steeling herself for the battle ahead. She motions for us to follow, dashing ahead. I take the middle of the pack, along with Laoise and Sebille. Sif is behind me, and Eva takes the rearguard. It's a solid formation, taking advantage of our individual strengths. The halls are eerily clear of soldiers.

Gráinne motions for us to halt as we reach an intersecting path. She signals me to her side. Around the corner, a group of soldiers lies wait in ambush, hiding behind barricades.

"It's going to be a slog if they've reinforced the central parts of the palace," I say. "Where's the hidden passage?"

"Still some ways away," Gráinne says. "I imagine that from here, we will find many such entrenched soldiers."

I furrow my brows. "Okay, I'll take out this group and push forward alone. You lead the others to the passage. Hopefully, my distraction clears the way."

"Alone?" Gráinne shakes her head. "No, I will not allow it."

"Don't worry about me, Princess." I wink. "I always destroy my enemies."

She purses her lips. "You had better come back to me, stubborn wolf."

I spare a moment to kiss her before rushing out around the corner. Gunfire fills my ears immediately. The nanomachines are adaptive little things, reinforcing my body in microseconds on impact. Bullets clang against me with almost no pain.

They realize too late that they aren't stopping me, and by the time they do, I am already carving through arteries. One of them takes a swing at me with the butt of their gun, only for it to shatter against my reinforced skull. Geysers of blood flow as one soldier after another is rent open.

I take less than a minute to clear out this group. Blood and viscera not my own coats me, the bodies of my prey strewn about. I wipe my knife clean, stowing it in its sheath. The others are gone by now, leaving me alone to hunt down my next targets.

From here the palace is swarming with pockets of guards, some patrolling, others forming barricaded footholds. I take out the patrols quickly enough, usually just a pair or a trio of soldiers at a time. The next large group, however, I take my time with. I give them an opportunity to call for reinforcements. My gambit works. Dozens upon dozens of soldiers flock to me.

It's only a matter of time to kill this many. Their weapons are useless against me, and I do not get tired. My cybernetic heart, lungs and synthetically reinforced muscles fuel my one-woman war on the emperor's palace army. A flicker of violet light flashes in the corner of my eye. I instinctively block with my arms as the powerful beam slams into me. I'm thrown back through a wall, stone and mortar crumbling around me. My flesh sizzles in pain.

"Gods below, did that kill her?" one soldier asks, panting.

"I'm shocked it didn't vaporize her completely. This gun can take a limb off a mech," says a familiar voice.

It's a voice I only heard a few times—at Fianna. Renault. Pushing through the pain, I get up from the rubble, dusting myself off. The nanomachines and my healing factor kick in to soothe my burnt flesh. Renault fires again, the massive gun barrel spinning to life. I dash to the left, the beam of light missing by mere centimeters.

The man is a giant, at least five meters tall and covered head-to-toe in powerarmor—a small mech. My knife will be useless against that, and so will any weapon I can pick up from the ground.

Fuck.

I leap into the air, dodging another blast from that gun—at the very least, it is slow to fire. I twist as I fall, slamming my foot down on his shoulder. Metal crunches under the weight of my kick, but he shrugs me off, slamming the gun into my ribs. The pain is dull, the nanomachines instantly reinforcing the area—which doesn't help with physics. I am launched into a pillar, my back smashing against marble as I go through it.

There isn't much pain, but I'm not going to win this fight like this. The massive gun spins up again, launching that deadly violet beam right at me. My first instinct is to dodge. I'm fast enough, but I brace myself instead, holding my arms out in front of me to block the shot. Searing pain courses through me at impact, but only briefly—something happens. Rather than the beam dissipating as it should across my body, the nanomachines seem to absorb the raw energy. I feel my muscles grow stronger. The exoskin surrounding me thickens, taking on a form rather like the Phantom Queen.

Renault fires twice more. Each time, my body absorbs the energy, transforming further. On the third shot, I move, not wanting to test the limit to the punishment I can take. The exoskin has become like metallic latex flowing down the contours of my body. Key parts of me—my arms, legs and chest are encased in thick armor. Even the HUD that flashes across my eyes is identical to my cockpit. The nanomachines must have somehow copied the software.

"What the fuck are you?" he asks, his voice raspy and tinged with fear.

"Don't know," I say, flexing my fist. "I'll have to figure that out once I'm done killing you."

I create a shockwave as I kick off the ground, slamming into Renault in an instant. He's knocked back, keeping his balance, but only barely. Even with his face obscured, I can sense his fear. The barrel of his gun spins up again. I pounce, grabbing the gun and tearing it apart with brute strength as it fires. The resulting explosion hurtles us both through the air. I catch myself easily enough, dashing back into combat.

He takes a swing at me, his massive arm like a club. I catch it in the air, twisting my body to throw him to the ground. He cracks the floor, leaving a small crater. I leap on top of him, pummeling him with my fists. His armor gives way to my fists, peeling away bit by bit. As if sensing my needs, the machines coursing through my body produce a lance—Gáe Dearg. I thrust the crimson tip down into Renault's head, twisting it as I feel it impact his skull.

He dies instantly; the powerarmor going limp underneath me. The remaining soldiers flee in terror. I don't give chase, as tempting as it is. Better for them to encourage the others to surrender. If not, well, at the very least, they may bring more reinforcements to me so that I can continue being a distraction.

The nanomachines return to their original state, my lance deconstructing down to its base parts. I'm now in a simple form fitting flightsuit. It's a gift to be able to manifest the Phantom Queen's weapons and that armored exoskin. I wonder if mother intended the little machines to be so useful or if this is simply the unintended side-effects of me being so heavily augmented to begin with. A question I'll only have time to ask later.

By now, I hope that the others have reached the passage at least. I open an encrypted comm line to them. There is a brief pause before Eva answers.

"Are you hurt?" she asks.

"No, I just finished up," I tell her. "Are you all in the passage yet?"

"We are," she says. "The bunker isn't too far from us. Sending location."

There's a ping in my ear and numbers display over my retina. "Right. I'm on my way. Before I forget: the nanomachines can become a remarkable exoskin suit. It was like being in a mech."

"Well shit," she says. "I'll pass that along to others. How did you figure that out?"

"Fought a man in powerarmor and one thing led to another. No idea how it works, only that it happened." I trod off away from the bodies littering the ground, heading towards Eva and the others. "I'm on my way. See you soon."

"You better."

* * *

Dia's distraction has paid off. The way to the hidden passage is mostly clear. We've run into a couple of patrols, but the five of us have been able to take them out quickly and quietly. Sif, in particular, is shining. Her sniper training is invaluable in keeping our presence quiet. The princess is proving a capable team leader, guiding us safely along the labyrinth of hallways in the palace. Laoise and Sebille look out for one another when we skirmish, proving quite capable.

Then there is me, and I am not coping well. I feel naked out of the Morningstar, weak and helpless—afraid. I am used to all eyes being on me and putting on a show of violence for the sake of entertainment. Somewhere along the way, I become nothing but a performer.

"We are close," Gráinne says, pulling me from my thoughts. "Two more turns, then into my room. Mother had the passage made in secret in case of invasion. I only ever used it to hide away."

"You're sure she never told your father?" I ask.

Gráinne smiles softly. "We had our secrets," she says. "For the many faults my mother has, she still resisted my father in her own small ways. This was one of them. Now it is our quickest path to victory."

We reach Gráinne's room without incident, the automatic doors sliding open as we approach. Once inside, she locks the room up tight. It won't stop a determined battalion, but it will buy us some time. Her room boasts opulent decorations of gold, silver, and marble. To say the room is extravagant would be an understatement.

"My poor plants," Gráinne says wistfully, walking over to the far corner of the room. She kneels, brushing her fingers along long dead flowers. "Father must have forbidden anyone from taking care of them when I left for Earth."

"How can you tell?" Sif asks.

"By the dust," Gráinne says, pointing out the specks on the dead plants. "The room is immaculate; the dust has gathered only here." She sighs as she rises. "One more thing, in a long list of things, that he has destroyed. My garden at the academy, too."

"I'm sorry, Princess," I say gently, placing my hand on her shoulder. "He's got a lot to pay for."

"Quite," she says, taking in a deep breath. "It is just as well that no one tended to them. The passage is here." She places her hand on the wall. A scanner activates, running a laser over her palm. There is a click, and a false wall opens to reveal the hidden hallway. "This will take us to the bunker."

I am about to speak when, unfortunately, a fist slams into my face. My back smashes into a wall. I cough up blood, my vision blurry. Six people, all equipped in powerarmor, step out of portals... I don't know how that's possible but I'm not going to question what is right in front of my eyes. The others open fire, but their weapons are entirely ineffectual against the six's armor.

One of them grabs Gráinne, their hand nearly as large as she is. She screams as she's tossed into an open portal. I try to leap in after her, but it snaps shut right in front of me.

"Target beta secured," one of them says. "Kill the others before target alpha arrives."

Fuck. Fuck. Fuck. Do they mean Dia? Fuck.

"Down the passage! All of you." I leap up onto one of the soldiers, smashing my fists into their head until my knuckles are bloody and raw. I make a few dents but nothing noticeable before being tossed off, slammed into the ground by my tail. If my bones could shatter, they would. I cough up more blood—I don't even want to think about all the internal bleeding.

The others run into the passageway, one of the hulking soldiers moving to stop them. I get up, smash myself into them and otherwise make myself a chaotic nuisance to distract them while the others escape. I don't know how much time I can buy them, but I am going to give them as much as I can.

My fists and feet smash into armor, my knife useless even when I try to slip it between joints. There's no weak point to target, and far too many soldiers compared to me. If not for my augmentations, I'd long be dead by now. How the hell did Dia kill even one of these guys?

I wish she was here. None of this would be happening if she were here. Am I going to die?

One of them takes a swipe at me, using their gun as a cudgel. I duck under it, scurrying away to get some distance now that I have their attention. Super-heated plasma shots fly past my head, melting the wall behind me.

Inside the Morningstar, I'm powerful. I'm not this weakling who can't stand on her own two feet. All I can do is stay alive, dodging desperately, hoping that Dia gets here in time to save my ass.

Fuck.

They took my girlfriend while I just sat there, stunned. Now, I'm hoping my other girlfriend saves me? So much for being among the best.

I'm pathetic.

One of the six boosts towards me, moving faster than I can react. I get another face full of steel across my jaw. They kick me to the ground, stomping on my chest with their massive boot. I cough up more blood as I'm crushed. They chuckle at my helplessness, grinding their heel into my ribs. My bones creak under the strain.

I can be broken after all—maybe I've always been broken.

Dia can't save me, neither can the princess or the others. It's just me. Just me getting ground down into pulp. I'm so sick of being a useless punching bag. From the very start of this, I've been so out of my depth. Only now do I realize the real reason I didn't join Dia to begin with—I was afraid I would just hold her back. It wasn't death that scared me; it was being worthless.

I will not die, not like this.

I dig my fingers into the boot, desperately trying to shove this asshole off me. They stick their gun in my face, the barrel spinning to life. Fury and fear take hold of me as I push back against my impending death. Strength I shouldn't have courses through me, the soldier gets shoved back half a step. It's enough.

I roll out from under their boot just as they fire; the beam melts the floor. There's not a single part of me that isn't in pain and bruised, but I'm alive. I'm alive and I am pissed. The soldier shoots again. I rush towards them, slipping the beam by a hair's breadth before smashing into them. They get shoved back again, that same otherworldly strength still running through me.

I press my attack, punching them hard enough that my fist craters their chest.

"Stop wasting time and kill her!"

"I will not die here, you fucks," I say, smashing my fist into my hand. "You're all dead. You just don't know it yet."

My vision goes black for a split second before the all too familiar HUD of the Morningstar appears. I don't know how it happened, and I don't care, but the exoskin has finally decided to work. The soldier aims their gun at me, shooting off a round. I leap into the air, an axe forming in my hand as I come crashing down. The heavy blade slices through the armor, cleaving through the pilot's head. They crumple, falling to the floor with a thump.

"Shit."

The six, now five, surround me, cutting off my movements. They are exactly where I want them. I can fight; I can win. My axe, a perfect replica of the Morningstar's, will cut every one of these assholes down—I have a princess to save.

I slash through violet plasma, my axe blade becoming cherry red. It slices through the arm of the soldier like butter, splitting limb from body. They barely have time to scream before I twist in the air and bring my axe down through their skull. Four to go.

Deadly feathers dance around me as I dash about. I don't even think about it, I just control them the way I do the swarm-bits, sending them off to cut my enemies down. Unlike my knife, the feathers find purchase in the joints of the armor, spilling blood as they slice through the pilots inside. Between feather and axe, I kill the remaining soldiers, leaving six bodies scattered about.

I am alive; I won.

"Damn, Eva," Dia says, stepping through the hole in the wall. "That was a hell of a fight."

"Hey," I say weakly. "How long were you watching?"

Her tail flicks behind her, her ears swiveling in search of sounds. "Long enough to worry that I made a mistake. I'm glad you're okay. You're not allowed to die on me."

I smirk. "Not planning on it. Thanks for letting me handle that on my own—I needed that."

"I know," she says softly. "The others went down the passage?" She scans the room, her brows furrowed.

"Except the princess," I tell her, casting my gaze down to the floor. "They came in through portals. Don't ask me how that works, and threw her in one. I have no idea where she is."

"Fuck," she spits. Her eyes close briefly. When she opens them, they glow bright white. "She's still in the palace. I'm getting a weak ping, but no signal is reaching her." She blinks, her eyes going back to normal.

I stand up, the exoskin fading away, along with the axe disappearing into my body. "You were the other target."

"It's fucking Cleopatra—again."

* * *

I hang from the ceiling, shackles bite into my wrists. A wicked woman smiles up at me, obsidian hair flowing behind her like void made liquid. Cruel red eyes bore into me; I'm dressed but feel utterly naked before her gaze. Even without introductions, I know to whom I am in front of.

"You," I spit.

"Me," she says, running her tongue along her lips. "You are exquisite; it's a shame my men failed to capture the pretty wolf."

I smirk, unable to help it, because of course my wolf would ruin her plans. "You are obsessed."

"True," she says, running her hand along my face, cupping my chin firmly. "I know perfection when I see it. Unfortunately, perfection is notoriously hard to tame. We have little time to speak before she and the others burst in to save you."

Her touch is not like that of lovers. She repulses me. I struggle against the shackles to move away. "You are unwise to think I need saving, Cleopatra."

"We'll see." She removes her hand, grinning widely. She'd be stunning if not for the malice in her smile. "I couldn't help myself, you know, I just had to meet you finally. I have been watching—waiting—for longer than you can imagine. It's difficult to articulate my joy when you all found one another on your own. I'm particularly impressed with the Lion's growth—that was unexpected."

I test the shackles subtly; I won't be able to slip them but, with enough force, I can rip out the anchor above me. "What do you want?"

She turns her back to me, the lights of the bunker coming on in full. My father is lying on a surgical bed, unconscious but alive. "Everything, Princess. I want everything."

She takes out a long syringe, squeezes out some of its contents, and then jabs it into my father's neck roughly. He wakes up, howling in pain, his eyes going wide with fear.

"I'm so close, too," she says, her voice dropping low. "So close to taking what I want." She giggles, a disconcerting sound from someone who is colder than death. "Play with this toy for a while; I no longer have use for it."

Father writhes, his flesh bursting as his bones twist. He breaks free from his restraints, his body growing rapidly into a hulking mass of flesh and protruding cybernetics.

"What a pathetic creature you are, Cormac," she says, stepping out of his way. "At least you will have some purpose in death." She snaps her fingers, tearing a hole in reality. She turns back to look at me, her red eyes glowing. "Do survive, won't you? The three of you make my existence interesting." She chuckles as she steps through the portal. It closes behind her, as if it was never there.

Before my eyes, my father grows several meters in height, arms and legs swelling to brutish proportions. I came to accept that he lost his humanity a long time ago—not in body, but in heart. It's fitting that the thing in front of me can hardly be called human. There is some justice that this is his fate, the man who stole the humanity of so many others reduced to this in the end.

I yank down hard on my restraints; the anchor gives way. I am shackled still, but the long chains will prove useful. Father thrashes about, mindlessly destroying the bunker. He recognizes that I'm here finally, his mouth opening to unleash a horrible screech.

"Good to see you, too," I say, circling around him.

He rushes towards me, clawed hands outstretched. I whip him with the chains, smashing them across his face. The metal cuts through his eye. He clutches his hand to the wound, snarling even as it heals shut. I whip the chains towards him again, wrapping it around his leg. He lunges for me again. I roll out of the way, pulling the slack out of the chain.

He trips, the crash rattling the entire bunker. I am launched into the air; the shackles snapping off my wrists. Nanomachines course through me, transforming my body into a living weapon—an elegant mixture of platinum and flesh opposed to my father—a colossal mass of blood and iron.

I come crashing down on him, my hands now adamantine claws that rip and tear, my tail a keen blade. He swipes at me with a clumsy fist. I leap away, twisting myself around and slicing through his arm, severing it at the elbow. Blood pours from the stump, soaking into the floor.

The door to the bunker bursts open. Dia and Eva jump through, shining and gleaming even in the dim light. My wolf has her twin lances, my lion her massive axe. The explosion distracts the beast that is my father. The three of us act without hesitation, digging claw, axe, and spear into him relentlessly. His regeneration knits his wounds back together, but not quickly enough. We overwhelm him with our combined might, removing limbs and puncturing organs.

In the end, he dies the same as everyone else—with a gurgle and a whimper.

"Here lies Cormac MacAirt," I say coldly, "the immortal emperor." I turn my back on his corpse. "Long may he rot."

The fight now over, my body returns to normal, the exoskin seems to almost dissolve into me. There is a part of me that thought I might feel relief, or even regret, at the sight of him dead, but I feel... nothing. He is just another dead man.

Laoise and Sebille enter the broken bunker. When they lay eyes on my father, his dead and broken form, they embrace one another and kiss. That brings me joy, too. The shadow that man cast was long and dark—the galaxy is a brighter place for his absence. Father's blood is fertilizer for a new, vibrant future.

Even vile soil can produce beautiful flowers.

"I'm going to the throne room." I stride out of the bunker, my thoughts filled with what I might say.

The others follow behind, silently, as we head towards the final dissolution of the Fomorian Armory. The throne room is as I remember it, gaudy and tasteless. There are some royal guards here, tending to the wounded or gathering the dead. They look surprised when we emerge from my father's sanctuary, but they do not attack.

I ignore them, heading for the throne itself. Never have I dreamed of sitting where my father sat, looking out at people as if I am better than them. Dia watches from below, giving me a single nod of encouragement.

"Open a broadcast to all the Armory."

A nearby guard obeys without question. I pause, allowing a moment for those across the stars to tune in. It's custom that when the emperor addresses the people in this way, that all stop what they are doing.

"Citizens of the Fomorian Armory," I say, forcing my voice to stay steady. "This is my first and last address to you all as empress." I take a breath, gathering my words, keenly aware that what I say now will shape the days ahead. "This throne represents your pain, the cruelty of your rulers, and has caused much of your suffering. I promise you a new age, one of freedom and equity. The empire is dead."

The guards look at one another hesitantly but otherwise do not act. I motion for Sebille and Laoise to join me. They walk up slowly, standing at my flanks.

"I give the floor to these two women," I say. "Some of you know who they are as leaders of the labor unions that fought for your rights."

Another breath, nervousness rising in my chest. "It is with great honor and pleasure I give the empire back to you, its people. The days ahead will be difficult. There will be those who try to sow discord and fill the vacuum left by this throne. That will not be tolerated." I bow to the camera, to my people across the stars. "I am empress no more."

My lovers embrace me as I return to them. Weariness takes hold. I lean on Dia's shoulder to keep myself upright.

"You did well, Princess," she says, running her fingers through my hair.

Eva nuzzles into my neck, her arms wrapping around my waist. "It's over."

Stress flows out of me like a river, exhaustion seeps into my bones. I wish I could sleep here and now, but there is still too much to be done. "I love you both."

We stand there for a time, Sif taking a protective posture as we steal a moment for ourselves. I do not even hear Sebille and Laoise's address to the people, though it seems their words do a great deal of putting even the guards at ease.

For now, at least, there is calm.

* * *

The staff and soldiers abandoned the palace in the wake of our assault. Those who survived gathered and buried the dead. We have won the day and are now on our way home. Eva and Gráinne sleep peacefully in our bed aboard the Banféinní. The princess passed out almost as soon as her head hit the pillows and Eva was soon to follow.

Cats.

It is nice to be alone with my thoughts, to process what has just been done. The powers of the galaxy have realigned. What comes next is beyond my ability to calculate. What I do know, however, is that my crusade is far from over. M.E.T.A Corp, Blackstar Industries, and Titan Technologies all still stand, their people still suffer under the yoke of oppression. Still, in the end, they are merely corporate empires among the stars. Time, patience, and skill will see them all destroyed.

Cleopatra is who I fear the most.

A ping sounds in my ears, Hatsuko's name flashes across my eyes. I cringe internally as I say, "Yo."

"Hello, Diarmuid," she says, her tone painfully neutral. "I'm glad you're alive."

I get up, moving across the room to put some distance between myself and my sleeping lovers. "Well, I'm very difficult to kill."

"Smart ass," she says. "I saw the news, heard about what you've done."

"And?" I ask, preparing myself to get chewed out.

Hatsuko sighs, as she is wont to do when I annoy her. "I had a whole lecture planned, about how irresponsible you are and about the ramifications of this... but I know you are already stressing about them. Yelling at you would only make *me* feel better." She pauses, the silence deafening. "What I will say instead: I owe you a drink and an apology."

"You don't," I tell her. "In fact, this is weird... yell at me like I thought you were going to."

She chuckles now, the sound frightening me considerably—she never laughs. "You proved me wrong, kid. You left me with a shitshow to manage and organize, to be sure, but you still proved me wrong. Come back to Earth soon."

"We are," I tell her. "I'm getting married, you know."

"I've heard."

It's my turn to sigh now, which I do liberally to let her know she's getting on my nerves. "Yes, you are invited."

"Ah," she says. "Was I ever not?"

"That's not what I meant, Hatsuko." I sigh again. "Besides, it's not as if I could stop an admiral from doing what she'd like anyhow."

"That's true." She chuckles again—I can hear the pleasure she is taking in my irritation. "One last thing, before I let you go. You can keep the ship. You're going to need it for... whatever the fuck you plan to do next. Stay safe, Commander."

"Am I being called to duty?" I furrow my brows. "I don't recall coming off leave."

"No," she says firmly. "You are being supported."

I chew on my lip for a moment, thinking of how to respond. "No strings, Hatsuko. I will just fucking nuke this ship if it comes with strings."

"No strings, I promise."

"So do I," I tell her. "See you at the wedding." I cut off the call.

My lovers, precious creatures they are, have not stirred from their sleep. I strip out of my clothes, haphazardly tossing them to the floor before getting into bed, entangling myself with the pair of sleeping beauties. Tomorrow, I will worry about how to take on the rest of the galaxy and the evilest woman I know. For now, anyway, there are no battles to fight. Right now, there are just two women whom I would do anything for in my bed.

"Hey," Gráinne whispers, snuggling into me.

"Hi, Princess."

She nuzzles her face into mine, tracing her hand over my neck. "Thank you, Dia," she says.

"What for?" I stroke my fingers through her raven hair, kissing the top of her head.

"Keeping your promise—the one you made in my garden."

Epilogue

Birdsong gently wakes me; the warmth of a lover nearly puts me back to sleep. Gráinne's arms are wrapped around me in her sleep, her tail coiled around my leg. I shift slightly to face her, pressing my lips to the top of her head. As with every morning, the stuffed animals are scattered along the floor around the bed, kicked or tossed off in our sleep. It's become something of a ritual to place them back on the bed once we're all fully awake.

Sunlight streams in through pale blue curtains, softly illuminating the room. The model mechs Dia collects line the dresser at the other end of the room. The mini-Seraph and Caliburn stand out in front of the others—makes me feel special to see where she has them placed. In a few months it'll be her birthday, I make a mental note to get her the Morningstar as a gift. It'll be fun to build it with her and the princess.

The smell of cooking food wafts into the room; Dia woke up early as usual. It's been a week since we got back to Earth and every day, she's brought us breakfast in bed. Gráinne rouses, the noises from the kitchen making her ears perk up and swivel towards the sound. She hums in delight, snuggling closer to me.

Life is good.

"Morning." I stroke my fingers through her hair, peppering her face with soft kisses. "What do you think she's got for us today?"

"No idea," she says, "but it will be delicious. Think we have time before she finishes?"

"Not likely." I chuckle as she sinks her teeth into my neck. "I don't mind waiting."

"Mm, but I do," she says, straddling my hips and rubbing herself against my hardening length. "She will keep the food warm for us."

I can't help but groan as she rocks her hips back and forth, her hands massaging my breasts. "Or just join in."

"Well, I would not complain." She licks along my jaw, her body sliding along mine. "Though, I also like it when it is just the two of us."

"Do you?" I say, feeling quite stupid the moment the words leave my mouth.

She stops moving, lifts herself off my chest, and just stares at me. "Yes," she says, her brow furrowing. "I love *you*, Eva, not just the three of us. Have you been worried?"

I nod, fighting back the tear forming in my eye. "Sometimes," I admit. "But I don't want to sound jealous."

"I am sorry." She kisses me tenderly. "Rather give voice to those kinds of concerns. You will not come across as jealous."

"Okay," I say, my heart pounding in my chest. "I get into my head about our relationship—with Dia, we have a history, but it's different between you and me. I'm afraid that you two took pity on me, and that I'm just an addon—a useless third wheel."

Gráinne kisses my collarbone as I talk, holding herself tight to my chest. "You are not," she says softly, "you are my precious, lovely lion."

I take a deep breath, focusing on her tender touch and not the swirling anxiety. "Thank you."

She gets off me to sit up on the bed, her violet eyes peering down at me. "I realize that I have not asked this of you, and that I maybe even took your answer for granted—will you marry me, Eva?"

"Um." I blink several times. My words get stuck, and my mouth goes dry. "I think my brain is broken."

Gráinne chuckles, getting up off the bed to open the curtains. She stands in all her naked glory, the morning light making her skin shimmer. She peeks back at me; her tail rising and curling at the tip as if to say hello. My mouth somehow gets even dryer as I stare at her.

She smirks over her shoulder. "I am a greedy woman, I know. My entire life spent rejecting love because it had to come from men—marriage was another cage. Yet now I have the two of you and want both of you as my wives, to be your wife, for you to be one another's wives. That, to me, would be perfection. That would be *living*."

I slide off the bed, walking over to her and wrap my arms around her waist from behind. We stand in the light that now pours into the room. The cityscape extends out further than the eye can see, the people below us are tiny specks of activity. Flowering vines grow along the buildings, splashing color across the horizon. Here we stand, the princess in my arms. I stand on the tips of my toes to reach her face, planting a kiss on her cheek.

"You really want all that?" I ask, whispering the words.

Her hands find mine, our fingers intertwining. She relaxes into the touch, leaning against me. "Yes," she says, "more than anything."

My heartbeat slows, my anxieties washed away. "I think you get to be greedy," I tell her. "You aren't the only greedy woman in this relationship, anyway. It's a quality we all share."

"Without a doubt, I am the greediest of all." Dia stands in the doorway, wearing nothing but her underwear. She smiles at us, the corners of her eyes crease. It's a soft look, a loving look. "Sorry that you felt left out, Eva."

We turn to look at our wolf; her hair is down, combed over to the side in a long silvery cascade. Her tattoos are on full display like this, sprawling out like vines across her chest and shoulders—it's hard to look at her without my knees going weak. "How much did you hear?" I ask.

Her ears flick, her smirk fading into a gentle simper. "All of it," she says, "and I want you to hear it from me: you were never an addon, Eva."

"Right," I say, chuckling softly. "Thanks—both of you."

Gráinne smiles, pressing her head to mine before kissing me. "Dia, darling. Would you mind keeping the food warm for us?"

"Yeah, of course," she says. "You two have fun."

* * *

Marriage—a linguistically meaningful term, now excised from its horrific history of treating women as property. It's an informal promise, made and ended on the whims of lovers. The princess, however, still wants to have a party—to dance without masks.

It takes several days to organize the event and even longer for people to arrive off-world to join in the festivities. Between the three of us, we have many people who want to trek across the stars to come see us in fancy clothes and say we love one another in flowery speeches. It makes Gráinne happy, and there is nothing I wouldn't do to put a smile on her face. Eva is, likewise, thrilled to party. To my great shock, she is going to wear a dress; I can't remember the last time she wore a dress.

I finish getting ready, taking a long look at myself in the mirror to make sure I'm done up the way I want to be. My tux is perfectly tailored and tight on my figure. It's black, with silver embroidery along the collar and down the front. I don't bother doing anything unusual with my hair; my typical style is how I like it best.

Mom is waiting for me outside the changing room, and like me, is wearing a tux though hers is a little loser, giving her an imposing silhouette. She grins at me. "Daughter of mine, you look sharp. If those girls weren't already nuts about you, they would be after seeing you in this."

"Thanks." I return the grin, flashing my fangs. "That's the idea."

Her expression sobers as she embraces me, squeezing me tightly. "Feels like yesterday you were building your first mech kits with me and your mother. You grew up so fast, kid."

"Mom," I say, returning the tight hug. "It's just a wedding."

"I know," she says, pulling away. "Indulge my sappy sentimentality. You just make me real proud to be your mom."

"You're going to make me cry," I tell her. "Thanks for always being here for me, especially when I'm being stubborn."

She grins again, placing her hand on my shoulder and giving it a squeeze. "Always."

Mother steps out of another room into the hall. She walks towards us, her heels clacking against the stone. A new reptilian tail hangs down from her back. Chitinous silver-blue horns protrude from her head, the sharp points are covered by sapphire jeweled caps with chains that connect to a tiara laced through her hair. Her dress, a deep blue that matches her hair, completes the ensemble. If I didn't know she was my mother, I would think she was a draconic queen from some distant planet.

"My darling," she says softly. "You look beautiful."

"I think you're the beautiful one," I tell her. "The new look really suits you."

She chuckles, preening toward mom who then goes red in the face. "Thank you, dear," she says. "I'm sure she has said this already, but I also want you to know I'm proud of you, Dia."

"Why are you two making such a big deal out of a wedding?" I ask, fighting the urge to chew on my inner cheek. "I think of all the things I've done, getting married is the least impressive."

Mother smirks, lifting her hand to pat me on the cheek. "Honey, toppling an empire is one thing, but making a relationship work longer than six months is the true mark of maturity."

"I…" Words fail me as I become redder in the face than I ever have before in my life.

The pair of them snicker at me. Mother can barely hold back her giggles. I rub the back of my neck sheepishly, unsure of what to say.

"Alright, I maybe deserved that one." I sigh, shaking my head.

Mom grins. "Just a little."

Mother embraces me tight. "That's for lying to me when you said you wouldn't fall in love with Gráinne in three weeks while already being in love with her."

"Yeah," I say, smirking. "I did do that."

"We love you," they say.

"I love you both," I say, taking a deep breath to calm my nerves. "I'm ready."

The three of us share one last hug before they link arms with one another and head into the main room where the many, many guests are waiting. I stand in front of the door as it closes, waiting for the signal. Gráinne wants pageantry, and there is nothing I wouldn't do for her. A minute passes. Then two minutes. At the third minute, our song plays. It's a merry, upbeat tune from a holofilm the three of us enjoy.

I step out of the door and into the grand hall. My wives come out at the same time; both take my breath away. Gráinne's gown is black and violet. There's a slit up one side, showing off her well-muscled thigh. The bodice is deep cut and studded with amethysts across the bust. Her long black hair is up in a loose bun, curled locks dangling down her face. Her empire may be gone, but she still looks every inch a princess.

Eva's dark emerald dress lacks embellishment, the fabric drapes off her, fitting snuggly to her powerful body. For once, she's tamed her crimson hair and tied it back into a tail, fully revealing her face to the world. Her eyes are bright, her smile broad. I cannot recall the last time she looked so filled with joy.

We walk towards one another, Gráinne taking her spot in the middle, her arms linked with mine and Eva's as we parade down the carpeted walkway. No one officiates the wedding; the practice died out centuries ago—no one gives us away either. We walk together as equals, lovers bonded in the fires of battle, towards the next chapter of our lives.

Everyone that I know and care about is here; it's a struggle not to cry. I'm just a pilot, a warrior on a crusade—yet so many came to be here. It beggars belief. Ceridwen sits next to my mothers, leaning on my mom who sits in the middle.

They seem quite close.

Layla gives us a small wave. Quinn flashes a wide grin. Brigid is sitting in Sif's lap, both looking quite pleased with themselves as they focus their attention on us. Hatsuko catches my eye, her lips twisting in a shit-eating smirk.

I love and hate that woman so much.

The three of us form a circle at the end of the walk, each holding the other's hands.

"I've never really been any good at this," Eva says, her gaze fixed on Gráinne and me. "Big fancy speeches and promises, I mean. It was just an ordinary day when you two came storming into my life. I didn't even want to pick up the call." She takes a deep breath, her face forming a grin. "Fuck, I am glad that I did. I can't even imagine a different life now. What do I say? I'm just happy to love both of you, and to be loved by you."

Gráinne squeezes our hands tightly, as if she might float away if she doesn't. "For my entire life, I existed in darkness—no control, no freedom, no hope." She looks between us, her expression gentle, but the look in her eye reveals a fierce resolve. "Now, I wake up every day and I get to *live* in the light. The two of you are my joy."

It's overwhelming to hear what they have to say; tears form in my eyes and it's difficult not to break down into sobs here and now. I had prepared vows to share, but now they feel so terribly inadequate. Gráinne, as if sensing my anxiety, lifts my hand to her lips, kissing the tips of my fingers. Eva squeezes my arm, winking cheekily and hitting me with her trademark grin.

"I also don't know what to say," I tell them, my voice cracking. "My entire existence, my entire purpose, has always been for the sake of others. I don't think I deserve anything, and yet I have so much. Loving you two and being loved in return makes me feel like I can be a little selfish. You're my gifts."

With vows exchanged, tears now flowing from our eyes, we kiss one another—each of us brides.

* * *

Sunset, the liminal space between day and night. There is tension while watching one, a somber excitement as you ponder your day and look forward to the treasures that night holds. My wives are with me, one on each side. This field with trees and wildflowers growing in vast patches all around us is beautiful and made all the better for the company I get to share it with. One day I will rebuild my garden; I am, after all, spoiled for choice in what to grow.

The grass crunches under the weight of someone's footsteps. A woman nearly as tall as Dia approaches, her equally white hair hanging down her back. Also like Dia, her eyes are white—curious. I'll solve that mystery later.

Most striking of all is that she's wearing a military uniform, an admiral of Central's Navy.

"Hatsuko," Dia says, her lips pursing into a thin line.

The woman smiles, bowing her head slightly towards us. "Diarmuid," she says. "That was a good wedding. I'm glad I got to make it."

"Yeah me too," Dia says. "Are you here for some small talk, or are you leading up to something?"

Hatsuko chuckles, shaking her head. "Always so impatient," she says.

"It's my wedding." My wolf scowls, though her voice isn't as harsh as I'd expect, given her expression. "If you want to talk, we can talk, but if you have other intentions, I'd rather you be out with them now."

"Fair enough," Hatsuko says. She pulls out a small datapad from her jacket, handing it to Dia. "There is a situation brewing on Uruk-3 I thought you'd like to know about."

Dia glances at the datapad, her brows furrowing, her eyes glowing a soft white as she scans it. "That's a Blackstar world," she says. "Local warlord named Gilgamesh is taking over more and more territory in the underworld there. What are you suggesting I do with this?"

"Go meet her." Hatsuko shrugs, stuffing her hands into her pockets. "I figure with your charm and skills, you may be able to take advantage of this. These aren't orders—I'm just here to support you."

"Good." Dia hands the datapad back, her eyes returning to normal. "Because I'm choosing to be selfish and going on honeymoon. If Gilgamesh is worth her salt, she'll be alive in a month or two."

Hatsuko nods, her expression pained. "Right," she says. "You know—I heard your vows, and I'm sorry."

"Not right now, Hatsuko," Dia says, squeezing my arm gently. "I can't have this conversation. Before I leave to deal with this, we'll grab a drink like old times. Just not now."

"Fair," she says. "You three have a good night." She walks away without another word.

I have never asked what happened between these two; the anguished look on Dia's face breaks my heart. She turns back towards us, her eyes downcast.

"It'll get better," Eva says. "That was the best it's been."

"I know," Dia says. "If it's all the same to you two, I'd like to head back. I cannot deal with the amount of people anymore."

"Of course." I kiss her cheek softly. "You two go. I will deal with the goodbyes; after all, what good is my training in dealing with dignitaries if I cannot use it to help my wives escape?"

Brief goodbye kisses are exchanged before I go back into the reception hall. To save time, I make a general announcement, wishing the guests well and that if they so desire, they should continue to dance and eat. I depart, leaving my mother in the capable hands of Maeve and Viviana. That is something I will try not to think about too much—she seems happier than I have ever seen her besides.

By the time I'm able to get away, the sun has already gone down and night blankets this part of the Earth. It's a clear night, the skies overhead gleaming with the light of the Orion Arm. I catch Dia leaning against the transport, her expression filled with yearning as she gazes up. She doesn't even notice my approach until I place my hand on her chest.

"You are itching to go back up there," I say, leaning into her, my head resting comfortably under her jaw.

"Almost always," she says wistfully, wrapping her arms around me.

I smile softly, humming in contentment. The night air is chilly, but Dia radiates warmth. "I think if you could marry the stars, you would."

"I would," she says, chuckling. "Hm, we should go to Eden for a month."

I whistle sharply; the planet is reputed to be the greatest luxury resort in human history. "I have never been," I say. "Is it really all they say?"

"Better," Dia says. "You can't really live there, or I can't anyway—it's too stimulating, but it's the perfect place where we can get lost in one another there without a care."

I nod into Dia's chest, clinging to her sturdy frame. "Let us go then—soon. Tonight, there is a different paradise we should enjoy."

Eva exclaims her agreement from within the transport. Dia laughs as she runs her fingers through my hair.

"Home?" I ask, taking her by the hand.

"Home."

Dia gets into the driver's seat; I get in the back with Eva. I am pounced on almost as soon as the door closes, her tongue down my throat. Happily, I kiss her back as our wolf drives us home. It is not a long drive, Dia drives very fast. Still, Eva's efforts leave me nearly out of my dress by the time we arrive. We hurry inside, leaving a trail of clothes in our wake.

They toss me onto the bed, mouths and fingers exploring my body—my mind delirious with pleasure. I know who is touching me, even through the haze of ecstasy in the darkness. Dia's skillful tongue brings me to the edge; Eva's ravenous hands play with my breasts. My wives fuck me; they fill my mouth and my cunt, sometimes at once, as they pass me around like precious treasure. Dia sinks deep into me, her mouth on my breast while Eva takes me from behind.

I scream and I moan as they have their way with me, lost in the bliss of being taken by them at once. Eva pulls my head back by my hair, Dia's fangs pierce into my neck. They hold me tight as they thrust, their rhythm taking my breath away. I lose myself in them as I cum, and I cum and I cum again. I don't bother counting how many times they bring me to orgasm, nor how many they have inside me.

By the time we exhaust ourselves, the sun is rising above the horizon. We lie together, legs and arms and tails wrapped around one another. Dia's face suddenly gets very red before she laughs.

"What?" I ask.

"Nothing," she says with a sigh. "I just realized that we didn't take the stuffed animals off the bed and they saw all that."

Eva chuckles then. "You're ridiculous."

"Shut up."

I kiss Dia gingerly, running my tongue across her lips. "It is a bit silly, but very cute. Never change, my perfect, pretty wolf."

Her blush deepens. "You're both insufferable."

"As if you'd rather us be any other way," Eva says. "Do we sleep, or do we eat?"

"I swear that's all you think about when you aren't piloting." Dia lets out an exasperated breath. "*Cats.*"

"For what it is worth, I am too tired to think about eating," I say, squeezing my wolf tight. "I say we sleep now and plan our trip when we wake up over your pancakes."

"What she said." Eva curls into me, her arms wrapped around my waist. She is almost instantly asleep, a remarkable skill.

"As you wish, Princess. Her snowy eyes close, a small smile on her face as she drifts off to sleep.

I stroke her hair, fighting off my enervation until I am sure she is dreaming.

A month's reprieve, maybe two before we face new challenges. Anxiety grips at my chest, intrusive thoughts of my wives' death plague me. I push them down, focusing on their breathing, matching mine to theirs and reminding myself of what we have already accomplished. I refuse to be robbed of my joy. Not now, not ever. I kiss my wolf's forehead; I entwine my fingers with my lion's.

Whatever comes next, we will be ready for it.

Coming Soon

Book Two of Mechanized Hearts

COMING SOON

FAE'RYNN

SHATTERED STAR

The galaxy has irrevocably shifted, the crew of the Banféinní saw to that.

Deep in the heart of Blackstar, a warlord–Gilgamesh–has risen to power. Her might is uncontested; her loyal bodyguard, Enkidu, is her greatest weapon. Powers align to crush them lest their meteoric rise threaten the system-state itself.

Eden has been a time of bliss for three new wives, away from battle, from their crusade. Yet the fight continues, and their honeymoon must come to an end. They have a new target, and new potential allies. The only problem? The destruction of the Fomorian Armory has made them the most wanted criminals in the galaxy.

Mechanized Hearts continues in this neo-noir cyberpunk thriller!

About the Author

Fae'rynn is a trans woman, a simple lesbian, who spends her days thinking of women and how to tell their stories while drowning herself in coffee.

You can connect with me on:
- https://twitter.com/Faerynnistired
- https://bsky.app/profile/faerynn.bsky.social
- https://www.patreon.com/faerynnbooks